If you liked *Pleasure Games* and
Legal Attraction, why not try

Burn Me Once by Clare Connelly
Boardroom Sins by J. Margot Critch

Discover more at millsandboon.co.uk

PLEASURE GAMES

DAIRE ST. DENIS

MILLS & BOON

For Steena, Elena and Trish.
True friendships are where sanity and insanity collide.

PLEASURE GAMES

DAIRE ST. DENIS

LEGAL ATTRACTION

LISA CHILDS

MILLS & BOON

First Published in Great Britain 2018
by Mills & Boon, an imprint of HarperCollins*Publishers*
1 London Bridge Street, London, SE1 9GF

Pleasure Games © 2018 Dara Lee Snow

Legal Attraction © 2018 Lisa Childs

ISBN: 978-0-263-26644-3

MIX
Paper from
responsible sources
FSC™ C007454

This book is produced from independently certified FSC™ paper
to ensure responsible forest management.
For more information visit www.harpercollins.co.uk/green.

Printed and bound in Spain
by CPI, Barcelona

CHAPTER ONE

LUCA LEGRAND COULDN'T decide whether he had the best luck in the world or whether he was actually cursed with the worst fucking luck ever. At the moment, sitting in a holding cell that stank like piss and rancid sweat, he was pretty sure it was the latter.

"Legrand!" A uniformed member of the Paris Police Prefecture banged on the bars. *"Votre avocat est ici."* *Your lawyer is here.*

Pushing himself to his feet, Luca waited for the man to unlock the cell and then followed him down the hall to a cubicle not much larger than a toilet stall. François Chevalier, the lawyer for the Legrand Estate vineyard, was already waiting inside, reading a newspaper at a steel table that was bolted to the floor.

François glanced up when the door opened. He didn't stand, and did not greet Luca, but rather drummed his fingers on the metal tabletop as he waited for Luca to take the seat across from him.

Once the door was shut behind the officer, François went back to reading the paper. More specifically, he perused an article with the headline, Héritier

de Legrand Vineyard en Prison Pour Voies de Fait.
Heir to the Legrand Vineyard in Prison for Assault.
Beneath the headline was a blown-up image of Luca
being shoved into a police car.

"It's not as bad as it looks," Luca said.

"Really? Because it looks bad," François said
calmly, though his mustache twitched.

Luca leaned back in the hard metal chair, folding
his arms over his chest. He gazed directly at François, not willing to look away because he was not
contrite in the fucking least.

"It's not my fault," he said.

"Is that so?" François leaned toward him, palms
on the table, forcing Luca to look up at him. His
face—though always red—was now the color of a
sun-ripened heirloom tomato. "You punched a reporter. You broke his nose. You smashed his camera. How is that *not* your fault?"

He stood up and swept a hand around the tiny
room that smelled like mildew and stale cigarettes.
"The first Legrand man to ever be arrested. Yet still
you sit there and say it's not your fault?" He made
a sour face, as if tasting a too-green wine, one that
should be spit out immediately.

Slowly, Luca got to his feet, all six feet two inches
of him, so François had to look up at *him*. "The man
deserved what he got."

"I don't care what he deserved. All I care about
is your legacy. Which you have single-handedly destroyed." He glared at Luca. His heavy lids and the
bags beneath made it nearly impossible to see his

eyes, but Luca was determined to hold François's gaze. The fact that François looked away first did not give him any pleasure, however.

"The value of our champagne has dropped significantly since you took over. Do you realize that?"

Luca ground his teeth, forcing himself to count to five. *Un, deux, trois, quatre, cinq...* But counting did not stop the deepest part of his gut from rumbling with liquid fire that was amplified with every breath. Through clenched teeth, he said, "The value of our champagne dropped the day my father died."

It was true. His father had run the estate for thirty years, continuing in the footsteps of his father and grandfather and two hundred years of ancestors before that. His father had been a robust, healthy man and it had seemed as if he would live forever. Not that Luca had seen much of him in the past ten years while he was competing on the Grand Prix motorcycle racing circuit.

"This cannot continue—" François gestured toward Luca's chest. "These scandals."

Here we go. Luca leaned against the wall, crossing one ankle over the other. Waiting for François to detail each of his latest "scandals." There was no point in defending himself.

Ticking items off his finger, François began the lengthy list. "Disturbing the peace."

Disturbing the peace? Luca had broken up with his girlfriend, Anika Van Horn, a model he'd quickly learned was more interested in the fame and fortune of the Legrand name than in Luca himself. She did not take the breakup well. In fact, she'd slapped him, making sure to do so at an outdoor café, causing a scene that spread in seconds via social media. He still wasn't sure how charges had come of it.

"Public drunkenness."

He had attended a fellow Monster teammate's bachelor party. While Luca had had his fair share of drinks, he had not been nearly as drunk as the groom-to-be, whom Luca had rescued from the Fontaine Stravinsky.

"Public nudity."

It had been his friend, the bachelor, who was naked. But the press had a way of spinning things so that it sounded like Luca was the one who'd disrobed, jumped into the fountain and done lewd things to a colorful, busty mermaid with water spouting from the tips of her breasts.

Sighing, Luca waved for François to keep going with the damning list, knowing what was coming next.

"Then. Just to up the ante…a sex video gone public. And not just any sex…" François paused, arching his brow for effect. He sniffed instead of finishing his sentence. "Such a boost to the prestige of your esteemed family name." François grimaced with sarcasm.

Luca opened his mouth, the excuse—the fact that the video was meant to be private and that Anika had obviously been the one to leak it online, either for publicity to boost her career or to publicly humiliate him—was ripe on his tongue. But what good would it do to explain this to François? It didn't change the outcome.

"And now, one week later, here you are." François's eyes leaked with moisture born of anger, like a grape in the press right before it was about to pop. "Assault and destruction of property. How noble."

The paparazzi had been relentless since the sex scandal. Luca had been unable to leave his flat. To go to the market. To do anything without being accosted. When one particularly pushy reporter, who had been doggedly harassing him night and day, had stepped in front of Luca while he was on his brand new Yamaha VMAX, causing him to swerve and nearly crash into a lamppost, Luca had lost it. He wasn't proud of his actions, but if faced with the same situation again? He wouldn't change a thing.

He'd parked the bike, walked straight up to the man who had the camera attached to his face like it was an appendage and asked him—civilly—to erase the images. When the man ignored him in order to take more pictures, Luca had simply snatched the camera away with the intent to erase the memory. The man shoved him, which resulted in Luca dropping the camera, smashing it on the cobblestones.

Oops.

Then the screaming idiot had thrown a punch, which Luca had easily dodged before acting on pure instinct. One punch. That's all it took to drop the *petit connard*. It wasn't his fault the man had started something he couldn't finish.

Again. No point in explaining any of this to François. The man cared about one thing and one thing only. The value of the estate. Which had, indeed, plummeted since Luca took over.

"I get it." Luca returned to the chair and sat down. "I'm a big fucking disappointment. Now, when are you bailing me out of this shit hole so I can get to work to rebuild the 'family name'?"

"Bail you out?" François laughed. "I'm not bailing you out. *Non*." He shook his head. "This is the safest place for you. You can't get into any more trouble if you stay locked up."

The molten metal that swirled in his gut erupted, filling Luca's veins, forcing every muscle to contract. He grabbed François by the collar and hauled him across the table toward him. "What did you say?"

The only sound François was able to manage was a sputtering plea for his release, which resulted in spittle spraying Luca in the face. For the first time that day, Luca felt remorse for his actions. François had been loyal to the family for three decades, yet he barely knew Luca, and for all he did know, Luca was indeed the fuckup that the media was making him out to be.

The sex scandal was one thing, but Luca couldn't understand the rest of it—the charges and the constant bad press. As a Grand Prix driver and a Legrand, he was used to being in the public eye, but lately the media seemed out to get him. Why? Was it because of the sex tape, or did he simply keep ending up in the wrong place at the wrong time?

Softening his grip, Luca raised his hands in appeasement. "I'm sorry."

"Sorry?" François's voice was high. "This behavior of yours is unacceptable." The lawyer straightened his shirt and tie where Luca had crumpled it. "You are an embarrassment to your family name."

"François, I recognize the…" Luca swallowed. With difficulty. "The *folly* of my recent actions. But I can't very well right wrongs from a prison cell."

Blinking rapidly, his eyes so puffy they were mere slits in his face, François said, "I don't think you understand the full implications of your actions."

"Then explain them to me."

François removed a sheaf of papers from a briefcase beneath the table and plopped them on the table.

"Do you know what these are?"

Luca slid the papers toward him. "Company bylaws." He slid them back across.

"Yes. And, if you were to read them, you would know that there is a code of conduct clause." He paused. "For *all* employees." He flipped to an earmarked page and shoved the document back across the table.

Luca glanced down. The words "grounds for dismissal" were highlighted as well as, "appropriate conduct."

"I know the bylaws. I am the CEO." It was sort of true. He'd been too busy running the company to pay much attention to them.

"So it should come as no surprise that the board is discussing your removal as CEO."

"What?" Luca guffawed. "They can't do that. I'm the only heir to the estate and I own fifty-one percent of the shares of the company."

"Well…"

"Well, what?"

"There has been discussion about your father's will being contested. In light of all that has occurred." He gestured toward the room in general.

"Contested? By whom?"

"Marcel Durand."

Marcel was only a few years younger than Luca and had only worked for his father for maybe five years. "Why would Marcel Durand contest *my* father's will?"

"Because Marcel is your half brother."

The first thing Jasmine Sweet did after finding her seat in first class on the Air France flight to Paris was to ask for a glass of champagne. The second thing she did, once she had the glass in hand, was to turn away from the large and empty seat beside her and sip the bubbly liquid until it disappeared. And the third thing she did was twist off the platinum band with the four-carat princess-cut diamond and shove it into the inside pocket of her purse. This was all accomplished before the plane had finished boarding.

"Excuse me." Jasmine held up a finger to signal the unfairly beautiful and terribly refined French flight attendant. "Do you have any berries? Blueberries, raspberries, that sort of thing?"

"Berries?" The woman asked with what Jasmine decided was a disdainful tone. *"Non."*

"Too bad. Just another champagne, then, please."

The woman pursed her lips before settling into a bored smile. "Would you care for orange juice with that or perhaps something to eat?"

"No, thank you," Jazz said, waving her hand dismissively. "Just the champagne."

Before the attendant moved past, Jasmine stopped her again. "Oh, and if it's not too much to ask…" Jasmine glanced at the seat beside her and lowered her voice. "This seat is empty." She pulled tickets out of her purse. "I have both tickets. Would you see if someone from economy would be interested in an upgrade?"

Both delicate brows arched at this request as the woman took the tickets from Jasmine's hands. Her full lips pursed together. "Yes, I see." Handing the tickets back to Jasmine, she said, "I will inquire."

"Oh, and make sure they like champagne. That's a must," Jasmine called, but the woman didn't turn around. "Thanks," she shouted. "You're a peach."

The flight attendant carried on through into coach, ignoring her while she made sure all carry-on items were stowed correctly.

Well, what had she expected? Friendliness? Kindness? Empathy?

Ha! So far her experience with the French was that they were aloof, intimidating and gorgeous. But, she supposed, she wasn't even off American soil yet. Things would be better once she landed in Paris.

She rubbed the bare spot where her ring had been only moments before. Her skin was lighter where the band had circled her finger for the last sixteen months, a promise of the life she'd always dreamed of, as if her skin wasn't quite ready to give it up.

She closed her eyes, imagining that she and Parker Wright had gotten married yesterday, as planned, celebrating their union at the Waldorf Astoria in Chicago with three hundred of their closest friends and family—Parker had a large family. And lots of friends. Well…work colleagues and friends of his parents, really. But whatever. And now they were on their way to Europe for their honeymoon. With eyes closed, she observed the physical sensation of the plane taxiing along the runway before accelerating, the seat beneath her vibrating as the plane took off.

A week in Paris, another week in the South of France, then on to Italy: Venice, Milan, Tuscany—ahh!—before returning to Paris for the final few days. She'd planned the whole thing, poring over hotel web pages and travel forums for what to do and where to stay.

"Money's no problem," Parker had said. "It's our honeymoon, after all."

Yes. It was their honeymoon and she'd booked all these gorgeous boutique hotels close to the sights, restaurants and shops—shopping was something they both loved to do. And then, after a day of exploring, she'd thought they would return to their hotel and make love—tenderly, passionately. Definitely trying new things now that they were married (like the new furry handcuffs she'd picked up and the ridged vibrator—yes, please!). As her imagination strayed to creative ways to use the toys, her hand strayed to the seat beside her, encouraging Parker to take her hand and clasp it in his warm fingers.

Instead, her hand came into contact with a large, hairy arm that was a smidge damp. Jasmine's eyes popped open and she swiveled to face the person seated beside her. He appeared to be in his late fifties or early sixties with thinning hair and a friendly face. He wore a tie-dyed T-shirt that stretched across an ample frame, and as he met her gaze, he pushed square glasses back onto the bridge of his nose before dipping his hand into a party-sized bag of Doritos. Jasmine noticed bright orange crumbs dotting the front of his shirt and the armrest.

"Doritos?" he asked, as he held the bag out to her.

"Don't mind if I do," Jasmine said, taking a handful. She waved at the glass of champagne sweating on her pull-down table. "Do you want something to drink? It's free up here, you know."

The man smiled and Jasmine tried not to stare at the orange residue stuck between his two front teeth. "Don't mind if *I* do."

Jazz pressed the button to signal the attendant and the woman materialized beside her seat. "Another champagne for my friend, here."

"I'd prefer beer if you don't mind."

"I don't mind." Jasmine smiled sweetly at the man before turning her beaming face toward the French woman. "Beer for my friend. And another champagne for me. In fact," Jazz added, indicating the first-class cabin with a wave of her hand, "Why don't you bring out champagne for everyone!"

The woman rolled her eyes but Jasmine didn't care. Was it the champagne making her feel light-headed and carefree?

"Toodle-oo, now." She motioned with just the tips of her fingers, hoping to give the woman—who wasn't even attempting the bored smile anymore—the brush-off. Then she turned to her seatmate.

"I'm Jasmine." Jazz stuck her hand out and the man beside her took it, shaking it with a surprisingly firm grasp.

"Neil."

"Nice to make your acquaintance, Neil. So, tell me about yourself."

The two exchanged pleasantries: where they were from, what they did for a living, whether they'd been to Paris before.

See? Jasmine consoled herself. *Look how calm I am, making nice with a complete stranger as if everything is normal.*

As if her whole world hadn't been turned upside down a mere forty-eight hours ago and she hadn't received the worst shock of her life.

Their drinks arrived, though Jasmine noticed her champagne was a little on the glass-half-empty side.

Bitch.

"So, Neil, what's in Paris? Business or pleasure?" She downed the champagne in three swallows and pressed the call button again.

Two can play this game, gorgeous French woman.

"Oh, a comic convention. It's the biggest one in all of Europe. I'm an illustrator." He brushed a wisp of hair off his forehead.

"Interesting." Jasmine helped herself to another handful of Doritos. "What kind of illustrations?"

"Do you want to see?"

"Why not?"

Neil unfastened his seat belt and retrieved a bag from the overhead compartment, taking out a sketch-book before replacing the bag and sitting down. He flipped open the sketchbook to cartoons of—well, Jasmine was having a hard time focusing, to be honest.

"The cartoon is called Betty Boobs. It's a play on Betty Boop. It's very popular in Europe."

Jasmine blinked and squinted. Big-chested, naked cartoon women with a bit of 1930s flare graced the pages of his sketchpad. Getting it on. Porn. The guy drew cartoon porn.

Cool.

"Neil, can I ask you something?"

"Sure."

"Do you know what a beard is?" She blinked at him, forcing herself to swallow. That last sip of champagne had burned.

"You mean like facial hair?" He stroked his chin.

"No. The other connotation. Do you know it?"

His bushy brows drew together and then rose up his forehead as if filled with helium. "You mean like a gay guy who—"

"Yes." She poked him on the arm. "That's exactly what I mean. For example, my fiancé—well, ex-fiancé—asked me to marry him, right?"

"Okay."

"Unbeknownst to me, I was his beard." Reaching over to the little table in front of Neil, Jasmine snagged the can of Bud that he'd barely sampled and guzzled a good third before continuing. "We were supposed to get married yesterday."

"Really?" His gaze was on the beer, not her.

She nodded.

Wow. She was really doing it. No tears. No temper tantrums. Just reporting the facts as if it had happened to someone else or like she was completely over it. Jasmine was proud of herself.

She drank deeply again before leaning close and placing her hand on Neil's sweating forearm. "Yep. I'd have never known, except the night before the wedding, while I was supposed to be staying at a hotel with my friends, I came back to my apartment to pick up something I'd forgotten—something borrowed, or was it something blue?" She tapped her lips. "Hmm. Either way, that part doesn't matter. What matters is that I caught my fiancé in bed with his best friend. They were booping. *Betty Booping*, if you will."

"Holy shit," Neil said, still eyeing the beer in her hand. "That must have been a shock."

"Oh, yeah." She pointed to the seat he was occupying. "My new husband was supposed to be sitting where you are sitting right now, but he's not. Because he's gay."

"I'm sorry."

"He never loved me." Jasmine fell back into her seat, staring at the headrest in front of her. "He was only using me. God. And I was so blind because he gave me whatever I wanted."

"Hey." The guy patted her hand where it lay on the shared armrest. "You okay?" He carefully retrieved his nearly empty beer from her slack fingers.

"A gorgeous penthouse apartment. Fifty-thousand-dollar limit on my credit card."

"I can't imagine…though a limit like that would be nice…"

"You know what the worst thing was, Neil?" She lolled her head toward him. "After I caught him? He was relieved. *Relieved.*"

"It's hard to live a lie, I guess…"

"And he said nothing had to change." She poked him in the sternum, above the orange crumbs. "Can you believe it? He still wanted to marry me!"

"Umm, you might want to keep it down a bit—"

"A housekeeper and cook if I wanted…whatever I wanted, really. Bribery." She shook her head. Her neck was stiff. So was her jaw. Tight, like it was wired shut. "All fucking bribes and distractions," she said through clenched teeth. "Distractions from what, you might ask?" She turned to face Neil and the rest of the story came out of the deep hole where her heart used to be. "So that *my* soon-to-be husband could take business trips with *Robert*. That's

the fucker's name. *Robert Miskey.* I'm a fucking
cover so Parker can be-boop Robert *fucking* Miskey."

"You're not allowed to shout on planes these
days." Neil blinked nervously.

"Am I making a scene, Neil? Am I?"

"Umm, yes."

"Don't you think finding out that you're a beard
on the eve of your wedding warrants a scene?"

The man was now frantically pushing the attendant call button.

Unbuckling her seat belt, Jasmine stood, address-
ing all the people in first class. "I'm supposed to be
married. I'm supposed to be on my way to Europe for
my honeymoon. And instead I'm here with Neil, who
draws cartoon porn." She glanced at Neil and said in
a marginally more controlled voice, "Sorry, Neil."

His smile wavered and his hands said, *No problem, crazy lady.*

"Doesn't that give me the right to make a scene?"
She tried to meet the other passengers' eyes, but there
were no takers. "Doesn't it?"

Cool fingers circled her upper arm and an accented voice said calmly, "Please return to your seat
or we will be forced to make a stop in New York
City where you will be escorted off the plane and
detained. Do you understand?"

Jasmine attempted to tug her arm out of the attendant's grasp but the woman was freakishly strong.
Fucking French.

"I—" When she turned her head she was met with
the sincerest smile she'd received from the woman yet.

"Please," the woman said soothingly. Her sincerity came as such a surprise that Jasmine's knees buckled and the woman had to help her back into her seat.

Jazz caught a whiff of the woman's perfume—Coco Mademoiselle by Chanel, if she wasn't mistaken—as the flight attendant leaned over her to secure Jasmine's seat belt. Tasteful, subtle, perfect.

"I'm very sorry you're having a bad day. Please don't make it any worse." Before standing, the woman tucked a handful of tissues into Jasmine's fist and, moving close to her ear, whispered, "Whoever this man is who hurt you? He did not deserve you."

CHAPTER TWO

THE SECOND JASMINE opened the door to her hotel room, she smelled roses.

Ugh.

Towing her bag behind her like it was an old, arthritic dog who was too tired to go for a walk, Jasmine made her way through the suite she had so lovingly booked months ago. Months ago when she thought she'd be sharing this room with the man she was supposed to spend the rest of her life with. But he'd been lying to her the whole time! Asshole.

The room was gorgeous—dammit! Twelve-foot ceilings and original crown molding from when the hotel was a mansion owned by a famous jeweler who had bought it for his mistress during the Renaissance. Now the beautiful, airy suite only mocked her. The Louis XIV furniture taunted her, reminding her that she'd chosen it for Parker. She preferred country chic. The filmy white drapes only served to remind her of the ten-thousand-dollar wedding gown that hid in her closet like a shameful secret, never to be worn.

But the worst was what she found on the polished cherrywood table in the sitting area: a plate of chocolate-covered strawberries, with an envelope addressed to Mr. and Mrs. Parker Wright propped between the berries and an ice bucket. Inside the bucket was a bottle of champagne sitting at a jaunty angle, chillin'.

Like a villain.

Stupid champagne.

Jasmine plucked the bottle from the bucket, unwrapped the foil on top and popped the cork. It ricocheted off what she hoped was an imitation painting, then off the crown molding, landing somewhere behind a potted plant. Not bothering with the crystal flutes, Jasmine drank directly from the bottle like it was water and she was dying of thirst.

"Hair of the dog," she muttered, wiping her lips with the back of her hand. She set the bottle on the table, unconcerned with the wet patch left on the highly polished tabletop, and rummaged in her bag for aspirin. Instead of the travel-sized bottle of pills, she located her cell phone.

According to her phone it was 3:23 and there were forty-seven—yes, forty-seven!—texts waiting for her. Reminding her—as if she needed any more reminders—of the ordeal of the last forty-eight hours.

With a groan, she tapped the message app…

Five from her mother. Delete.

Two from her father. Delete.

Thirteen from her best friend, Ashley…hmm. Maybe she'd read those later.

Twenty-seven from Parker.

The man was desperate.

Her finger hovered over the delete button, but instead of deleting the messages, she deleted him from her contact list.

"Liar. You're dead to me," she muttered before tilting her head way back and letting the bubbly burn down her throat.

Parker's voice rose between her ears, *C'mon, Jazz. I figured you knew. Nothing has to change between us. I still love you, you know, as a best friend.* He'd made that statement while sitting in bed beside his lover. Then he'd gotten out of bed and approached her, hands out, pleading. *You can have whatever life you want, I won't interfere. All I ask is that you keep my private life secret.*

Honestly? In this day and age, why did he need to pretend? Well, she'd asked him that question directly. *It's my father. He's homophobic, okay? I'll lose the trust fund.*

God! So, all of this was for the money? He'd deceived her for years just so he could maintain his precious lifestyle?

Not that she'd minded the lifestyle. It was what had kept her from making demands, from thinking too hard about the lack of intimacy and passion she'd yearned for. Parker's generosity seemed proof enough he loved her, and she'd been so wrapped up in their perfect life, she'd failed to see what was happening right in front of her.

With bottle in hand, Jasmine wove toward the

window, pushing the drapes aside so she could admire the view.

And what a view. The rounded Parisian rooftops, the Eiffel Tower—so close she could practically lick it. The view was the reason Jasmine had chosen this suite, a dream come true...

Opening the French doors, Jasmine stepped out onto the wrought-iron balcony. Fresh air. That was what she needed. She plunked herself down in the chair and set the bottle on the glass-topped bistro table as she gazed out at the magnificent sight.

And she had no one to share it with. She was completely and utterly alone. She sighed, slumping with the weight of self-pity. Wasn't she allowed? She'd been ready to give Parker everything, thinking he'd felt the same way. She shut her eyes. Maybe her ex-fiancé cared for her, even loved her, like he'd said. But it wasn't the kind of love she'd thought it was. The love she'd always craved. And she wasn't ready to forgive him for tricking her into believing that it was. Her phone chirped, and Jasmine automatically glanced down. Another message from Ashley. Tapping on the message app, she skimmed the messages.

Jazz? Are you okay? Call me.
Please, let me know you're okay.
Your parents are worried. You should call them.
Jazz? Are you in Paris?

Instead of replying to the text, Jasmine touched the FaceTime button. Her best friend answered immediately. The video was grainy, but Jasmine could still see the dark circles beneath Ashley's hazel eyes and that her fine blond hair had yet to be combed.

"What time is it there?" Jasmine asked by way of a greeting.

Ashley blinked. "It's twenty to ten."

"In the morning?"

Ashley's eyes narrowed. "I knew it. You went to Paris, didn't you?"

"See for yourself," Jasmine said, panning her phone to give Ashley a panoramic view of the Paris skyline.

"Holy shit," she heard Ashley comment. "Nice."

Switching the screen back to face her, Jasmine half smiled. "It's nicer now that I have you to share it with." She sighed. Damn if her lip didn't start quivering. "If I had been thinking clearly, I would have changed the other ticket and brought you with me." Her lip quivered for real and she covered her mouth to quell the shaking.

"If you had been thinking clearly, you would have at least told me—told someone—what you were doing. Jesus, Jazz. We've been so worried."

"I know. I'm sorry. I just…" She had to stop talking because the trembling in her lips spread across her face, pricking the backs of her eyes until tears spilled over her lashes. She shook her head since words were impossible at the moment.

"Have you talked to Parker?" Ash asked softly.

"No." Jazz wiped her cheek with the back of her hand. "I'm not going to, either."

"Understandable. What about your parents?"

"I will." She passed back through the French doors into the hotel suite and plopped down at the table, plucking a sweating strawberry from the plate and popping it into her mouth.

"So, what are you going to do?" Ash asked. "God, those strawberries look good, by the way."

Jazz grabbed another berry and bit into it. "They are good. Really sweet." Her voice cracked on the last word and the chocolate-covered berry suddenly tasted like ashes in her mouth. She swallowed the lump with difficulty.

After a pause, Ashley piped up, "I'll tell you what you're going to do."

"What?"

"You are going to have yourself an adventure."

"An adventure?"

"Yep. You want to forget about Parker? Go have fun. Do all the things that you want to do. Shop on the Champs-Élysées, go on wine tours and see the sights. Hell, take a train to Monte Carlo and rack up Parker's credit cards."

Something hot yet icy lanced Jasmine's gut. "Oh, God. The credit cards." She shook her head vehemently. "I don't want to use them."

"What do you mean?" Ash asked, leaning closer to her phone camera. "After all you've been through? You deserve to spend some of Parker's money."

"No. I can't do it. I can't live off of him anymore. It's just so…" She squeezed her eyes shut. "Symbolic of my life with him. Dependent and lame."

Even from across the distance, Jasmine heard Ashley's deep inhalation, followed by a long exhalation. "But, how are you going to survive if you don't?"

The reminder that she had no way of supporting herself slammed through Jasmine. When she'd met Parker she'd been working as a stylist in an upscale salon. She'd liked the job—loved it, actually—but as her relationship with Parker progressed, they'd seen little reason for her to keep it. He made more than enough to support them.

"I don't know. I guess I didn't think about money before I left."

Ashley rubbed her jaw, her gaze sliding up and to the side as she considered this possibility. Her gaze returned to the screen. "Where's the ring?"

"What ring?"

"Duh…your engagement ring?"

Jasmine's gaze automatically searched her ring finger only to find it bare. Her purse! She reached inside, found the cold platinum and held it in front of the phone for Ashley to see.

"Get rid of it."

"Like, chuck it?"

"No! That thing cost Parker a fortune. Go sell it. Use the money to do something wild and crazy. And whatever's left? That's what you use to start over."

Jazz held the ring up, seeing it in a new light. Could she do that?

Hell, yes, she could. The ring was *hers*. Parker had given it to her when he said he'd love her forever.

Now she was heartbroken, fucked over and desperately in need of a break. Parker probably wouldn't even care.

Jazz bit her lip. "I'll sell the ring, but I don't know how to do 'wild and crazy'."

"Oh, my God." Ashley slapped her forehead. "I've known you most of my life and if there is anyone who knows how to be wild, it's you."

"Ash…"

"Don't Ash me. You know what you need?"

"A drink?" Jazz held the champagne bottle aloft.

"I think you've self-medicated enough," Ash replied with pursed lips. "No. Here's what you need. Go find yourself some smoking-hot Frenchman who knows how to treat a woman. And then you need to have a month of raunchy, nasty, awesome sex." She snapped her fingers. "A sex-venture."

"A sex-what?" Jasmine rolled her eyes.

"I'm not kidding. You need a release from all this tension—what better way than good sex? You're totally single now."

Jasmine groaned.

"I'm sorry, hon. But that's why you need a passionate, torrid, love affair. Feed some romantic French dude chocolate-covered strawberries. Let him lick champagne off your body…"

"Seriously?"

"Go to one of those sex districts and buy awesome European sex toys…or…" Ashley's eyes lit up. "No, wait! Buy yourself a gigolo. A super-hot one!"

Jazz couldn't help laughing at Ashley's suggestion. It felt good to laugh. "You are insane." She blew her bangs out of her eyes. "And you should be here," she finished softly.

"Yeah, well..." Ashley stood and patted her rounded belly. Her friend was tiny, so her third trimester of pregnancy made her look like she had a basketball tucked up under her shirt. "I'm not exactly in the best form for sex-ventures. Plus, I'm pretty sure I would scare off any potential hotties."

Jasmine touched her finger to the screen as if touching Ashley's belly. "That is one lucky kid to have you for her mother."

Ashley's lips twisted. Her friend had worries of her own with her first child due in under a month.

"Thanks, Ash."

"Hey. What are friends for? You know I'm here for you. Anytime. I'm just a FaceTime away."

Jazz nodded.

"Oh, and Jazz?"

"Yeah?"

"Let me be your cautionary tale..." Ash rubbed her belly. "As soon as you sell that ring and before you embark on your sexy time?"

Jazz groaned. "Uh-huh?"

"Buy condoms. Lots and lots of condoms."

Two weeks had passed since Luca had been released on bail. The agreement he'd made with François was that he'd not only stay out of the limelight, but that he'd disappear completely while François worked behind the scenes to change the board's mind. He had hired Myra Monte, publicity guru to the stars, to try to salvage the Legrand brand—promos, charity donations and the like.

"Give me a month," François had said. "During that time, I don't want to hear about you, read about you or have to bail you out."

"But wouldn't it be better if I talk to the board? Prove to them I'm competent?"

"No. You have to trust me."

Luca did trust him. Thus he was lying low, as requested, staying out of the press, staying out of trouble. The problem was, scandal had followed him for the last year like a stray dog he'd fed on a whim, a dog that wouldn't leave him alone. It was that feral beast he didn't trust.

Bad luck? Luca wasn't so sure anymore.

He stopped his Ducati Diavel Cruiser at the red light, considering for the thousandth time the information François had revealed.

What if he was being sabotaged? If he was, Luca knew exactly who was behind it.

Marcel Durand. His half brother.

Luca still had a hard time processing the news. Marcel was blond, but with blue eyes—like Luca's. He had shown a real interest and talent for running the exclusive champagne empire. Yet, his father had left the estate to him. Not Marcel. Did that mean he wanted Luca to run it? That he'd forgiven Luca for his mother's death?

Something tightened in his chest.

His father had died before Luca had the chance to

ask if he'd forgiven him. He'd also died before telling Luca about Marcel. Had he wanted Marcel to inherit and run the Legrand estate?

Luca revved the engine.

He'd never know what his father wanted, but whatever it was, it didn't change the fact that what Marcel was doing was shitty. He'd almost confided his suspicions to François but decided against it. Since his mother's death, Luca had always taken care of his affairs himself. This was no different, and if he was right, if Marcel was manufacturing these "incidents"—which only required an anonymous call to a tabloid divulging Luca's whereabouts, readily available on Google Calendar—then Luca would figure out a way to take care of Marcel himself.

The first step was to take a hiatus from his high-profile life, making sure no one would know where he was. So he'd rented a flat in a quiet part of town through a discreet agency, he'd started growing a beard—which itched like mad—and he'd been driving his Ducati around Paris. No one would suspect Luca Legrand, professional driver, to be on a Ducati, a make driven by an opposing team. He'd even bought himself a new phone with a new number so he wouldn't be contacted by friends…or tracked by Anika.

Only one problem.

He was bored stiff and had no idea if this hiatus would help with the mess he'd created.

No. The mess Marcel has created.

Grinding his teeth, Luca revved the engine again,

released the clutch and sprang forward just as the light changed to green. The thing was, before he'd known who Marcel was, he'd liked him. The man was smart, competent and had seemed like Luca's only ally when every other employee of the Legrand estate—*they aren't employees, they're family*, his father had always said—had shown him little more than polite but cold deference. Something else his father had always said was that trust takes time. Then there was forgiveness...

Luca took the next corner hard and when he spotted a police car at the other end of the street, he reminded himself to slow down. "You don't need to break any more fucking laws," he muttered to himself.

Just to be safe, he turned down a narrow side street—the kind that drove tourists crazy because they went unmarked on tourist maps—and then turned down another, which was narrow and deserted.

No, it wasn't deserted; there was a motorcycle—a Honda Shadow—parked at the side of the road beside an antique shop. The man astride it glanced Luca's way, watching him as Luca drove past. At the corner, Luca checked his rearview mirror.

Something was off. He could feel it by the way the man's helmeted head followed his departure. After Luca turned the corner, he stopped the bike by an empty storefront and parked. Leaving his helmet with the shaded visor on, he walked back to the corner and peered down the street.

The man was in the process of pulling off his helmet, and under that he wore a balaclava. With a final surreptitious glance up and down the street, the man strode into the shop with a crowbar hanging from his fingertips.

Fuck.

It was just his luck.

Luca's one goal was to avoid trouble and here he'd stumbled across a robbery in the middle of the goddamn day.

For the first time in two days, Jasmine forgot everything that had happened and wandered with delight through the shop she'd found using Google maps. It was off the beaten track, down some lonely little cobblestone street. And it was full of treasures.

This was not the type of pawnshop she was familiar with from the United States—a seedy place with bars on the windows where a greasy man wearing an undershirt picked his teeth behind an enclosed counter. This was a delightful boutique with beautiful items carefully displayed, everything from lamps and pots to clothing and jewelry.

"This is so…Paris," she said quietly to herself as she gazed about the tiny space.

There were so many exquisite pieces in the shop to choose from: necklaces, bracelets, earrings. There were also hand-embroidered silk scarves, funky original hats and handbags. There were antiques and what had to be one-of-a-kind items, like the silver oil lamp that reminded her of the stories Auntie Bibi used to whisper at bedtime when she slept over at her cousins as a young girl. Adventures and genies from *Arabian Nights*. She picked up the lamp, considering. Maybe this lamp was a sign that she should have her own adventure, just like Ash encouraged.

Though, a sex-venture?

Jazz smiled to herself. Crazy.

"Est-ce que je peux vous aider?" the man behind the counter asked.

"I'm sorry," Jasmine said, making her way toward him, the lamp, a silk scarf and a necklace clutched in her hands. Not that she needed any of the items but the prices were so good and Jazz was a sucker for a good deal. "I don't speak French. Do you speak English?" She leaned on the display case, her gaze drawn to the gorgeous jewelry inside.

"Yes, a little."

"Those are so pretty," she said, pointing to a pair of emerald-drop earrings.

"Would you like to take a look?"

Oh, yes please, she nearly gushed before she remembered her reason for being there. She absently rubbed the polished silver of the lamp and said, "I have a ring I'd like to sell."

"To sell? May I see?"

She set the lamp down on the counter and reached into her purse. Room key. Wallet. Cell phone. Passport. Hmm...where had she put that ring?

"It's in here somewhere." She dug around. Seriously, where the hell was the ring and what would she do if she'd lost it? She was sure Parker had paid about twenty grand for it. Not that she'd looked it up online or anything.

Okay. Maybe she had.

She located the ring at the bottom of her bag and placed it on the counter for the man to inspect, straightening her shoulders as he picked it up and scrutinized it through the lens of a loupe.

"C'est belle," the man murmured as he checked the ring from all angles.

The bells over the door tinkled but she didn't bother to look because something inside of her had shifted. An unknown weight lifted from Jasmine's shoulders, making her feel like a brand-new person. Could she really put her broken engagement behind her and be the woman Ash had described—carefree and adventurous? A woman who lived in the moment and was on the lookout for a sex-venture…

"Mettez-vous par terre!" a deep male voice shouted.

She turned toward the voice but nothing about the man behind her made sense. It was like she'd stumbled upon the set of a movie and her already muddled brain was having a hard time computing why a man would be wearing a ski mask in spring and brandishing a crowbar.

To her bewilderment, he strode forward and smashed the display case she'd been leaning on with one massive blow.

What the…?

"Écoutez-moi!" He shouted right in her face.

So weird. Was she dreaming? Because this whole

thing had an otherworldly quality to it and it just got worse when the dude reached into his beat-up jacket, pulled out a gun and pointed it at her.

"Par terre!"

Before Jasmine had time to consider what the man was shouting, he grasped the back of her neck and shoved her to the floor.

Oomph!

That hurt.

But now that she was on the ground, the thief ignored her and she lifted her head to find him swiping handfuls of jewelry and dumping the items into a leather satchel. Her ring was among the things he took.

Something inside of her gut, something hot and heavy and furious, was not about to lie benignly on the floor while some petty criminal robbed this delightful shop.

And her.

After all she'd been through? She deserved that fucking ring. Or, rather, she deserved the money from that fucking ring so she could move on from the disaster that was her life.

With energy she had no idea she possessed, Jasmine sprang to her feet, grabbed the outstretched arm of the thug and clung to it like her life depended on it.

"You fucker!" Jasmine growled, twisting his arm in a move she'd learned in a self-defense class, forcing the man to drop the gun. She grabbed the strap of the satchel, pulling it off his shoulder.

"Salope!" The man swung the crowbar catching the side of her head.

The pain in her temple was so sharp and stinging, that warrior-Jasmine drained out of her system as she curled on the ground, gripping the satchel like a beloved teddy bear, feeling like she might vomit from the pain. What happened next would have confused her at the best of times, but her head was still spinning from being clocked and her body was still pumping with adrenaline, lack of sleep and jet leg...

There was a crash.

Followed by a wet *thunk* and a man cried out in pain.

A body crumpled heavily half on, half off her.

A hand appeared in front of her face, gesturing for her to take it in order to help her to her feet. *"Ça va?"*

And then Jasmine was standing on noodle-y legs, gazing into the face of a stranger. The man wore a black leather jacket and a black helmet with the visor raised, revealing a face with a scruffy beard, dark brows and...the clearest, bluest, most amazing eyes she'd ever seen.

And then there were four eyes, then six...

"Mademoiselle?" He snapped his fingers in front of her face.

She shook her head, and then wished she hadn't as stars appeared, dancing in front of her open eyes. She would have fallen if not for the strong hands gripping her arms, holding her up.

However, there were equally strong hands tugging on the strap of the satchel she was still clutching. The thug on the floor grappled for the bag and two things happened simultaneously. The bag slipped from her hands, spilling the contents on the tile floor just as a black leather boot swished past her line of vision, kicking the thief in the face and knocking him out. The rest happened in slow motion. Rings, earrings and necklaces scattered, jumping and skittering across the polished tile floor like live things freed from captivity. Jasmine caught sight of her ring bouncing along the hard floor, ricocheting off the bottom corner of the counter and landing—plunk— inside the passing boot of the stranger.

Without thinking, Jasmine lunged for the man's leg, reaching into the top of his boot for her ring, but he shook her off, glaring down at her and speaking harshly—probably cursing—in French. Then the man stilled, his head jerked toward the door and the street and Jasmine became aware of the sound of sirens approaching.

"Merde!"

With one powerful shake, the six-eyed man dislodged Jasmine from his leg and strode toward the door.

"Wait!" Jasmine scrambled to her feet and hurried out after the stranger in black. Once on the street, she saw him jogging toward a corner and Jasmine took off after him, calling, "Please, wait! You've got my ring!"

However, running in high heels was nearly impossible on the cobblestone street, so Jasmine paused to pull off her sling-back sandals and hurl them away—

she'd grab them later. Then she ran the rest of the distance in bare feet. Her head pounded like a drummer was between her ears, playing a solo at a heavy metal concert.

When she got to the corner, her legs wobbled and she could barely see straight.

There.

The man with her ring was straddling a motorcycle, the engine roaring to life as she stumbled toward him, stepping onto the road, holding her hand up to stop him.

Her brain must not have been functioning, because just as the man revved the engine of the motorcycle the world went sideways, and where once there was a street, a man and a motorcycle, there were now only quaint French rooftops, an impossibly blue sky and a bird flying at an odd angle.

Then everything went black.

CHAPTER THREE

JESUS FUCKING CHRIST.

Why couldn't Luca mind his own damn business?
Not only had he found himself caught in a robbery,
the police were only a block away and now a foreign
woman—based on the fact she was shouting in English—had fainted right in front of his bike.

"Non. Non, non, non." Luca put the bike in neutral, jumped off and bent down beside the crumpled
woman. He shook her shoulder. *"Reveillez-vous."*
Wake up.

The woman moaned, her lids fluttered and then
she passed out again. He could see the beginnings
of a bruise blossoming along her hairline.

"La vache!" The words scraped the back of
his throat. Glancing up and down the street, Luca
weighed his options. What if he propped her unconscious body in a doorway…

A quick survey of the street revealed that the two
closest doors were covered in paper with signs in the
window advertising space for rent.

Not good.

The sirens were loud and close.

Dammit. He couldn't leave her. And he definitely couldn't get caught at the scene of a crime. He'd wind up in another media shitstorm.

Luca fit his hands beneath the woman's arms and lifted her to her feet. She briefly came to, giving him just enough time to instruct her to straddle the bike. However, once she was astride, she slumped forward.

The sound of more sirens approaching from another direction got Luca's pulse racing. He scooted the woman's body forward on the seat—God, she wasn't very big, was she?—and then straddled the seat behind her. He shifted into first and then wrapped his left arm around the woman's waist to hold her steady while he slowly drove the seven blocks, down side streets and alleys, to his rented flat. The ride only took ten minutes and would have been faster if he could have shifted into a higher gear, but that was impossible to do while holding on to an unconscious woman.

The fact she was still out cold was not a good sign.

She better not die.

What the hell was he doing, bringing an unconscious foreigner back to his flat? He must be out of his mind. Luca could see the headlines smeared across the papers and news channels: Dead Foreigner Found in Luca Legrand's Secret Residence. Foul Play Suspected.

But what choice did he have?

Luca parked his motorcycle in the underground lot, carefully scooped the woman up into his arms and carried her to the elevator that would take him to the fifth floor.

Once inside the flat, he laid her on his bed, got an ice pack out of the freezer—one he kept for when his leg ached—wrapped it in a towel and placed it on the woman's temple.

"Ne me quitte pas," he whispered, brushing hair off her forehead and temple so he could press the cold pack against her wound.

"What does that mean?" she asked softly, her eyes still closed.

Oh, thank God. "I'm asking you not to die. Please."

A small smile touched her lips and she covered his hand with hers. Her touch was light and cool, and Luca felt a stirring of tenderness toward this complete stranger.

"Okay," she murmured. "I'll try."

Then she passed out again.

Rubbing his temples, he gazed down at the slight woman who took up less than a third of his bed. She was showing all of the signs of a concussion; he'd seen it too many times to count on the racing circuit, and although he couldn't risk taking her to a hospital or calling an ambulance, he had to get her medical help.

Back in the bedroom, in the drawer of the small bedside table, was his old phone, the one he hadn't turned on in two weeks. He grabbed it, booted it up and typed a name into his contact list. Then he pressed the call button. As the phone rang, his heart beat fiercely in his chest.

It wasn't anxiety, nor was it adrenaline. This was something else, like he was teetering on the edge of a precipice, vertigo pulling at him, forcing him to jump, and just as he felt himself fall…he noticed the rocks below.

Jasmine woke up to the sound of her own groans. She lay there for a few minutes, listening to the pounding cymbals inside her head, each clash punctuated with a sharp pain that lanced the side of her skull and reverberated through her temples down to her jaw.

Random images from the last few days flashed through her brain. Her wedding had been cancelled, she'd boarded a plane to Paris…

Jasmine's stomach heaved dryly as she recalled nearly getting kicked off the plane. But she hadn't, had she? She'd made it to Paris, right?

Then what…?

Hmm…? Why was it so hard to remember? Was she hungover? She sat up and her head swam like she was wearing glasses with the wrong prescription. Wait a second, she didn't wear glasses, did she?

She touched her face. No glasses. Then Jasmine rubbed her eyes, and when her vision cleared, she took in her surroundings. She didn't recognize a thing.

Where the hell was she?

"Ah, our patient is awake."

Jasmine turned her head—too quickly—causing her to squeeze her lids shut in pain. When she opened her eyes, she saw a man she'd never seen before. He was tall and thin, wearing a tailored shirt and pants. His face was all angles with sunken eyes and cheeks that made his cheekbones prominent. He had close-cropped salt-and-pepper hair and smiled kindly.

"Who are you?"

"My name is Hugo Caron. I am a doctor." The man spoke English slowly, with a French accent.

"Where am I?"

"You are in a private residence in Paris."

"In Paris?"

"Yes. You have bumped your head and I believe you have sustained a concussion. I need to perform some tests to see how serious it is."

When the man stepped to the side of the bed, Jasmine realized there was someone else in the room. Another man who stood in the shadows.

"Who's that?" she asked, pointing.

The doctor turned, as if he also hadn't realized there was someone there. "That is…" he began slowly, "the man who found you. You were unconscious on the street. He brought you here and called me."

"Oh."

Why was everything so foggy? Why did none of this make sense? What had happened to her once she'd arrived in Paris?

"Oh!" She put her hand to her mouth, a snippet of a memory returning.

Have yourself a sex-venture. It was Ashley's voice in her head.

Slowly this time, Jazz took in her surroundings.

The queen-sized bed with the dark sheets and comforter. A masculine choice. The room, a foil to the suite at the hotel—oh, wait, she remembered the hotel! It was airy and light and decorated with antiques—this room was painted taupe and had modern furnishings.

"I'm going to do some tests and then ask you some questions, okay?"

Jazz nodded but stopped herself when the motion caused instant nausea. "Okay," she whispered.

The doctor shone a light in each of her eyes and then asked her to follow his finger as he moved it from side to side in front of her face. He checked her ears with a scope, and her hearing by speaking quietly into each one. With gentle fingers, he touched a tender spot on the side of her head.

"Ouch."

"I'm sorry." He tilted her head up and to the side to get a better look at whatever injury she'd sustained and he *hmm*ed.

"Okay. Straighten your arm out to the side," the doctor instructed. "Now I'm going to push down, try to resist. Good." He changed his grip so that he held the underside of her arm and asked her to push down against his hold and then he did the same on the other side.

Following that, he helped her to stand and asked her to balance on one leg and then the other, and each time he instructed her to touch her finger to her nose while balancing on one foot. There were some more balance and coordination tests before he helped her back onto the bed. He pulled up a chair right beside it and leaned forward.

"I'm going to ask you some questions, okay? You might not know the answers to some but don't worry. It's normal to experience some short-term memory loss after a head injury."

"Okay." Jasmine touched the side of her head gingerly.

The doctor proceeded to ask her full name, where she lived, what she did for a living. All of those were easy to answer. She may have fibbed that she was still employed.

"How long have you been in Paris?"

"Just a day. I think. What day is it? The twenty-fifth?"

"Yes, June twenty-fifth. Good. Where are you staying in Paris?"

"Um…a hotel. It's very pretty, very posh."

"Do you remember the name?"

"Ahh…l'hotel…d'something?" Jasmine bit her lip. "I can't remember, but it's near the Eiffel Tower."

The doctor raised a single brow. "I see. So, what brought you to Paris?"

"It's my honeymoon."

The man straightened. "And where is your husband, madame?"

"My husband?" Jasmine put a hand to her forehead. "I'm sorry. No. It's not my honeymoon." She shook her head and then wished she hadn't. "I'm not married. I just always wanted to come to Paris on my honeymoon." The words came out in a flurry.

"So, are you here with anyone?"

"Um…no. Just me. By myself." Jasmine was vaguely aware of the doctor getting up and going to speak quietly to the man who had been observing from the corner of the room.

"What happened to me?" Jasmine asked.

The doctor didn't answer as the conversation between the two men increased in volume. Were they arguing? Over what? Surely not her?

"Excuse me?" She waved. "Hello?"

Still the men did not respond. The doctor was gesturing at her and speaking rapidly in French. The other man made some guttural remarks and then threw his hands in the air.

"Hey," Jasmine called. "Can someone please tell me what's going on?"

"*Oui, bien sûr.*" The doctor turned toward her. "We were just discussing your situation. You have a mild concussion. It's nothing to worry about. However, you must be observed for twenty-four hours." He glanced back at the man in the corner. "I can take you to the hospital—but you have no passport."

"Oh, yes I do," Jasmine said. "It's in my bag."

"And where is your bag, *mademoiselle*?"

"It's—" She bit her lip. Blinked. "Isn't it here?"

The doctor turned to speak quietly to the other man who answered quickly. "*Non.* You have nothing here except for what you are wearing."

"Really?" Where the hell was her bag? It would have everything. Her phone, her hotel key, her ID, Parker's credit cards!

Dammit!

"So," Jasmine said slowly, "what will happen to me if I go to the hospital?"

"You will be asked to show identification and because you don't have any, they will have to contact the embassy and your next of kin."

Jasmine held up her hand. "No." The last thing she needed was to have to contact her parents, or worse, Parker, and ask for help after being in Paris only one day. She wasn't ready to face him yet. Absolutely not an option.

"What are my other choices?"

"That you stay here. My friend has kindly offered to observe you for twenty-four hours."

The man standing in shadows muttered something beneath his breath. Whatever it was, it didn't sound like he was thrilled with the idea of *observing* her. Well, Jasmine was not overly keen on being watched by a complete stranger, either, thank you very much.

"There must be some other option."

"You don't know where you're staying. You are here alone and have no identification or money. Unless you know someone in Paris, you do not have many choices, *mademoiselle*."

Slowly—very slowly—Jasmine tilted her head to the side. "What about you? Can't I stay with you?" She pointed at the doctor.

"*Je suis désolé*. I'm sorry but it is impossible. My work has me flying to Italy this evening." The doctor turned toward the other man and gestured him forward. "Luca is a good man." The doctor coughed as if to cover up a chuckle. "He will take excellent care of you until you remember where you are staying."

"What if I can't remember?"

"Your memory should return soon. But if it doesn't, I'm sure the two of you can figure things out." The man's lips twisted as if to repress a grin. "Now," he glanced at the watch on his wrist. "I really must go before I miss my flight." He nodded to Jasmine. *"Au revoir, mademoiselle."*

The doctor exited the bedroom and the other man—Luca—followed. Jasmine could hear the two of them continuing their heated discussion outside the door, though it became more muted as they moved farther down the hallway.

She pressed the heels of her hands to her eyelids, willing herself to remember what had happened. Something.

Anything.

But for the life of her, the last thing Jasmine remembered was Ashley saying, *Buy condoms, lots and lots of condoms.*

"She can't stay here," Luca insisted once the bedroom door was closed.

Hugo, who was the team physician for Luca's racing team, had not only treated Luca after various wipeouts—including the shattered leg that had ended his career—he'd been a close friend ever since Luca joined the team five years ago. While he'd briefly explained his predicament with the family estate, and Hugo understood his need for discretion, Luca had kept most of the details to himself. Including the robbery.

"I'm sure she'll remember the name of her hotel by the morning. Anyway, you know how important observation is in these first twenty-four hours. This woman has no one to watch her." Hugo smiled gently. "Except you."

"Isn't there another way? I am supposed to be lying low. Not harboring an amnesiac tourist."

"It's only for one night."

Luca groaned in defeat.

Hugo patted his arm. "Everything will be fine." Just then, Hugo's phone dinged and he tapped on it. "My cab is here." He tucked his phone into his pocket and headed for the front door.

"Hugo, wait." Luca exhaled. He hated the fact that he had to say this. "You can't breathe a word of this to anyone, do you understand?"

"Of course." The expression Hugo wore was kind. And most welcome after the way others had treated him since the sex scandal. "Give her acetaminophen for the pain. You know the drill. Rest. No TV." Hugo reached for the door handle. *"Bonne chance, mon ami."*

Luca banged his head—once, twice, three times—against the closed door after Hugo left, and then a noise from down the hall had him spinning around. The woman stood there, eyes wide, her feet bare, thick waves of dark hair shadowing half her face.

"I'm sorry."

Her soft apology did more to diffuse Luca's anger than he would have expected. "Why are you sorry?"

"For putting you out." She gestured to his flat in general. "It's obvious you don't want me here." She walked toward him, taking careful steps. Whether it was because her head hurt or because she was scared of him, Luca couldn't tell. "It's just…" She seemed to be weighing her words. "I don't think I could deal with a hospital waiting room or the embassy right now. I'm still feeling a bit dizzy."

Hugo was right…whoever this woman was, she needed to be taken care of. "It's okay," he said eventually, forcing a smile. "I've changed my plans for this evening." *Plans? What plans, Luc?*

"Oh." A little wrinkle formed between her brows.

"Please. You are welcome to stay the night."

"Are you sure?"

"Yes."

She took a tentative step forward and then another until she stood right in front of him. The top of her head came to just below his chin, her face was tilted up so she could meet his gaze. Her lips were pink and full—the kind of lips Anika would have paid a fortune for—but it was her eyes that captivated him. Liquid brown, like melted chocolate, with smudged mascara that rimmed her wide eyes, only making them appear larger.

There was no fucking way he could say no to those eyes.

"My name is Jasmine. Jasmine Sweet." Her lips trembled with an uncertain smile as she extended her hand. "And you are Luca…?"

"Luca. Luca Deschamps," he lied.

CHAPTER FOUR

THE MAN UNNERVED HER.

There was an intensity to those blue eyes—so dramatic against his dark brows, dark hair and olive skin—that made her feel as if his gaze was boring inside of her, seeking something. But what? It left her feeling shaky and…tingly.

Could be the concussion.

Still…somehow, she felt comfortable here. She'd only half lied when she'd told him why she wanted to stay. The truth was, he was doing her a favor. Now she could put off dealing with Parker and her family until later. Plus, it was one thing to be traveling solo when she knew where she was staying. It was another when she was concussed, confused and without any identification.

"Are you hungry?" the man asked.

"What time is it?"

He flipped his wrist to check his watch. "Seven thirty."

As if on cue, her stomach rumbled and she laughed, though it sounded false to her ears. "I guess so."

"Come. Sit."

She followed him into the open-concept kitchen, dining room and living room. Like the bedroom, the space was stark. Wood floors, a plain gray leather couch, white walls with dark beams overhead and the floor-to-ceiling windows that seemed to be the norm in Paris.

Jasmine sat on a gray leather barstool at the breakfast counter, leaning her elbows on the granite surface, her hand going automatically to her aching temple.

"Un moment." The man—Luca—strode back down the hall, returning a moment later with the ice pack and two tablets. He first placed the pack against his cheek, murmuring something in French before passing it to her. "It's still cold. It'll help with swelling and bruising."

"Thank you."

Then he dropped the tablets into her upturned hand, his fingers accidentally grazing her palm.

There were those damn tingles again.

She frowned, which hurt. Still, her gaze followed him as he opened a small refrigerator, removed a glass jug of clear bubbling liquid, poured it into a tumbler and handed it to her. She took a sip of the sparkling water, which burned quite pleasantly as she swallowed the pills.

"Are you okay to sit? Do you need to lie down?"

"I'm fine, thank you."

His lips turned up at the ends—not a real smile—as he prompted her to apply the ice pack by taking her hand and placing it against her head.

"It will help."

Jasmine closed her eyes as she iced, ignoring the tingles—and certainly not thinking about the source of the tingles. Once again, she willed herself to re-member what had happened after her arrival in Paris, but there was nothing behind her lids but blackness interspersed by shards of light that flashed with each beat of her pulse. For some reason, trying to remem-ber made her head hurt more, so instead, she simply listened to Luca work in the kitchen.

Cupboards opened and closed. The sound of a nearby drawer as it was sliding open and closed on its runners. A knife against a cutting board. Slicing. Another drawer and the sound of cutlery. The clink of glass against the granite countertop followed by the pop of a cork and the gurgling of liquid being poured.

When she opened her eyes, a glass of red wine sat in front of her, as did a plate of various cheeses, finely sliced meats, nuts and olives that he'd placed in the middle of the counter between them.

Luca was tipping his own wine glass back and Jasmine noticed the movement of his Adam's apple as he swallowed. He had a strong neck. Lots of ten-dons and muscles that worked in harmony.

And then he caught her staring. "Yes?"

She cleared her throat and pointed at her glass. "Should I be drinking?"

"Just a glass. It's good for you. But then water." He gestured to the platter of food. "Please."

Hesitantly, Jasmine reached for a piece of cheese.

Oh, it was good, and the more she ate, the more hungry she felt.

When was the last time she'd eaten?

Glancing down, she noticed her dirt-smeared blouse. When was the last time she'd changed? Showered? Turning and tilting her chin in a way she hoped was inconspicuous, Jasmine gave her pits a sniff.

Ugh. Not the freshest.

"Um…" Jasmine began after eating a handful of nuts and three slices of meat. "I hate to trouble you, but would I be able to take a shower?"

The man turned from where he'd been pulling items out of the small refrigerator. "It's not a good idea."

"Excuse me?"

"Taking a shower is not recommended. If you faint, you could hurt yourself." He poured flour onto a plate and added spices with his fingers from pinch jars on the counter. After wiping his hands on a nearby towel, he said, "Come with me."

Jasmine eased off the stool onto her bare feet. The act of standing made her light-headed and she kept a hand on the wall as she followed Luca slowly down the hall, right to the end where there was a large bathroom tiled in slate-colored travertine. There was an ultramodern glassed-in shower big enough for two and a large free-standing soaker tub with a washing wand propped at one end.

"Don't fill the tub," Luca said, gesturing to it. "There are towels here." He pulled a thick white towel out of a cupboard. "I'll find some clothes for you and leave them in the bedroom."

"Oh, thank you."

"Dinner should be ready in forty-five minutes."

"Okay."

Jasmine leaned on the counter for support and turned to find blue eyes scrutinizing her, making her already wobbly knees feel weaker.

"Do you need help?"

Jasmine swallowed.

Was he serious? Would he actually help her? She glanced at his hand propped on the side of the doorframe. Tanned. Nicely shaped fingernails. Big hands.

What would it feel like to have them removing her clothing?

Helping her into the tub?

Washing her body?

Oh, God.

The tingles she'd been feeling all evening spread from her extremities down her lower back and abdomen, culminating at the very juncture of her legs.

"*Mademoiselle*? Are you okay?"

Jasmine realized her breaths were coming in short little pants and she was gripping the counter like a life vest in an ocean of orgasmic waves.

"Fine," she said quickly. "I'm totally fine."

"Do you need my help?" he asked once again.

She met his gaze. There was concern there and nothing more. This man was not coming on to her, as insistent as her imagination was. Luca was simply being helpful. And kind.

She smiled what she hoped was a reassuring smile. "I'm all good."

"Bien." He stepped back out the door. But before he left, he ducked his head inside the bathroom one more time. *"Mademoiselle?* Please, keep the door open."

Luca left the woman in the bathroom and went to the wardrobe in the bedroom. There was very little to choose from that would fit her, as the collection of clothes he'd brought was sparse. In one drawer he found a pair of shorts that could be tightened with a drawstring and one of his favorite T-shirts from the Red Bull Ring MotoGP event in Austria, 2016.

He left the items on the bed and then went to stand outside the door of the bathroom. It was partially open. He raised his hand to knock, but before he did, his glance went to the mirror, visible through the opening.

Jasmine's back was to him—her bare back.

Merde...

Her spine swayed gracefully and there were two delightful little dimples at the top of her buttocks. Her skin was a flawless caramel color, a contrast to the dark hair that cascaded in waves between her shoulder blades. Her ass was...

Jesus, her ass...

Clenching his fists, Luca turned away from the barely opened door. What the hell was he doing? Now he was a fucking voyeur? This woman's mere presence was trouble enough. The last thing he needed to be doing was ogling her through a semi-closed door. He certainly did not need to be entertaining thoughts of running his finger down the indent of her backbone, dipping into one dimple and then the other and cupping the glorious globes of her ass in each of his hands.

Squeezing before exploring...

Enough!

With a strengthened resolve, he knocked on the wall beside the partly open door. *"Mademoiselle?"*

"Yes?" Her voice sounded startled. And hopeful.

What the fuck?

"I've left some clothes for you in the bedroom. I can launder your clothes tonight so they are clean for tomorrow. Just leave them on the bed."

"Oh." Her voice sounded breathless. "Thank you."

Luca marched down the hall without another word. He needed to focus his attention on tasks like preparing the fish for dinner. Unfortunately, his body wasn't exactly cooperating.

It's been a long time, Luca...and that ass...

"Silencieux!" he muttered to himself.

There was no way he would get involved with an amnesiac, concussed tourist. Honestly. It was a bad idea all around. No matter how much his libido thought differently.

Twenty minutes later, when the fish was warming in the oven, he glanced down the hall with a hint of worry. Should he check on her? What if she'd ignored his recommendation and had filled the tub with water, then fallen asleep or passed out and drowned.

Shit.

He hurried down the hall and was just about to push open the door when Jasmine came out wearing nothing but a towel. The scent of his own shampoo wafted about her and he was forced to squash the insane desire to bury his nose in her hair and breathe her in.

Before tugging the towel from her body and tasting that warm skin.

"Hi." The woman's eyes were wide and gorgeous, and appeared much more innocent, sans makeup. That should have quieted his libido.

It did not. Quite the opposite.

He purposefully took a step back, tipped his head and said, "Dinner is ready. I hope you like fish."

He didn't wait for a response but simply spun around and made his way back to the kitchen where he poured himself a large glass of wine and drank most of it before Jasmine made her appearance.

Jesus.

If he'd thought she looked good enough to eat wearing nothing but a towel and the scent of his soap, he was mistaken. The sight of her in his too-big clothes was—fuck—an instant and immediate turn-on.

"Whatever it is, it smells wonderful," she said, softly. Shyly.

Seriously, she was killing him.

"It's sole meunière. Very simple. Just fish, lemon, butter and parsley. Oh, and potatoes."

She sat down at the counter and shrugged. "Sounds good to me."

Luca took the plates from the oven and set them on the counter. He slid cutlery across, refilled her water glass and went around the counter to join her on the other side. Ten minutes ago he had been famished. Now, sitting within touching distance of the American woman, Luca's senses were so enraptured by her that his hunger for food was displaced by an even stronger hunger. Her skin was still warm from the bath, so warm he could feel heat radiating off her. With the heat came the scent of his toiletries but somehow feminized when combined with her own natural scent.

Then there were her eyes.

Whenever their gazes met, he found himself captivated by her large brown eyes, as if sinking into them in a wonderful way, like Charlie at the river of chocolate in Willy Wonka's chocolate factory. He wanted to stay there, drinking it in, forever.

It was Jasmine who broke his stare, turning her attention to the food in front of her. She delicately cut off a piece of fish and placed it on her tongue.

"Mmm…my God." She closed her eyes while her fork was still aloft. "That is so good." Opening her eyes, she smiled at him. "That's more than just fish and lemon and parsley."

"*Non*. That's all it is. But everything is fresh, of course."

"Of course." She took another bite. "You French really know how to cook."

Luca grinned. It was a cliché, and yet coming from this woman her remark pleased him. They finished their meal in relative silence—except for the odd sound of orgasmic enjoyment, which was not helping to cool his libido in the least—and once their plates were clean, Luca took them to the sink and washed them.

"Thank you."

He looked up. "You don't need to thank me every five minutes."

"I know but…" She played absently with a strand of hair. "Your kindness means so much…" Her voice caught but she recovered quickly. "Particularly when I'm a complete stranger to you."

"Really, it is nothing."

She exhaled softly. "Can I ask you a question?"

He glanced up. "Of course."

Her fingers strayed to the lump on her head. "Is there anything else you can tell me about how you found me?"

Luca pulled in his lower lip. His new beard felt strange against his mouth. "*Non*. I found you passed out on the road."

"Where?"

"Not far from here. Maybe seven or eight blocks away."

She touched her head. "And I was alone? No bag, no shoes?"

"Yes."

"Was I mugged?"

"Perhaps. I really don't know." *Liar.* But something in his gut told him that the less anyone knew about this whole ordeal, including her, the better. She might be trustworthy, but he didn't know for sure. Jogging her memory might be like opening Pandora's box, unleashing a situation he couldn't handle right now. He'd let her stay the night, then tomorrow morning he'd figure out his next move.

"God, I wish I could remember."

"Mmm." Luca cut some more slices of cheese and added them to the platter from earlier. Not because they needed more cheese or more food, but to give him something to do during this conversation.

"I've tried to remember, but…"

"It's normal." Luca pushed the platter closer to the woman. "To have a lapse in memory. It will return. Sometimes the more you try to concentrate, the harder it is. You need to rest. Tomorrow you will remember and be able to go back to your old life."

"You speak as if from experience."

Luca broke a piece of cheese and ate it, considering his answer. "I have had a concussion before."

"How did you get yours?"

"I—" Luca paused, only for a second "—have ridden motorbikes since I was eight years old. I have had a few accidents." The last of which ended his career. A ninety percent recovery wasn't enough when it was your gear foot.

"Don't you wear a helmet?"

"Of course. Helmets have saved my life. But you can still get a concussion with a helmet."

She tilted her head as she gazed at him. Her brows

drew together as if a thought—or a memory—had just come to her.

"What is the last thing you remember?"

Jasmine plucked a piece of cheese from the plate. She had nice hands, her fingers slim and delicate, her nails painted a neutral color.

"I remember flying to Paris. This was supposed to be—" She glanced up. "A girl's trip with my best friend, but she's expecting a baby—unexpectedly—and…"

Luca waited silently for Jasmine to continue.

"Anyway, I decided to come by myself."

"Sometimes traveling alone is the best way." Luca had enjoyed a few trips to Greece on his own. Just to get away from…everything.

Jasmine took a sip of water. And then another. She had one more before finishing. "Anyway, I drank a lot on the flight. And…" She massaged her neck. "I may have drunk a lot in the twenty-four hours before that." She glanced his way. "Not sure I ate a whole lot during that time." She rolled her shoulders and sighed. "I also haven't slept very much. So it's possible my head injury was simply a result of me passing out from exhaustion, hunger or the world's worst hangover. Likely a combination of all three."

"It is possible," he said slowly. "But by the look of the bruise, it was probably more than that." What was wrong with him? Why didn't he simply agree with her, put her to bed and get rid of her in the morning?

Jasmine shrugged. "Maybe. Which would explain

my missing bag. And shoes." Her frown deepened. "Shit. What am I going to do?"

"You will have to go to the embassy. Apply for an emergency passport."

"How can I do that when I don't have any identification?"

"What about in your hotel room? Is there anything there? A copy of your passport? Other ID?"

The woman narrowed her eyes as she thought and then slowly shook her head. "I don't think so. Maybe. But…" She laughed awkwardly. "I don't even know where my hotel is."

Luca stood. This conversation wasn't helping. "You said you didn't sleep much."

She nodded.

"You should get some rest. Sleep is important."

"Let me help clean up, first."

"Non, merci." He indicated the hall. "There is a new toothbrush in the drawer in the bathroom. Please."

"Okay." Jasmine stood and Luca could see that her balance was off because she grabbed the countertop. After a pause and a couple of breaths she made her way down the hall to the bathroom, shutting the door this time.

Damn.

No, not damn. What was he thinking?

When he heard the door open a few minutes later, Luca called, "Jasmine?"

"Yes?"

"I will be waking you up throughout the night. To check on you. Please, don't be alarmed."

CHAPTER FIVE

I will be waking you up...to check on you.

There was nothing sexual about that comment. Absolutely nothing. In fact, it was the opposite of sexual; it was merely a statement made by a man who had been forced to take care of a strange American woman he'd found passed out on the street.

So why did she feel turned on?

She stood in the bedroom doorway, staring at the kitchen. Luca stopped working at the sink to glance down the hall, and even from a distance, Jasmine was immobilized by his gaze. After an indeterminate amount of time, he looked away and the spell was broken. Jasmine hurried into the bedroom, pulled the covers back and crawled between the sheets. The cotton was cool and welcoming to her overheated body. The bed was soft, and for the first time in days, Jasmine relaxed.

Even the throbbing pain in her temple had mellowed to a dull ache.

She turned her head and breathed in. The subtle fragrance of Luca's aftershave clung to his pillow.

Spicy. Masculine. Delicious. Lying on her side, she stole the other pillow and hugged it, burrowing her nose into the faint scent. God. What would it be like to have sex with him? To feel the scruff of his unshaven jaw against her sensitive skin? His hands—those strong hands—touching her body? Exploring. Squeezing. Penetrating.

His mouth—oh, yes, she'd sneaked glances at his mouth during dinner. Full lips. Expressive. The kind of lips that were made for kissing.

French kissing.

And maybe more.

Weren't French men known for enjoying kissing a woman…everywhere?

Jasmine rubbed her knees together.

She'd never experienced that.

Apart from some serious groping in high school with a shy cowboy, Parker had been her first and only. He had wooed her with romantic dinners and expensive gifts. He'd complimented her all the time, but with words, never touch. When he'd told her he wanted to wait until marriage to have sex, Jasmine had put her foot down and nixed that idea. She'd read an article in one of Parker's men's magazines about the importance of being compatible in bed and had even shared it with him.

The following night they'd had wine with dinner—lots and lots of wine, now that she thought about it—and that had been their first time. Her first time, period, so she hadn't had anything to compare it to.

Well, except her imagination.

But she'd been too uncertain to ask for what she wanted, at first, and later Parker had been so busy with work they could never find the time. And he was so generous about everything else, she didn't want to pressure him.

But doubts had crept in and she'd started to wonder if she was somehow inadequate.

She rolled onto her back, the pillow lying unhugged on top of her. How had she not seen what was going on with her ex-fiancé?

Jasmine had found there were only two ways to alleviate her unsatisfied arousal. Masturbation and fantasy.

Highly detailed sexual fantasies.

They had been her form of counting sheep every night after Parker had nodded off.

She wrapped her arms around the pillow on top of her, letting her mind drift, calling up her latest fantasy involving a sexy space crime fighter, an outlaw in an intergalactic universe.

In this reoccurring fantasy, her hero rescues her from an evil alien's harem and whisks her away to a secluded tropical planet on the outskirts of the galaxy. Her outlaw takes it upon himself to teach her to enjoy sex again. He starts slowly, touching her—only touching—every fucking inch of her body until she is moaning with desire. Then he leaves her wanting on a bed made of some super-awesome alien material that heightens a person's sexual desire when they simply lie on top of it. He returns the next day, this time kissing and licking her entire body.

In her mind, everything was crystal clear…

He's lying between her spread legs, his strong hands pushing her thighs wider, his dark hair—almost black—brushing her belly. A firm tongue nudging her clit one way and then the other. When her hips buck, he holds them down, pressing her into the mattress that sends blasts of arousal across the surface of her skin and into the very depths of her body. When next she raises her hips, he lowers his mouth until he's sucking on her most vulnerable parts, her ass in his hands, kissing, licking, sucking until she can't stand it…

Jasmine's hand roved down beneath the sheets. She wasn't even aware of untying the string at the waistband of the shorts until her fingers delved into her wet heat, mimicking the tongue of her fantasy lover.

God.

You like that?

"Yes, oh, yes," Jasmine murmured against the pillow.

You want this?

"Yes." The word was said on a gasp as she rubbed her clit with the pads of her fingers.

*Oh, baby…*another lick, another suck, *You've got the sweetest pussy. I can't get enough…*

Jasmine lifted her hips off the bed as her fingers penetrated her slick channel. The man in her fantasy looked up from what he was doing. Dark hair. Dark brows. A week-old beard. The bluest eyes.

This wasn't the man from her fantasy.

It was Luca.

Her orgasm hit her like a rogue asteroid, knocking her out of orbit, shattering her as she pressed one hand on top of the other between her legs lest she literally explode.

Luca stood outside the door. The woman was moaning. In pain? Should he go in? He put his hand on the doorknob and was about to turn the handle when she cried out.

Then everything went quiet.

That was not good. He didn't want to walk in to find her passed out. Or worse. He waited a few seconds before knocking.

"Jasmine? Is everything okay?"

"I'm fine," she called in a high-pitched voice.

"*Bien*. I'll wake you around midnight, okay?"

"Yes. Okay. Perfect. That's good. Thank you."

Luca's hands lingered on the door before he moved to the bathroom to wash up. It was early, yet, for him, only nine thirty, but he should try to rest if he was going to rouse the woman every four hours.

"What else do you have to do?" he asked his reflection. "You've got two more weeks to wait before returning to work. You should be glad for the distraction."

Distraction was fine, but this distraction was a little too…distracting.

He dried his face, the image of Jasmine's naked back burned into his irises.

"She'll be gone tomorrow," he muttered, then he hung up the towel and turned the light off.

On his way to the living room, he paused outside her door, listening. No more moans. No more sounds. He hoped that meant all was well. He moved past and settled his frame onto the sofa, reaching for the laptop that sat on the coffee table. Like every night for the past week, he navigated the web to the Legrand website.

When Myra Monte took over the estate's publicity, she convinced Luca to auction off one of three remaining bottles of the Legrand Goût des Rubis. The exclusive rosé blend had been commissioned for the marriage of Grace Kelly to Prince Rainier in 1956, and the bottle included a two-carat ruby in its label. While the bottles were meant to be passed down through the family, Luca had readily made the decision to give one up for the auction if it meant he could maintain control of the estate.

Already the international interest from collectors had been a distraction from Luca's dishonor and prompted an uptick in champagne prices.

Luca entered a name into the search engine: Marcel Durand. He'd done the same thing every night for a week. Watching for any new article or item to show up. He creeped his social media pages and watched for any indication of the slimy eel Luca knew him to be. But, he had to admit, the guy knew how to keep his nose clean.

Luca could almost hear François's voice telling him he could learn a thing or two from this young man.

Salaud! Bastard!

"Literally." Luca ground his teeth.

He was just about to type in another search when he noticed something new. An announcement of Marcel's engagement to Lydia Fournier—hmm… the name sounded familiar. Luca must have met her at one of the functions the company had held in the last eleven months. She was blonde and tall, almost as tall as Marcel, who stood beside her in the photo that had been posted in today's paper. Luca skimmed the article, reading that she had been attending university in Madrid. Then he stopped reading.

So, Marcel was living a perfect life. That would end when Luca exposed him for what he was, though he still had no idea how to go about doing it.

Probably because it was difficult to make a move when he was in hiding, rarely going out during the day. Of course, today had been the exception. This morning, he'd gone for a long ride along the Loire River valley. Riding was the only thing that kept him sane.

But instead of sanity, what had he gotten? An American damsel in distress.

The polar opposite of sanity.

Worse, this damsel just happened to have gorgeous, thick hair, soul-melting eyes and the nicest ass he'd ever seen…

Luca pinched the bridge of his nose. He was a

sucker for a beautiful woman in need. Wasn't that how he'd met Anika? She'd had too much to drink during a party on a yacht. He'd held her hair while she got sick.

Without thinking about what he was doing—maybe it was a reminder of why not to get involved with the devil that was woman—Luca typed "Luca Legrand sex video" into the search engine.

Despite the fact that Luca's team had had the video taken down—and wanted to take legal action against the original site that posted it—it had spent far too long online before he'd become aware of the situation and had it handled. Millions of viewers had seen it.

Merde.

And millions were still talking about it, if the current search results from blogs and gossip sites were any indication. Luca didn't doubt the internet was rife with illegal copies that could still be viewed somewhere. The whole situation was a nightmare—one that felt impossible to contain. Some sadistic need to punish himself had him opening the original copy of the video and hitting the Play button. The video was dark and amateurish—because when he and Anika had made it, it was for their eyes only—but her face was clearly distinguishable. As was his as he tied her up, spread-eagled, to the bed. An act that took ultimate trust had been corrupted by exposure to the public.

Luca rubbed his forehead before exiting the video. He returned to the search results online and clicked on the first hit, then scrolled to the comments beneath the article. He knew he shouldn't, but he couldn't help himself. More figurative self-flagellation.

What an asshole.

Luca Legrand can tie me up anytime.

Anika deserves better than that sadistic pig.

He should be thrown in jail...

With a growl, he snapped the laptop lid closed, pushed the computer back onto the coffee table, got to his feet and paced the length of the small living room. What his surfing had confirmed for him was that he could not afford another scandal. He needed to get rid of the American woman first thing without her or anyone else finding out about his involvement.

He could drop her at the embassy—but she had no money and no one to vouch for her.

He could take her back to the street where the shop was to see if she would remember anything. Maybe her bag was still at the shop. Or, more likely, it was at the police station.

He opened the French doors onto the small balcony and went to stand at the rail, breathing in the night air, considering his options. The woman's memory was faulty and she didn't know his real name. Even if she tried to describe him to the police, what were the chances they'd find out it was him? He could vacate the flat, go somewhere else, maybe head south of the city to the villa he'd avoided for twelve years. Perhaps if he just dropped her off at the police station and then drove away...

No. The possibility that someone local would see him and recognize him was too much of a gamble. Once again, it was François's voice in his head telling him it was too risky.

He leaned his elbows on the rail and gazed out.

Wait.

He stood up straight.

Maybe he should call François and get him to help. François was as intent on keeping things quiet as Luca was.

That wasn't a bad idea.

Why hadn't he thought to call the lawyer sooner? He'd do it first thing in the morning.

With the decision made, Luca went back inside and settled onto the sofa, his bed for the night. The ride and fresh air this morning had tired him out. Worrying about the woman had taken the last of his energy and he was tired. However, instead of sleep, images of Jasmine's sweetly curved spine appeared behind his closed lids. Why he let his mind wander in that direction, he couldn't say. Maybe because she'd be gone by morning.

Luca saw himself kneeling behind her, hands on either side of her sloped hips, his tongue tracing the indent of her spine at the top of her ass. Circling those delicate dimples, kissing high up on the globes of her cheeks.

Luca?

"Hmm?"

Will you kiss me? Please?

She turned herself around, presenting the front

of herself. There was a silky patch of hair over her mound, so soft and glistening he had to stroke…with his cheek. "Where do you want me to kiss you?" he asked, gazing up at her.

Everywhere.

"It would be my pleasure," he mumbled quietly.

"Luca?"

Luca's eyes popped open. Jasmine was standing above him, gazing down at him with a—smirk?—on her face.

Fuck.

Sitting up quickly, Luca hoped to hide his raging erection from the woman who had caused it because she'd been starring in his fantasy only two seconds ago. "Jasmine?" He cleared his throat. "Are you okay?"

She nodded and then winced. "I'm fine. But I was lying in bed…" For some reason her cheeks turned pink. "And… I…" Her gaze met his. Her eyes sparkled.

Jesus, was she psychic and able to read his mind? Did she know what he'd been fantasizing about?

"I think I remember what happened."

CHAPTER SIX

SHE MUST HAVE woken him up. He'd sat up abruptly and looked startled by her appearance. Whatever he'd been dreaming about, it must have been good, based on the noticeable bulge behind the fly of his designer jeans. God, his girlfriend was one lucky woman, because that was one sizeable erection.

Hmm. Did he have a girlfriend?

Jasmine realized—with a start—that, first of all, she was staring at the man's crotch, and second of all, she really didn't know anything about him, other than that he drove a motorcycle and had had a concussion before.

"So, what do you remember?" he asked, looking as though he might stand but then thinking better of it. Jasmine hid her smile.

Who was she to judge? She'd been lying in bed totally fantasizing about *him*—in glorious detail—when out of nowhere a memory had surfaced. A quaint little shop on a narrow cobblestone street. A lamp. A scarf. And…a thief.

She'd been caught in a robbery.

It took her a few minutes to describe what she recalled while Luca listened carefully. "And what is the last thing you remember?"

"There was this man wearing a ski mask yelling at me in French. I didn't understand and then he pushed me…" Her hand went to her temple. "Or maybe he hit me." She frowned. "I kind of feel like he did both. Anyway, it's foggy, but that's the last thing I remember." She sat down on the edge of the couch.

Luca nodded slowly. "I'm so sorry, Jasmine. The thief must have taken your bag in the robbery."

"Yes. Probably." She rested her elbows on her knees.

Luca stood and went into the kitchen. "Anyway," he called, "I am happy that your memory is returning. Tomorrow, I'll help you figure out the next steps. You should be back in your hotel and back to your regular life in no time."

"Ye-es." Jasmine drew out the one-syllable word.

"Get some rest. Tomorrow will be busy." He gestured for her to return to the bedroom.

But Jasmine didn't want to return to the bedroom. She didn't want to waste what could be her one and only night with this enigmatic Frenchman by sleeping it away in his bed.

Alone.

Not to mention, she didn't want to go back to her hotel. In her mind she had a flash of the suite: the high ceilings, sheer drapes, a wrought-iron balcony—the room only served to remind her of the fact she was not on her honeymoon and that she was in Paris.

Alone.

She eyed Luca from beneath her curtain of hair. What she really wanted to do was to get to know him more.

No, what you really want to do is to ask him to take your clothes off—slowly—and do terrible—wonderful—things to your body.

"You know," Jasmine said, getting up and going to sit at the breakfast bar. The act of standing had made her feel light-headed all evening, but for some reason this time it didn't. That had to be a good sign, didn't it? "I don't actually feel that tired. I feel kind of…wired."

"Wired? I don't understand what that means." Luca poured himself a glass of water.

"It means I feel the opposite of tired. Is that normal, with a concussion?"

Luca tilted his head to regard her. "No. I don't think so."

"Hmm. Weird." Jasmine rested her elbows on the breakfast bar. "So, I gotta ask," she began. "Does your girlfriend mind that you have a strange woman spending the night in your apartment?"

Luca blinked. "Girlfriend?"

"Yes." She focused on her hands.

"*Non.* I'm not seeing anyone."

Her head snapped up. "Really?"

"Really."

"Huh.".

"What is this 'huh'?"

"Nothing. I'm just surprised." With a new bold-ness, Jasmine leaned across the breakfast bar, pulled Luca's sweating glass toward her and drank from the same spot he had drunk from.

His eyes followed her. "Why?"

"Because." She examined him from the corner of her eye. It seemed impossible that he was single. He was…well, what she knew of him was all positive. He was kind to strangers, for sure. He had the nicest hands—she couldn't look at them without imagin-ing them on her body. He filled out his clothes in all the right ways—she tilted her head to eye his crotch again. Very nice.

And then there were his eyes.

He had "I'm going to fuck you" eyes.

And she was here to say yes to those eyes.

But Jasmine wasn't ready to say any of that, so instead, she shrugged, turned the glass on the wet spot it had created on the counter and said, "You just seem like a good person."

He made a deep, guttural sound. "You don't know me."

Jasmine glanced up. "Are you saying you're not a good person?"

Luca shook his head and poured himself a sec-ond glass of water. When he didn't answer, Jasmine pushed herself to her feet and wandered into the liv-ing room, running her hands along the spartan book-shelves, pulling out copies of books—novels?—in French and a guide to Paris in English. She picked up an ornamental bowl made of alabaster and weighed it in her hands before setting it down again and moving on. What quickly became apparent was that there was not one personal item in this space. No photographs. No personal papers or keepsakes. No clutter. It was completely neutral.

She turned to Luca. "Who's apartment is this?"

"It's mine," he said, though it sounded defensive. Even with the sexy French accent.

"No, it's not."

He cleared his throat. "It belongs to a friend of mine. It's mine for now."

Jasmine was just about to ask why he was staying at a friend's place, when Luca answered the question for her.

"My girlfriend and I broke up six months ago. It wasn't…amicable. I've been staying here since." He turned his back so she couldn't see his expression.

Was he angry? Heartbroken? Something else?

Hmm. Well, he was single and his explanation made sense. Her gaze swept the room once more and she spied his laptop sitting on the coffee table.

"Hey, can I borrow your laptop?" She strode over and flipped it open.

"Attendez!"

Startled, Jasmine jumped back. Luca strode over and snatched the machine off the coffee table before taking it into the kitchen and setting it on the counter facing away from her. He tapped rapidly on the keyboard before using the touchpad, and after a couple minutes, he brought the computer back and set it on the coffee table in front of her, open to a search engine.

Interesting. What was it that he didn't want her to see? Considering someone had been sporting a healthy erection when she'd woken him up, Jasmine could guess. Was it the head wound or just the fact that she was starting to feel like her old self that gave her the courage to blurt, "Were you surfing porn, Luca?"

"Pardon?" He reached into a cupboard overhead and retrieved two clean wine glasses.

She smiled to herself as she leaned forward to check email.

What the hell was her password?

"Porn," she said absently as she typed some random phrase into the field. She glanced up at him. "You do know what porn is, don't you?"

"Of course I know." He had the good grace to look uncomfortable for approximately three seconds and then his lips twitched and a slow smile spread across his face. He poured wine into the glasses he'd gotten out of the cupboard and came to sit beside her on the couch.

With the warmth of his thigh pressed against hers, Jasmine really couldn't think as each password she tried only resulted in an error message. She was so used to logging in automatically from her phone app—when was the last time she'd needed her password?

"And if I was?" Luca asked, so close to her ear it tickled.

She shivered at the pleasant sensation, her hands hovering above the keyboard like they were as frozen as her email account would be if she failed too many more attempts. Jasmine shut the lid of the laptop, the turn of the conversation seeming more important than email at the moment.

She turned to face him. "I guess that's your business."

He handed her a glass. His gaze was as intense as ever, but something had changed. Something subtle. It wasn't like he was searching; it was like he was trying to convey something. Something important. Something fierce.

Whatever it was, her body responded.

Hard.

Her lips parted and her mouth was suddenly dry. She wet her lips, and Luca's searing gaze dropped to her mouth, lingering there. "Should I be ashamed of watching people make love?" His nostrils flared, as if he was a predator, scenting her. His gaze narrowed as it returned to hers, and the quirk of his lips was on the cynical side.

"No." Jasmine shook her head, unable to break eye contact. "I don't think so."

He nodded and drank. When his stare focused elsewhere, Jasmine was able to take a sip of wine herself.

God, it was good. Smooth, like silk slipping down her throat...

"What kind of an American are you, Jasmine Sweet?"

"Huh?"

"There are stereotypes, you know. About Americans."

"I'm sure there are." Americans had plenty of stereotypes about the French, too.

It went both ways.

"So," she said, raising a brow. "Are you going to tell me what they are?"

His nod was almost imperceptible. "There is the puritan American. Someone who thinks the body and bodily functions are dirty."

Jasmine bit her lip.

"Is that you, Ms. Sweet?" He leaned forward.

She held her breath.

"Or..." He backed up and cocked his head to the side. "Are you the kind who enjoys being a woman, physically and sexually, but who pretends she doesn't like sex because she's ashamed of her pleasure?"

The breath that Jasmine finally dragged into her lungs was ragged. When Luca didn't continue, Jasmine asked in a breathy voice, "Are those the *only* stereotypes you have for American women?"

Luca shrugged.

"What about..." Jasmine began. "The American woman who enjoys sex *and* isn't afraid to admit it?"

"Does such a woman exist?"

"Oh, yes." Jasmine set her glass down beside the computer and scooted closer to Luca. "What about the American who likes to try new things?" She reached for his face, wanting—no, needing—to know what his beard felt like against the tips of her fingers. Against her cheek. Her mouth.

As much as Jasmine was willing herself to be this bold, confident sex-venturer, her fingers still shook when she touched him. But she didn't care. And he didn't stop her.

Or turn away.

Or capture her hand and place it firmly in her lap.

No. He simply sat there and let her explore.

His eyes assessed her from beneath lazy lids while she brushed the contours of his face. His beard was both wiry and soft, and under that she felt the strength of his jaw.

In fact, his jaw suddenly hardened as if he was gritting his teeth.

Wasn't that an interesting response?

"What about the American who isn't afraid to ask for what she wants?" Jasmine whispered, her fingers sliding from beard to mouth, tracing the seam and then the top and the bottom lips. Oh, Jasmine was lying her face off right now, but it felt good.

The subtle parting of Luca's lips was an invitation, she was sure of it, and two of her fingers slipped in, just to his teeth and then past. Good lord, his mouth was wet.

And incredibly hot.

Why was he letting her do this? Why was he encouraging her?

Jasmine had no clue; all she knew was that his mouth was completely and utterly seductive, and when he closed his lips around her fingers and gently sucked, Jasmine realized that the simple sensation of suction on fingertips was more erotic than anything she'd experienced.

She pulled her hand from his mouth and without thinking, sucked her fingers into her own mouth, never breaking his heavy-lidded gaze.

"Are you saying *you* are this kind of woman who is not afraid to ask for what she wants?"

With fingers resting against her mouth, Jasmine nodded.

"Tell me, Jasmine. What is it that you want?"

Was there anything more sexy than hearing that question—deep and guttural—from a hot guy with a French accent?

No. There wasn't. Not that Jasmine could think of, anyway.

She dragged her fingers down her bottom lip, past her chin, to her throat. She'd never felt more seductive, more wanton, more womanly. God. If she had only one night to spend with this man who had turned her into a sex fiend with a simple stare and a question, then dammit she was going to make the most of it.

Jasmine wanted to know what it was like to have something this irrational.

Something that would rock her world.

Not only that, she was going to ask for it.

"I want you to fuck me."

The only reason Luca had been playing along was because he was angry. It was that stupid video—the comments in particular. No one knew the context of that video and he was so tired of being judged for it.

He'd almost longed for her disapproval so that he could unleash some of his angst on her. But she didn't judge. Oh, no. She'd flirted. And then she'd touched him, with a mixture of sensuality and innocence that was so disconcerting Luca found himself caught up in a new game that too closely mimicked his earlier fantasy.

When she'd asked him to fuck her, he nearly lost it.

All of his control was on the cusp of melting away and Luca had to use everything in his power to fight the urge to pull his own too-big T-shirt up over her head and then tug the shorts from her hips. He ground his teeth as an image of him burying his face in her hair and sucking on that tender spot at the base of her neck flashed across his vision.

And that was just to start.

Get a grip, Luca. "I don't think—"

She reached out, took his wine glass from his hand and set it down on the table on the other side of the computer. Then she framed his face with her hands. They were so small and gentle, and they still trembled, which turned him on more than if she was truly this sexual goddess she claimed to be. Her gaze was on his mouth, like she had zeroed in and locked on her target.

"Jasmine—"

Suddenly one of her hands slipped down between them to cover his hand. Jesus. When had he planted his left hand on her bare thigh, trailing his fingers on her supple skin? Luca couldn't remember, but when Jasmine pushed his hand higher up her bare leg, inching beneath the leg of the shorts, he didn't stop her.

In fact, when she got up on one knee, suddenly giving his hand easy access to the silky skin that stretched up her inner thigh, Luca completely forgot about stopping.

How could skin be so fucking soft?

His hand inched higher and he knew—just knew—her pussy would be bare. The damp heat that was only centimeters from the tips of his fingers teased him, like a wet whisper, asking him to touch. When Jasmine swung her leg over his in order to straddle him, his fingers found the taut cord that marked the juncture of her thigh and pelvis.

God. Her body was so close. So alluring.

He wanted her.

But somehow he refrained from taking what he wanted, from playing with the soft skin of her labia before plunging his fingers deep inside.

She finally settled herself in his lap and Luca groaned because the heat of her body was scorching, even through the cotton of her shorts and his jeans.

"Please…" she whispered against his lips.

It was his fucking fantasy come to life, and yet Luca needed to stop it.

Her mouth was on his, pressed against his, kissing softly as she made little sounds at the back of her throat.

If you don't stop now, you won't.

"Jasmine," he whispered in between kisses. "We can't."

"Why?"

"Because."

"Because, why?"

Oh, Jesus.

Luca gave up. He threaded his fingers through Jasmine's lush hair and held her hard so he could kiss her properly. Her mouth tasted of wine and honey, and he sucked her sweet nectar both voraciously and with care, like he was a ravenous bear and she an un-predictable beehive. She reacted to his kiss by dig-ging her fingernails into his shoulders, all the while rubbing herself against the fly of his jeans. All he'd have to do was pop his fly and slide the legs of the shorts to the side, and he'd be able to bury himself inside of her.

She'd be wet.

And hot.

And probably fucking tight.

God, he wanted her tight little pussy. His cock ached with need, and as she ground down into him, he held her hips and thrust his toward her.

Non!

This could not happen, no matter how much her sweet little pants and gyrating hips made his cock feel like it was going to explode. It was exactly these thoughtless encounters that got him into trouble. He had to stop. Now. Before it was too late.

"Jasmine." He held her hips still and turned his face away. "We can't do this."

She blinked. "Why? I'm single. You're single." Her breath was coming fast from arousal. "There's no reason to stop."

"Yes. There is." Luca searched her face, and when he saw the bruise on her temple he realized he had his excuse. "You should not be exerting yourself, physically."

She touched her head and frowned.

"Hugo made me promise. Believe me, I would like nothing more than to continue this—" He indicated the space between them. "But I am worried about your well-being."

Her lower lip trembled and then hardened. "I see." She sat for a moment, her face turned away, though he saw how she wiped her cheek.

Oh, God. She wasn't crying, was she? He hadn't meant to make her cry. "I'm sorry."

"It's okay," she said, still turned away. "I should probably go to bed."

"Yes."

She drew in a long, shaky breath before climbing off his lap. She still hadn't looked at him. "Good night, Luca."

"Jasmine?"

She stopped and slowly turned. There were no tears on her cheeks, they were simply red. From embarrassment? Luca didn't know which was worse, making her cry or embarrassing her. "Sleep well."

She nodded and then walked quietly back down the hall. The sound of the door closing only made his balls ache more than they already did. A beautiful woman who had no idea who he was, who was willing to go to bed with him? And he'd refused?

Was he out of his mind?

Or was he really changing for the better?

CHAPTER SEVEN

JASMINE WOKE THE next morning with a headache and a sense of remorse. The headache was explainable, but the remorse was confusing, because last night she'd experienced the best kiss of her life.

And then Luca had pushed her away, and all her feelings of inadequacy around sex resurfaced. Even when he'd woken her up in the middle of the night, he had been clinical. Making sure she knew where she was before leaving her alone again.

She sat up in bed, rubbed her eyes and gingerly touched her temple. There was still a tender lump on the side of her head.

Lovely.

Flipping back the covers, she swung her legs over the side of the bed. On a chair next to the wall was a pile of clothes. Her clothes. All laundered and folded.

Seriously?

Not only was Luca a good caretaker, a good cook and super-D-duper hot, he did laundry? And folded it? The man was a catch.

She picked up the clothes and made her way out

to the hallway. Just as she was about to turn the knob on the bathroom door, it opened and Luca stood there surrounded by clouds of steam, the masculine scent of expensive aftershave wafting about him while he wore nothing but a towel around his waist.

Low on his waist.

She stared as she hugged the clothes to her chest lest she give into her base urges and reach out to touch him.

His chest—lickably bare—was ripped. Hard pecs covered in lovely dark hair that only added to his masculinity. His abdomen was mostly hairless, which allowed her to count the ridges. An eight pack? Was that even possible? Apparently. And from his navel a line of hair drew a dark course leading down to what promised to be dark pleasures.

Jasmine's mouth watered and her fingers twitched with need.

"Good morning," he said.

"Uh-huh." She couldn't tear her gaze away.

"Jasmine?"

"Hmm?"

He snapped his fingers in front of her face.

Jasmine gave her head a shake and glanced up. "Yes?"

If she thought his eyes had said "I want to fuck you" last night, she read a whole new message this morning. They shone with such an immoral light it was as if they were now saying, "Here's what I'm going to do to you. I'm going to tie you up, have my way with you and only after you've come five times will I fuck you."

Of course, that could have been her imagination.

Was there time for her to have five orgasms before she had to leave? Hell, she'd settle for one...

"I phoned my friend an hour ago. He will be here to pick you up at 9:00 a.m."

"Huh?"

"My friend François. He'll take you to the embassy so you can apply for an emergency passport. I'm sure they'll help you contact your family so they can wire money and you can continue your vacation."

"Oh."

It was as if he'd poked her with a pin, deflating her.

He motioned her into the bathroom and then went into the bedroom and closed the door. The sound of the door locking was not the same as the high-pitched wheezing of a deflating balloon, but it may as well have been because that was how it made her feel.

"Well, there goes my chance for good sex," she said beneath her breath as she closed the bathroom door.

She showered slowly, letting the scent of Luca's shampoo and soap encompass her. "I'll never wash again," she said to herself as she brought a handful of suds to her face to sniff. Wanting to remember this scent forever.

You know how pathetic you sound? Her inner critic asked.

"Yes."

Her ride to the embassy was going to be here in an hour, which gave her no time to enact any sort of seduction plan. But the worst part was, once she arrived at the embassy, she would have to suck it up and call Parker. He was the one who had all of her documentation. Copies of her passport, her birth certificate and driver's license—all of it was in the desk drawer in the living room.

She turned and let the strong spray hit her directly in the face.

Fuck that. There was no way in hell her first conversation with him since their breakup would be one where she had to ask Parker for help. She needed to find a way around that.

Jasmine turned off the shower and dried herself. Getting ready didn't take long when she didn't have any toiletries besides a toothbrush and a men's comb that didn't even make it through her hair. Without foundation, she was unable to cover up the discoloration at the side of her face.

At least her clothes were clean.

And her panties—which were folded very nicely.

Luca folded my panties. And my bra.

It seemed like such an intimate thing to do.

"Enough," she said to herself. "You have got to get this fantasy under control. It's not happening, Jazz. So just stop."

After running her fingers through her damp hair, Jasmine finished dressing and padded barefoot down the hall to find Luca in the kitchen making breakfast.

The first thing she noticed was the wonderfully

rich smell of coffee that had a hint of melted dark chocolate. So decadent. On a plate was a baguette cut in half along with a pot of butter and preserves. There was also a plate of eggs and two glasses of orange juice.

"Thank you," Jasmine said, as she stood in the kitchen entry.

Luca nodded and then glanced at her bare feet. "You need shoes."

Jasmine glanced down at her ruby-red toenail polish. "Yes, I suppose I do." She must've lost them along with her purse.

"I'll tell François to take you to a shop first."

"I don't have money."

"He'll buy you a pair."

Jasmine went around to the breakfast bar and sat. "François must be a very good friend."

Luca made a face. She couldn't tell if it had a positive or negative expression. "I've known him all my life."

Jasmine had hoped that Luca would at least join her for breakfast, but he'd obviously already eaten because he was in the process of washing his plate. Once it was set in the rack over the sink to dry, he refilled his espresso cup and took it down the hall to his bedroom.

This really was it. Her sex-venture was over before it had even begun. Such a shame. Watching the clock over the stove like she was an inmate on death row eating her final meal as she awaited the appointed hour, Jasmine decided she would call her parents first, once she got to the embassy. They could contact Parker if need be. Once she had travel documents, she'd change her flight and go home.

What had she been thinking, coming here by herself? She wasn't an adventurer, and certainly not a sex-venturer. This whole thing had been one big mistake. Running away from a situation she didn't want to face was never a good decision.

Just as she finished the last bite of baguette, a telephone rang. Luca strode back down the hall to retrieve it. He checked the screen and said, "It's François."

Her stomach sank. If she looked down, Jasmine was sure she'd find it flopping around on the hardwood floor. With a sigh, she carried her dishes to the sink to wash. However, before she'd finished wiping her plate, she noticed the volume and tone of Luca's voice, and she stopped what she was doing to listen.

Something was wrong.

While she didn't understand the French language, she understood *body* language and Luca's said one thing. He was angry. He paced the room while gesturing wildly with his free hand. His voice was deep and guttural and he spoke so rapidly his words sounded like machine-gun fire.

"Non. Je ne peux pas le croire."

That did not sound good. Jasmine leaned her elbows on the counter as she watched the exchange with great interest.

Luca opened the sliding doors off the living room to the balcony and peered down at the street below.

Something was going on because Jasmine heard the cacophony of a crowd even from where she stood.

"Non, non, non, non," Luca said, slamming the doors shut.

Okay, she understood that. It was a lot of no's. Definitely indicating something was making Luca unhappy.

When Luca finally hung up, he slammed the phone against the counter, which surprisingly did not break it, and growled like a caged beast before pacing some more. His head was down and he gripped his hair as he moved back and forth across the small space.

Finally he stopped, turned to her and said, "Okay. Change of plans." He marched to the wardrobe in the front hall and came back with two helmets, two leather jackets and a leather bag. "Put this on," he said, shoving a helmet and jacket at her. "We leave in five minutes."

Jasmine stood barefoot at the front door, stunned by this change in events. Luca stomped down the hall muttering angrily and returned moments later stuffing clothes into a leather satchel and slinging the strap over his shoulder. Then he donned his helmet, took her hand and dragged her out the door and down to the parking garage.

When he started up his bike, she stood beside him with her visor raised and said, "I thought I wasn't supposed to ride."

"You're fine. Now get on and wrap your arms

around my waist." He flipped down the passenger foot pegs and waited.

As soon as she'd done as he asked, he put the bike into first, opened the garage door and ripped up the ramp and onto the street, narrowly missing a van and then another one before skirting a group of people that were milling about between the vehicles, toting microphones and cameras.

What the hell was going on?

"Hold on tight," he called over his shoulder as he changed gears and wove between cars as he headed for a main street.

Jasmine leaned against his back, her toes curling painfully around the teeth on the metal pegs as she watched Paris slip by at high speed.

Holy shit! Was that the Louvre? She'd seen so many pictures of the palatial landmark, but now, as they roared by the building, weaving in and out of the tourist traffic, it seemed surreal. But the building and crowds were gone before she'd had a chance to really take it in, then Luca turned onto a street that paralleled the Seine.

"Oh, my God," she whispered to herself a few minutes later. With hands gripping the leather waist of Luca's jacket, she sat up so she could get a better view. They were on the other side of the river from Notre Dame Cathedral. The central spire, the ornate stonework, it was such an impressive, distinctive Gothic structure, and even though she'd seen hundreds of pictures of it, seeing it in person took Jasmine's breath away.

So did the speed at which they were traveling.

Luca drove like a madman, changing lanes at speeds that were certainly illegal and highly unsafe.

She'd never felt more thrilled in her life.

When a car driving in the opposite direction turned on its lights and siren, and then spun around to pursue them, Jasmine felt something else she'd never experienced. A tingling at the base of her spine that spread out across her lower back and into her abdomen.

"Hold on," Luca commanded for the third time.

She leaned into him and closed her eyes. This could very well be the last day of her life and if it was…she didn't care.

She was having an adventure!

How the hell had the fucking paparazzi found him? Luca had no idea. François said they were out in full force at the front of the building milling about, waiting for him to emerge. Did they know he was in the company of a concussed, shoeless American woman?

He hadn't had time to think about who might have leaked his whereabouts, he'd been too busy driving and trying to get the hell out of Paris. His adrenaline had kicked in, causing him to drive like he would in a race. It was the best fucking feeling in the world—next to an orgasm, of course—because it was the closest thing to flying that you could get while still staying on the ground. Time moved differently, like breaking speed limits actually broke the veil of physics and hurtled him from the laws of this world into the next.

It was a spiritual experience.

So when the police siren had started up behind him, Luca barely noticed or cared, other than realizing he'd never be able to take Jasmine directly to the embassy while the police were on his tail. He'd taken the corner onto Boulevard Périphérique so tightly an amateur would have spun out, and Jasmine had screamed behind him, burying her hands in his pockets as she mashed herself against him.

He continued speeding along Périph, headed toward the A6 that would take him south of Paris. It wasn't until he was on the A6, the police lost somewhere in traffic, that Luca had had time to think about who might have exposed him—once more—to the press. Had Hugo said something to someone?

No, his friend wouldn't do that.

Who else could have known? Had Anika had him followed? What about Marcel? Maybe Marcel had overheard his conversation with François and alerted the press. Or had Jasmine told someone when she used his computer last night?

He pulled the clutch and changed gears, rage feeding his need to push the bike to its limits. There was only one problem; something in his boot, a rock or something, was driving him crazy. He'd noticed it as soon as he'd put his boots on but hadn't had time to stop and shake it out. He wouldn't be stopping, either, not until he got to Nemours, where he planned to drop Jasmine off at a train station before he traveled another hour south to his final destination in the Loire Valley.

By the time he turned off the highway onto D403 into Nemours, the rock in his boot was a constant annoyance, also reminding him that Jasmine was still shoeless. After an hour on the bike, her feet would be getting sore from the metal pegs. He needed to find a shoe store.

Once turning onto the Rue d'Paris, he saw a little shop on the corner and pulled the bike over. He flipped up his shaded visor and turned in the seat. "You see that store, Chaussures Sigal? It will have shoes." Opening up the flap on his bag, he found his wallet and peeled three one-hundred-euro notes from a stack just as Jasmine dismounted and pulled off her helmet.

Her eyes were saucer shaped as she took in the bills. He thought she was going to comment, but she didn't. She snatched the money out of his hand and padded barefoot into the store. That gave Luca time to take off his boot and shake the rock out of it.

Except it wasn't a rock.

No, that wasn't true. It *was* a rock, a *big* fucking rock. Luca picked the ring up off the road and inspected it. The band was small and platinum, made for a delicate finger. The diamond was...huge. Three, maybe four carats. This was an expensive engagement ring.

"Jesus," he muttered to himself. Was it Jasmine's ring? Was that why she'd been chasing him yesterday on the street? Had the ring somehow gotten lodged in his boot during the chaos of the robbery?

What was he supposed to do with it now?

Tell her? But then she would know that he'd been in the store, seen what happened and lied to her. No. He couldn't tell her, but he did have to give it back to her.

Somehow.

If it was hers.

But if it *was* hers, what did that mean? Was she engaged? Where was her fiancé? What the hell was she doing with him?

Luca tucked the ring into his wallet—maybe he'd slip it into her pocket while saying goodbye at the train station. If it wasn't hers...oh, well. Twenty minutes later, Jasmine emerged from the store wearing a pair of sandals and holding another bag in her hand.

She held the bag aloft and said, "I borrowed some money to buy some clothes, too—I got great prices on two pairs of shoes, a blouse, a skirt *and* a dress." She smiled wide, showing her teeth. "I hope that's okay."

"Of course." He swung his head to indicate the seat behind him. "Get on."

"I'm a very good shopper," she continued, as if he'd commented about it. Which he hadn't.

"Great. Now, get on."

"Yeah. I don't think so."

"Excuse me?"

"I'm not getting on until you tell me where we're going, why you're driving like a maniac..." She eyed the bag he had slung across his chest. "And why you have an enormous wad of cash in your wallet."

Dammit. He had no intention of answering any of those questions. Well, he could answer the first one. "*We* aren't going anywhere. I am dropping *you* off at the train station and you are returning to Paris."

She set the bag down, crossed her arms over her chest and said, "No."

"No?"

"I'm not going back to Paris."

"Yes, you are."

She shook her head. "Nope. And I'm not getting on the bike, so…"

"Fine." Luca pulled his wallet out of the bag again and peeled off a few more notes. He held them out to her. "You've got shoes now. You can walk to the train station." When she didn't take the money he leaned over, picked up the shopping bag and dropped the notes inside.

She glanced down at the money and then said, "You know what I think?"

"*Non.* I don't."

"I think you're on the run from the police." Her eyes lit up. "And I think you're worried that I'll turn you in."

If she thought he was some criminal on the lam, why the hell were her eyes so bright and her cheeks so pink? It was like the notion turned her on.

And—bam—like that, *he* was turned on.

Fuck. He had to get rid of her. Quick. She was a liability. "An interesting hypothesis." He pointed to the end of the street. "Take this street across the river and then turn right. The train station is maybe five hundred meters north."

Jasmine's lips twitched. "So, you're saying I need to walk right past that official-looking building on the other side of the street?" She pointed. "Because that's the police station." She smiled. Wide. "I asked the girl in the store. She pointed it out to me."

Oh, for fuck's sake. Luca started the engine and lowered his visor, ready to call her bluff. "*Au revoir*, Jasmine. *Bonne chance*." He was just about to drive away when he remembered something.

He still had her ring.

CHAPTER EIGHT

FOR A SECOND, Jasmine thought she'd been wrong about Luca, that he didn't care about the police and might actually drive away.

Except he didn't.

Oh, he revved the engine like he *wanted* to drive away. He even put the bike into gear. But after some muffled sounds that Jasmine was certain were a string of curse words, he lifted his visor and said, "What do you want from me?"

Jasmine glanced up and down the street. There was no way she could articulate *exactly* what she wanted from this man. Half of the things were illegal—maybe only in Alabama, but still. "I want to come with you." She wet her lips. "Wherever it is that you're going." She had no idea where he was going but she was pretty sure it wasn't back to Paris. And if he wasn't going back, either was she, but for very different reasons.

She blinked as a random imaged popped into her brain…

Luca standing bare chested before his shower, only this time he invited her to join him...

He cut the engine. "Why? Why don't you want to go back to Paris and continue your nice holiday? Why would you want to come with me? You don't know me."

How could she answer that without sounding ridiculous? She wanted to stay with him because when she was with him, her senses were heightened. Colors were brighter, food tasted better and nothing was predictable. He was the first man to make her feel alive. She knew it wasn't a forever thing, but that wasn't what she wanted. She wanted to experience more of how Luca made her feel.

Electric. Sensual. Feminine.

He was exactly what she needed at this juncture of her life. He was the key to her getting over the disaster of her engagement.

He was what she needed to move on.

But of course she couldn't tell him any of that. So she told another equally true story. "The person who has all the papers and documents I need for a passport is not someone I'm keen to speak to right now." She didn't even have to pretend. The excitement and thrill of the motorcycle ride evaporated instantaneously at the thought of talking to Parker. For the first time in over an hour, the lump on the side of her head throbbed like someone had shoved a knife into her temple. Once the pain abated, she said softly, "I know I have to, at some point, but not yet. I'm not ready."

Reaching down into the bag, she fished out the notes and tried to pass them back to Luca. "Please. I promise I won't cause any problems. Let me come with you, just for a few days."

He tilted his head to one side, his blue eyes so much bluer in the sun. She could see the wheels turning and a spark of hope filled her when he exhaled heavily and took the proffered notes from her hand. *"Bien."*

"Does that mean good?" She kind of recognized that word, but the way Luca said it made it sound like it was anything but good.

"It means fine. Come with me. For now."

Jasmine fought the urge to clap and jump up and down. She had to play it cool. She had to show him that he was making the right decision by taking her with him—and she was going to make sure she paid him back.

In whatever way possible.

Preferably on her back.

Or on her knees in front of him.

Perhaps on her hands and knees with him behind her.

Oh, God…

Jasmine climbed onto the back of the bike, her clit throbbing against the leather seat as she snugged herself up against him, the bag of clothes squished between their bodies as she shoved her hands into his pockets.

Yes.

This felt good. It felt right.

"So, where are we going?" she called.

"You'll see."

Without another word, Luca took off, doing a U-turn in the street and heading back the way they'd come in order to merge back onto the highway. While he still drove fast—maybe about ninety miles an hour?—it seemed positively leisurely compared to the earlier frenetic speeds.

The traffic was lighter when they got farther south. And the countryside? Well, the traditional French landscape was like something out of a movie. Rolling hills of pastureland, vineyards and fields of wildflowers. On the top of every other hill sat little villages built out of stone with black tiled roofs, and every so often she caught sight of a river as the road wound up and down and around.

But nothing could have prepared her for their destination. Luca turned off the highway heading for one of the little villages with old stone and brick buildings rising crookedly along narrow winding streets. Luca turned down one street on the outskirts of the town, and between the trees that lined it she could see glimpses of the river. The steeply sloping roof of a large villa rose at the end of the road.

Was that where they were going?

Luca turned down a lane that also had trees on either side. At the end of the lane was what must have been a twelve-foot-high metal gate, and to the right of the gate was a humble stone cottage. Luca stopped in front of the house, turned the bike off and engaged the kickstand. "Wait here."

He pulled off his helmet and hung it from a handlebar, ran his hands through his hair and slowly made his way to the door. An elderly gentleman opened it, looked Luca up and down and then gave him a bear hug.

Was that his father? Had Luca brought her home?

Luca and the man spoke for a few minutes before the man disappeared and then reappeared with a stout, elderly woman who practically mauled Luca. She gestured wildly and even from the distance, Jasmine could tell the woman was inviting Luca inside. He pointed to where Jasmine was sitting. The man tipped his head in greeting from the door but the woman only seemed to be frowning at her. Luca spoke again and gestured to the house and the man disappeared inside. When he reappeared, he handed something to Luca and, in return, Luca opened his bag and found something that he gave to the man.

What was it? Money?

After one more hug from the woman, Luca jogged back to join her. Considering he had obviously been reunited with people of significance to him, his expression was grim.

What was going on?

She had no time to ask because he popped his helmet back on, and without bothering to do up the strap, he straddled the bike in front of her and started it up. He drove slowly to the gate, climbed off the bike again, took a ring of keys that he'd obviously been given by the man and used one to unlock the gate. He swung it open, came back to drive through, stopped, and then closed and locked the gate behind them.

He mounted the bike again and they drove down the lane until a house came into view.

No. Not a house.

This was a French villa. Or a château or something.

It was a large, whitewashed, two-story structure with a steeply pitched roof of black tiles and vines creeping up the corners.

Luca stopped at the doors of the two-car garage and turned off the bike.

"We're staying here?" Jasmine asked after she pulled off her helmet.

"Oui."

"Who's place is this?"

"It's mine."

"It's yours?" Jasmine asked, aghast.

Shit, he thought. *That slipped out.*

Luca quickly shook his head. "It's mine, just for the season."

"So, who does it belong to?"

Luca should have been planning a story during the drive, but he'd been bombarded by too many memories. Summers here by the river. Rebuilding and riding his motorcycles all over the countryside. That one summer, nearly fifteen years ago, when he and his mother had been returning from town, his mother letting him drive her Aston Martin DB9. The sudden thunderstorm. The dark road. The pools of water.

Driving too fast.

The crash.

"It belongs to an aunt. She's in Switzerland at the moment."

Jasmine studied him as if she wasn't quite satisfied with the story, but she didn't press him as her attention was captivated by the grandeur of the house. The Gauthiers—the elderly couple who lived in the caretaker's cottage—had done a superb job of keeping up the place. Even the ivy wasn't overgrown, considering no one had stayed here for twelve years.

"And she's okay with you staying here now?" she asked over her shoulder as she started to make her way up the gravel path.

"I called her while you were buying clothes," he lied, adding to the lengthening list.

The walk was well groomed, flowers had been planted in beds edging the walls of the house and the trees were all pruned. Considering what he paid the Gauthiers to maintain the property, he would have been extremely disappointed if things hadn't been kept up. The deal was that the house was supposed to appear lived-in.

It did.

Yet for Luca, the residents were all ghosts.

"And who are the people who live outside the gates?" Jasmine asked as she waited for him to unlock the front door.

"Madame and Monsieur Gauthier. The caretakers."

He recognized the house key among the seven on the ring and unlocked the door.

"They seemed happy to see you."

"I used to come here sometimes as a boy. It's been many years. I'm surprised they remembered me," Luca said quietly as he swung the door open, prepared to be greeted by stale air, dust and spirits.

Instead, the air smelled like lemon and the marble floor shone. Not a speck of dust. His money had been well spent.

"Ho-ly." Jasmine gazed at the sixteen-foot-high ceilings and the curved stairs that led to the second floor. Without being invited, she wandered in through an arched door to the living room, which had the same high ceilings with original beams overhead. The room had an enormous fireplace at one end, and French doors opened up to the terrace out back that stretched the entire length of the home.

The only things that made the house seem uninhabited were the dust covers draped over all the furniture. Luca followed Jasmine from room to room as she explored. It was a one-sided conversation, as she made appreciative comments in each room and he stayed silent. So many memories.

Too many.

After touring the entire main floor—which consisted of the living room, dining room, kitchen, two bedrooms, bathroom and WC—they returned to the front entrance.

"What's up there?" Jasmine asked, pointing up the stairs.

"More bedrooms and bathrooms. But the main floor should be sufficient for our needs."

She bit her lip, and by the way her eyes glowed, he could tell she wanted to investigate further. However, his old room was upstairs and he wasn't in the mood to revisit it.

"Out back there's a pretty park and a pigeon loft that dates back to the seventeenth century, when this was a monastery."

"Are you serious?" Her eyes shone and she took his hand and tugged him toward the door. "Let's go."

Despite the melancholy that Luca had initially felt upon his return, Jasmine's enthusiasm for the estate—a place he had always loved—was contagious. For the rest of the tour, he showed off the property with the pride of someone who had a deep fondness for the place. The large park that led down to the boathouse on the banks of the Loire River. The vineyard to the south, the only part of the estate that was showing neglect. He didn't expect his elderly caretakers to handle that job.

They strolled between the overgrown rows of grapes, and Jasmine stopped. "What kind of grapes are these?"

"Mostly sauvignon blanc, but this vineyard still has some pinot noir vines and some cabernet franc." Luca gazed out over the rows, amazed at how peaceful it was here.

"Why isn't this being cultivated? It seems like such a waste."

"It's a lot of work for…my aunt."

Though Luca could imagine it, suddenly. Cleaning up the rows. Pruning. Weeding. Picking. For the first time since he'd taken over the Legrand estate, the thought of producing wine and champagne seemed more than just a duty, it excited him.

He glanced down at Jasmine, who was watching him with a puzzled expression. "What?"

"Nothing."

They took a path back to the main garden. "You're lucky to be able to stay here. I'm surprised you didn't come here sooner."

"It's a little remote."

"It's gorgeous!"

"You like it here?"

"Are you kidding?" Jasmine's enthusiasm bubbled out as if from a spring. Her cheeks were pink, her eyes sparkled and her hands moved expressively. "This is like a fairy tale." She gazed up at the nearest tree. "What is this? A pear tree? And what's that? Apples? Is this an orchard?"

Luca laughed and then, for the first time that day, he noticed how badly the side of Jasmine's face was bruised. Considering all the excitement of the trip, she hadn't complained once.

"How's your head?" he asked, taking a step closer and reaching out to gently touch her face.

She sucked in a breath. From pain?

"Sorry."

"It's okay," she replied quickly, turning toward him. "I'd actually forgotten about my goose egg."

"Goose egg?"

"Lump on my head." She covered it and winced.

"This place could make a girl forget just about anything."

She gazed up at him and everything was forgotten. The paparazzi, the betrayal, the road trip and the ghosts of memories. All Luca could focus on was her.

This petite American woman who gazed at him with a heady combination of longing and lust. Who, despite his distant and questionable behavior, seemed to find his company enjoyable. He reached for her hand and drew her close.

"Jasmine?"

"Yes?" The word was breathy and hopeful. She placed her hand on his chest, and Luca longed to feel her slim hand against his bare flesh. To let her touch him, her trembling fingers exploring him with the same wonder she'd explored the estate.

"Luca?" A male voice called from the terrace.

The spell was broken and Luca's head snapped to attention. Monsieur Gauthier stood up on the terrace, his hand shading his eyes from the sun.

"Ah. Supplies are here. I don't know about you, but I'm starving."

CHAPTER NINE

THE PLACE WAS like something out of a storybook and Jasmine couldn't contain her sense of excitement, excitement that made no sense. Here she was, without a penny to her name, no ID, no passport, stuck on a remote and practically abandoned estate in France with a man who was running from someone, most likely the police.

And yet things had never felt so right.

There must be something wrong with her.

Maybe it was the fact that Luca had almost kissed her in the orchard.

You are getting some tonight! Her inner critic had even traded in her sarcasm for a little bit of excitement.

With a skip to her step, Jasmine followed Luca up to the terrace where the older gentleman waited for them. He spoke rapidly to Luca, pointing inside the house and then gesturing to the grounds. After they finished, the man met her gaze and bobbed his head.

"Bonjour, mademoiselle."

"Bonjour," Jasmine said, liking the feel of the French word on her tongue.

"Monsieur Gauthier, this is Jasmine," Luca introduced them.

In halting English, the man greeted her and welcomed her before turning his attention back to Luca. They ended their conversation with a handshake and the man left by way of a path around the house. When they went back inside, there were three baskets full of staples waiting for them on the kitchen table. Bread, cold meat, cheese, butter, milk, flour, sugar, coffee, and fruit and vegetables that were not in plastic bags but looked like they'd just been pulled fresh from the garden…there was even a box full of pastries.

In addition, stacked in an ironed pile, were freshly laundered linens.

"Why don't you go make up the beds," Luca said, "while I put lunch together?"

Beds? Did Luca say beds?

Oh, hell, no. There were not going to be any "beds" for them. *One* bed. One for both of them. However, that would all be sorted later, so Jasmine took the linens—which smelled like sunshine—to the first bedroom on the main floor. She pulled the dustcover off the queen-sized mattress and got to work. Once she was done, she couldn't help but lie down on top of it. The mattress was a little firm, but that was okay. She gazed up at the high ceilings with the old beams running across. There was a gorgeous antique chandelier above the bed—a little dusty, but still pretty. The bed had one of those old-fashioned canopies arching up from the headboard, which contributed to her sense of being caught up in some modern-day fairy tale. The furniture wasn't buffed to a high polish like the furniture in her hotel, but was nicked and worn, as if well used.

She shut her eyes, and just like last night, images of Luca filtered through her brain, though with less clarity than her constructed fantasy.

Luca, damp after his shower.

Luca's hard body in front of her as they raced through the streets of Paris.

Luca, smiling seductively with the sun dappling his face through the foliage in the orchard.

Luca kissing her in a way no one had ever kissed her.

Luca…just Luca…

Where had she gone? How long did it take her to make up a couple of beds?

When Jasmine didn't return, Luca went in search of her and found her curled up in the middle of the bed in the master bedroom. Sound asleep.

Instead of closing the door and letting her rest, like he should have, Luca walked softly into the room and sat on the bed beside her. What was it about this woman that compelled him to do such irrational things, like watch her sleep? He'd only known her for twenty-four hours, yet already he felt the need to crawl up beside her and fit her slight body within the circle of his arms and hold her.

Protect her.

Make love to her.

Then do it again and make her scream in ecstasy...

What the fuck is your problem? You barely know her.

Luca got up carefully, so as not to wake her, picked up the rest of the linens and left the room to make up the bed in the room down the hall. After that was done he went back to the kitchen and ate, though his thoughts were still on his unwanted guest.

Unwanted? Really? Or is it that you want her too much?

With a groan, Luca put together another open-faced sandwich with a thick slice of bread, a slab of meat and some creamy cheese, and decided it was time to get busy. He spent the next hour removing dust covers from furniture, testing light bulbs and fixtures to make sure everything was in working order, and then going to check on the hot water boiler. There was an old bag of wood pellets—he had to get some more soon—that he dumped in the burner before lighting the pilot light. Hot water should be ready in thirty minutes. Then he made his way to the garage.

He spent another couple of hours in the garage and in the boathouse, cleaning and checking the old vehicles and boats. After so many hours working in the dust, he returned to the house and headed straight for the bathroom. After cranking the stiff tap and letting the water run through pipes that had grown rusty from disuse, he stuck his hand under the spray to test it. Scaldingly hot. Perfect.

He dropped his clothes and stepped under the spray, rubbing the dust from his skin and hair. There hadn't been room to bring anything other than their toothbrushes and a change of clothes, they'd have to pick up toiletries tomorrow.

How long would she want to stay?

How long did he want her to stay?

Honestly? Luca didn't know. He was completely conflicted over his surprise American guest. His logical side insisted he drive her to Nevers tomorrow so she could catch a train back to Paris.

His physical side?

Luca glanced down, noting the growing evidence of what his physical side wanted. He wanted her naked. On her back. Her legs parted. Her dark hair fanned out on a white pillow. Her lips swollen from having been wrapped around his cock...

He grasped his erection. Jesus, he needed some relief. There was an old cake of soap on a shelf and though it was as hard as a rock, after moistening it, it eventually lathered, giving off a honey and lavender scent. Once he had created some suds in his hand, Luca slid it along his length. He leaned against the tiled wall and shut his eyes, letting his imagination take over as he fisted himself.

Fuck, it had been too long.

"May I?"

Luca's eyes popped open.

He dropped the soap and stood dumbfounded, his erection pointing straight at the object of his desire.

Jasmine stood just inside the curtain—she was stealthy, this one—completely nude. Luca took in her naked body, as if the vision of her could be absorbed through every pore. Her hair, her sultry gaze, her parted lips, her narrow shoulders and full breasts. Her slim waist and curving hips.

Her bare pussy.

He'd known it.

"Would you like me to?"

"To what?" His question came out as a growl.

"To finish." Her gaze dropped to his erect penis. "For you."

Luca fought with himself for all of a nanosecond.

Then she wet her lips, biting down on the bottom one before slowly raising her gaze, a sinful question in her shy smile.

That was it. Battle over.

She had won.

"Yes. Oh, fuck, yes."

But when she grasped the backs of his legs so that she could lower herself to her knees in front of him, her mouth level with his erection while water sluiced down into her upturned face, Luca realized Jasmine hadn't won.

He had.

She'd woken up disorientated. But it hadn't lasted long. Particularly when she'd padded out into the hallway and heard the water running in the bathroom.

Luca was taking a shower.

This was her fantasy. Except she wasn't imagining it; it was happening right here in real time.

Fuck fantasy.

It was time to start living instead of spending so much time wrapped up in her imagination. Without wasting one more second, Jasmine had stripped out of her clothes and left them lying in the hallway. She'd thought for sure Luca would hear her coming into the bathroom so she'd moved straight up to the curtain and pulled it back, only to come face to face with the rawest, sexiest thing she'd ever seen.

Luca was leaning against the wall, naked—a fucking Adonis—with the nicest, hardest cock held firmly in his fist.

Pumping.

She'd blurted, "May I?"

The second Luca had opened his eyes and stood there, all naked and proud, she knew he wouldn't say no.

And he hadn't.

Without even thinking about what she was doing, Jasmine dropped to her knees in front of him and took him in her hands. He groaned at her touch. Groaned. Like what she was doing felt good to him. Like he liked it.

God. It made her feel so…powerful.

Wrapping her fingers around him—sweet Jesus, the man was well proportioned—Jasmine tried to mimic his earlier movements. She must have been getting it right, because his stomach muscles contracted as he thrust his hips forward and he muttered darkly in French.

Reality and fantasy merged, and Jasmine didn't even have to think anymore. She just did. She lifted her face to the spray and opened her mouth, catching water until her mouth was full and leaning forward, guiding Luca into the warm bath between her lips. Displaced water gushed down her chin as she took him in.

The harsh, guttural sounds he made encouraged her to take him deeper, and then deeper still, until she couldn't breathe. Then slowly, slowly, she withdrew until his tip rested against her lips. She circled the head of him with her tongue; he tasted faintly of lavender soap and man, and it was like nothing she'd experienced before.

Better than her fantasies.

Better than—

"Jasmine..."

She'd never heard her name spoken in that tone before, with reverence, like her name could invoke magic...dark magic. Hazarding a glance up through the spray, Jasmine met Luca's lust-crazed gaze while she played his cock back and forth across her parted lips.

This was what she wanted. What she'd always dreamed about in a lover. Someone to look at her with absolute desire. She couldn't get enough. She loved the way his penis pulsed in her fist. She loved the way Luca's hands had found their way to her hair, threading though her damp tresses and holding on with a ferocity that spoke of carnal need.

She loved the savage grunts he made, seemingly against his will.

Opening her mouth wide, she took him inside again, sucking in a way she hoped matched his ferocity. This time, when she withdrew, she gently dragged her teeth along his length, not caring about whether he liked it or not, but simply doing it because *she* wanted to.

By his reaction—thrusting his hips toward her—he liked it. So she licked and sucked and trailed her nails up the inside of his thighs, beneath his balls and then down his length and Luca cried out.

"Fuck, woman." He took hold of his cock and turned himself away. Then he reached down and pulled her to her feet. "You're going to make me lose it."

"I thought that was the idea."

"Non," he said softly.

Jasmine's heart would have plummeted from insecurity if not for the obvious flame of desire in his gaze.

"I need to make you come first."

CHAPTER TEN

"You want to…" she gasped as if the sentence was hard to finish "…make me come?"

"Yes."

She drew in a shaky breath and then exhaled again. "Do you have…condoms?" she asked, looking like some combination of innocent school girl and sultry vixen.

"Condoms?" he frowned. Then he shook his head.

She gnawed on her bottom lip. "Damn."

Pulling her body close and running his hand down the curve of her spine—better than he'd fucking imagined—he left his hand on the top of her ass and whispered, "There are plenty of ways to make you come without having to use condoms."

Because her body was so close, he felt the deep tremor that coursed through her, like his words had evoked a shock of some kind. Jesus, if simply telling her what he was going to do made her body react like this, what would this woman be like in the throes of an orgasm?

Luca couldn't wait to find out.

"But first…" He tilted her chin up and kissed her. Her mouth was warm and wet and sexy as hell. He pulled her closer and she parted her legs so that his cock fit snugly up into the warm apex of her thighs. He was so fucking tempted to simply adjust the angle and slide into her…

But not yet.

Something told him that she was not as experienced as she claimed. Could be the way her body trembled when she touched him. Or the way her eyes changed so often from a lust-filled haze to clouded with uncertainty.

With regret, he pulled back and smiled down at her. "Now…"

"Yes?"

There it was. That hopeful innocence he'd detected that told him to take it slow—now that he'd made the decision to fuck her.

"We dry off, get dressed and eat."

She blinked up at him in confusion. Oh, this was going to be both painful *and* too much fun. He ran the backs of his knuckles down her cheek and then swiped his thumb across her parted lips. She shut her eyes and automatically opened to take him in. Fuck, her mouth was to die for. So soft and sweet and innocent and sexy all at once.

"You enjoy tempting me?" he asked harshly.

Sucking deeply on his thumb—just like she'd done to his cock—she finally pulled his hand away and said, "I enjoy having parts of you inside of me. If that tempts you…" She shrugged.

And there was the other side of the coin that was Jasmine. A sexual force like a hurricane that had a calm center but could easily wreak havoc and destruction.

"Come." He took her hand and coerced her out of the shower. There was only one towel and he dried her off first: her torso—she had pretty, dusky hued nipples, so fucking suckable. He moved down to her belly, then he dried the length of each leg before carefully rubbing the towel between. After that, he dried her hair.

She stood completely still, her lids fluttering as if she found it difficult to keep them open as she let him towel her off.

"Go get dressed," he instructed with a light slap on her bottom. "I'll meet you in the kitchen."

She blinked. There was the tiniest wrinkle between her arched brows. Then she turned and padded toward the door. She did not glance back, but she did sashay her ass in a way that was obviously meant to entice him. Her swaying backside prompted an urge to stride after her, grab her shoulder, spin her around and take her—hard—up against the door.

It would feel so fucking good.

Luca was in desperate need of release...

Non.

He would save that maneuver for later. For now, he wanted to take his time, build her arousal and get her body so fucking ready for him that she would fall apart without his even touching her.

She wore her new dress, the one she'd picked up at the shop, the one the shop girl had oohed and aahed over. It was white and sheer with spaghetti straps and a hemline that was high in the front and low in the back. It made Jasmine feel both sexy and virginal. When she swept into the kitchen, her heart beating a million miles a minute—though she did her best to maintain a cool, seductive smile—she was rewarded by a grumbling sound Luca made at the back of his throat. There was also a spark in his blue eyes and a smile that only lifted one corner of his mouth.

"You are beautiful."

It was such a simple statement. And yet the huskiness of his voice suggested he wanted to tear the fabric from her body and finish what they'd started in the bathroom.

How would he do it? How would he make her come? With his hands? His mouth?

Oh, please. Let it be with his mouth.

He'd already begun preparing a meal, and while Jasmine wanted to help—she was no slouch in the kitchen—he seemed to have things completely under control. Actually, that summed him up. Luca was a man who liked to be in control of situations. Even when he was ripping along at inhuman speeds on the motorcycle, Jasmine had known intrinsically that Luca was in *complete* control.

Supper was a thick, fluffy omelet with bits of cured meat, cheese and fresh herbs. To accompany it, Luca had opened a bottle of wine, a light white, that was absolutely delicious. They ate on the terrace as the sun began to set. Jasmine was ravenous. She hadn't eaten since breakfast.

"So," Luca said, his wine glass in hand, his eyes hooded. "Before I…" He paused. A subtle smile touched his lips as if he was thinking something irreverent—what was it?—then he changed the subject. "Tell me more about yourself."

"Before I tell you any more about myself, it's your turn to tell me a little bit about you."

Luca's posture changed from open and alluring to rigid and guarded. "There is not much to tell."

"Who are you running from?"

She didn't think he was going to answer. He stared out at the horizon and drank. Finally, he said, "I had an altercation with the police a few weeks ago."

"Are you a fugitive?"

He shrugged. "Depends on your definition."

So…she was aiding and abetting an outlaw. That thought should have terrified her. Instead, a thrill raced through her, not unlike the thrill she'd experienced on the back of his motorcycle. That, combined with the lingering arousal from the shower and the desire that Luca's mere presence elicited, meant Jasmine had never felt more alive.

"What do you do? For work?" She paused. "Or… do you work?"

He regarded her carefully as if weighing what to say. Finally he said, "I used to race motorcycles. But I don't anymore."

"So now you…?"

"I am on vacation from my job." He lifted the glass of wine. "I work for a vintner."

So that was why he knew so much about the vines in the vineyard.

"And now your turn. What do you do, when you aren't visiting Paris, losing your belongings and finding yourself concussed on a street corner?"

"You make me sound like a prostitute."

He cocked his head to one side and Jasmine couldn't decide if she should be offended or not.

"Don't look at me like that. It was not an insult."

He'd read her mind. Or perhaps he'd simply read her body language. Either way, it felt good to be read so easily by him. Like he was actually paying attention to her.

Luca refilled her glass. "Do you want to know what I think?" he asked.

"I don't know, do I?"

He set his wine glass down and reached across the table to caress the back of her hand. "I think you came to Paris looking for something."

"Why do you say that?"

"Because if given the choice between a planned vacation and a…hideout in the French countryside, most people would choose the former."

"Maybe."

"The question is, why? Why do you want to be here? With me?"

She tugged on her hand but he held it firmly. So instead of pulling away, she squeezed. "Honestly? I can't quite explain it. I just know that at this moment in time, there is nowhere I'd rather be."

Luca regarded her carefully. Though he gave very

little away, the fact that his thumb caressed the back of her hand told her he was pleased by her answer. But his question did stay with her as she sipped her wine. What was it about him that compelled her to act so irrationally?

God. It was everything about him. His tone of voice—the French accent didn't hurt—his intense stares, his touch, his words, his mouth, his hands, his hard body...

Yes, it was all of that, but most of all it was the fact that he desired her.

Her.

That, in itself, was the most intoxicating thing.

What was it about this woman that made him so hard? She was stunning, particularly right now with her dress glowing against the darker tone of her skin and her large eyes that seemed to capture what remained of the sunset, only to reflect the light back at him. She was absolutely beautiful. But, Luca had been with beautiful women before. No. There was something else about her. Maybe it was her passion tempered with a delicious degree of innocence. Luca couldn't really pinpoint what drove him to want to give this woman what she asked for.

Non, Luca didn't want to give her what she asked for; he wanted to give her more. Much more. Starting right now. "Do you have a good imagination?"

"Excuse me?"

"Do you like to fantasize?"

Jasmine made a strange face, like she'd been caught in a lie, which was an interesting reaction.

"Everyone fantasizes, Jasmine. It is not a crime."

"I know," she said quickly, suddenly finding something very interesting about her wine glass. "Of course I fantasize about things."

"About sex?"

"Mm-hmm." It was more of a squeak than an acknowledgment.

"Tell me one."

"You want me to tell you what I fantasize about?"

"Yes. You said you aren't afraid to ask for what you want, right?"

"Yes."

"Well, our fantasies are our deepest desires. So, tell me one of yours. What is it that you want?"

Was she blushing? He reached across to touch her cheek. Jesus. She was burning up.

Why did her charming blush send blood right to his balls?

"Have you ever envisioned being tied up?" he asked when she didn't supply an answer. The question just came out, revealing more about himself than he should be sharing.

She sucked in a breath and nodded.

"Why don't you tell me about it?" he pressed.

Jasmine swirled her wine glass, thinking. Luca could hear her breaths, coming faster and faster. What was going on in her head? Was she envisioning something right now?

Softly he asked, "Have you ever imagined a man taking control of your body?"

Her gaze rose to meet his. He noted both excitement and fear in her fevered gaze.

"Are you able to trust this man in your fantasy enough to let go, so that you can experience pleasure beyond anything you've known before?"

She drew a sharp breath between her sweetly parted lips as she stared at him.

That was what this fantasy meant for Luca. It wasn't about control. It was about trust. A lover who was willing to place her pleasure in his hands was the biggest turn-on.

Maybe because trust was so very rare, in Luca's experience, as Anika and her fucking video had confirmed.

Finally, Jasmine tipped her glass to her mouth and finished her wine.

"I have imagined something along those lines," she said quietly.

"And do you trust me?"

"I do." The little wrinkle formed between her brows. "I mean, I probably shouldn't, because I barely know you." She wet her lips. "But I do."

Luca set his glass down, pushed himself to his feet and held his hand out for her to take. Jasmine's felt warm and small in his as he pulled her to her feet and walked her back inside, leading her down the hall to the master bedroom. The moment the door was shut, Jasmine turned in his arms, went up on tiptoes and kissed him.

Luca kissed her deeply before gently pushing her away. It was too easy to get carried away with this woman. If he wasn't careful, he'd have her clothes off—and his—and would find himself buried deeply inside her body before either of them knew what was happening.

Non.

He had other plans for her.

"What are you doing?" she asked as he held her at arms' length.

"I'm going to fulfill your fantasy."

"O-kay."

"And I'm going to make you come. All without touching you."

She frowned. "I don't understand."

"You will." Luca moved to an armchair that sat in the corner of the room. He dragged it closer to the bed. "You are going to do exactly as I say. Do you understand?"

She opened her mouth to reply but only ragged little breaths emerged. So she nodded her head.

"Now, take off your dress."

She stayed where she was, regarding him for a few minutes. "Why don't you take it off for me?"

"That's not how this works." He sat down and leaned back in the chair. "Take it off, Jasmine. Now."

Her arms went behind her back and she unzipped the dress. Then she nudged each strap until they hung down her arms. Finally, as if it was a sentient being, the dress slipped, slithering down her body and pooling around her feet.

Luca took a deep breath through his nose as he gazed at her in her cream-colored lace undergarments.

"Lie down on the bed and raise your hands above your head beside the pillow." He waited until she complied before continuing. "Spread your legs. Wide."

"Like this?"

"Yes." He dragged the chair closer so he could see her better. "Now, imagine your limbs are tied to the bedposts."

Jasmine rubbed her lips together. "Okay."

"You have a gag around your mouth so you may not speak. Do you understand?"

"Yes."

"You just spoke."

She nodded to show she understood.

"Good. You are waiting on the bed, blindfolded. Waiting for the sound of a man to come into the room. You are completely at his mercy. This scares you and yet excites you, as well."

She made a soft sound at the back of her throat.

"You have been fantasizing about him, though you barely know him. You think about his hands, how it would feel if he were to touch you…"

Her fists opened and closed. Shit, she was so responsive. Of course she was.

"You have watched his lips when he speaks, wondering how they would feel, on your mouth, your breasts, your thighs…your clit."

She writhed at the mention of the word *clit*. Luca smiled. "But it is his cock that keeps you up at night. You can't stop thinking about it. Longing to know how it would feel in your hand. The skin. The tip. The weight of his balls. You hunger to taste it, to suck it gently into your mouth, to explore it with your tongue. But most of all, your pussy aches with the need to feel it rammed up inside of you. Slowly at first, wonderfully, painfully slow, until you cry out for more and only then, when you are on the verge of tears, does he slam it home..."

Her hands clenched the comforter and her legs strained against invisible bonds. She shifted her ass. Why? To create friction to ease some secret itch?

Luca's body responded to hers. His dick throbbed behind the denim of his jeans. He popped the button and let the zipper slide open. "The door opens and someone comes in. It's the man. You can tell by his footsteps. He is there in the room with you."

Jasmine moaned.

Fuck.

Luca shoved his hand down the front of his jeans, needing to pull himself free. He was so fucking hard it hurt.

"Would you like me to tell you what he's going to do to you?"

She didn't say yes. That would be breaking the rules of the fantasy. But her answer—nodding her head while making needy sounds at the back of her throat—was clearly consent.

Jasmine's body was on fire. No one had ever spoken to her like this before. Not even close.

"He gazes down at you, naked and tied to his bed. His to do with as he pleases."

She sucked in a breath. Why did that statement excite her? It shouldn't...but it did. It did so much.

"He has watched you, touched you, even kissed you, and now he is going to have you. Just the way he wants you."

Oh, God. Maybe this was too much...

"He starts with the toes on your left foot. Painted so prettily, like little candies."

He'd noticed her toe nail polish?

"Sitting on the foot of the bed, he caresses your toes before leaning down to suck on each one, drawing them into his warm mouth. Your body responds violently and with pleasure."

Jasmine's hips flew off the bed in response to the imagery. Her toes sucked? She'd never imagined such a thing. But now? She could practically feel it. Warm and wet, his mouth lapping at her. Sucking on her.

"He touches your feet, made more sensitive by the bonds, the bottoms, the tops, your ankles, before sliding his hands up your calves and thighs. You moan as he caresses higher and higher. Showing him where you want him to touch by the way you lift your hips off the bed."

It was like he was there. She could feel him kneeling between her legs, and her clit throbbed with the idea that she was spread before him.

"Your bare pussy is exquisite and he lightly strokes over your mound, dragging the backs of his knuckles over your clit. Circling the inside of your thighs and lightly pressing just the tips of his fingers into your wet heat."

Oh, God.

"So soft. So warm. He leans over and breathes hot air against you as you strain your hips toward his mouth. Wanting touch. Wanting that mouth to suck on you. Lick you. Penetrate you."

Holy…fuck. She lifted her hips toward this imaginary lover. Needing…

"But you are his captive. His prisoner to torture and tease. He nudges your swollen clit with the tip of his tongue before moving on, enjoying the sound of your muffled cries of frustration."

Jasmine grunted.

"He drags his fingers up from your hips, past your belly, clutching your sides so he can lean down and play inside the sweet indent of your navel. Your hips strain beneath him, your pussy jealous of the way he licks your belly and of the attention he gives to your breasts, pinching your pretty nipples, preparing them for his mouth."

Oh, God, oh, God…

"Slowly he continues in an upward direction, kissing and licking your sides, your rib cage beneath your breasts, circling round and round until he finds a nipple made taut by his fingers."

Her breasts ached as if they had been fondled, but not hard enough…

"No touching. Put your hands back up over your head, Jasmine, or I won't finish."

Dammit. She hadn't even noticed she'd done that, but her breasts were so sensitive, so needy.

"He sucks on one nipple and then the other. He sucks hard and you cry out. While he does that, he places a knee between your parted thighs and grinds back and forth across your swollen cunt."

That word. No one had ever used that word with her before. She hadn't thought she liked it, but… now? Now her pussy wept at the carnal image the word painted.

"You're so fucking wet, you're staining the knee of his jeans with your arousal."

Jasmine gasped; her pussy throbbed.

"The man slides to the side so that he is propped beside you, gazing down at your perfect body, caressing you with his gaze before giving in to the need to touch, following the cords down your neck to your collarbones and your breasts, barely skimming his fingers over your skin, leaving gooseflesh in his wake.

"He plays with you, draws circles and patterns across your breasts and abdomen before finally hovering just above your mound. You lift your head, as if to see. Needing to watch when he finally buries his fingers inside of you. But the blindfold prohibits it and you moan with frustration."

With her eyes closed, Jasmine enacted his words, lifting her head off the bed as if unable to see her lover lying between her legs.

"He needs to taste you. He's longed to suck the

sweet honey from your pretty pussy lips, so swollen and rosy with desire."

A soft whine formed at the back of her throat as a tingling sensation that simultaneously started at the tips of her fingers and toes rushed through her limbs to coalesce low in her belly.

"He spreads you even wider, holding you open with his thumbs and then leans in for a taste. Lapping along your slit, sucking on you and fucking you with his tongue…"

Oh, shit…oh, shit…

The tingling, throbbing mass swirling in her abdomen exploded, tugging on all her parts until Jasmine swore she'd disintegrate. Crying out, she clutched at her throbbing crotch with both hands in an unsuccessful attempt to quell the orgasm raging through her.

"That's it, Jasmine. Come for me."

Her eyes popped open.

She was lying on the bed, legs splayed, still wearing her bra and panties. Luca stood over her, his cock in his hand, stroking.

"Did you like it?" he asked, his voice gruff.

"Yes," she managed, keeping one hand clamped between her legs and reaching for him with her other hand.

He stepped closer and let her cover his hand with hers.

"I'm going to come on your belly. Is that okay?"

"Oh, fuck, yes."

He grunted. Placed a knee on the edge of the bed

and pumped his cock like a piston. Jasmine could barely keep up with the pace. But she knew he was close by the sounds he was making and by the pained expression that flicked over his features.

"Jesus," he muttered darkly. Then he leaned over her, gripped his cock and spewed come into a hot pool across her stomach and rib cage. He remained poised above her for a few breaths before zipping himself up and telling her to stay where she was.

He returned moments later with a warm, damp cloth to wipe her clean. When he was done, he left her once again.

"Wait," Jasmine called before he shut the door behind him. "Where are you going?"

"To sleep in the other room."

"Why?"

He stood in the open doorway, just a dark shadow. Finally he said, "I can't sleep beside you without fucking you."

He didn't wait for her answer. He simply closed the door and left her to her own thoughts.

Aftershocks continued to quiver through her already trembling body. She'd just had an orgasm. An amazing, body-shattering, mind-blowing orgasm. But more than that, she'd had it without any physical stimulation whatsoever, not from him and not from herself.

He'd made her come with words.

Maybe people did this all the time. With phone sex and stuff. But Jasmine had never had phone sex. In fact, she'd never had an orgasm with a man present.

Period.

God, Jazz...if you came that hard just by him talking to you...imagine what it would be like to really be with him. To do all the crazy things you've fantasized about.

"I don't think my imagination is even capable," she whispered to herself in the dark. Shedding her bra and panties, Jasmine crawled naked between the sheets. She lay on her back staring at the dark ceiling. She should have felt elated at the notion of being with Luca, but she'd realized something very important. Luca was clearly an expert in bed.

What would he do when he found out she wasn't?

CHAPTER ELEVEN

It was Wednesday morning. Luca rose early and the first thing he did was drive to the nearby village of La Charité-sur-Loire to pick up a few things that Monsieur Gauthier had missed. Namely, toiletries and condoms.

Merde.

It had taken him a while to fall asleep last night, knowing Jasmine lay sleeping just down the hall. Her responsive body primed and ready for him.

She was probably still soaking wet.

Now, ten hours later, the thought of her wet pussy made Luca's dick instantly hard. Yet he still wanted to take things slow. It was so rare to find a woman his age who was both ready and willing to engage in exploratory sex but was still relatively innocent— for whatever reason.

It was a mystery. Jasmine was a gorgeous, sophisticated woman who obviously enjoyed sex. So why was she so fucking innocent?

Do you really care?

He shouldn't care, but strangely, Luca did.

He parked his bike at the pharmacy, debating about whether to leave his helmet on or not. He didn't want to risk anyone recognizing him. It had been many years since he'd been here, and with his beard and grown-out hair, he didn't look like the Luca Legrand in all the promotional pictures and from the tabloids. Still, he couldn't take the chance. He simply raised his visor, went inside and picked up the items he needed.

There was an elderly man behind the counter, and when he glanced at Luca there was no sign of recognition. Thank God.

A few more stops and Luca was on his way back to the villa. When he got back, he smelled freshly brewed coffee and something being fried in butter.

"Morning," Jasmine said over her shoulder. "Where have you been?"

In different circumstances, he might have felt annoyed by the question. Who was she to question his whereabouts? But he didn't feel annoyed. He only felt one thing.

Aroused.

He came right up behind her, wrapped his arm around her waist—she was wearing a skirt and tank top—lifted her mane of hair and kissed her neck. "I was buying some necessities." He plopped the paper sack on the counter in front of her.

Jasmine reached inside, squealing with thanks over the shampoo, conditioner, hairbrush and soap.

"Oh…" she said, dragging out the vowel. "What's this?" She held up a box of condoms. "Twenty-four?"

Luca didn't make any excuses; he just smiled, pulled her close and slid his hand up the inside of her thigh. That was all it took for her to melt against him, her body molded to his, her hands on his forearms. "Luca?"

"Mmm." He nuzzled his face into the curve of her neck and shoulder.

"I need to tell you something."

Her voice was flat and serious. He released her and backed up a step to regard her but she avoided eye contact.

"What is it?"

"Can we talk while we eat?"

"Of course."

She poured him the coffee—nice and strong, which was a pleasant surprise—then slid eggs onto a plate with a slab of toasted bread and sliced tomatoes.

Sitting across from him at the kitchen table, she fiddled with her utensils. Shit. She was about to confess something.

What?

"I'm not who you think I am."

Okay, that wasn't what he'd expected her to say. He took a bite of egg, pretending not to be surprised, and then washed it down with a gulp of coffee. "You mean, you're not American?"

She chuckled softly. "That's not what I mean." She took a small bite of bread that took an overly long time to chew. "I mean, I'm not as experienced as you."

Luca hid his smile. Did she think he didn't already know that? "Really?" He drank more coffee, watching her. She kept her gaze averted and suddenly Luca had a flash of what she was going to confess.

"Jesus," he said, putting his coffee cup down. "You're a virgin."

She shook her head. "No. I'm not." But the little lines between her arched brows told a different story.

Fuck. How did he feel about that? It was a shock, that was for sure. Yet…his cock twitched at the notion, as if excited by the prospect. Not good. As much as some primal part of him celebrated the idea of being the first man to claim this incredible woman, his logical side kicked in. This was supposed to be a meaningless tryst—just a bit of fucking—only for a couple of days. It wasn't supposed to be an initiation.

That was too…meaningful.

She slid her hand across the table and covered his. Her fingers trembled and now he understood those tremors. "Jasmine, I don't think it's a good idea if we continue—"

"Wait. Don't say it." She finally met his gaze, her large brown eyes pleading with him. "I'm not a virgin, but…" She pulled her hand away and made a harsh sound at the back of her throat. "God, it's so…"

"What?"

"The last man I was with, actually, he was the only man I've ever been with. And…"

"And?"

"Well, he…" She paused, and her face contorted in pain.

Oh, fuck. Some shithead had hurt her? This was

worse and he should be packing her up and driving her to the train station. Right now. But, instead, he took hold of her chin and forced her to look at him. For some odd reason, his gut clenched and his other hand grasped his knife as if he meant to use it as a weapon. "Tell me," he growled.

"He used me." She shrugged and tried to turn away.

Luca didn't let her. "What does that mean?"

"God, Luca. Do I have to say it?"

"Yes." He ground his teeth.

Jasmine stood up and moved to the sink, turning her back to him. He pushed his chair away and followed her, going to stand right behind her, though he didn't touch her.

"He pretended to be something he wasn't. He used me to keep up his facade."

"And what facade was that?"

She leaned against the counter. "That he was straight."

It took a moment for her words to sink in. Then, with hands placed gently on her shoulders, Luca turned Jasmine to face him. "Are you telling me that the only man you've ever been with was gay?"

She bit her lip and nodded her head.

"And this man…" Luca suddenly thought of the ring that he'd tucked in his wallet. "Was he your fiancé?"

She nodded, her lip quivering. "I walked in on him. With his best man."

Jesus.

Luca gazed down into her tortured eyes. A voice in his head—that sounded suspiciously like François—was telling him this woman was damaged and that he should stay away from her. That continuing any kind of sexual tryst was taking advantage of her vulnerability. But Luca didn't want to stay away. Fuck, no. He wanted to enfold her in his arms and hold her. He wanted to kiss away the tears that glistened at the corners of her eyes and to tell her that this other man was a *salaud*, a bastard, for trying to use her. More importantly, he wanted to show her how beautiful she was, how desirable she was, and to teach her the absolute joys of making love to someone who couldn't contain his lust for her.

So he settled on something somewhere in between those two extremes. He held both sides of her face and leaned down to kiss her softly. Then he backed away and said, "I think it's time we explore this passion between us, don't you?"

Her lips trembled when she smiled, and Luca experienced a bizarre combination of tenderness, desire and dread.

Jasmine wanted to be thoroughly and completely fucked by this man, but she also wanted him to know what to expect—or not to expect—from her. She had been terrified to tell Luca the truth. Had stayed up half the night trying to figure out what to say or whether she should just go on pretending to be someone she wasn't. But when she saw that box of condoms, she'd known she had to come clean.

Now she was so glad she had. He kissed her. Sweetly. Then he grabbed the box of condoms and led her back to the bedroom.

Her legs felt wobbly as she stood there, watching him hang his leather jacket on the back of a chair. Her knees nearly gave out when he stalked back to her, his hair mussed, his gaze intent, his jaw firm. He yanked her close and threaded his fingers through her hair, holding her head steady for what he was about to do, which was to devour her mouth until she couldn't breathe. His lips were everywhere. On her lips, on her cheek, in her ear, on her neck, back on her mouth, inside her mouth. Not just kissing but biting and licking, sucking and owning.

She pulled away, not because she wanted to stop but because she needed a moment to catch her breath. After a lungful of air he moved them forward, easing her onto her back, dragging her up onto the comforter beneath him.

"You have driven me crazy from the very first, do you know that?" His words were dark and dangerous as he kneeled above her, gazing at her like he didn't want to just devour her lips but her entire body.

Yes. Yes, please.

"Knowing you were here in this bedroom last night was torture." He tugged the front of her top up, taking her bra with it, exposing her bare breasts and licking his lips like she was dinner. "Watching you come was my undoing." His hands moved to her legs, pushing the skirt up and up until it was gathered at her waist, revealing her white panties.

"Jesus. Are all of your undergarments fucking virginal?" He groaned.

"I like white. And I'm not a virgin."

He slid his hands up between her legs, parted them and then moved in between. He kneaded her upper thighs, sliding higher until his thumbs reached beneath the lace of her panties. "Do you know that first night I lay on my couch thinking about this? Thinking about the texture of your skin, the taste of your pussy. How soft and wet you'd be."

Did he mean it? Jasmine didn't know, but the way he looked at her was intoxicating and made her girl parts tremble with the need to climax.

He caressed over the white lace, slipping fingers under and grunting with pleasure as he explored between her folds.

"I can't decide if I want to fuck you with these panties on or not."

A fiery bolt of electricity slammed through her at his suggestion. The idea that he'd shove part of the lace aside and enter her that way was so erotic. God, she loved the way he talked dirty to her.

Her body reacted to his words and his touch, her hips meeting his hands, gyrating against his fingers. Wanting what he was doing but wanting more, too.

"Take them off. Please."

He granted her wish, but when he revealed the bare skin beneath, it was as if it pained him because something sharp flashed across his features. After tossing the panties to the side, he spread her wide and slid two fingers into her body until his knuckles bumped against her clit. Lowering himself to her side, he observed her expression as he twisted and pulsed inside of her.

"Do you like being finger fucked?"

"Yes," she said, her voice sounding on the verge of a sob. "I love it."

There was that expression again. Like this was hurting him.

With her free hand, she smoothed the wrinkle from between his brow and whispered, "Harder. Do it harder. Please."

He made a low rumbling in his chest but he gave her want she wanted, withdrawing his hand and then slamming his fingers back inside, watching her carefully the whole time.

"Oh, yes!" Her hips flew off the bed. The pressure his fingers created, the friction, the growl he made as he did these things to her. He was enjoying this as much as she was.

"Mon Dieu."

To Jasmine's dismay, he pulled his hand away, though what he did next made it okay. Bringing his fingers to his nose, he inhaled deeply before licking them.

But when he pushed one of her legs wider so he could crawl back in between her thighs, she wriggled with the knowledge of what was about to happen. Her favorite thing to fantasize about. The very thing she'd never done before.

Could she do it? Could she let him…?

Too late.

He spread her wide and then buried his head between her thighs, feasting on her. That was the only way to describe it. She grasped his thick hair with both hands. Seeing him there, the top of his head and dark hair positioned between her legs, the feel of his tongue, teasing her clit before sucking on her, his thumbs sharing entry inside of her, was all more than she could take.

"Luca…" she moaned, clutching at his hair. Desperate. "Please." Please what? She had no fucking clue. She just knew she needed something.

He didn't let go but rather increased the pressure on her, moving his head back and forth rapidly, penetrating her with his tongue and fingers together. Then…oh, yes…he squeezed his pinky finger into the tight opening of her ass, something no one had ever done, something she hadn't been sure she'd ever like.

She didn't like it; she *loved* it.

Her pussy erupted inside his mouth, her body bucking out of control with the severity of her orgasm as she kicked and tugged frantically at his hair.

"Luca…yes, yes, oh, God, yes!"

Jasmine thought she might start crying, not out of sadness but out of the weight of release. It was Luca who slowed things down, who cupped her pussy, holding on to the aftershocks of her orgasm as if he was going to keep them for later. He crawled up beside her, stroking her face, calming her until she opened her eyes and saw him there, watching her.

Softly he kissed her, his mouth so warm and tasting of sweet sex.

"You are a beautiful woman," he said softly. "But when you come? You are a fucking goddess."

How had this amazing woman never experienced oral sex before? He'd known she was not as experienced as she claimed, yet she'd given him an un-fucking-believable blow job yesterday in the shower.

"Thank you," she whispered.

"For kissing you?"

She nodded, smiling shyly.

"Did you like it?"

"Yes." Her smile faltered as she tugged her wrinkled shirt back over her breasts.

"What are you doing?"

"Getting dressed."

"Why?"

"Because—"

Oh, no, she wasn't. "Come here." He rolled off the bed and extended his hand, offering to help her up. She took it and stood, uncertain, her skirt hanging askew around her hips.

"We are not done here, Jasmine."

"We're not?"

"That was only the entrée." He licked his lips, her flavor still lingering there. Fucking delicious.

"But, isn't the entrée the main course?"

"No." He lifted her shirt up and off, and tugged the skirt down her hips so that it fell about her bare feet. "In France, the entrée is only the first course."

"Oh."

Lord, he could gaze at her naked body forever. Her skin had a beautiful rosy flush to it that was in delicious contrast to her dark hair.

"So, now what?"

"Now you are going to do exactly as I say."

Her gaze flew up to his, her swollen lips parted, his words and meaning making her gasp. Not in fear, but in excitement and willingness.

"Undress me."

Her brows rose and then she nodded, her fingers moving quickly to the buttons on his linen shirt.

"Not so fast. Enjoy every moment."

With her fingers on the third button, she gazed at it before slowly slipping the button through the hole. She moved on to the next and he felt the pressure of her fingernails on his skin.

Divine.

She continued, as if the act of buttons coming free of their buttonholes was fascinating, until his shirt was undone and she parted it like a curtain at the start of a play. The soft grunt she made after running her hands over his bare chest elicited a growl from him. Her touch was so wonderfully erotic. Tentative and sensual all at once.

"My God," she murmured as she leaned close and rubbed her cheek against him. "You have the nicest chest."

The statement made his already hard cock twitch.

"And you smell delicious." She ran her tongue in between his pecs and then circled one of his nipples before lightly clamping her teeth on the other. "Taste even better."

For an inexperienced woman, there were times when she sure as hell seemed to know what she was doing. Luca fought the urge to twist her lush hair around his fists and to position her where he wanted her. But that was *not* what he wanted, not for Jasmine, anyway. He wanted to savor every fucking moment, which meant he had to control his more basic urges—no easy feat when the mere sight of her made him desperate to bury his cock in her warm body. But taking his time and building anticipation always made it better, and that was what he wanted for her.

Maybe there would come a time when she would welcome some of the other forms of lovemaking he enjoyed, where he could express his more dominant side. The idea drove him to distraction, but for this first time…

Wait.

How many times would they be doing this?

Well, you did buy twenty-four condoms…

He had, but he also had other things to worry about and this—whatever this was—couldn't last more than a couple of days. Jasmine needed to get back to her own life.

Jasmine's hands brought him back to the here and now as she slipped them beneath the shoulders of his shirt, pushing it off and tugging on the sleeves so the garment fell to the floor.

Her hands fluttered down his arms and back up again. Her soft pants were audible in the quiet room and Luca held himself perfectly still as she explored the terrain of his body.

"Do you like touching me?"

"Yes."

"Had you thought about it, while you were in my bed at the apartment?"

Her hands stilled and she slowly raised her gaze. "Maybe."

"Did you wonder if I had plans to…touch you?"

"Yes."

"Did that excite you?"

"Yes." She slid her hands up his chest to his shoulders, following the line of his collarbone. Up his neck her fingers went, to his jaw. "But I was worried, too…"

"Worried about what?"

"That you didn't want me."

He took her hand, kissed her fingers and directed them down his chest to the fly of his jeans. "I want you."

"Oh, my God…" she whispered reverently as she squeezed his erection.

"Undo my belt."

Eagerly, her hands whipped the leather through the loop but he covered her hands again. "Slowly."

She tightened the leather in order to release the prong before sliding the belt off him completely. It made a wonderful hissing sound sliding through the loops and brought to mind other ways he wouldn't mind using the belt.

Not yet.

Once the belt was on the floor, her hands rested on the waistband of his jeans. Could she feel his cock twitching beneath the fabric? Luca wanted her to both hurry the fuck up *and* keep up the leisurely pace of this slow-dance prelude to lovemaking.

Carefully, she popped the top button before slowly unzipping his fly and parting the fabric to push it down his hips.

"Shorts, too."

His cock needed to be free. That was all there was to it.

Fitting her hands beneath the material, she pushed shorts and jeans down his hips, kneeling in front of him—oh, God—while she tugged his clothes all the way down his legs.

Did she have any idea how erotic that was, her kneeling before him, her gorgeous mouth in line with his erection? Looking up at him with such willingness—just like she had in the shower—like she'd do whatever the fuck he asked? His erection bobbed at the notion, straining toward her as she slipped her hands back up his calves, the backs of his knees, pausing on the front of his thighs, not touching him. Yet.

"You're so…"

"So what?"

"Hard."

Oh, fuck. She wrapped that small hand of hers around his cock and squeezed. Luca hadn't had such a sustained erection for so many days and just the simple act of her touch was more than he could take.

"Get a condom from the box and put it on me."

She didn't move, like she hadn't heard him, and licked her lips as if she wanted a taste. No. He would explode in her mouth if she did that. He was way too fucking close.

"Do it now, Jasmine," he commanded through gritted teeth.

His tone broke through to her and she obeyed, getting up and returning quickly with a condom between her fingers.

The fact she was so adept at rolling it over his length meant she'd done this before. She'd said as much, so why did that thought disturb him?

"Lie down on the bed. Spread your legs."

He couldn't help it; his dominant side was taking over, but Jasmine didn't seem to mind. No, in fact, she seemed to be enjoying this. Her pretty little nipples were tight with arousal and the smell of her drifted through his senses, her own personal scent made stronger by the warmth of her flushed skin.

"Show me your pussy."

God, she had the most beautiful cunt he'd ever seen. Rosy and swollen, and when she pulled her pussy lips open, she revealed the most delicious pink center, covered in a lovely sheen of arousal.

He needed her.

He needed her right fucking now.

CHAPTER TWELVE

OH, GOD. JASMINE had never needed something so badly in her life. Luca towered over her, magnificently male, deliciously nude, his face inscrutable, his fists opening and closing at his sides. What her eyes were drawn to most, however, was that *very* male part of him that rose erect and proud from his groin.

"Please," she said in between pants, as she fondled herself.

He crawled onto the bed, moving on top of her, making her feel so small and feminine beneath his bulk. With one hand wrapped around the back of her neck, he raised her face to kiss her. Deeply. His mouth was warm and commanding as he moved leisurely over hers. But when she slipped her tongue between his lips, he groaned and his hips ground in between hers, forcing her thighs wide, adjusting so the tip of him was situated right at her entrance.

"Please, Luca."

The kiss deepened. His hips shifted and then…oh! He was inside of her—finally!—filling her wholly and completely. Her body reacted like a bow pulled taut, arching against him while the entire length of his penis created beautiful friction moving all the way up inside.

"Ahh." He sighed into her hair, holding himself flush for a second before slowly withdrawing again. "So good."

He nuzzled her neck and her temple while he supported himself on one arm and Jasmine clutched that arm, marveling at the sheer power of this man.

So sexy.

What was even sexier was when he backed up onto his knees so she could see him, the sheen of sweat on his chest, the play of muscles across his taut abdomen that danced while he thrust between her parted thighs.

"You are incredibly beautiful," he murmured. His gaze settled at the point where their bodies joined and the thrusts increased in tempo while he watched himself drive in and out of her. Jasmine couldn't decide if it was sexier watching him disappear inside or watching the passion on his face.

Suddenly his expression changed from passion to purpose and his tempo increased. Everything he did was unexpected, three quick thrusts followed by one hard one followed by a slow withdrawal.

So good. So, so good.

He shifted, releasing her ass to reach for her legs, placing them flat against his chest, her ass flush with his hips. Gazing down at her, he kissed one instep and then the other, reminding Jasmine of how he'd talked about sucking on her toes. Was he going to do that now? Her pussy pulsed in anticipation.

He didn't. Oh, no.

Instead, he raised her ass, leaned forward and…

"Oh!" she cried with wonder.

The position created friction in new and sensitive places and the pressure inside of her swelled as he leaned into her upright legs, bending her in half while his cock drove into her again and again.

"Luca," she moaned because he hit a part of her that sent a frisson of pleasure to the tips of her toes and the crown of her head. Release gushed between her thighs and she cried out again. This was not an orgasm; this was something else, something that had never happened to her before.

"Jesus…" he muttered, holding her legs tight and moving in short, sharp bursts before finally parting her thighs and lowering himself on top of her, moving at a frenetic pace as he watched her face.

"Come for me, Jasmine. I want to see you come."

"I already did. I don't know if I can again."

He guided her hand down between them.

"See how wet you are? How much your pussy likes this?"

Oh, God.

"Play with your clit while I fuck you. Make yourself come for me. I want to feel it while I'm inside of you."

She pinched herself, though she didn't need to. His words alone were enough to push her over the edge, tension from her core, her ass, her thighs and that new, oh-so-sweet spot inside of her, all strained together at once before releasing simultaneously in a cataclysmic wave of rapture.

"Yes, oh, fuck, yes." He urged her on as he increased the pace, driving into her harder and faster until Jasmine couldn't breathe. Until she couldn't take it anymore because it all felt so good. Too good.

And just when she thought he couldn't go harder, he did, and instead of abating, her orgasm expanded, sending shockwaves up into her chest and down her thighs to the backs of her knees.

"Luca!"

He growled in response, gripping her hips and driving into her one last time before squeezing his eyes shut and shouting something in French.

The woman was insatiable. Was there any wonder? She was a passionate, sensual being who had never been able to express that part of her. So Luca had no problem with the fact that they spent the next five days in bed. He warned her she might feel sore, but she never complained.

Probably because she was always so fucking wet.

They'd laundered their clothes and hung them on the line to dry—they should really pick up some more—but so far they'd had very little need for clothing. Their last few days had consisted of waking up, fucking, eating, showering, fucking, napping, eating…fucking.

He still had another week before he could return to his normal life. The Legrand champagne had increased in value thanks to the magic of Myra Monte, and his absence hadn't hurt. Checking the prices was the only thing he'd used his cell phone for, which he only did every other day now. If he had to bide his time out of the limelight, then spending it in bed with Jasmine wasn't the worst way to do it.

The only problem was, he needed Jasmine to go back to her own life at some point. So why did the thought of her leaving create a strange ache in the pit of his stomach?

Maybe because she had helped him forget about the pain he had always associated with this villa and the loss of his mother. Or maybe it was because, for the first time since his mother had died, Luca felt as if someone saw him for who he truly was. Not Luca Legrand the hotshot Grand Prix motorcycle racer. Not Luca Legrand the heir to a fortune.

Just Luca.

It was late afternoon, and they were lying in bed after another hot and heavy session. Her body was warm and pliant in his arms, and while she was drowsy, he could tell by her breathing that she was still awake.

There was nowhere else Luca wanted to be at that moment. Not even on the racetrack. Holy shit. That was saying something.

Jasmine shifted in his arms and reached for the box that stood open on the nightstand. She pulled out the line of condoms, counted them and then stuffed them back inside. "We have four left. You know what that means?"

"We've used twenty?"

"Your math skills are astounding." She laughed. "Do you think we should get some more?"

"At the rate you're going, we'll need more by the end of the day."

She slapped him playfully on the chest before lying back down. "I never imagined it'd be this way," Jasmine said quietly, lost in thought as she lazily drew lines up and down the length of his torso.

When he didn't respond, she continued, "I mean, I'd imagined it…lots of times. All the time, actually. But I kind of thought it wasn't real. That maybe I was deviant because I thought about sex all the time, you know?" She propped her chin on her hand so she could gauge Luca's expression. "I didn't think people really did it this much. Is it normal?"

He stroked the hair at the side of her head. "Yes, it's normal. And you are not deviant." His smile grew. "Well…maybe a little, but the good kind of deviant."

She returned his smile and laid her head back down, pressing her ear to his chest. Was she listening to his heartbeat? He pulled her closer, liking the idea.

"Is it like this with other men?"

A grumble erupted deep inside of his chest. "Other men?"

"Are all men like you?" She shifted onto his shoulder so she could see his face. "Do they like doing it as much as you?"

The deep, rumbly sound inside of him intensified.

"Why are you growling?" she asked, propping herself up again.

"I'm not growling."

She patted his chest. "Yes, you are."

He lifted his head and gazed at her. His smile had disappeared and he felt his nostrils flare.

"Are you angry?"

"I'm not angry. I just don't know how to answer your question. I don't think about the sex lives of other men."

"Well, you've been with other women, obviously." She flopped back down. "A lot, I'm sure."

Jesus. What was wrong with him? Why did her semijealous tone gladden him, and why the hell did the thought of her going out and having amazing sex with someone else drive him to want to punch something?

In the throat.

"Can I tell you something?"

"Yes." He hoped she was changing the subject because this topic was aggravating him.

"There's something I remember, before the whole robbery thing in that shop in Paris, it might be the last thing I remember…"

Luca's stomach tightened and his arm twitched beneath her.

She propped herself up on his chest. "I remember this lamp. It was an antique silver lamp that reminded me so much of these stories my aunt used to tell to me and my cousins. *Arabian Nights*." Her eyes lit with remembrance.

"Oh?" Luca relaxed his arms and exhaled a breath he'd been holding.

"I rubbed it." She smiled with a faraway look. "Almost like I expected a genie to appear and grant me three wishes." She met his gaze and stroked his jaw where his beard had gotten thicker. "I think it must have worked."

Luca laughed. "You think I'm a magical genie?"

"I think what you do to me is magical and I'm pretty sure I've been granted more than my share of wishes."

He snuggled her closer. "You sure you don't have any unanswered wishes or…desires?" They'd just made love and yet Luca's cock stirred at the thought of trying something new.

"Well…" Her expression changed from thoughtful to playful. "Remember when you asked me about my fantasies?"

"I might remember a conversation about fantasies." Luca was purposefully vague.

She laid her head back down on his chest and drew circles on his abdomen. "I have this one fantasy…"

Seriously. He should be exhausted. Spent. There should not be one ounce of arousal left in him. But for Jasmine? There was. "I want to hear this fantasy."

"I loved fairy tales as a kid. They've sort of informed my adult fantasies."

"Is that so?"

"Yes. And there's one where I'm dressed in a red cloak…"

"Like Little Red Riding Hood?"

"Maybe." She lifted her head. The uncertainty that he hadn't seen in a couple of days had returned. "Is that silly?"

"No. Tell me more."

Her gaze slid to the side, recalling. "I'm walking through the forest and... I'm being followed."

"By a wolf?"

She shook her head. "No. By a man." She stroked his face. "I've always been more fixated on the huntsman than the wolf. Of course, he's a shirtless man with a beard."

"I am shirtless. I also have a beard. That is an interesting coincidence."

"Yes." She bit her lower lip.

"And then what happens?"

"He chases me."

"Does he catch you?"

She nodded.

"And once he catches you?"

"He eats me. There's a bit of wolf in him, after all."

Luca groaned. His cock was rock hard.

"But first, he ties me up..."

How was it possible the woman had just described one of his own favorite fantasies? Easing her body off his, Luca rolled from the bed and went in search of something to wear. He bent down to grab a damp towel left discarded after their morning shower and fixed it around his hips.

"Where are you going?" she called.

"To get our clothes from the line. And then you're going to town to find yourself a red cloak."

She hadn't found a red cloak when she took the bicycle to the village to shop, so she'd settled on a red dress, instead. In addition to that, she'd picked up some new underwear. Not that she was wearing any right now.

"Put on the dress," Luca had commanded after she'd arrived back at the villa. He'd insisted on staying behind for who knew what reason.

Whatever the reason, it had evoked goose bumps along her arms despite the warm weather.

Jasmine had gulped. God, she loved it when he was authoritative. Maybe because she knew what it meant. He was going to take control of her body and give her the most mind-blowing gift of pleasure imaginable.

"Oh, and Jasmine," he'd said over his shoulder. "Don't bother with panties."

Now Jasmine was out in the garden behind the house picking fruit. Clouds were gathering overhead and a breeze lifted the skirt of her dress and caressed her nether regions in a delightful way, reminding her of her pantylessness. She didn't feel exposed, however—she felt positively content.

No. Not content.

Alive.

Electric.

Sensual.

Luca had said she would know when he was about to pursue her, but he didn't tell her how she would know.

"Go out into the garden and wait for my signal."

"What signal?" she'd asked.

"You'll know when you hear it."

"And then what?"

He'd smiled wickedly. "And then you run…"

She took a bite out of a pear she'd just picked. It wasn't ripe yet and was bitter on her tongue. That was when she heard the engine of Luca's motorcycle roar to life.

Oh, shit!

He wasn't supposed to pursue her by motorcycle. That was cheating!

Jasmine dropped the pear and dove behind a tree. Already her heart was beating like crazy and her palms were sweating. She peeked around the trunk of the tree, and when she didn't see any sign of man or motorcycle, she made a run for the boathouse, about seventy yards from where she had been crouching. When she got to the boathouse she tried the door. It was locked.

Damn.

She shouldn't be breathing so hard after running such a short distance but she could barely catch her breath. Talk about fantasy and reality merging. There was no reason to be frightened. It was only Luca out there, and they were merely playing a game—her game—this wasn't real.

But it felt real.

Maybe because she didn't know what he would

do to her once he caught her. The one thing Jasmine had no doubt about was the fact that Luca *would* catch her. Particularly given he was on the motorcycle. Pressing her body against the wall, she maneuvered around to the back of the structure. Only once she was on the far side did she hazard a quick glance around the corner of the wall to see if there was any sign of Luca.

Nothing.

However, the sound of the bike was louder.

Where the hell was he?

She needed a plan.

The dovecote was about fifty yards away to the east. In the opposite direction was a meadow of wild flowers and beyond that was the overgrown vineyard. That's where he would expect her to go.

So, where should she go? Should she be predictable or should she play for real, attempting to evade him?

She leaned against the wooden wall and listened. The sound of the bike changed. He was on the move. She pressed a hand against her churning stomach and shut her eyes.

"Okay, Jazz. This is your fantasy. If you're going to play, you're playing for real, got it?"

She took a deep breath and peeped around the corner again. The sound of the engine was definitely moving in the direction of the vineyard. Dovecote it was, then. She slid along the wall toward the eastern corner and then, when she was positive the coast was clear, she dashed out into the open, heading for the cylindrical structure. It was shaded by large walnut trees, and soon Jasmine felt protected by the cover of foliage. There was no door on the crumbling building, just a rectangular opening, and she ducked inside.

Light filtered in through openings in the conical roof and Jasmine stared up in wonder. There must have been at least two or three hundred nesting sites honeycombed into the walls, all empty now. She'd never seen anything like it.

What would it have looked like filled with birds?

Suddenly the sound of the bike grew closer and Jasmine realized she'd chosen a hiding place with only one entrance. Her heart pounded against her rib cage as if trapped and desperate to get out.

The bike drew closer, driving slowly. He was in the garden now.

Shit!

It was difficult to breathe.

Jasmine searched the interior of the structure. There was a small ledge halfway up the wall. Maybe if she climbed the nests she could hide on the ledge. She tested a stone pocket that had served as a nesting site. It seemed solid enough.

The sound of the bike came closer and Jasmine held her breath.

Shit. He was right outside!

Without another thought, she began to climb. It was easier than it looked, the little ledges for the nests made the perfect hand- and footholds. It would have been even easier if her palms weren't so damp from sweat. She could see the ledge up above almost within reach. A couple more feet.

Then Jasmine realized something. At first she hadn't noticed because of the blood pounding between her ears, but now, suddenly, she did.

Silence.

Luca had turned off his bike.

She glanced down to find him standing there, wearing nothing but his jeans and boots, a triumphant smile on his face. "Hi, Jasmine." He stepped closer to the wall and peered up at her. "The view from here is fucking spectacular."

She gasped.

A crack of thunder from outside startled her and her leg trembled, her toe slipping on the ledge just as the stone she'd been clutching crumbled beneath her fingertips.

From there, everything happened in slow motion, her body barn-doored—one hand, one foot still holding on as she swung out into thin air—and then she fell.

It was only four or five feet but it seemed to go on forever.

Oomph!

Luca broke her fall, catching her shoulders so that she landed with very little impact on her feet. His look of triumph was replaced by a look of fear. "Are you okay?" He smoothed hair away from her temple. It was still tender, even after a week. "Jasmine?"

She smiled up at him. "I'm fine."

The dovecote was lit by a flash of lightning, which was quickly followed by a very close crash of thunder.

"We should—" Luca began.

Jasmine didn't wait for him to finish. She spun around, ducked out the door and sprinted toward the house.

CHAPTER THIRTEEN

WHAT WAS IT about a fleeing woman that evoked the instinct to chase? Seeing Jasmine dash across the lawn—skirt flapping, dark hair streaming out behind her—resulted in adrenaline surging through his veins followed immediately by a burst of energy. Making it almost too easy to catch up with her.

She squealed with what sounded like a mixture of fear and laughter when she glanced over her shoulder and saw how close he was. The sound only pushed him harder. He barely noticed that the skies had opened up and rain had begun—not until Jasmine slipped on the wet grass, almost losing her footing.

It was at that moment that he pounced, catching her off balance. He rolled so that when they hit the ground she landed on top of him, and before she had a chance to blink, he rolled her over beneath him, pinning her.

That didn't stop her from struggling.

Jesus Christ.

Suddenly, her body went slack.

Dammit. Had he taken this fantasy too far? "Are you okay? Did I hurt you?" he asked.

"You should let me go."

Instinctively, Luca climbed off of her and Jasmine scrambled to her feet. Too late, he saw the gleam of mischief in her expressive eyes.

"See you, sucker!" With a squeal she took off in the other direction.

A simple lunge and he had a handful of her skirt. He yanked her into his arms, spun her around, bent down and kissed her with the ferocity that chasing her had evoked. It was while she was moaning into his mouth that he grabbed the ties from his pocket and then twisted the fabric around her wrists, tying her hands together.

"Hey, that's cheating," she complained without conviction.

"I don't recall any rules to this game other than you run and I chase."

She panted while she looked up at him, her gaze hazy with desire.

"Do you like chasing me?" she asked, glancing knowingly at the crotch of his jeans.

"Strangely…yes." Thinking the game had come to an end, Luca took Jasmine's arm and started leading her toward the villa. He glanced down. "Did you like being chased?"

"Strangely, yes." She winked, and with that, Jasmine bolted. Again.

God damn.

How had he found such a woman? Someone who matched him so well? There was nothing like it to get his blood pumping and this time when he caught her he wrapped his arms tightly around her slight body.

"Let me go." She wriggled against him, her breasts brushing against his arms, her skin hot and wet against his bare chest.

"I'm not falling for that again."

Luca held her tight with one arm while he reached around the front of her, bunching up the material of her dress in order to get underneath. He needed to touch her. He needed to know if she was as aroused by the chase as he was.

She was so turned on, her sweet pussy was weeping tears down the insides of her thighs.

Luca groaned into her hair and plunged his fingers inside of her. Jasmine keened, a primal, animal sound. Luca had heard that cry before. At least twenty times before. And he knew what it meant.

Jasmine fucking loved this as much as he did.

Luca was tempted to lay her back down on the grass and fuck her. He had a condom in his pocket and it would feel so good. For both of them. But the rain was falling in sheets and they were drenched. So, instead, Luca decided to stick to the original plan.

He pulled his hand out from between her thighs and sucked his fingers into his mouth. "You taste good, Little Red," he whispered harshly in her ear. "I can't wait to feast on you."

Her knees buckled and he caught her, throwing her up and over his shoulder.

"Let me go!" She even went so far as to pummel her small fists against his back, but the resistance was all feigned as she nuzzled her face against his bare back and licked him.

Then she bit him.

Luca held the backs of her thighs tight against his shoulder as he trudged the rest of the distance to the terrace, enjoying the feel of Jasmine's mouth on his skin. Kisses, licks and bites included. Instead of taking her to the master bedroom, where they'd spent most of their time thus far, he took her to the cellar door—that he'd made sure to leave open—and carried her down into the extensive wine cellar beneath the house. It was cool in the cellar, and Jasmine would probably feel a chill because of her wet dress.

That was fine; he'd have it off her momentarily.

The cellar was lit by every candle he'd been able to find in the house, giving it a warm and sexy glow. There was a worktable he'd set up as a tasting area and another one set against a grate on which he'd thrown a thick comforter. That was where he was going to tie her up.

But first, the dress. He fingered the zipper at her back.

"Holy shit," Jasmine whispered, gazing around at the cellar. "I like the candles. But seriously? How much wine does one person need?"

The cellar was a remnant from when his mother's family was a producer in the area. His father hadn't wanted to continue cultivating the grapes here—it wasn't champagne from the Champagne region, so what was the point?—but there were still thousands of bottles in the cellar.

Luca wasn't looking at the wine, however. He only had eyes for Jasmine. Dripping wet, hair hanging in her face, her dress now unzipped and hanging off her shoulders. She was a magnificent sight.

The only problem was, with her arms bound, he had no choice but to use a knife to slice the thick straps at her shoulders.

"Luca!" she gasped.

"Shh," he commanded. "No talking."

She blinked at him, her lips turning up in a half smile as he peeled the wet material from her body.

"Unless you want me to gag you for real."

She gnawed on her lip and shook her head.

"I am going to blindfold you. And you don't get a choice about that." Luca removed the other strip of cloth—shockingly still dry—from his pocket and placed it over Jasmine's eyes, securing it behind her head.

She made soft little sounds at the back of her throat, and Luca took an extra blanket left folded by the table and rubbed her damp skin. Taking a step back, Luca took a moment to gaze at her—her faced turned blindly toward him, her hands tied together in front of her, reaching for him.

Trusting him.

Un-fucking-believable.

Warmth infused him as he carefully untied the rope from the bindings around her wrists, picked her up—blanket and all—and laid her down on the comforter. He secured her wrists to the grate by her head. The table wasn't long enough for her entire body, ending at her knees so they bent over the edge. It was perfect for what he had in mind.

"Spread your legs," he commanded.

She shook her head.

Damn. That wasn't what he expected. He'd thought she was finished with the facade. Apparently not. But maybe this was better.

"Spread your legs, now."

A soft mewling sound slipped past her lips, but she acquiesced. Luca's dick throbbed with fierce need and he pulled out another couple of ties, eased her thighs even wider—to the accompaniment of gasps of pleasure—and tied each ankle loosely to a leg of the table.

The sight of her tied like that was almost more than he could handle.

"You shouldn't have run. You shouldn't have fought me," he said, his voice coarse.

She wet her lips before continuing to breathe through her mouth.

"You leave me no choice…" He went to the table where he'd set up four bottles of wine ranging from crisp white to thick dessert. "Now I'm going to have to punish you."

The sound of her sucking in a breath echoed against the stone walls.

"Would you like to know how I'm going to punish you?" He poured a glass from the first bottle and moved right up beside her.

Her head bobbed in a circular movement, a mixture of yes and no.

He leaned down, very close to her, and dipped his finger into the glass of wine before running it along her lips. Whispering in her ear, he said, "First I'm going to taste you." He licked the sheen of wine off her lips. "Then I'll drink from you." He poured a tiny bit of wine between her parted lips and before she could swallow, he fixed his mouth to hers and drank the wine from her mouth. "Suck you." He poured a little pool in the hollow at the base of her neck and bent to suck. Wine and flesh. So fucking delicious.

"And finally?" Luca caressed her cheek, drew his fingers down her throat, between her breasts, past her belly until his hand cupped the top of her mound. "I'm going to eat you."

It was like Luca had attached electrodes to all her best bits—her nipples, her clit, her mouth, her ass—and sent thousands of volts of electricity through her, because her entire body went rigid with the shock of desire.

Never had she imagined she could feel this way. Not even close.

He dribbled wine—a delicious white—into her mouth, down her chin and throat and across her breasts.

"I'm starting with a chenin blanc. This is a new wine I purchased in town. Fresh." He licked her neck and whispered, "Fruity." He circled her breasts. "Exquisite."

It was all made so much better by the fact she was blindfolded. *And* tied down. All she could do was lie there and feel. The pressure of his tongue, the warmth of his mouth, the abrasion from his teeth. The suction.

God.

She heard the *glug-glug* of more wine being poured—was it from a new bottle?—and then Luca moved up by her head. "Do you have any idea how hard you made me when I was chasing you?"

She shook her head.

He untied the cloth from the grate, directed her still-bound hands close to him and then placed them against his crotch. Oh! He was monstrous. Luca ground her hands against him before finally, with a groan, drawing them away. That was when he dipped her fingers into cool liquid and stuck them in his mouth. His tongue ran between her digits, lapping at her before sucking.

Hard.

His mouth was so warm and soft inside. She wanted more but instead he stopped. She made a sound of protest but he once again tied her hands to the grate above her head, anyway.

"I think I need to torture you a little more," he whispered before dripping wine down her inner arm, catching the trail with his mouth. He poured some onto her breasts and sucked it off the sides, the place between…then right off the tips of her tight nipples.

She moaned in ecstasy when he chewed gently on those tips, like they'd been marinated.

"Do you have any idea how much I want you right now?"

"Luca," she moaned.

He pressed a finger to her mouth. "Shh. This is a sauvignon blanc from this cellar. It's fifteen years old, which some think is too old, but I think is perfect. Do you want a taste?"

She nodded, and he carefully spilled some wine into her mouth. It could have been vinegar and it still would have tasted amazing. But it wasn't vinegar. It was the most heavenly wine she'd ever tasted.

Luca moved away again and Jasmine strained to hear what he was doing. Ahh, pouring more wine. How many bottles? She couldn't remember. She'd been too taken by the fantasy of being lugged—kicking and screaming—down into a cellar by her shirtless savage.

The mere thought of the short-lived chase sent a fresh wave of blood to her clit, resulting in a heady throbbing sensation that made her writhe.

"This is one of the estate's finest. A pinot noir. There used to be many pinot grapes in the region. Now they are rare." He poured this wine on her stomach, and Jasmine could feel it pooling in the indent of her navel and spill over her sides. "Just like you." He sipped from her skin.

He was getting so close to where she wanted him that, even with her limbs secured, Jasmine lifted her hips, forcing her midsection toward him.

"Ah…my little captive…"

Right. She was supposed to be fighting him. Well, it was her fucking fantasy. She could do whatever the hell she wanted, and right now she wanted to encourage him to suck the throbbing place between her legs that was in desperate need of release.

He slid damp fingers over her mound to the swollen flesh at the top. He pinched and she cried out. "Is this what you want Jasmine?"

She squirmed, feeling completely exposed with her legs pulled apart.

"You want me to touch you here? Pour wine over you? Suck it off you?"

She whispered, "Yes. Oh, God, yes."

But did Luca grant her wish? Maybe he wasn't a genie, after all. He poured wine on her thighs, on her belly, her knees and lapped it all up, but he avoided the place she wanted him most.

"Please, Luca," she moaned.

"Please what?"

"Please touch me."

"Like this?" He flicked his finger briefly across her clit and she moaned in frustration.

"Harder."

"Like this?" He pressed down with his thumb, moving her clit around in firm circles.

"More. Please." She was panting now. Panting because it felt so good, panting because she knew it would soon feel even better and panting because she couldn't see and had no idea what he was going to do next.

Starting at the top of her mound, something thick and cool trickled down over her clit, between her folds, and Jasmine even felt slick coolness entering her.

"This is my dessert wine. The grapes were picked

by hand. It is made only for the family." He licked the spot just above her clit. "Very rare." Now he sucked her clit into his mouth. "And it's never tasted better."

With strong hands on her thighs, Luca finally bent his head to her—oh, she wished she could see. He started off gently, just making passes with his tongue. But that didn't last long. Thank God. His fingers dug into her flesh as his mouth consumed her. Licking, sucking, penetrating...

Jasmine raised her head from the bedding as if to watch. She couldn't see but her imagination filled in the blanks. Luca's thick, dark hair, bobbing between her thighs. The veins on his hands popping with the strain of holding her. A different angle now, as he moved to flick her clit with his tongue, raising his gaze to catch hers, a wicked smile in his eyes as he tortured her with his mouth.

Oh!

His mouth became brutal. Licking and biting, nipping at her folds and holding them between his teeth as he slipped a finger inside of her. Jasmine felt an orgasm building along her buttocks and spine; it was a deep one, but for some reason, she wanted to stave it off. This was all too good. It couldn't end yet.

"Come for me Jasmine. I need you to come." Luca growled as he plunged more than one finger inside of her.

"No," she moaned, rolling her head from side to side. "Not yet."

"Yes." He slammed his fingers inside, wriggling them back and forth against her walls. "Right now."

Despite Jasmine's efforts to keep her orgasm at bay, her body had other ideas. Contractions starting from the backs of her knees joined forces with the mounting pressure at the base of her spine, tightening her abdomen and her ass, and pulling on her innards as if to bring everything inside her body together, only to blow them apart again.

But they didn't blow...not yet.

She cried out with the massive orgasm that was lurking so close to the surface. "Luca!" She screamed his name over and over again.

He grunted and stopped what he was doing.

No!

But then the ties on her legs were loosened and she could move, not that she wanted to. Then her hands were released from the grate and he tore off the other ties that had bound her hands together.

The blindfold remained.

He pulled her off the table onto her feet, turned her around and pushed down on her back, bending her over. "I need to be inside of you," he grunted.

And then he was. So fucking deep.

That's all it took for her to shatter.

Jasmine could barely support herself as her body disintegrated with pleasure while Luca drove into her from behind, again and again, harder and harder, deeper and deeper. And just when she thought she was coming down from her orgasmic rapture, Luca cried out, held her hips flush against his and erupted inside of her.

Jasmine came all over again.

CHAPTER FOURTEEN

LUCA COULDN'T REMEMBER enjoying a day so much. After the cellar, they took the opened wine bottles to the kitchen and cooked a meal together while finishing off a couple of the vintages. During dinner, he'd inquired about any other fantasies she might have hidden deep inside of that deceivingly innocent exterior.

"Well, there is this one where we're in a public place…a museum or something."

"Really?" He leaned close to kiss her neck. "You never cease to surprise."

Now they sat in the living room, a fire crackling in the fireplace to foil the dampness of the evening. There was no television, at least not a working one, and they cuddled on the couch while Luca read out loud from a book of short stories. The one he'd chosen was called, *La Vénus d'Ille*. He would read a passage in French—Jasmine had insisted, said his reading in French was turning her on—and then would translate it for her.

It was an old story about a bronze statue of Venus

that was cursed, came to life and eventually killed a young man who was about to be wed by taking his wife's place in the marital bed. It ended with the statue being melted down into a bell, which then cursed the village with poor crops.

Jasmine sat up at the end of the story, a frown marring her features. "What kind of story is that?"

"A classic French tale."

"But it's so tragic."

"Not all stories have happy endings." Luca closed the book and put it down on the table.

Jasmine took his hand and threaded her fingers though his. "They should." She turned her head to him.

"Don't tell me you believe in happy endings."

"Of course I do."

He was about to say something about the fact that her engagement had not had a happy ending, but decided not to. Instead, he cupped her chin and kissed her. There was something so endearing about her optimism. Even if it was misguided.

"Luca," she said, after they broke apart. Her eyes were large and full of something that wasn't lust. For once. What was it? Curiosity? Concern?

Shit.

"I've told you all about me. I've even told you some of my darkest fantasies…" She rubbed his fingers. "But I still don't know anything about you."

She was right. He'd barely told her anything. Not about who he really was, not about why he was hiding out. He hadn't even come clean about how he'd met her. Why? Because he was still afraid she would expose him?

He wasn't afraid anymore.

"What do you want to know?"

Jasmine chewed on her bottom lip. "How about we start with this place. Who's is it, really?"

"What do you mean?"

"You know where everything is. You know all about the wine stored in the cellar. You know about the boats and the old cars in the garage and—"

"You're right," he interrupted. "This house belonged to my mother. When she and my father married, she kept this as our summer house. Every summer, I came here with her while my father worked."

"Where are your parents now?"

"Dead."

"Oh. I'm sorry." She squeezed his hand. "When did they die?"

"My father died about a year ago." He glanced around at the walls of his mother's house as if they were listening, too. "My mother died when I was sixteen. It was a car accident." He turned his gaze back to Jasmine. "I was driving."

He'd never told anyone before. It was strange how easily it came out.

"Oh, Luca. I'm so sorry."

He caught the hand that was about to stroke his cheek and held it aloft. "My father never forgave me. At least, I don't think he did. I never had the chance to ask."

"Luca…"

From somewhere down the hall, a telephone rang. It was such an out-of-place sound, both he and Jasmine jumped, as if it wasn't an everyday noise but a message from ghosts of his past.

Luca pushed off the couch and strode down the hall to where he'd left his phone in the bedroom. The call went to voice mail but he recognized the number. François.

Luca immediately called him back and heard the relief in François's voice.

"Good news," François said. "You can come out of hiding."

"What's going on?"

"Prices are up and we've pushed the date of the sale of the Legrand Goût des Rubis to tomorrow. I need you in Paris for the press conference. Show the board you can handle it and I think we can sway favor your way."

"Press conference? Wait, how do you know I'm not in Paris?"

"Luca, I've known you all my life. There's only one place you'd go after the paparazzi fiasco last week."

Of course François would know where he was. He'd worked for the family for decades.

"So," François hedged. "What did you do about the woman?"

Luca glanced toward the door. "She's still here, with me."

He could hear the disapproval dripping through

the silence on the line. Finally, François said, "Press conference is at eleven tomorrow morning. You need to get rid of her by then."

"Get rid of her? What do you mean?"

"Take her to the police station. There's one a few blocks from the hotel where we're holding the conference. Let her figure it out from there. She is not your responsibility, Luca. You can't risk another scandal, not tomorrow of all days. Do you understand?"

"Of course," Luca said, though he wasn't exactly sure how Jasmine was a scandal.

He hung up the phone and stood in the dim silence of the room for a moment. This was good news. He should feel elated. He could return to his normal life, a week earlier than expected, no less. Yet it all came with a strange heaviness.

This week had been…un-fucking-believable. Jasmine was un-fucking-believable. But it wasn't real. It was just like he'd tried to explain to her not twenty minutes ago. Real life had no happily-ever-afters. Life was nothing more than a combination of events: some happy, some sad, most in-between. And then?

It all ended.

While this last week had been one of the happiest he'd ever experienced, like everything in life, it had to end.

He was taking her back to Paris. Just like that. After the most monumental day of her life…it was all coming to an end.

After the phone call, Luca had returned and pro-

ceeded to explain that he needed to return to Paris
and that it was time she return to her life, too. Their
"fairy tale" existence—if sex several times a day
was a fairy tale—had come to an end. Then he'd
taken her hand, led her to the bedroom and made
love to her.

One last time.

Sometime in the night he'd gotten up and slept in
the other bedroom, leaving her alone.

"What did you expect, Jazz?" she whispered to
herself as she reached across the empty side of the
bed. "Did you really think he'd invite you to stay?
Did you think this was anything more than a holiday tryst?"

Yes.

It was true. Last night, before the phone call, Luca
had finally opened up to her. For a brief moment,
she'd entertained ideas about sharing a life with him.
God, she was such a hopeless romantic. She'd been
living in a fantasy world, and even if this fantasy
world was *so* much better than any she'd been able
to construct in her imagination, it didn't change the
fact that it wasn't real and never had been.

After barely sleeping, Jasmine decided to get up
once the sun peeked through the drapes. Time to
face the day she'd secretly hoped would never come.
She showered and made her way to the kitchen to
start the coffee. There was an old stovetop espresso
maker—a moka pot?—that made the best coffee.

She gazed around at the kitchen. Old cabinetry, an

old gas stove that was finicky, a refrigerator that was barely larger than a bar-sized one she had at home.

Home?

Where the hell was her home?

She had none.

She'd lived with Parker for two years of their three-year relationship, and while his penthouse apartment was ultramodern, with all the conveniences she could ask for, she felt more at home here in this outdated kitchen than she ever had in Chicago.

"That must be the sex talking," she muttered as she turned on another burner to fry up some eggs. Luca was right. It was time she stopped avoiding her life and face what had happened back in Chicago. It was time she found herself.

The hard part was, she'd never felt more like herself than she did right here.

A noise from the hall had her turning around. Luca stood in the doorway of the kitchen. At least... she thought it was Luca.

"Your beard. You shaved it."

"Yes."

But it was more than his clean-shaven face that made him appear different. His black curls had been slicked back in a way she'd never seen before. He wore clean jeans and a button-down shirt that had been pressed. There was almost nothing about this man that resembled the sexy brute who had pursued her—and captured her—yesterday.

Nothing except his eyes.

And in those startling blue eyes that she'd come

to adore was a distance that told her everything she needed to know without him having to say it.

The fairy tale was over.

She turned back to the eggs, not wanting Luca to see the emotion she feared was written quite clearly across her face. While she did that, he sliced some meat and cheese, and poured orange juice, and they sat and ate in silence. It was while they were cleaning the breakfast dishes—when had they gotten into such a familiar routine?—that Luca finally spoke.

"I left the bag on your bed so you can pack your things. We'll leave in half an hour."

Not trusting her voice, Jasmine simply nodded.

The leather satchel that Luca had brought from Paris lay open on the bed. Jasmine took her pile of clothes out of the drawer and set everything beside the bag. She spread the bag open and was about to plop her clothes inside when she noticed Luca's wallet in the bottom. She glanced toward the open door and tiptoed back to pull it shut.

Was snooping wrong at this stage of the game?

Maybe.

But Jasmine didn't care. In a couple of hours, she'd never see Luca again. She opened the wallet to the slots that held all of his credit cards and ID. The picture on the driver's license was the clean-shaven version of Luca who had appeared this morning. He had credit cards. Lots of credit cards. She pulled each one out before slipping it back inside. Then she studied his driver's license picture again.

Something was off. What was it?

Luca Legrand.

Legrand? Hadn't he said his last name was Deschamps? She checked his credit cards again. They were all in Luca Legrand's name. Why the hell had he lied to her about his last name? It made no sense.

She opened the bill compartment and pulled out the wad of cash. The man was carrying thousands of euros. Why would he need to carry so much cash when he had credit cards? And...wait...what was this lump at the very bottom of his wallet?

Jasmine fished inside and came out holding a ring between her thumb and forefinger.

Her engagement ring.

Why the hell did Luca have her engagement ring?

Who the fuck was he?

Luca found Jasmine at the front door. She wore the same outfit she'd been wearing that first day, the leather bag sat at her feet and she stared at him with a strange expression on her face.

"Are you ready?" It was a stupid question. She was clearly waiting for him.

"Luca?" she said, moving toward him.

"Yes?"

"What happened on the day you found me?"

Her question took him by surprise. It'd been a while since they'd talked about that. Luca simply reiterated the story he'd told all along about how he'd found her on the street.

"Are you sure?" she asked, gazing into his eyes, as if testing him.

"Of course I'm sure. Why?"

"It's funny. I seem to remember—vaguely—trying to sell a ring of mine." She turned her head to the other side, regarding him. "And I was wondering if you had any idea what might have happened to it?"

Fuck.

He'd forgotten all about the ring. Where had he put it? In his wallet, maybe? Luca couldn't remember. He checked his watch. It was eight thirty. It would take them two hours to get to Paris, which didn't give him much time to spare before the press conference. He didn't have time for this conversation. Particularly for the lengthy explanation that the conversation would entail. Once life got back to normal, he'd track Jasmine down and send her the ring.

Anonymously.

But right now? They had to go.

"Sorry," he said as he picked up the bag and slung it over his shoulder. "I don't know anything about a ring." He waved Jasmine out the door and locked it behind them. His bike sat waiting for them and he passed her a helmet before putting his on. She slid hers on without another word, and when she climbed on the back behind him, she held onto the leather of his jacket. Not him.

Something was up. Probably the fact that things were over and he was being distant. But what choice did he have?

The two-hour ride back to Paris was uneventful, apart from some wet roads from yesterday's storm. Yet how different it felt from the ride out of Paris little more than a week ago. It felt more like a month, a year, a lifetime ago.

At the exit to Nemours, he slowed, turned and asked Jasmine if she needed to stop for any reason, but Jasmine just shook her head so he drove straight through. She'd been quiet the entire ride, not that they could talk while riding a motorcycle, but she seemed different. Detached.

Well, so was he.

Even when he turned onto the Avenue de la Grande-Armée, which led to the famous roundabout circling the Arc de Triomphe, Jasmine remained quiet. Barely holding on to him.

It shouldn't matter to him, he was going to be saying goodbye to her in a matter of minutes.

Yet it did.

He took Avenue Kléber to Rue de Longchamp. The 16th Arrondissement Police Commissariat was only two blocks east. Luca pulled his motorcycle up to the front of the commissariat and stopped.

"What are we doing here?"

"This is a police station. I'm dropping you off."

Luca engaged the kickstand, removed his helmet and stood. Then he took the satchel off his shoulder to pull his wallet out before handing the bag to Jasmine, who'd also gotten off the bike.

She'd taken her helmet off along with the leather jacket he'd loaned her, and she hugged the bag against her chest, as if it were a shield. "So that's it?" Her lower lip quivered. "You don't have anything else to say to me?"

What the hell was he supposed to say? I care for you more than I should? I don't want to leave you but I have to if I want my life back?

This last week with you has been the best time of my life?

Luca simply shook his head. "*Non*. I have nothing to say."

Pain flashed across her face.

"Jasmine," he said sharply and grabbed her arm. She tried to tug away but he held on. "Please understand. I'm not who you think I am."

"So, who are you?"

"It doesn't matter. But you? You are..." God. What could he tell her? The truth, for once?

"Jasmine, you have this exceptional capacity for love. You need to go and find someone who deserves you."

It was the best, most honest statement Luca was capable of making. And what did he get for his effort? A slap across the face.

He stumbled in shock and then grabbed her hand again, needing to...what? Straighten things out? Explain?

What?

"Let go of me." She tugged but he wouldn't let go.

Suddenly people were running out of the police station. Police officers had guns drawn, shouting to get down. Luca pulled Jasmine into his arms, an automatic response.

"What's going on?" she shouted.

"I don't know."

More officers, maybe ten in all, surrounded him and Jasmine. All with guns drawn. All pointing at them.

What the fuck?

"Laissez-la partir!" an officer shouted. *Let her go.*

"Luca?" She searched his face, panic written all over hers.

"It's okay. It's okay," he reassured her, though there was not one part of him that believed things were okay.

"Luca Legrand, laissez-la partir, maintenant!"

"You need to go to them," he said as calmly as possible. He dropped his arms from around her and gave her a gentle push toward the nearest officer. Jasmine glanced back with a worried expression before slowly walking away. The officer jumped up, ran to cover her and then scurried her away.

What happened next happened so fast, Luca couldn't process it. The officers pounced and he was forced onto his stomach on the pavement. A knee was pressed into his back, the cold clasp of handcuffs were forced onto his wrists and an authoritative voice said, "Luca Legrand, you are under arrest for the kidnapping of Jasmine Sweet."

CHAPTER FIFTEEN

NOTHING WAS MAKING SENSE. There were too many people surrounding her, too much chaos, all of it happening in a language she didn't understand. The next thing Jasmine knew, she was being escorted inside the police station where more officials were waiting.

"What's going on?" she asked, over and over again, but no one answered her until a female dressed in uniform approached. She had sympathetic brown eyes and brown hair pulled back into a ponytail.

"Jasmine?" she said. "My name is Danielle. Please, would you come with me?" She held out her hand as if Jasmine was supposed to take it.

"Where are we going?"

"Somewhere quiet." Her thickly accented voice was calm and soothing, and Jasmine followed the woman to a room where two male officers were seated.

"Please, sit," Danielle said, indicating one of two empty chairs. "First of all, we are so happy to find you safe and sound."

Jasmine frowned. "People knew I was missing?"

"Yes. We've all been looking for you."

Oh, shit.

"Your family has been very worried."

Oh, God. Her family. She'd meant to email her parents and then had totally forgotten. Or rather, been distracted by mind-blowing sex…

With a man who had turned out to be a cold-hearted asshole.

She was such an idiot.

"Can I speak to them? I need to speak to them."

"Of course. We will let you speak to them momentarily. But first, I need you to answer some questions, okay?"

"Okay, but…" Jasmine looked from the woman to the men. "Do you know what happened to me?" Maybe finally she'd get some answers about the theft and the concussion.

The female officer glanced at the men, giving them some kind of meaningful look. What it meant, Jasmine had no idea.

"Your belongings were turned in to the police over a week ago."

"Belongings?" The woman was speaking English but she may as well have been speaking French for all the sense she was making.

"Your bag. With your passport, ID, money and hotel key."

"You found my bag?" Jasmine said, sitting up. What a relief. She wouldn't have to contact Parker for her documents, after all.

"Yes." The woman went on to explain how the police had contacted the hotel to return her belongings after they'd been picked up from the scene of a robbery, only to find out she'd never returned. They'd used the information on her passport to contact her next of kin. When no one had heard from her, she became a missing person. "You have become an international incident."

"Are you fu—" Jasmine stopped herself. "Are you serious?"

"Yes. Now," the woman said. "Tell us about Luca Legrand."

Jasmine had figured Luca was in trouble with the law, but this seemed a hell of a lot more serious than what she'd supposed. What had he done?

Then suddenly, she remembered what she'd found in his wallet.

"Is this about the ring? Was Luca involved in the robbery?"

"The robbery?" She shook her head. "Luca Legrand is the heir to the Legrand estate, worth billions. I doubt he'd be involved in petty theft."

Jasmine stared open-mouthed.

Billions?

The woman tilted her head in that very French way and turned to the man writing notes with a raised brow. "But then, where that man is concerned, who can be sure of anything?" She spoke softly to the two male police officers, the one who was taking notes slid the paper in front of Danielle and then the men exited the room.

Once the door was shut, Danielle found an envelope from the pile of paperwork from which she withdrew a stack of photos and slid the first in front of Jasmine. "Can you identify the man in this photo, please."

"Yes," Jasmine said slowly, it was promotional picture for the Grand Prix circuit. "It's Luca. He lied about his last name, but I saw his ID. It's Luca Legrand."

The woman nodded. "And you have been with Monsieur Legrand since you went missing?"

"Yes, but…"

"And he held you captive?"

"No."

"No?" The officer spread the other photos out across the table, in order. "I need you to describe what is happening here."

Hesitantly, Jasmine slid the photos closer and looked at the first. Then the next and the next and the next until she'd seen all twelve images.

Holy fuck.

The pictures were grainy because they'd been taken during a storm—yesterday's storm—and they told a story. A sordid story.

Dear God.

Who the hell had taken these? And how did the police get them?

It was like time-lapse photography. Luca chasing her and tackling her. Pinning her. Tying her up. Jasmine trying to escape and Luca chasing her down again. There was even a picture of him manhandling her. Then there were images of him hauling her up and over his shoulder and carrying her back to the house.

"Look," Jasmine said. "This isn't what it seems."

"Mmm." The woman gathered the photos back up into a pile. "I think this is exactly what it seems." She patted Jasmine's hand. "It is very common to feel a sense of…" She paused as if searching for a word. "*Kinship* with your kidnapper."

"Luca didn't kidnap me."

"*Mademoiselle*, I know it may seem that way. Men like Monsieur Legrand can appear charming, but—" The woman smiled with such understanding, yet she didn't understand anything.

Jasmine put her fingers to her temples and winced as she pressed on a still tender spot. "Please, I need to explain."

"Of course. I want you to tell me exactly what happened, and I want you to start from the beginning."

Luca had no idea how long he'd been in the interrogation room. The police had confiscated his watch and everything else on his person. When they'd first shown him the pictures, he'd been too shocked to answer any questions.

Who the hell had taken those pictures? How the hell had they found him? What the fuck was he going to do now?

When he'd finally found his tongue, he'd gone over his story about fifty times with the police, explaining that Jasmine was a tourist he'd come across who'd had an accident. That he'd simply helped her and everything was consensual and that this was one big fucking mistake.

Of course they didn't believe him.

When François finally appeared. He sat down across from Luca looking ten years older than the last time he'd seen him.

"We have to stop meeting like this," Luca attempted a joke.

It did not go over well.

"I don't even know what to say," François said.

"Say you'll talk to Jasmine. Say you can get the story straight and that you can get me out of here."

François's reply was a single raised brow followed by a sad shake of his head. He slid the pictures that had been sitting in the middle of the table toward him and went through them. Slowly.

"It's not what it looks like," Luca said to fill in the terrible silence.

François raised his gaze and then removed his glasses to clean them.

Before Luca had a chance to add anything, there was a knock on the door and François got up to open it. An officer stood outside and spoke quietly to the lawyer. Luca heard Jasmine's name mentioned but that was the extent of it.

When the conversation ended and François returned to the table, Luca noticed the door had been left open.

"She's refusing to press charges," François said, as if this was a bad thing.

Luca stood. "Then it's all over."

"No. It's not." François sighed. "The photos were sent in by an anonymous tipster. There's no stopping them being leaked to the press. Criminal investigation or not, the public has already condemned you."

Fuck.

"I don't even know what to say to you anymore. It's over, Luca. You've ruined us." He got up and walked to the door, then stopped to say, "Oh, and the American woman wants to talk to you, apparently. She'll be here shortly."

Luca stood, scrubbing a hand up and down his face. How could things have gone so awry? There was only one way. He'd been set up. Again. And there was only one man who would do it.

Marcel.

Luca kicked the wall in anger just as the door opened. Jasmine stood there accompanied by a female officer.

"I'd like to speak to him alone, please," Jasmine said to the other woman.

"I don't think—"

"Please."

"Okay, but I'll be right outside if you need me." It was clear by the woman's tone that she didn't like the idea of Jasmine being in a room alone with him. Based on the fucking photos, he couldn't blame her.

"Jasmine," Luca began. "Thank you for—"

She stopped him with a fierce look before he could say another thing.

"Why did you lie?"

"About what?"

She threw her head back and laughed. There was not one whit of humor in it. "Let's see, about your name. About who you really are. About this…" she shoved her hand into her pocket and pulled out her ring.

Fuck.

"Jasmine, let me explain. Please."

"You had plenty of time to explain." She paced the room. "Days to explain." She stopped. "I asked you point-blank this morning about my ring and you lied to my face." She came to stand right in front of him. "Why?" She narrowed her gaze. "Did you rob the store and knock me out and then try to hide that fact by whisking me away?"

"No. God, no. That's not what happened."

"Then for the final time, tell me the truth about what happened. You've got two minutes or I press charges for theft." She tapped her toe, a permanent scowl on her face.

Luca began slowly, explaining how he'd stopped the robbery that day. How she'd chased him out of the store and he didn't know why. How she'd collapsed. How he'd found the ring later and had planned to return it. How he'd been lying low because of previous scandals he'd been involved in and that he was in danger of losing his family fortune. There was so much that it all became tangled together in his explanation.

And it all sounded terribly lame.

"So, your name is really Luca Legrand and you are heir to the Legrand champagne estate?"

"Yes. You've heard of me?"

She made a face. "The police were kind enough to explain a few things to me." She walked straight up to him and poked him hard in the chest. "Here's what they were unable to explain. Why you didn't trust me with the truth."

He'd never seen her angry. It was a sight to behold. "Jasmine. I couldn't tell you the truth. I had to lie."

"That's bullshit."

"You don't understand. I was afraid of—"

"Of what? Huh?" She poked him harder. "What the hell were *you* afraid of?"

"This." He waved to the room, the pictures, the police station at large. "I was afraid something like this might happen. Everything was at stake, my reputation, my inheritance. Everything. And, based on what has happened to me this year, I couldn't trust anyone. Not even you."

She shoved him. "And it made no difference to you that I told you *everything* about me? That I trusted you enough with *my* secrets. That I let you tie me up, for fuck's sake? But you couldn't even tell me your real name?"

"Jasmine…"

She took a step back and cocked her head to one side. "You know what, Luca," she said. "You're no better than Parker, using me so that you wouldn't lose your trust fund." She closed her eyes and lifted her chin. "Jesus," she muttered to the ceiling.

"I never used you."

"No?" Her laugh was an angry sound. "You're saying you *didn't* use my body for your own pleasure? You *didn't* use my company to make your exile more palatable?" She shook her head.

Luca had had enough of being misunderstood. "You're accusing *me* of using *you*?" he snarled in frustration. "What about you? *You* blackmailed me so I'd agree to take you with me to the villa. *You* showed up naked in my shower. It was *you* who asked me to do all of those things to your body." He grabbed her shoulders. "I didn't ask for any of that, Jasmine. It was all you."

Jasmine's mouth hung open in shock. She blinked. When she spoke, it was slowly and carefully. "Are you saying you were just doing me a favor? That you fucked me out of pity?"

Her lip quivered.

Luca's anger dissolved the second he saw tears welling up in her eyes. "No. That's not what I'm saying."

She backed away, holding her hands up as if he was an evil entity and she needed to ward him off. "You're an even bigger asshole than Parker." She spun around and marched to the door, banging on it with her fist to get the officer's attention.

"Jasmine, wait," he called. "I'm sorry."

She walked out the door and slammed it behind her, and that was when Luca realized something.

Something huge.

He didn't want Jasmine to think that he was the

fuckup everyone else in the world thought he was. He wanted to go back to the villa, to the times when she'd gazed at him like he was the most amazing man in the world.

And most of all, Luca realized that he didn't care about losing everything. But he did care about losing Jasmine.

CHAPTER SIXTEEN

WHEN JASMINE FLEW back to America, she didn't even stop in Chicago but flew directly to Denver to be with her parents. She didn't plan on staying long, just until she could figure out the shit show that was her life. She also flew home to hide. Her sex-venture in France had become international news. Big in Europe first, because of the Legrand family fame, then across the Atlantic, when it became known an American was involved. Pictures of her being chased and carried off by Luca were all over social media, and since no one knew the full story, the public was left to interpret what was really happening in the condemning photos. Blog posts and new memes showed up daily, with sometimes corny but mostly offensive captions. If she thought her experience with Parker had been humiliating, she was sorely mistaken.

She now understood the true definition of humiliation.

Which made speaking to Parker somehow more bearable. She'd finally phoned him and asked him to ship her belongings, and she had to admit, he'd been accommodating. At least he wasn't still suggesting they work it out between them. She'd offered him his ring back. He refused to take it, at first, but she'd insisted.

Jasmine had to make it on her own. No more relying on men. Especially if they were only capable of lying to her. The truth was, she'd finished being angry with Parker a long time ago. Luca had helped with that. Had made her feel things she'd never thought possible. Now she was only upset with herself. She was the one who'd fallen twice for men who'd deceived her.

She was afraid her infamy would hurt her job prospects, but she got a job at the first hair salon she applied to. Once word got out about who she was (Luca Legrand's scandalous sex slave) she was booked solid for the next six months. So the upside of her disgrace was that her income was guaranteed and she would be able to move out of her parents' house sooner rather than later.

Her second week on the job, one of her coworkers came running back to her chair while she was cutting an elderly lady's hair.

"Jasmine! That guy who abducted you is on TV. Come see."

She'd given up setting people straight about her supposed kidnapping. No one listened because fiction was way more interesting than fact.

When Jasmine rounded the corner where the overhead television was perched, one of the girls turned up the volume just as Luca took the microphone in what appeared to be a press conference.

"God, he's hot. I wouldn't say no if he kidnapped me."

A rumble erupted in the pit of her stomach but she didn't say anything because she wanted to hear what Luca had to say. He spoke in French and it was translated by a female. It started with something about the sale of a rare bottle of champagne that had sold to a collector for half a million euros. The man who'd purchased the wine stood up and nodded as he was presented with a bottle amid the flash of numerous cameras.

Once the clamor died down, there was silence. Luca paused, seeming to weigh his words. Then he spoke some more. The translator seemed caught off guard and spoke quickly to keep up. "The Legrand champagne estate has been run by Legrand men for many generations, and while I am the last Legrand…" Luca glanced at a man sitting beside him. "I will be resigning as CEO and announcing a successor as soon as possible." There was a flurry of flashing cameras, and the crowd grew louder as reporters vied for further comments.

Jasmine frowned.

Luca was giving up his birthright? Why?

Then Luca raised his hand for silence and began speaking in English.

"And now, I have a message for Jasmine Sweet."

O-oh, shit.

There were gasps from the other women in the salon who had gathered round.

"Quiet," Jasmine said. "I can't hear."

Someone turned up the volume as Luca began to speak. "Jasmine, there are so many things I regret. I regret that you have been the subject of this malicious international media frenzy. I regret lying to you. I regret some of the things I said and some of the things I did."

Flashes went off in his face and he turned away for a moment before continuing. "But there are many things I do not regret. I will never regret the time we spent together. I certainly do not regret the things we did together. Most of all, I do not regret falling in love with you."

The salon went silent. All eyes turned to her.

The press conference was a nightmare, even worse than the last two weeks with relentless paparazzi hounding him. He couldn't believe what he'd just done. Yet Luca felt a strange lightness after announcing that he would be stepping down as head of the family business.

It wasn't planned. He was supposed to show up today and announce the new owner of the rare Legrand vintage. Then he'd been going to use the press conference to tell Jasmine he was sorry and that he loved her. He was sure she'd hear him this way. But as he'd stood onstage, thinking about that love, of all the things he wanted to give her, he knew she was his only priority now.

Even over his family legacy.

He refused to subject her to any more of Marcel's vindictive machinations and there was only one way to accomplish that.

Quit. So he did…on television, before he could change his mind. Now Marcel would have no reason to make his life, and Jasmine's by proxy, a living hell.

The thought of Marcel winning should have angered Luca, but he only felt relief.

Luca had just stepped into his office when Marcel appeared. "What the hell was that?" he asked, his voice angry and clipped.

Luca was too exhausted to fight with his half brother. "You have outplayed me at every turn. Take the position—it's yours. And if you want to contest the will? Go ahead."

"What are you talking about?"

"I know what you've been up to. Arranging the scandals, the paparazzi at the worst possible moments. Having me followed. Taking those pictures. You won, Marcel. At least be gracious in victory."

Marcel shook his head. "Luca, I don't know what you think I did, but I would never try to ruin you like that."

"Of course you would. You knew the board wanted you to lead the company and that the only way to do that was by contesting my inheritance. I'm just saving us all time and lawyers' fees."

"What are you talking about? Your father wanted *you* to run the company. It's yours, Luca. He already made generous provisions for me."

Luca stared hard at the man he'd blamed for his misfortune. What surprised him was how genuine Marcel appeared. Luca ran his fingers through his too-long hair. "But if you didn't do it, who else would—" Just then, François walked into the room with Marcel's fiancée, Lydia Fournier. Now Luca realized why he'd recognized her last name, she went by her mother's.

And her mother was François's ex-wife.

Lydia Fournier was François's estranged daughter.

Though, by the looks of things, she was not so estranged now.

"It was you," Luca said, striding up to François. "You're the only one who knew where I was. Both times. All the time." He blinked, dumbfounded. "It was you all along."

There was a gasp from Lydia who released her father's arm as she eyed the two men in shock.

Luca turned and paced, his fingers threaded through his hair. "I trusted you. I confided in you. And you betrayed me."

"You're mistaken." François's voice was eerily calm. "It is you who betrayed your family name." He shrugged. "I just made sure the world saw you for who you truly are."

"Oh, my God." Luca stumbled backward as if François had pushed him. "Why would you do that?"

"Do you know what I have done for this company? The long hours. Being your father's right-hand man for thirty years. I gave up my own family for yours. My wife left me, my only daughter wouldn't talk to

me for years." He adjusted his glasses. "Then you
came along. Luca Legrand, the prodigal son who
never gave a damn about the company. You were
going to destroy everything I worked for. Everything I sacrificed." He shook his head. "I couldn't
let it happen. So, I destroyed you, instead."

"Papa!" his daughter cried as she leaned against
Marcel.

"I did it for you, Lydia." Finally he looked at his
daughter.

She shook her head and clutched Marcel, who
stared at the lawyer in disbelief.

"François," Luca said. "You're fired."

"You can't fire me. You're no longer in charge."

"François," Marcel said, stepping forward.
"You're fired."

It had been three days since she'd seen Luca on TV
and Jasmine couldn't stop thinking about him. He
loved her? How could that be?

Did she love him?

Yes, of course you do, stupid.

"I can't believe he gave up all that money for you,"
her friend Ashley said via FaceTime. "It's so romantic. We're talking billions of dollars here, people."

"I doubt he gave it up for me," Jasmine said, waving off her friend's comment. "I'm sure he was forced
to."

"Well, he certainly wasn't forced to profess his
love for you in front of millions of viewers world-
wide." Ashley wagged her brows suggestively.

Jasmine shook her finger at the camera. "Don't you have a baby to go birth?"

Ashley lowered the camera to show off her stomach. "Yep, overdue by three days." She groaned. "I'm about ready to explode." She raised the camera again. "Now, stop changing the subject. When are you heading back to France to snatch up that smoking-hot Neanderthal?" She tapped something on her phone and suddenly a meme popped up on Jasmine's messenger app. It was the picture of Luca carrying her over his shoulder, but instead of clothes they were dressed in hides like cavemen, with the caption *Why Luca Legrand's dating profile says Old-Fashioned.*

"Very funny," Jasmine said. "I don't think I want to be your friend anymore."

"You have to. You're going to be my baby's godmother. Now answer the question."

"I'm not going back to Paris. I've got a very good job here in Denver and I don't need a man to take care of me."

"Uh-huh. But he did take care of you, right? Like all of your nasty lady needs were *well* taken care of?"

"Okay, horny pregnant person, some of us have to go to work now. Bye!"

She ended the call before Ashley delved any deeper into how she really felt. Which was…confused.

During Jasmine's break she went to the deli next door to buy a sub, and when she got back, the receptionist stopped her. "Package for you, Jazz." The woman gave her a curious smile.

Jasmine took the package into the staff room and opened it while she ate her lunch. It was a rectangular wooden box about the size of a small toaster with a sliding lid. There were no markings on the box, nothing. Inside was something shiny and heavy. She pulled it out. It was a silver oil lamp, like the one she'd seen in the shop in Paris that fateful day. She dumped the box to see if there was a note. Nothing.

After finishing her sandwich, she washed up and went back to her station. A man with shoulder-length hair wearing a leather jacket sat in her chair with his back to her. She stopped in shock. She recognized that jacket.

Luca.

"What the hell are you doing here?" she asked, a mixture of relief, rage, surprise and pleasure making her voice sound weird.

He turned in the chair. She'd forgotten how startlingly blue his eyes were. Well, she hadn't forgotten, they were just so much more striking in real life than in her imagination.

"I need a haircut. Obviously."

She took a couple of steps closer and pulled her scissors out of the jar of disinfectant. "And you trust me to be near you with a sharp object?"

"I absolutely trust you," he said with a soberness that made her cheeks tingle.

"Okay. I'll cut your hair. But that's it."

"That's all I asked for."

It took her twenty minutes to do the job, and she couldn't decide if it was the longest or the shortest twenty minutes of her life. He smelled so good and he was so close, and with every snip of her scissors, memories flickered in and out of her mind's eye, making it difficult to keep her lines straight.

"There," she said as she dusted hair off his shoulders. Oh, she'd forgotten how lovely and broad his shoulders were.

The bastard.

"You look a little less like a Neanderthal now." The meme that Ashley sent her that morning flashed behind her lids and she suppressed a smile.

"Did you get my package?"

"The lamp? Yes. Are you here to grant me more wishes? Because I don't want any more."

He stood. Another thing she'd forgotten. How tall he was. He was imposing and…gorgeous.

It took her breath away.

"No. I'm not here to grant wishes. I'm here to ask *you* to grant *me* three wishes."

"Why on earth would I—"

He stopped her with a quick kiss. It was nothing compared to the searing ones he'd bestowed often during her stay at the villa, but it still resulted in her knees turning to pudding.

"All I ask is that you listen. You may decide about granting them after."

"Fine." She waved for him to proceed, hoping to hide the fact that she was finding it hard to breathe.

"First, I wish for you to return to Paris." He pulled a ticket from his pocket. "There is so much you missed, so much I want to show you. So much I think you would love."

She took the proffered ticket with exaggerated reluctance and placed it on the counter of her workstation.

"Second, I wish for forgiveness. I said and did many things I regret. I would like a chance to make it up to you."

She opened her mouth but he held up his hand before she could speak. "Let me finish." His chest rose and fell as he took a deep breath and released it. "I wish for you to tell me if my love for you is reciprocated or not."

He pressed a finger to her lips. "Don't answer now. Take your time." He handed her a small envelope. "Here are instructions if you should choose to use the ticket. The flight leaves in four days."

Luca leaned forward and kissed her softly once more, whispering in her ear. "Oh, and you may want to destroy those instructions after reading. They are for your eyes only."

When he walked out the door, every pair of eyes in the salon watched him go.

Jasmine's hand shook as she opened the envelope. She skimmed over the message once and then read it again, slowly. As she reread it for the third time, her heart fluttered in her throat when she reached the last line.

Panties optional.

CHAPTER SEVENTEEN

WOULD SHE SHOW? Luca's doubts far outweighed his confidence. He was also taking a big risk—no, a huge risk—by suggesting this rendezvous. But if there was one thing he'd learned, Jasmine was worth the risk.

Thankfully, the paparazzi weren't quite as fierce as they had been a few weeks ago. There was always a new scandal somewhere for them to prey upon. Besides, his televised declaration of love seemed to have swayed public opinion, especially when it'd been followed up with an announcement that he'd be running the estate, after all…with his *brother*. Now the world knew there were *two* Legrand heirs.

He waited in the shadows of salon five in the Musée d'Orsay, the old train station in Paris that had been converted into a museum. It was not nearly as large as the Louvre, and it was much quieter. A necessity for what he had in mind.

He checked his watch. It was five minutes past the appointed afternoon time. And then it was ten.

Fifteen.

She wasn't coming.

Suddenly a woman appeared in the entrance of the salon. She wore a red dress—bless her heart—a black bag over her shoulder and black heels that did amazing things to her already shapely legs. Her dark hair fell in stylish waves past her shoulders. She stopped inside the salon, glanced around, referred to a pamphlet in her hand and moved inside.

She stood in front of *L'âge d'or: La nuit* by Léon Frédéric, just as Luca had instructed. He'd chosen this salon for its remoteness in the museum.

He walked up behind her quietly, hoping she wouldn't hear him.

However, perhaps she felt his presence, as he did hers, because as soon as he was within earshot, she spoke. "Americans should adopt the European attitude toward the naked body." Her voice was low and husky.

"Do you think so?"

"Oh, yes. We're much too uptight." She tilted her head to take a better look at the rendition of a group of people, mostly naked, sleeping together in a field. "The human body is very beautiful."

He brushed hair from her shoulder. "*You* are very beautiful," he said softly against her skin. Then he raised her chin and turned her toward him.

Her eyes were large and liquid as she gazed up at him.

"I'm so glad you're here."

She blinked and he felt her soft breath on his

cheek. "You're a hard man to say no to, Luca Legrand."

Relief filled him. "I hope that's a good thing."

"Sometimes." She smiled up at him.

He recognized that smile. A lethal mixture of sensuousness and innocence.

His relief grew. "I would like to thank you for making the trip."

She bit down on her lower lip. "How would you go about doing that? Thanking me?"

"There are so many ways, Jasmine." It was true. He wanted to be so many things to this woman. Her lover, yes, but more, too. He wanted to be the man she woke up to, the man she shared her fears and hopes and dreams with. He wanted to laugh with her, cook with her, read books together on a cozy couch. He wanted to share his life with her.

While her presence suggested much, he needed desperately to know that she believed in him and there was only one way to find out.

"Do you trust me?"

She crossed her arms over her chest. "I don't know, you've given me very little reason to trust you." She shifted from one foot to the other. "Why?"

While she was playing it cool, Luca could feel the warmth emanating from her skin, telling him that she already knew where this was going. He had been explicit in his letter…

He leaned close and whispered in her ear. "There is a fantasy of yours I would very much like to fulfill."

Breath stuttered inside her throat. "Oh?" She was trying to sound coy. It was so fucking sweet.

"But it requires trust." He paused. "Can you forgive me enough to place your trust in me?"

She blinked up at him, carefully considering his question. Good, because it was critical to him that she knew what she wanted. What he wanted.

"Please?"

"O-kay…"

Relief washed over him and Luca curbed the urge to shout with joy. Instead, he took her hand and led her into an even smaller and quieter gallery adjacent to the one they'd just been in. Luca directed her to the corner, so she was standing behind a display of a statue and he stood close behind her, their backs to the wall. "Look at the sculpture. Read the inscription."

"But I can't read French…"

His hand slid beneath the hem of her skirt, moving upward. "Try. Say it out loud."

"Um… Jean Hugues…" Her breath caught as his fingers explored higher: her thighs, her bare ass—Jesus!—the front of her.

"Luca?" She glanced over her shoulder. "Are you sure?"

"Shh," he whispered. "Spread your legs, lean forward and keep reading."

Instead of words, a soft gasp slipped out of her mouth.

The result was a fierce tightening in his groin. "There is no one else in this room. The light is dim.

No one can see." He was barely touching her, yet he could feel heat on the inside of her thighs and her skin was lightly damp. "Read."

"Torse de jeune-..." She grunted when he delicately parted her soft lips.

"Go on," he murmured, pressing his fingertips into her warm core.

"Fille." She angled her head. "I'm not saying that right, am I?"

"You're doing fine." His other hand slid beneath her hair and around her neck as two fingers slid deeper inside of her.

"What...what does that mean?" She panted.

"Torse de jeune-fille means torso of a young girl." Curving his fingers, he pressed against the satiny walls of her channel.

"Ahhh..." Her back arched as she raised her ass into his hand.

"Tell me, do you like being fingered in public?"

"Yes." She rocked back into him.

"Are you worried someone will see?" He withdrew his fingers from her heat and rubbed the moisture across her pussy and clit before playing around the tight little opening of her ass.

"Maybe...but...no. Not really," she said, followed by a soft whine.

Christ. So many things he still wanted to do with this woman. She was so willing and passionate and ravenous in her sexual appetite.

And she was here. She'd come. That had to mean

something. She wouldn't have come all this way just for sex. It had to mean more.

It did for him.

A man walked into the room, glanced in their direction and then moved to study the Renoir near the entrance. Jasmine squeaked softly against his palm.

"Shh," he murmured in her ear. His hand drifted from her mouth to her jaw and down to her shoulder where he brushed hair away to place a soft kiss on her bare skin.

"Luca." His name was a soft moan.

"I'm not going to stop until you come." He nibbled her ear. "I want your come in the palm of my hand."

His comment resulted in her grinding into his hand.

"This sculptor? Jean Hugues? How do you think he knows a woman's torso so well?" He paused, even though he didn't expect an answer. "By touching her." He rubbed her fat little clit with his thumb while he vibrated his fingers inside of her. "Caressing her." While his hand on her shoulder and throat was gentle, the one beneath her skirt was not. "He probably fucked her in every way possible," he whispered softly in her ear.

The low whine, which Luca had come to learn meant she was close, started deep in her chest.

"Shh, *ma colombe*." He rubbed his jaw against her hair while he placed his palm flat between her legs, cupping her. "You need to keep quiet when you come."

Her whole body flinched within the circle of his arms and a surge of moisture filled his hand.

"Yes, just like that." He buried his face in her hair. "Luca." She clung to him and he loved it. God he loved it.

In fact, he loved it so much—loved her so much— he swept the hair away from her ear and told her how he felt.

Oh. My. God. She'd had an orgasm in a museum. With other people in the room. It was…unbelievable! But even better—like a billion times better— was the fact that Luca had told her that he loved her.

And this time she believed him.

After the museum, Luca took her to the Eiffel Tower and they went up to the top where a wind gust threatened to expose her, literally, to the world. As if she hadn't been exposed enough in the last month. But none of that mattered anymore because she was here, at the Eiffel Tower, not gazing at it from a balcony alone but sharing it with the man she loved.

It made all the difference.

Once they were back down on the ground, Luca unpacked a picnic lunch and spread everything on a blanket on the grass. Before he let her sit, however, he wrapped his arms around her, held her close and whispered wonderful things in her ear.

Not naughty things—well, there may have been a couple of naughty suggestions—but mostly it was about how he felt about her. How scared he'd been that she wouldn't show today. How he wanted to make her dreams come true, and her fantasies—like they'd just done. But mostly he wanted to prove to her that this was about more than sex.

It was about connection and understanding and about two people who trusted one another.

She turned in his arms and linked her hands around his neck. "Luca?"

"Yes?"

"I forgive you."

"Really?"

"Yes."

"That simple?"

"Um…you call confessing your love on international TV, giving up your inheritance, flying across the country to give me a lamp and then flying me here, simple?"

He laughed. "Well, when you put it that way…"

She went up on tiptoes and kissed him soundly on the mouth. Then she tilted her chin up and said, "By the way, I love you, too."

He whooped at the sky, then picked her up and spun her around.

"Careful," she squealed so he'd set her down. She patted her skirt into place. "I'm not wearing anything under this, remember?" She laughed, wondering at how life could change. Luca brought out extremes of emotions, from the most pleasure she'd ever experienced to the greatest anger. In between those extremes, her heart had ached for him. All of it, all of the emotions—even the extremes—made her feel more alive than she'd ever felt.

They sat down and shared a lunch of bread, cheese, wine and pastries gathered from local shops. They were *not* the only picnickers in the park and Luca borrowed a corkscrew from a neighboring group.

God, she loved Paris. The people were so uninhibited.

Here she was drinking wine in a public place after being fingered in a public place, hanging out with a rich and famous man in a public place.

This was living.

"You're smiling."

"I'm happy." She gazed at him. "Thank you for inviting me here." She covered his hand. "And thank you for…" She bit her lip. "Saying what you said in the press conference. I hope you didn't really give everything up for me."

"Of course I did." He grinned and there was a flash of mischief in his eyes. "But, as it turns out, my brother is a better man than I am. I'd intended to make him CEO, but we have decided to run the company together." He took a drink of wine and a far-off look came into his eyes. "It's what my father would've wanted."

"Oh, Luca." She leaned over and kissed him.

He kissed her back with the freedom and joy of a Parisien in love.

"However, I have a new venture I am thinking about." He stroked her cheek. "Though I need a partner."

"Oh?"

"Yes. I want to market my mother's wines again. It's the area I love. The wines I love. It is a shame to let those vines go to waste."

"That sounds like an amazing idea."

"Yes. I think so." He took her free hand. "And I'm wondering if you would consider being my partner in that venture?"

She sat up, stunned. "You want me to come back to the villa?"

"Yes. It will be hard work and it may not be your passion, becoming a vintner. So, give yourself some time—"

"Yes!" Jasmine threw her arms around him before he could finish. "Yes, of course, yes." She smiled up at him. What he was asking her was so different from a man telling her he wanted to take care of her.

Being partners? That sounded like a dream come true. "From the very first, that place seemed more like home to me than anywhere else I've ever lived."

"It's not too...provincial?"

"No. I love it there."

"Bien." He handed her wine back to her and they clinked glasses. "You may have to learn French."

"J'ai déjà commencé." I've already started.

Jasmine smiled broadly at Luca's look of surprised approval. Then she squirmed when he whispered something about looking forward to teaching her more intimate French things while he inched his hand up beneath her skirt.

She playfully slapped his hand away and rearranged her skirt, grinning. Then Jasmine reclined so that she could put her head in Luca's lap.

"I told you," she said softly, eyes closed.

"Told me what?"

"That happy endings make the best stories."

She opened her eyes to find Luca gazing down at her with adoration in his eyes. *"Touché,"* he whispered.

* * * * *

LEGAL ATTRACTION

LISA CHILDS

MILLS & BOON

Special thanks to Megan Broderick—

for keeping me on track for all those things
like Dedications and Dear Reader Letters
and Art Fact Sheets.

I appreciate all your help!

CHAPTER ONE

DAMN IT! RONAN HALL had been seeing her everywhere. But then, Muriel Sanz was everywhere: on every billboard in Times Square and on the cover of every magazine in every newsstand in the city. Hell, in every city…

Ronan hadn't expected to see the woman here, though, in the lobby of the apartment building he'd just been about to leave. She'd walked in as he'd been walking out, but he'd turned around to follow her to the elevator. Maybe he should have expected her to be here, since he knew *they* were friends. Their friendship could cost him his law license if the bar association believed Muriel's lies and the evidence she'd manufactured against him.

Damn her!

As the elevator doors began to slide closed, he shoved his hand between them and held them open. She wasn't getting away from him. Not that she'd been trying. She hadn't seemed to notice him at all as she passed through the lobby of the building in the Garment District. While crossing the polished terrazzo floor she had been looking down at her cell phone, typing a text.

Who was she texting? Her friend Bette? A lover? Given what he knew about her and her insatiable appetites, probably a lover.

The doors started to close again—on his fingers. He cursed and used both hands to shove them open so he could step inside the car.

She stood alone in the elevator, at the polished brass control panel, pressing the button to shut the doors. She had definitely seen him now. Her naturally tan skin was flushed, and her pale green eyes were bright with anger.

She was so unbelievably beautiful—maybe the most beautiful woman he'd ever seen. That was why she was such a successful supermodel. Her hair had strands of every color in it, and her face was all cheekbones and full lips and those big, beautiful eyes. And her body...

Even though she wore a long, oversize sweater with black leggings, the green knit clung to every swell of her full breasts and curvy hips and ass. It just wasn't fair she had a figure like that.

And he suspected none of it was surgically enhanced or the media would have discovered and had a field day with that, just as they had every other aspect of her life.

That was why he saw her everywhere—even in his damn dreams.

"What the hell are you doing here?" she asked.

He'd been in the building to see her friend Bette

Monroe. He and his law partners, minus their managing partner, Simon Kramer, had come to talk to her on Simon's behalf. Bette was Simon's former assistant, and he was miserable without her—personally more than professionally. And it was Ronan's fault that she'd broken off her personal relationship as well as her professional one with Simon.

So, after his partners had left, he'd stayed behind, trying to decide if he needed to come back and apologize to her again. Or maybe for the first time. He wasn't exactly sure if he'd already apologized or not. But then, he wasn't exactly sure if he owed her an apology or not.

"I'm going to see *your friend*," he said, his decision made, and he reached for the control panel.

A button was lit up, but it wasn't for the tenth floor where Bette's apartment was. Before he could touch it, Muriel slammed both her palms against the panel, hiding the buttons but also pressing them all in the process. The doors closed, and the car began to ascend. The elevator was small, with smoked mirrors, polished brass and a floor that matched the terrazzo in the lobby.

"What the hell are you doing?" he asked.

The car stopped and the brass-plated doors slid open. But she didn't step out of the elevator. Instead, she jabbed the button to close the doors again. Then she pressed the button for the lobby, but all the other floors were already lit up. They would have to stop at every one going up before the car would bring them back to the ground level.

"You're not going to harass Bette anymore," she told him. "She is not the one who gave me the evidence I forwarded to the bar association."

"Evidence." He snorted. "That's not evidence. All of it is forged bullshit, and that's going to be easily proven."

Her wide eyes narrowed with suspicion. "If that's the truth, then why are you so tense? So nervous?"

"Because I'm pissed you'd go to such extremes to smear me." A former runaway who'd spent some time living on the streets, Ronan had worked hard to achieve everything he had, and he hated that anything—especially her lies—could put his career and his partners' law practice at risk.

She snorted now. "That I would go so far to smear you? You hired a PR firm to destroy my image! And for what? Just so you would win a bigger settlement for my slimy ex in the divorce?" Her long, thick lashes fluttered, but he doubted she was flirting with him. Was she blinking back tears?

He felt a twinge of something. Sympathy? No. He had none for women like her. The only thing he should feel for her was suspicion and caution. He had no doubt she would try to play him—just like she had her ex-husband when she'd had him sign that ridiculous prenup agreement before marrying him. The only way around it had been to prove who and what Muriel Sanz really was.

The elevator dinged, and the doors opened again. She jabbed the button to close them. "How can you sleep at night?" she asked him.

Not very well lately because he thought of her all the time, even when he was with another woman. He imagined Muriel's beautiful face, her sexy-assin body...

How could he be so attracted to a woman like her? What the hell was wrong with his dick?

"I could ask you the same thing," he said. "You're the master manipulator. Is that how you convinced Bette to give you the stationery with the Street Legal letterhead?"

He had started to believe that his partner's former assistant had had no part in Muriel's sick plot. Bette Monroe had seemed stunned when he'd confronted her about her friend filing the complaint with the bar association.

"I told you," she said, slowly, as if he was too dense to understand, "that Bette did not give me anything."

"So you took it from her without her knowledge?" It would have been easy enough to do had she ever visited the offices of Street Legal. But he'd checked, and she hadn't. Maybe Bette had brought some stationery home with her, though. He needed to ask her.

The elevator stopped and the doors opened again. She jabbed the button to close them. "I did not take a damn thing."

He snorted again. "I'll see if Bette remembers anything." He had already interrogated her once, and of course she had denied helping her friend. But maybe she would remember Muriel going through her purse or taking something from her apartment.

Would she admit it to him, though? Or would she continue to protect her friend?

"You and that sleazebag managing partner of yours have already treated Bette like crap," Muriel said. "You are not going to hurt her anymore." Now she jabbed the stop button, and the elevator jerked to a shuddering halt between floors.

"What the hell are you doing?" he asked as an alarm began to ring, echoing throughout the small car. His head started to pound, nearly as hard as his heart had been since the moment he caught sight of her crossing the lobby like she was gliding down a fashion-show runaway.

Ronan was not crazy about confined spaces—especially being confined with her. He punched the button to restart the elevator.

It lurched up, then began to drop—the car and his stomach. He'd been worried about losing his law license, but apparently that wasn't all that Muriel Sanz might cost him. He'd be lucky if he survived this elevator ride with her.

A scream tore from Muriel's throat as her feet left the floor. The elevator was falling faster than she was, plummeting down the shaft. Then the car jerked so abruptly to a stop that she tumbled forward, falling hard. But she didn't hit the terrazzo floor of the elevator car. Instead she hit a heavily muscled body that had fallen before she had.

Ronan Hall lay sprawled across the car, his legs stretched across the floor while his back and shoulders had slammed against one of the smoked glass and brass walls. Maybe his head had hit the wall, as well, since his eyes were closed.

Was he unconscious?

From where she'd landed against his chest, she stared up at his handsome face. His features could have been carved from granite; he was that chiseled—his jaw square, his cheekbones as sharp as his nose. His lashes were long and thick and black against his cheeks. They didn't so much as flicker.

Despite herself and all the many thousands of reasons she had to hate his guts, concern filled her, and she asked, "Are you okay?"

"I don't know," he replied, his voice low and gruff. "Did we stop falling yet?"

She was afraid to move, just in case they hadn't. That fear was the only reason she lay atop him, her legs tangled with his. Or else she would have scrambled off his body. But she didn't dare in case the elevator began to fall again.

She sucked in a breath and held it, and his scent filled her nostrils and her head. He smelled so damn good—not like expensive cologne that her ex had always worn. No. Ronan smelled like soap and...

A scent that was his alone.

Not only was he handsome as hell but he had to smell good, too? It wasn't fair, but she shouldn't have been surprised. Life had not been very fair to Muriel lately.

She was too positive to let that keep her down, though. She would not stay down now, either, once she was certain the elevator wasn't going to drop all the way to the bottom of the shaft and crumple like an aluminum can under a car tire.

"Are *you* okay?" Ronan's voice, even deeper with concern, asked the question now.

She glanced up at his face to find his eyes open as he studied her. She shrugged, then gasped as the car creaked. Ronan's strong arms slid around her, holding her still—or maybe she had already tensed because he'd touched her. Either way, she was frozen with fear—of falling and of how he was making her feel.

"Don't move," he said, his voice dropping so low that it was a deep rumble in his chest.

She had no intention of moving, but she couldn't control the frantic beating of her heart. It was pounding so hard that she felt her whole body shaking with the force of it. Hers wasn't the only one. His heart hammered in time with hers. Her breasts were crushed against his muscular chest.

"Can I breathe?" she asked, her lungs aching as she tried to control the panic making her want to pant for air.

"I don't know if we should…" he murmured, but his breath stirred her hair as he whispered the words.

A strand tangled in her lashes, but she didn't dare reach up for it. But that meant her hands stayed where they were, and she only just realized exactly where they were and what she was touching. Instinctively she'd extended them to break her fall, and since she'd fallen on him, her hands were on him. One was against his biceps while the other was braced on his thigh. Both muscles rippled beneath her touch, as if he'd just realized where she was touching him, too.

And his body, which had already been taut with tension, grew harder yet. Against her abdomen, she felt his erection straining the fly of his dress pants.

He must have come right from the office to see Bette, since he was still wearing a suit. In the pictures she'd seen of him in his downtime, he'd had on jeans and a T-shirt. Not that she'd seen that many pictures of him in his downtime. If he and his partners in the Street Legal law practice hadn't been as notorious as they were in Manhattan, he probably wouldn't have been photographed at all. But he and the others were infamous for being ruthless litigators and lovers. When they were photographed outside the courtroom, they were usually with a famous female—an actress or model or fashion designer…

She tried to shift her hips, so her mound wouldn't press so tightly against his cock. But he groaned. And one of his arms slid around her back as his hand grasped her hip.

Through gritted teeth, he warned her, "Do. Not. Move."

The elevator had stopped dropping. It had even stopped making those ominous creaking noises. "I don't think it's going to fall," she said.

"I'm not worried about the elevator," he replied.

"Then why are we lying on the floor afraid to move?" she asked.

He groaned again and his fingers tightened their

hold. But she doubted that he was in any real pain—
because his mouth curved into a slight, naughty grin.
"Maybe I was just enjoying you throwing yourself
at me."

She sucked in a breath of shock and wriggled,
trying to move off him. But his hands held her too
tightly, and all she managed was to grind her hips
against his groin. And to rock the elevator again.

The cables creaked. But they held. The car was
not going to tumble any farther down the shaft. She
was not worried about dying anymore. Instead, she
was worried about her reaction to Ronan Hall.

Instead of slowing down, her heart was beating
even faster. Her skin was tingling and hot everywhere her body was in contact with his—which was
pretty much everywhere. He was so muscular, so
tall and broad.

And when she'd sucked in that breath, she'd inhaled his scent again; it filled her head. The way he
would fill her...

His erection was so long and hard. Heat rushed
straight to hrt core, making her hot and wet. For him?

No. It wasn't possible. She could *not* be attracted
to the man who had destroyed her reputation, and
nearly her career and her life, as well.

"Let me go!" she demanded.

"Where are you going?" he asked. "We're stuck
in an elevator. So we might as well make the most
of this opportunity." The hand not clutching her hip
slid up her back to her head, which he held in his
palm while he pressed his mouth to hers.

As their lips connected, Muriel felt a jolt she wanted to attribute to shock. But she knew it was something else—something that had her nipples tightening and heat streaking to her core: lust.

He kissed her tentatively, at first, just skimming his lips across hers. Then she gasped at another jolt of desire, and he deepened the kiss, sliding his tongue inside her mouth. His kiss was hot, passionate and wild.

And that was how it made Muriel feel: hot, passionate and wild. She didn't want to desire this man, of all men. But he was so damn good-looking—not to mention muscular and skilled.

He was a master kisser—so good that he nearly made her come with just a kiss. But then he began to touch her, too, moving his hand from her hip up her side to cup a breast.

She sucked in a breath, which pushed her breast against his palm.

He gently squeezed, and her breath hissed out between their melded lips. And he groaned in response. He pulled back slightly and moved his hand to the buttons on her sweater, easily flicking them open.

She wore a camisole beneath the sweater. But it was one of her friend's designs, so it was super sexy with bows holding it up at the shoulders. Once he'd pushed the sweater from her shoulders, he reached for one of those bows.

If he pulled it loose, the camisole would slip down, would reveal her breast for him to see and touch…

She wanted his hands on her. She wanted him.

But she couldn't. Not really. Not after what he'd done to her—to her reputation, to her savings and to her sense of self-worth.

The only way she wanted Ronan Hall was…on his knees begging for her forgiveness. And she knew that wasn't very damn likely to happen. Ever.

Not until she'd inflicted the same hell on him that he had put her through.

CHAPTER TWO

RONAN'S HEAD SNAPPED back with the force of her slap. But he only grinned. Even though his cheek was stinging, that kiss had been totally worth it. He could taste her still on his lips. She was so damn sweet.

How could she taste so sweet when she was such a hard and vicious woman? Yeah, he'd needed that slap to bring him to his senses before he did something stupid, like pull that bow loose on her shoulder.

What would she do if he did that? Slap him again? Seeing her without the camisole, that would undoubtedly be worth another slap, though. He could see her tightened nipples pushing against the thin silk. She wore nothing beneath that camisole but her honey-toned skin. He wanted to close his lips around one of those distended nipples and tug at it until she cried out and begged for more.

His fingers still on that bow, he toyed with the end of it. One tug was all it would take.

But then she smacked his hand away and shoved him back with her palm against his chest. "Don't you dare!"

"Don't dare me," he advised her. He was the kid who would have stuck his tongue on the icy flagpole with the first dare. He wouldn't have even needed to be double dared. He lifted his hand toward her shoulder again.

She jerked up her sweater and wrapped it tightly around herself, as if he would have forcibly undressed her. As if anyone would need to. On all those billboards and magazine covers, she wore barely more than her seductive smile. Usually just a few scraps of lace or silk.

"What game are you playing?" he asked her. She was not a modest woman, but she was a cunning one. Those forged documents proved that. "Game?" she asked, her husky voice pitched higher than usual with outrage. "You're the one who kissed me."

"You trapped us in this elevator and climbed all over me," he pointed out. Was she trying to seduce him? Or just sexually tease him into madness?

"I fell on you," she said. "And *I* did not trap *you*."

He snorted. "I wasn't the one playing with the control panel, punching in every damn floor before you stopped it entirely."

"I stopped it," she said, "because I wanted to stop you from harassing Bette anymore."

"I'm not going to harass Bette," he said. For one— Simon would kill him if he did. The guy was already furious with him over some things Ronan had said to her. Poor Simon had fallen hard for his mousy former assistant.

But then, maybe Bette wasn't that mousy—to a guy who liked the sexy librarian type.

That wasn't Ronan's style. He didn't want someone repressed. He wanted someone as wild and adventurous and as into sex as he was.

Muriel stepped in front of the elevator doors, as if she could stop him. "No. You're not talking to Bette at all anymore."

He didn't want to talk to Bette. He didn't want to talk at all. He wanted Muriel back in his arms, her body pressed to his. She was the one, the female who might finally match his appetites in the bedroom and wherever else they might dare to do it…

"We're stuck here," he reminded her. And as he said it, the elevator rocked and creaked.

And Muriel gasped and shot forward—straight into his arms.

"Did you fall again?" Ronan teased her. "I wouldn't think a supermodel would be as clumsy as you are."

Despite glaring at him, she remained in his arms with hers locked around his shoulders. "Didn't you feel that? We're falling again."

"I've never fallen before," he told her. "So I'm not about to fall now…" And especially not for a man-eater like Muriel Sanz.

Then he realized what she meant even before she murmured, "I was talking about the elevator." Then she started laughing, and as she laughed, she stepped back and dropped her arms from around his shoulders. "I wasn't talking about falling for you. You can't believe I would actually fall for *you*."

He narrowed his eyes and glared at her. She made it sound ridiculous that she could care for him. Plenty of other women claimed that they had. But then, he hadn't had the relationship with those other women that he had with her. Actually, he hadn't ever had a real relationship with anyone.

Just sex...

And he would like to have that with her, even though she was trying to destroy his career. Because from that kiss, he knew it would be good between them. Hell, it would be better than good; it might be great.

He hadn't had great in a while—probably because every time he'd been with a woman the past few months, he'd imagined that woman was Muriel and he'd been disappointed when he'd realized she wasn't.

"I would never make the mistake of thinking you could love me," he assured her. "I don't think you're any more capable of really falling in love than I am."

"I was married," she said, "until you ended that."

"You ended that with your cheating."

She lifted her hand, but before she could swing it toward his face, he caught her wrist. Through gritted teeth, she told him, "I did not cheat."

He snorted again, almost amused over her show of righteous indignation. She could be one of those models who easily crossed over into acting; she had the skills. "So how did your ex find so many witnesses who testified otherwise then?"

Her green eyes widened. "My ex...? He found the witnesses? I thought you did—you or that PR firm."

"Yeah, that was your second mistake when you forged those notes that supposedly came from my case files," he said. "You made it sound as though I found the witnesses." He shook his head. "And that wasn't true."

She glared at him. "What those witnesses said wasn't true. They perjured themselves and you knew it."

"And that was your first mistake," he said. He stepped closer now, pressing his chest up against her breasts. "Trying to blame me for your bad choices."

"Bad choices?" she repeated. "My only bad choice was getting married in the first place."

He nodded. "In that, we are in complete agreement. Marriage is always a mistake." His parents' marriage had showed him that. Their constant fighting was why he'd run away from home for a while in his teenage years. "People aren't meant to be monogamous."

"Many people are," she said.

He shook his head now. "Not people like you and me, Muriel." He skimmed his fingertips along her jaw, down her throat to push her sweater from one shoulder. Then he toyed with that bow again. He was so tempted to tug it loose. So damn tempted.

His fingers twitched and the bow began to loosen. Then the elevator dinged and the doors slid open.

Muriel stepped back through the doors. But as she did, she reached out and struck a button on the control panel. The doors closed as she turned and ran down the hall.

Ronan wasn't sure what floor they had stopped on, or if it had even been her floor, or if she had just really wanted to get away from him. Before he could look at the numbers above the doors, the elevator began to move again—heading down—until it stopped in the lobby.

He hesitated a moment before he stepped through the open doors. He'd changed his mind about trying to apologize to Bette again. It was probably better for Simon if Ronan didn't talk to her at all. He suspected she'd already told him all that she knew. No. If he wanted to get to the bottom of the documents that had been given to the bar association, he needed to talk to Muriel again. But he would have to do that another time—because if he tracked her down now, after that kiss and seeing her nipples pushing against that camisole, he would do a hell of a lot more than talk to her.

Legs trembling, heart pounding, Muriel leaned back against her apartment door. She'd turned the deadbolt, so even if he'd followed her, he would not be able to get inside her place. But she didn't think he'd followed her. The elevator doors had closed before he'd had a chance to step through them.

But he could track her down…especially now that he knew where she'd moved after the divorce. While the building was nice, her apartment was small—much smaller than her old place. Maybe Ronan didn't realize she lived here; maybe he'd thought she was just visiting Bette.

Then she should have gotten off on another floor…because she wouldn't put it past him to knock on every door until he found her.

He was furious with her for reporting him to the bar association. Why was he so angry? Because he'd been caught? Or because he hadn't suborned perjury, as he'd tried to claim?

She could understand his anger if he'd done nothing wrong. That was how she'd felt over her divorce proceedings. She'd been maligned in court and in the media, and she hadn't done anything of which she'd been accused. She had definitely not cheated.

She'd taken her vows seriously. She'd been monogamous. That was all she knew. Even before she'd gotten married, she'd never dated more than one man at a time. And since the disastrous divorce, she hadn't even started dating again.

Maybe that was why Ronan Hall had affected her so much. Or maybe it hadn't been him at all. Maybe it had been the elevator malfunctioning and making her fear that they were about to plunge to their deaths. With her emotions so heightened, it was no wonder she might feel attracted to him.

And it wasn't as if he wasn't good-looking and sexy…

But still, she should hate him, not desire him. And she did hate him.

But what if he *wasn't* responsible for those witnesses coming forward? What if those memos from his Street Legal law practice had been forged, as he'd claimed?

No. She couldn't believe that. She knew every one of those witnesses who'd testified. While they hadn't all been close friends of hers, they were acquaintances. They wouldn't have lied about her without some serious coercion. Arte wouldn't have done that. He hadn't been the man she'd thought he was, but he wasn't a monster or she wouldn't have married him in the first place. He'd once been so sweet and charming.

No. Ronan Hall was the monster. And she would prove it. In case those memos weren't sufficient evidence, though, she needed to find more.

Ronan had been attracted to her, too. And she didn't think it was because he'd been scared. No. He was attracted to her because of how she looked. Her looks were why—despite her reputation being smeared—her career hadn't suffered like she'd worried it would. Magazines and designers said she sold copy and clothes, maybe even more so since she had become so notorious.

But she hadn't wanted to be notorious. And she was mortified that so many people believed those lies about her and that her grandparents—the sweet couple who'd raised her—had heard those lies. About affairs and orgies and sex parties...

While they knew her too well to believe them, they had to contend with the comments from their friends, from their fellow parishioners, from their neighbors...

That was why she hated Ronan Hall. Not so much for what he'd done to her as for what he'd done to them. She wanted him to suffer like they had. That was why she'd turned those papers she'd received over to the bar association. But maybe she should have had them authenticated first. She'd thought Bette had given them to her, though.

But Bette hadn't known anything about them.

So who had delivered that envelope of memos to Muriel's door? And were they real?

She needed to know the truth. And she needed proof of it. The best way to do that was to go directly to the source: Ronan himself.

Could she use her looks to get him to admit to what he'd done? An audio recording of his confession would be indisputable evidence.

But what would she have to do that would compel him to confess? Seduce him?

Instead of disgusting her, the way the idea should have, she was strangely excited by it. Maybe that was just because it had been so long since she'd been with anyone but her vibrator. While that eased some of her tension, it wasn't like being with a man—like having his hands and his mouth on her.

Like Ronan's mouth had been on hers...

Heat flashed through her, and she headed toward her bedroom—and to the vibrator she kept in the table beside the bed. For tonight, it would have to do...while she planned how to seduce Ronan Hall into confessing to his misconduct during her divorce proceedings.

That was what she really wanted. His confession. Not him…

But she thought of him as she pulled the vibrator from the drawer. From the erection she'd felt straining against his dress pants, she knew he was bigger than her toy. And if it was possible, maybe harder…

He had wanted her. No matter how much they detested each other, they couldn't deny the attraction between them. And Muriel would use that to her advantage, just like she used thoughts of him as she shrugged off her sweater and pushed down her yoga pants. Then she lay back on the bed, and she imagined Ronan kissing her, touching her…

She tugged one of the bows of her camisole free and began to touch herself. There were two more bows holding her panties together. She undid those as she flipped the switch for the vibrator. And she imagined it was Ronan's long, hard cock as she slid it inside herself.

She came almost instantly, and to her horror, she cried out his name.

CHAPTER THREE

LIGHTS BLAZED, BUT that wasn't what had sweat beading on Ronan's brow. The heat flashing through him had nothing to do with the lights and everything to do with the woman posing beneath them.

She wore so very little on her gorgeous body—just some scraps of lace and silk and all that naturally tan skin. Desire slammed through Ronan with a force he'd never felt before. It knocked him back on his heels while making his cock rock hard.

Maybe coming here had been a bad idea.

But he wanted to come—inside her. He knew she was the only one who could relieve the unbearable tension that had been building in his body since he'd been trapped in the elevator with her a couple of nights ago.

"Muriel!" the photographer shouted at her. "You're not giving me what I want!"

She wasn't giving Ronan what he wanted, either—because he wanted her to untie that bow between the cups of her strapless black bra, wanted her to untie the bows on each hip that held up her panties.

But he wanted more than to see her naked. He wanted to feel her, taste her…and bury himself deep inside her.

Why the hell was he so attracted to this woman? He would have screwed her in the elevator if she hadn't pulled away and slapped him. But she'd kissed him back before she'd done that. Was she attracted to him, too?

He was counting on it—so that he could get the truth out of her. That was really why he was here, why he'd tracked her down at her photoshoot. It wasn't for sex.

He could get that anywhere. It wasn't as if he wanted or needed only her. Any woman would do.

No. What he really wanted from Muriel Sanz was the truth.

Her lips curved into a slight smile. "What do you want, Lawrence?"

"Bad," the photographer shouted back. "I need you to be bad."

She was bad, and Ronan had proved that in court. She claimed those witnesses had been lying, though. Why would they lie? Why would they risk perjury charges? They'd had nothing to gain from their testimony.

Muriel Sanz was the liar. And Ronan intended to prove it. He just had to get her to admit to forging those memos. Could he seduce her into a confession?

Those witnesses had claimed she was addicted to sex and that was why she'd cheated on her husband. So if she was addicted to sex, maybe he could get her addicted to sex with him—so addicted that she would confess all to him.

He knew it was possible for a person to get addicted to another person. That had been his father's downfall: his addiction to Ronan's mother despite how badly she'd mistreated him. She'd been a lot like Muriel Sanz—beautiful and selfish and completely devoid of a conscience.

"I need you to be the badass of Bette's Beguiling Bows," Lawrence said.

This photo shoot was for the line of lingerie Muriel exclusively modeled. That line had been designed by her friend and Simon's former assistant, Bette Monroe.

He had to admit that Bette had a talent for design. Her lingerie was the sexiest he'd ever seen.

Unfortunately, so was Muriel.

"Oh, I can be a badass," she assured the photographer. But she was looking at Ronan now. He could feel her gaze on him, and his skin began to heat even more. She raised her husky voice a little more, probably making certain he would hear, and added, "I can be very, very bad…"

Ronan chuckled. She'd already started confessing…and he hadn't even touched her yet.

The camera clicked.

She ran her fingertips down her deep cleavage to the bow between her breasts. And she toyed with the ends the way he'd toyed with the bow the other night…in the elevator.

Too bad that bow hadn't been between her breasts,

too. Then he could have touched her, like she was touching herself.

As she stroked her fingertips up and down her cleavage, she sank her teeth into her bottom lip then swiped her tongue across it.

And Ronan groaned. The photographer echoed the sound and shot a glance at him. Instead of admonishing him for trespassing on the set, the guy grinned at him. "You must be the reason for that sudden spark in her eyes," Lawrence said. "You made her bad."

Ronan chuckled. "Nobody made Muriel that way." Least of all him. She'd already been bad.

"I'm good," she said. And she tilted her head provocatively. "Very, very good..."

And both men groaned again.

Lawrence muttered, "Now I understand why her ex..."

"What?" Ronan asked when the guy trailed off. "Why he what?" Divorced her or married her?

The photographer just shook his head. "You can stay," he told Ronan. "But don't distract me."

"What about me?" Muriel asked.

"He's a good distraction for you," Lawrence said.

Could he be? Could Ronan distract her enough that she would withdraw her complaint to the bar association?

He had to try, at least. That was why he was here. That and the fact that thoughts of her and that damn kiss had been keeping him awake.

He wanted more than a kiss.

* * *

He was not a good distraction for her. But as Muriel peered over Lawrence's shoulder at the computer monitor at the thumbnails of all the photos the photographer had taken, she couldn't deny that Ronan had certainly inspired her. This was by far the best shoot she'd ever had and she had been modeling since she was fourteen years old—more than a decade.

"If you're not going to take that man out for a drink, I will," Lawrence said. "He got you to the money shots, baby!" He turned around and kissed her lips. "You have never looked more gorgeous!"

Muriel chuckled at the photographer's enthusiasm. "I'm sure he's already gone."

She couldn't imagine why he had showed up to begin with…unless he was after the same thing she was.

The truth…

He probably wanted to know how she'd gotten her hands on the memos she'd turned over to the bar association. At least he must have finally accepted that Bette hadn't given them to her. That was good. She never would have used them had she known the problems it would cause for her friend.

"I'm still here," a deep voice murmured.

That was not good.

She glanced up to find his long, muscular body leaning against the doorjamb of Lawrence's office. He was wearing a suit; he must have come either straight from the office or from court. Who else's life was he ruining?

She was afraid it might be hers again if she dared to try her plan to seduce him into a confession. Could she take the chance?

"I can leave," he offered, "if I'm interrupting…"

"You interrupted the shoot," she said. "And you didn't offer to leave then." Hours ago. He had stayed through changes in wardrobe, hair, makeup and backdrops.

Why had he stayed so long?

"He improved the shoot," Lawrence said. "Your best work ever…" He turned back to the computer monitor with all the frames and murmured, "Maybe mine, too."

A little thrill chased through Muriel, but she worried it had less to do with the praise than with how Ronan was looking at her, with how he'd been looking at her the past couple of hours. With every wardrobe change, his eyes had gotten darker and his body even more tense. Despite the way he was leaning now, she could feel that tension; it fairly radiated from him.

So that she felt it, too—coiling low in her body, pulsing in her clit. She couldn't remember ever wanting a man more, which was crazy. She had been in love before and hadn't felt this powerful attraction. But this man—this man she hated—she wanted more than any other.

Maybe she had lost her damn mind. That was the excuse she was going to use for what she was about to do. "So, how about it?" she asked as she walked toward the doorway. "Do you want to go for a drink?"

His dark eyes narrowed as if he was as suspicious of her offer as she was of his showing up at the photo shoot. Now a little chill moved through Muriel, raising goose bumps on her skin despite her having changed into street clothes of jeans and a sweater. She hadn't felt a chill like this when he'd been staring at her, when she'd been wearing nothing more than a bra and panties. Then she had felt hotter than hell. And it showed in those photos.

But wondering how he'd tracked her down unnerved her. How had he found her?

She hesitated as she neared the doorway where he stood. But then he stepped back into the hall. "I didn't come here just to watch," he said. "That's not my thing..."

She narrowed her eyes with suspicion. Was it just that everything he said sounded like sexual innuendo or was he actually implying that there was something between her and Lawrence?

Of course, he had seen Lawrence kiss her. But Lawrence kissed everyone. *Everyone.*

"Good night," she called back to the photographer. He barely glanced up from the computer monitor to wave.

As she walked down the hall of the old warehouse, she turned to Ronan and asked, "Why did you come here? And how did you find me?"

"I have my sources," he said.

And that chilled her blood even more. "I am well aware of that," she said. "But I can't believe they actually got it right this time."

He stopped at the elevator and turned toward her, his dark eyes narrowed. "So all those witnesses were lying and you're the only one telling the truth?"

"Yes," she said. Her grandparents had raised her with values—one of which being that it was never okay to lie, not even little white ones. Too bad those *witnesses* hadn't been raised the same way she had.

"Why would everyone else lie?" Ronan asked her.

"You tell me," she challenged him. "Did you pay them?" He must have. What else could they have had to gain, except for some time in the horrible spotlight that the scandal had shone on her?

He chuckled. But he didn't answer her question. He just turned and pressed the button for the elevator.

What would it take to get him to confess to somehow coercing those witnesses into lying? He was rich. So he didn't need money. He had probably used his own to pay them off since Arte hadn't had much money until he'd taken most of her savings—and the apartment and car—in the divorce. He didn't even know how to drive.

The elevator dinged, and the doors slid open with a swoosh of noise and air. Muriel sucked in a breath at the thought of getting into another elevator with Ronan Hall.

He stepped back and waited for her to pass through the doors in front of him. "Come on," he said. "As long as you don't mess with the control panel this time, we'll be fine."

She hesitated. "We could take the stairs…" It would probably be safer—for a few reasons.

"We're on the twelfth floor," he reminded her. "Did you take the stairs up?"

"No."

"So you don't have a problem with using the elevator," he said as if he was cross-examining her again, the way he had on the witness stand. "You just have a problem with taking the elevator with me."

While his cross-examination had been ruthless, he hadn't shaken her. But then, she'd had the resolve of the truth on her side. He didn't have that, so maybe she could shake him. But she was not going to get a confession out of him unless she was alone with him. Dare she go through with her plan? Dare she be alone with him?

Because she knew what was going to happen…

The attraction between them was too strong— so strong that it could probably even overpower the anger and resentment and distrust between them.

She stepped into the elevator car. And when she automatically reached for the control panel, she pulled her hand back to her side. She was not going to risk getting stuck with him again.

He chuckled as he stepped inside with her. Then he reached for the panel. She didn't see which button he pushed; she just assumed it was for the lobby. In the heart of the Garment District, the building's tenants were mostly fashion designers along with a few photographers. There was no place to have a drink there.

Muriel really needed that drink. Hell, she needed more than a drink. She couldn't remember the last time she'd eaten. And she was not the type of model who starved herself. She enjoyed food too much.

Fortunately, the fashion industry appreciated curves now over skin and bones. Or she wouldn't have been able to get any work. Now she was sought after...

Professionally. Personally—not so much. Men weren't eager to date the man-eater the media had painted her as being. She'd overheard people talking about how she was too intimidating to the opposite sex now.

Ronan Hall hadn't appeared too intimidated the other night. And he must not have been or he wouldn't have sought her out again.

The doors closed, shutting them into the stark car together. This elevator wasn't nearly as fancy as the one in her building; it was all bare metal and wood, and it was bigger—big enough to carry crates of garments from one floor to the next.

She didn't have to stand anywhere near Ronan. But it didn't matter how far away she was from him; she could feel his presence. It was as if electricity arced between his body and hers.

Her skin tingled, and her blood heated, pumping hot and fast through her veins. "We should go somewhere with a kitchen," she said. "I'm hungry, too."

She felt a hollowness inside, but she wasn't sure that it was one food could fill. Maybe only he could...

He reached for the panel again, jabbed a button and the elevator shuddered to a stop.

"I'm hungry, too," he said as he reached for her. He wrapped his arm around her waist and reeled her in until her body pressed against his. He was so big, so broad, so tense.

His erection strained against his pants—and against her hips. Instinctively she arched and rubbed against him, and he groaned.

"And with every outfit you changed into, I got hungrier," he said.

"You didn't have to stay." But she'd been glad that he was still there—every time she had stepped out of the dressing room after a wardrobe change. She'd wanted him to see what she was wearing; she'd wanted him to see her, and she'd wanted to see his reaction.

"I couldn't leave," he said, his voice gruffer now as if he was in pain.

"Why not?" she asked.

"Because I didn't get what I came for…"

"And what did you come for?" she asked.

He lowered his head to hers and kissed her—deeply—hungrily. His lips moved over hers, nibbling and plucking at them until she gasped with pleasure.

"I came for you," he said, his voice a gruff whisper. "I came for this…"

His hands moved over her, lifting her sweater up and over her head. He uttered a lustful sigh. "I was hoping you were still wearing this…"

It was the black bra with the bow in the middle. Bette was a genius designer. She somehow made the bras so that the one bow held the cups together and provided support. Muriel's breasts swelled over the top of it.

"Why?" she asked, and she wasn't faking the breathlessness in her voice. Her heart was racing so fast that she could barely draw any air into her lungs. But as she tried, her breasts swelled even more and nearly spilled over the top of the black bra.

Ronan reached for that bow, tugging on the ribbons, and the bra fell away, freeing her breasts. She panted for air now as excitement coursed through her. Her nipples tightened and ached for more than the touch of his gaze.

"That's why," he replied. "I've been dying to undo that bow."

Muriel had been modeling lingerie and swimsuits for most of her career, so she had long ago gotten over any qualms she might have had about modesty. But there was something about the way that Ronan Hall was looking at her that made her feel more naked than she had ever felt before.

He wasn't just looking at her body. It was as if he was trying to peer into her heart and soul. Maybe he was wondering if she had one.

She did. She doubted that he did, though. So what the hell was she doing getting half-naked in an elevator with the man who had nearly destroyed her?

CHAPTER FOUR

RONAN'S HEART POUNDED in his chest and in his cock. He couldn't believe how damn beautiful she was. Her breasts were full and perfect mounds, her nipples ripe and rosy. He wanted to close his lips around one so badly. But when he reached for her, she stepped back.

Her green eyes widened with panic and she lifted her hands to cover her breasts.

He glanced around the elevator. Was there a security camera in it? He hadn't thought about that, although he should have. But after watching that photo shoot, he hadn't been able to think at all. He had only been able to feel, the desire coursing through him.

He wanted her more than he could remember ever wanting anyone else. He wanted to become an addiction for her, but now he was afraid that it might be the other way around—and that was before he'd even had her.

Maybe this was a mistake. Maybe he should be taking a step back like she had. He felt a punch of the same panic he saw on her face. But it wasn't nearly as strong as the punch of desire that had his stomach tightened into knots.

"What the hell are we doing?" she asked, her voice shaking with horror.

He shrugged. It wasn't as if he could admit to wanting to seduce her into telling the bar association the truth. She might not even know what the truth was anymore. His mother had gotten that way—so caught up in her own lies that she'd begun to believe them.

"I hate you," she told him, her voice shaking with anger. "I hate what you did to me."

And now he felt another kind of punch—of regret. But he'd only been doing his job—getting the best deal for his client. "*I* didn't do anything…"

…That she hadn't had coming. She'd put her husband through hell. He hadn't seen a man that broken since his father. He flinched as he felt that jolt of panic again. But he didn't have to worry. He wasn't like her ex or his father; he was too smart to fall for a pretty face. Hell, he was too smart to fall for any face. Ever…

Her breath hissed out between her teeth. And she leaned down to grab her bra up from the floor of the elevator. "How can you say you didn't do anything? You hired a PR firm to smear me!"

"It's not like your career suffered for it," he pointed out. "In fact, I think the whole trial helped your career." Now everyone knew her name and her face, whereas before they might have only known her body. While she had been modeling lingerie and swimsuits for years, she hadn't become famous until her divorce drama.

She shook her head, and her titian hair swirled around her bare shoulders. She had yet to put on the bra. She still held her arms across her breasts.

He wanted to see them again. He wanted to touch them. Taste them…

"You should be thanking me," he said, grinning as he goaded her.

She lifted one hand away from her breasts to swing it toward his face. But before her palm could connect, he caught her wrist and jerked her body against his.

"That's not how you thank someone," he admonished her. And he lowered his face to hers. "This is how you thank someone…" The minute he touched his lips to hers, he forgot all about teasing her. Or the panic he'd felt.

He forgot everything but how much he wanted her. Her soft breasts pushed against his chest, and he could feel the tightness of her nipples through the thin silk of his dress shirt. He swallowed a groan as his body tensed and throbbed with desire. Then he swallowed her moan when a soft one slipped through her parted lips. He deepened the kiss.

He slid his tongue inside her mouth, and she stroked hers over his. They mated and tangled around each other, teasing, tasting…

It was the hottest kiss he'd ever had—all panting breath and moans. It was wet and wild. And he wanted her the same way. He wanted her wet and wild for him. So he eased her body back from his, and he touched her.

He moved his hands over her beautiful breasts, skimming his fingertips over her silky soft skin before stroking them over her tightened nipples.

She moaned again.

Then he lowered his head to her breasts and he replaced his fingers with his lips, closing them over one of those taut nipples. He gently tugged, teasing her.

Her hands slid into his hair, grasping his head. But she didn't pull him away. She clutched him closer. Her fingers moved from his head to his neck, and she jerked his tie loose before tackling his buttons. Once she parted his shirt, she raked her nails down his chest.

His stomach clenched as desire punched him hard in the gut. He pulled back, but she followed him, pressing her breasts to his bare chest. She felt so good against him, so damn good in his arms.

He tightened his arms around her and just held her for a moment. But his body heated and the tension built. And just holding her would not be enough.

He had to have her—had to taste her—had to be inside her. He moved his hands to her waist and undid the button of her jeans. The zipper rasped as he lowered it. And his pulse pounded harder from the noise. She'd let him do that, just as she'd let him take off her sweater and bra. But would she let him push down the jeans?

She stepped back before he could reach for them.

And his breath caught and trapped in his lungs. She was going to stop him.

He could understand why...

She blamed him for her coming out on the losing end of her divorce and in the media. But, as he'd pointed out, it hadn't hurt her career any, not like she was trying to hurt his by turning in those forged memos to the bar association. Since she'd done that, he should be so damn mad that he shouldn't be attracted to her at all.

And he *was* damn mad, more pissed off than he could remember being in a long time. But even then he couldn't find her repulsive. She was too damn beautiful and sexy to resist. Not that he wanted to resist.

He wanted her too much for that and, more important, he wanted her to want him too much.

But he wouldn't be able to do that if she kept stopping him.

She just stared at him now, her gaze on his bare chest like a caress. He could feel her touch, feel her skin even though a couple of feet separated them now.

Then she took another step back and turned away from him toward the control panel. He held his breath, waiting for her touch a button and get the elevator moving again.

But if she were going to do that, wouldn't she first put her bra back on and her sweater? Instead of reaching for her discarded clothes, though, she pushed down her jeans and revealed a tiny bow on a G-string at the top of her perfect ass.

Ronan fisted his hands at his sides so he wouldn't reach for her. Just because she'd undressed didn't mean she intended to have sex with him. Maybe she only intended to torture him. Maybe—like turning those documents over to the bar—it was her way of getting revenge on him.

Seeing her like this—so bare and beautiful—and not being able to have her, might be worse than losing his law license…

What the hell was she doing? Muriel asked herself the question again, but like before, she couldn't come up with an answer. Sure, she knew what she'd thought she was doing: carrying out the plan she'd concocted to bring Ronan Hall to his knees and get him to tell her the truth.

But nobody brought men like Ronan Hall to their knees. Not women. Not men…

They were too tough. Too powerful.

In their lives and most especially in the bedroom. She'd heard all the stories about him—not just how ruthless he was in court but how ruthless he was in relationships. She'd worked with some of his ex-girlfriends. He was always the one who'd ended things and always too soon for the women concerned.

No matter how ruthless he'd been, the women had wanted more. Some had even admitted begging.

So Muriel was the one who needed to worry about being brought to her knees. Again.

He'd already done it once—in the courtroom. Now she had to worry about him doing it here. Because when he touched her…

When he kissed her…

He made her want him more than she'd ever wanted anyone before. Just like all those other women had told her.

He wasn't kissing or touching her now. She could put her clothes back on and restart the elevator. But when she bent over to pull up her jeans, a strange noise filled the car.

It was raw and guttural, a groan full of pain, as if the man who'd uttered it was being tortured. Ronan was the only other one inside the elevator, so she turned toward him.

He was on his knees now. But even on his knees, his head was above her waist. He was so damn tall and broad.

And so damn sexy.

His breath was hot as it whistled between his clenched teeth and brushed across her abdomen. Her stomach muscles tightened as tension wound inside her, streaking from her nipples down to her core.

"You're perfect," he murmured as his lips brushed across her skin.

She could have snorted and reminded him that that was not what he'd claimed in court. Then she had been anything and everything but perfect.

But she couldn't say anything. She couldn't even move. She was frozen as she waited for him to touch her again.

His lips skimmed softly across her stomach to her hip, then lower over the lace of her panties. And through the thin lace, she could feel his hot breath move over her mound. He touched her with his hands, too. They moved to her ass, cupping it in his palms. And somehow his fingers must have tugged so gently at the bow that she hadn't felt it release. But her panties fell.

And nothing separated his mouth from the essence of her. He flicked his tongue back and forth across her clit as he lifted her, moving her legs over his shoulders. Then he feasted on her—sucking on her before sliding his tongue inside her.

And Muriel melted, heat and pleasure flooding her. He lapped at her—licking and sucking and driving her out of her mind. She whimpered, moaned and arched back. Without the wall of the elevator behind her, she might have fallen. The wood was cold and hard against her back. But she didn't care.

She had the heat and strength of Ronan. She clutched at his head as he continued to move his mouth over her. His tongue flicked and teased. And he raised one of his hands to her breast, sliding his palm over it and the taut nipple.

She cried out as she came, the orgasm shuddering through her with such intensity that tears burned her eyes. And she understood why women begged him for more.

Despite that release, *she* wanted more.

He hadn't pulled back. He continued to lap at her

as if he couldn't get enough of the taste of her orgasm. But that wasn't what she wanted now.

She wanted him. She wanted to feel him inside her.

She slid her legs off his shoulders and tried to stand. But her body was too limp from pleasure, her muscles too loose. And her legs folded until she was on her knees in front of him. She'd already opened his shirt, so she pushed that and his suitcoat from his shoulders. Then she reached for his belt.

But he caught her hand.

And she wondered now if he was going to stop her. She froze as she remembered all the times that had happened in her marriage. She wasn't the sex addict that her ex and those witnesses had claimed she was. But she'd certainly needed it more than her husband had.

He'd had an excuse every time. He hadn't felt well. Or he was tired.

But she'd always wondered if it was her fault. If she just wasn't that desirable...

But Ronan's dark eyes burned with desire for her. His thumb stroked over her wrist, over her leaping pulse. His voice was a rough rasp when he murmured, "If you touch me now, I'm going to come right away. And I want this to last."

So did she.

But just his words—and that gruff, sexy way he'd uttered them—had her on the verge of coming again, especially when his gaze moved over her like a caress.

He licked his lips, which were wet with her orgasm. And he groaned. "You taste so damn sweet. I could go down on you all night."

"We don't have all night," she reminded him. They only had until someone noticed the elevator wasn't moving and got working on the problem. "We have to hurry."

She didn't care if he came quickly. She just needed him to come—inside her. With a condom, of course, though. She always practiced safe sex. She reached for the bag she'd dropped onto the floor. She had to have some inside.

Didn't she?

She didn't need it. Ronan pulled one from his wallet. Then he was standing. He unclasped his belt and unzipped his pants.

Her breath caught and held as she waited for him to push them and his silk boxers down, and when he did, she released that breath on a gasp of shock and awe. He was huge—so long and thick and throbbing…

She wanted to touch him with her hands and with her mouth. She wanted to suck on him the way he'd sucked on her. But when she reached for him, he caught his fingers in her hair.

"We don't have time," he reminded her. And there was regret in his voice.

He wanted her to go down on him. She could see it on his face as he stared at her kneeling in front of him. She flicked her tongue out to tease him and that same groan of torture he'd uttered before filled the elevator car.

But he stepped out of his pants. And he ripped open the packet and sheathed himself in the latex condom. He must have had them specially ordered because it covered more of him than she imagined any store-bought ones would have.

"You are so big…" she murmured breathlessly as a moment of fear flicked through her. Would he fit?

She couldn't wait to find out. She lay down on the floor of the elevator. And as he watched, she ran her hand down her body—from her throat over her breasts, down her abdomen, to where she was already wet and throbbing. As she moved her fingers over her mound, she moaned and squirmed, so ready for him.

And that groan tore out of him again. "You're going to make me come just looking at you," he warned her. But then he dropped to his knees again.

Instead of moving between her legs, though, he lifted her so she straddled his thighs. Then he lifted her more, and she nearly stood so she could ease herself down onto his cock. She guided him inside her, her inner muscles rippling and grasping at him. Even as wet and ready as she was, she had to stretch and arch to accommodate his girth. She could feel his cock pulsating with the same desire that filled her.

And the tension was on his handsome face, in the beads of perspiration on his brow and the rigidness of his clenched jaw. He lowered his head and kissed her. And as his tongue slid into her mouth, he thrust deeper into her body. His hands caught her hips, and he guided her down, then up.

They moved together in a frantic rhythm as the pressure built inside...

Muriel nearly sobbed with the need for release. She was close to something she instinctively knew would be more powerful than anything she'd felt before.

With just his mouth, he'd given her an overpowering orgasm. With that cock...

That enormous, throbbing cock...

She couldn't imagine the pleasure he could give her. Then she didn't have to imagine, as her muscles began to clench. He reached between them and flicked his thumb over her clit—once, twice...

And she screamed as pleasure gripped her. She came and came...

And came...

Then he was coming, too, his hands gripping her hips tighter and he drove her harder against him. Then he tensed and yelled. And his body shuddered with release.

Shock gripped Muriel now. Instead of being frozen or limp, she was filled with panic. What had she just done?

That scream she'd uttered...

She'd never cried out like that before. But then, she'd never felt anything like that before.

And that scared the hell out of her. So she moved quickly. She jumped up from his lap and rushed around to grab up her clothes. Her hands trembled too much to mess with Bette's bows now, so she just pulled on her jeans and her sweater and shoved the lingerie into her bag.

Ronan dressed, too, but not as quickly as she did. And he glanced around the elevator as he did up the buttons of his shirt. His hands were completely steady.

And she hated him for that along with all the other reasons she'd already hated him. She hated that what they'd just done seemed to have had so little effect on him. But then, he had sex all the time.

She was the one who'd been reduced to using battery-operated partners for her pleasure—because of him. So maybe it was only fitting that he'd given her such pleasure.

He owed her.

But he'd also given her panic. Someone must have heard them, was probably investigating even now. She was going to wait a moment before she restarted the elevator, though. She didn't want someone to see them stepping off it and realize what they'd just done…

The whole damn car smelled like sex—like orgasm and perspiration.

Sweat trickled down between her breasts.

"Is there a security camera in here?" he asked. "Is that what has you so freaked?"

She gasped at the horrible thought. She was afraid they would be caught. She hadn't considered that they might already have been caught on camera.

Why hadn't she considered that there might be security cameras in the elevator? With her luck, there probably was, and then someone would sell the footage and her sex tape would be splashed all over the internet.

Her sex tape with Ronan Hall...

She should have been horrified. Instead, she felt a little flicker of excitement at the thought of being able to watch it herself, to see what he'd done to her. What she wanted him to do again. But if she turned to him now, he would think that everyone had been telling the truth about her—that she was a sex addict.

Her hand shaking, she slapped the button to restart the elevator. She had to find a security guard. She had to make sure that if there was a tape, she got the only copy of it.

"You can't even look at me?" Ronan asked.

And if she didn't know him better, she would have thought she heard hurt in his voice. But from all those weeks spent in court with him and all those interviews she'd watched that he'd given, she did know him better. She knew he didn't care about other people's feelings because he didn't have any of his own. There was no way she could have hurt him.

No way that she would...unless he lost his law license because of her complaint. She felt a twinge of regret over reporting him to the bar, but then she reminded herself of all those weeks in court, of all the lies that had been told about her, of all the reporters who'd hounded her for interviews.

She shook her head. No. She couldn't look at him now. And it should have been because she was disgusted over what she'd just done and with whom she'd done it. No, she couldn't look at him now with as much as she wanted him again.

Still…

Those orgasms he'd given her had only made her hungry for more. Her plan had backfired. She wasn't going to bring him to his knees, at least not in the way she wanted. But she was very afraid that he would bring her to her knees and she would stay on them, begging him for whatever pleasure he would give her. It was better that she never see Ronan again—except on video if that security tape existed.

She almost hoped that it did.

CHAPTER FIVE

TOO BAD THERE hadn't been a security camera in the elevator. Then Ronan would have been able to watch the tape and verify that he hadn't just dreamed what had happened that night over a week ago. He would have known for certain that he had actually had sex with Muriel Sanz, the most beautiful woman in the world.

He wasn't being romantic or fanciful when he thought that. He was just repeating the fact that the world had already declared. She had recently been voted The Most Beautiful Woman in the World by Celebrity International, and she was on the cover of every magazine and all over the internet. He couldn't get away from her.

And yet he hadn't seen her in several days. Now he wasn't sure that what had happened had actually happened. He hadn't gotten any release from the tension that gripped his body even now.

But maybe he was tense because of this meeting his partners had called. Before anyone at the conference table spoke, he knew what it was about: him.

Tuesday was their usual day to discuss Street Legal business. This was Friday. Of course, the meeting could have been about their partner Stone Michaelsen's upcoming murder trial. It was the highest profile case he'd had yet—representing a billionaire accused of killing his young bride. What if his case had been compromised? They suspected they had a mole in the office. Some notes from Ronan's partner, Trevor Sinclair's case files had been given to his opposing counsel. Trev still won the trial against the major pharmaceutical company, so it hadn't been a big issue for him.

Not like those *notes* about Ronan that had been turned over to the bar association. Even though those had been forged, they could still affect him. He could lose his license or at least be sanctioned. And if that happened, it could affect the practice, as well.

He glanced around the table at his three partners. These guys were more than business associates. They were friends—longtime friends. If not for them, he wouldn't have survived the time he'd spent on the streets as a teenage runaway. And because they were his friends, he needed to fix this so it didn't affect them at all.

"Don't worry," he told them, because it was clear from their somber gazes and rigid jaws that they were worried. "I've got this handled."

"You know who the mole is?" Simon asked hopefully. As the managing partner, he'd taken it upon himself to find the source of the leaked information, but he'd found love, instead.

Ronan would have preferred, and not just for self-ish reasons, that Simon had found the mole. It would have been less dangerous for his friend than risking his heart.

"No." Ronan shook his head. "I don't know that…" The source had to be someone in their office, someone who had access to their case files.

"We need to find out," Trevor said. He was still pissed that his big civil trial had nearly been compromised. Then he added, "You need to find out, so you know who the hell is behind this mess with the bar association."

Warmth flooded Ronan. Trev cared about him. They all did. And he, despite his reputation for caring about nothing but winning, cared about them.

"I'm sorry," he said.

"I'm the one who was supposed to find the mole," Simon said.

"And it's not like Muriel Sanz's claims are true," Stone added with unwavering support. "There's no way you would ever suborn perjury."

He was glad that they knew that, that they believed in him. If only Muriel could do the same…

She had to know the truth, or she wouldn't have had to forge the documents. And despite her claims to the contrary, she must have been the one who'd forged them. But if they were credible enough for the bar to investigate, they must have looked authentic. How had she pulled off that without some help?

"Thanks," Ronan said. "Glad you guys know that."

"You don't have to cheat to win," Trevor said.

"Not anymore," Simon murmured. He'd been a con artist, trained by his father at an early age to deceive people. Without Simon's cunning and charm, Ronan and his partners wouldn't have survived the streets. "But someone else is cheating. It was one thing to take notes from our files, but to forge them?"

"Maybe they only took the letterhead," Trevor said, "and that model forged the documents."

That was what Ronan believed—or had believed. After their interlude in the elevator, he wasn't sure what he believed anymore. He wasn't even sure he believed *that* had happened. He was still so damn tense and needy—for her. He hadn't even bothered trying to ease that ache and tension with another woman. He knew only Muriel would satisfy him now—until he'd had enough of her.

Stone snorted derisively. "You think she's smart enough to do that?"

Ronan tensed even more. "She's not some empty-headed bimbo!" he snapped in her defense. It wasn't like his friend to stereotype just because of her job. Ronan had known and dated plenty of smart models and so had Stone. "She's not an idiot."

Stone shook his head. "I looked over your case file. She had to be an idiot to marry *that* guy."

"A lot of intelligent people marry the wrong people," Ronan said. His father had been one of them, and he was a brilliant man in all matters but love.

"I don't doubt that," Stone said. "But you're the one who painted her as the empty-headed bimbo."

"He and Allison McCann," Trevor said with a sigh that sounded almost regretful.

He used Allison McCann's PR firm, McCann Public Relations, in all his trials, too. But then, Trevor handled the high-profile civil cases. Ronan handled the high-profile divorce cases.

Hell, everything Street Legal handled—down to the trusts and wills Simon wrote up—was high-profile because of their reputation and their clients.

"It wasn't just me and Allison," he said. "It would have been all those witnesses she claims lied about her, too." Was she telling the truth? He needed to know. He needed to know what the hell was fact and what was fiction.

Like if he'd really had sex in the elevator with The World's Most Beautiful Woman or if he had only dreamed it.

"Bette thinks they did," Simon said.

"Bette is her friend," Ronan reminded him. And that friendship went both ways. Muriel had defended Simon's former assistant, as well.

Simon tensed. "You don't still think Bette had anything to do with Muriel getting that letterhead?"

He couldn't rule it out, not until he had all the facts. And apparently he wasn't the only one. Both Trevor and Stone glanced at Simon then quickly looked away.

"You all think she could have?" Simon asked.

"They're friends," Trevor said.

"So are all of us," Simon said. But instead of adding on whatever point he'd meant to make, he cursed.

"And we'd all lie for each other," Trevor finished for him.

Simon sighed. "Yeah, we would. But Bette wouldn't lie to me."

Ronan snorted. He'd never known a woman who didn't lie. And he couldn't believe that his streetwise friend had become so naïve.

Yeah, falling in love was a mistake for everyone. It was a mistake that Ronan would never make.

Instead of getting angry, Simon just shook his head, as if he pitied Ronan. Simon was the one who'd tied himself down to one woman. His plan had been to seduce Bette to find out if she was the office mole, but she had wound up seducing him, instead. She'd conned the con.

Simon was the one deserving of pity. Not Ronan.

"Why do you think she won't lie to you?" Ronan asked. And he was honestly curious now.

"Because she loves me."

Ronan snorted again.

"She really loves me. It's not infatuation, not lust—it's real," Simon said.

And Ronan was sad for him, that he believed love was real.

"Too bad you couldn't pull that off," Stone said. "If you could make Muriel Sanz fall for you, you could get her to withdraw her complaint to the bar association."

"They're really taking that seriously?" Ronan asked. Stone had a source at the bar.

His friend grimly nodded.

"Damn it!"

"Try the seduction idea," Trevor suggested. "It worked for Simon."

Simon chuckled. "It worked because I could get close to Bette. Muriel Sanz hates his guts. She's never going to let him close enough to seduce her."

Oh, she had let him close—close enough to kiss her and touch her and taste her and fuck her brains out and his, too.

What if there had been a camera in that elevator?

They hadn't thought about that until it would have been too late. They hadn't thought at all. And Ronan hadn't talked about it. He hadn't told his friends about either time he'd run into Muriel. He'd figured they would get worried that he had only made the situation worse and pissed her off more.

He was kind of worried that he had. She hadn't even been able to look at him after…

Stone sighed. "And Ronan doesn't have your charm, either, Si. You're right. It would never work."

"Want to bet on that?" Ronan asked.

Simon laughed again. "What—are you playing truth or dare right now?"

They'd played that game on the streets, daring each other to take stupid chances or tell the truth about the shitty lives they'd run away to escape. Ronan had always taken the dare. He intended to play that game with Muriel Sanz now.

He dared to try to get the truth out of her. "It's a dirty job," he said, "but someone's got to do it."

"I would make the sacrifice," Stone said with a

lustful sigh, "if I wasn't just about to start this killer trial."

"I can do it," Trevor offered, and his blue eyes twinkled with lust. "I'd like to do The World's Most Beautiful Woman."

"No!" The shout surprised Ronan, especially since it had slipped through his own lips—just as some strange emotion coursed through him, tightening his stomach into knots and clenching his hands into fists. Was this jealousy?

It was something he'd never experienced. He had never been possessive of anyone before. Hell, he'd set up his friends with some of his exes in the past. Maybe that was the issue, though. He hadn't had enough of Muriel Sanz yet.

"I know you think she's a hellcat," Trev said. "But I can handle myself. In fact, I kind of like it rough." He chuckled.

And Ronan wanted to slug him. What the hell was wrong with him? These were his friends. He gritted his teeth and shook his head. "I will handle it," he said. "I've already talked to her a couple of times since she turned me in."

Trev leaned across the table and intently studied Ronan's face.

"What?" he asked, unnerved.

"I'm looking for the claw marks."

He touched his cheek.

And Trevor chuckled again. "She hit you."

"I had it coming."

"Oh, I'm sure you did," Trev said. "So what makes you think *you* can handle her?"

He wasn't sure that he could, but he damn well intended to try. "She's my problem," he said. "I've never had a problem I haven't been able to handle."

There was a sudden silence around the table. And they all glanced away from him like they had Simon when he'd been so certain that Bette wasn't lying. They knew there was one problem he hadn't been able to handle, not without running away: his parents.

But he wasn't going to run away this time. He sighed. "Come on, guys, that was a long time ago. I can handle Muriel Sanz." And he intended to put his hands all over her until she screamed again like she had in the elevator.

Or at least that was what he thought she'd done. He had to make sure he hadn't dreamed it all.

"Just remember what you're really after," Simon advised. "You want her to withdraw her complaint to the bar."

"And tell you where she got those documents," Trevor added with a quick glance at Simon.

Before they could start arguing again, Ronan stood up from the conference table. "Challenge accepted," he said, as he headed toward the door. But as he walked away, he realized Muriel Sanz might prove to be the biggest challenge of his life.

The doorbell pealed, making Muriel flinch. It had been ringing nonstop for days, ever since she'd received that ridiculous title that magazines made up to sell more issues. She wasn't certain who even voted on these things. Her—The World's Most Beautiful Woman?

Yeah, right.

The bell sounded again, so she picked her way through her suddenly overcrowded apartment to the door. When she peered through the peephole, all she saw were flowers—a colorful profusion of orange tiger lilies and red gardenias and yellow tulips. They were really beautiful. She couldn't refuse them. With a sigh, she pulled open the door.

"You must be getting tired of bringing all of these up," she said.

But then the flowers moved, revealing the face— the unfairly handsome face—of the man who carried them. It wasn't Howard, the gray-haired doorman with so many wrinkles he looked like a bulldog. This was the man who'd been haunting Muriel's dreams, keeping her awake in her tangled sheets.

He didn't look as though he'd lost any sleep the past week. What a damn good-looking man. He must not have come from the office because he wore jeans and a T-shirt now, which left his arms bare—the muscles bunched up impressively with the load of stuff he carried.

"What are you doing here?" she asked, her pulse quickening as she realized that he had somehow figured out which apartment was hers. Just the way he'd tracked her down at work, he had tracked her down at home.

He held up a bottle of wine that was in the hand not holding the arrangement. "We never went for that drink." His dark eyes gleamed with naughtiness as he must have been remembering, like she was, why they hadn't gone for that drink.

They had quenched their thirst in the elevator instead. No. That had just wetted Muriel's appetite for more...of Ronan Hall.

"You're not here for a drink," she said as his gaze skimmed over her.

She wasn't dressed like The World's Most Beautiful Woman now. She wore an old pair of yoga pants and a tank top. But he stared at her like she was wearing only her Bette's Beguiling Bows lingerie. Maybe he could see beneath the thin tank top and nearly threadbare pants.

He stepped forward, and she instinctively stepped back, which allowed him to pass in front of her and enter her apartment. Along with the wine bottle, he held up a big bag from which spicy and mouthwatering scents wafted. "No, I brought dinner, too. I remember you were hungry that night."

"That was over a week ago," she reminded him. "I've eaten since..." But she *was* hungry. It wasn't for the food in that bag, though. She was hungry for him. Then her stomach growled, and she remembered that she hadn't eaten lately.

He chuckled. "Not today."

She snorted. "Not for a couple hours."

He glanced down her body again. "You don't starve yourself?"

She laughed now. "I wouldn't look like this if I did."

He nodded and a little groan slipped out between his lips. "No. You wouldn't. I'm glad I didn't bother bringing a salad, too."

"What did you bring?" she asked, even as she knew letting him stay would be stupid.

They wouldn't just have wine and food. They'd have sex, too. And maybe that was why she was going to let him stay.

She really, really wanted sex with him again. She wanted to know if it was as good as she'd thought it had been in the elevator. Or maybe it had just seemed like that because it had been so long since she'd had sex with anything but her vibrator.

"I brought Carmine's."

She pointed to the bag. "I can see that."

"Pasta ragù and chicken parm…"

Her stomach growled again. "Good choices. And the wine?"

He held up the bottle again—it was in the same hand with the food. "Pinot noir."

How could he have known all of her favorites? Then she remembered. She'd had to do an interview for the magazine that had bestowed the ridiculous title on her. She narrowed her eyes as she studied his handsome face. "You've done your homework."

He didn't deny it. Just grinned that damned sexy grin of his again. And his dark eyes twinkled. "Lucky for me your favorites are also mine."

She didn't know if she believed that or not. She

doubted she could believe much of what he said. But she didn't care at the moment. She was too hungry, and not just for the food.

She took the bag from his hand as she led him toward her small dining area. The table overflowed with flowers, too, like the coffee table and the narrow foyer table. The flowers were the only vibrant color in the apartment she had wanted to be a serene oasis for her after the chaos the divorce had made of her life. The walls and ceiling were white, as was all the furniture. And the floors were bare with no varnish or stain darkening the white oak.

"Looks like a funeral parlor in here," he remarked.

"You're not the only one who read that article," she said. "These are all for congratulations." From people she'd never even met, from designers and photographers and even a few movie producers. She shuddered a little, thinking of all the attention she'd garnered.

He held out the flowers. "Congratulations."

She shrugged. "I had nothing to do with it." If anything, it was probably because of him and all the publicity over the divorce trial. But what she added was, "Just genetics…"

He laughed. "So you're not denying you're beautiful?"

"Should I feign some modesty?" Too many people had told her she was beautiful, starting with her very honest grandparents, for her to say otherwise.

"You'd be lying if you did," he said.

She gave him a pointed look. "And I don't lie."

He didn't argue with her. He just grinned again and held up the bottle of wine. "Screw?" The grin widened and his dark eyes glittered with mischief. "Corkscrew, I mean."

She stepped through an archway into her tiny kitchen and took one from a drawer in the white cabinets and handed it to him. Then she pulled down some plates and grabbed some silverware. This time she did intend to eat and drink first.

But she had no doubt what they were having for dessert: each other.

CHAPTER SIX

WATCHING MURIEL EAT was torture…

She closed her eyes and savored each bite, little moans of pleasure slipping between her lips. After swallowing the food, she would flick her tongue across her lips as if to clean up any drop of sauce or missed morsel. Then she would lift the fork to her mouth and slowly part her lips, beginning the decadent process all over again.

Ronan had never gotten hard watching someone eat before. But he was now, so hard that he couldn't taste the food in his own mouth. He could only chew it and wash it down with a sip of wine.

She was too distracting. Too damn irresistible…

His body was tense, his cock pulsating with the need to be buried inside her. No. He wasn't hungry anymore. After pushing his plate aside, he took another sip of the wine.

Then he murmured, "I'm surprised you let me in."

She glanced up at him as if only just realizing he was still in the room. She'd been so focused on her food that she might have forgotten all about him.

Ronan flinched as his ego took the hit. Nobody forgot his presence—until now.

"You're not the only one," she murmured. "But I was hungry."

"I'm glad I brought food, then."

"Thank you," she said. "You didn't eat much yourself." She gestured at his plate.

"I wasn't hungry..." For food. His stomach was clenched into too many knots for him to eat anything. But her...

He wanted to taste her again like he had in the elevator. Wanted to see if she was as sweet as he'd thought she'd been, as addictive.

Not that he would ever get addicted to anyone. He knew how dangerous that could be, and he was not about to make that mistake—not even for The World's Most Beautiful Woman.

"Why are you here?" she asked him.

Ronan opened his mouth and the truth almost spilled out because he had no problem with telling it how it was. But if he told her what he was up to—seducing her into dropping the complaint with the bar association—she would undoubtedly kick him out of her apartment. So he couldn't tell the truth. At least, not the whole truth.

"I came because I can't stop thinking about the other night in the elevator."

"That was scary," she said.

It had been scary. He couldn't remember ever wanting anyone the way he'd wanted her. But that had been then. He wanted her even more now, especially after watching her eat. He wanted to watch her do something else.

Him.

"I thought we were going to plummet to our deaths," she added.

Ronan realized what elevator incident she was talking about, and it wasn't the one he'd been thinking about, the one that had never left his mind, keeping him awake and hard every night and pretty much every other waking moment since it had happened.

But had it actually happened?

Or had he wet-dreamed the whole thing?

"It wouldn't have happened if you hadn't kept messing with the control panel," he reminded her.

Her green eyes twinkled as she stared across the table at him. "I like testing control."

Realizing she'd been teasing him, he grinned and asked, "Yours or mine?"

"Both," she replied. "But I failed that test in the elevator."

"Is that why you couldn't look at me afterward?" he asked. That had bothered him. Did he disgust her so much that she had been embarrassed she'd had sex with him? Or had she been embarrassed over where they'd done it?

She sighed. "I can't believe we didn't think about cameras." She looked at him with suspicion. "Or had you thought about them and just not cared?"

He shook his head. "Honestly, I wasn't thinking at all." Just feeling an overwhelming attraction to The World's Most Beautiful Woman.

Her eyes remained intent as she studied his face, as if trying to determine if he was being honest.

"You're the one who's famous," he said. "Don't you assume there are always cameras on you?"

"I don't know if I'm famous or infamous now," she said. And it was clear that she blamed him for that. "But I should be getting used to cameras always being on me."

There had been some paparazzi staked out in front of her building. But he suspected she was aware of that. It was probably why she was home on a Friday night. Of course, it was early yet. Maybe she intended to go out after dark.

"Yes, you should," he said. "I think you're going to have more than fifteen minutes of fame." He had already discovered she was more than a gorgeous face and perfect body. She was smart and strong, too.

She shrugged off his assurance. "The next scandal will come along, and the media will forget all about me."

He shook his head. "Not a chance."

Still staring at him, she sighed. "Not if I keep hanging out with you," she agreed.

"You think I'm going to embroil you in another scandal?" he asked.

"Just spending time with you is a scandal," she said. "You're the man who represented my ex in court, the man who destroyed me."

He leaned back a little and was able to reach through the dining room archway into the living room. Her place was small, but she'd lost the penthouse in the divorce—thanks to him. He picked up the magazine he'd seen on an end table and held up the cover with her face emblazoned across it. "You don't look destroyed."

With all her recent success, she should be able to afford a bigger place than the one she'd lost.

"I'm resilient," she said.

"Yes, you are." He could relate. He'd survived a lot so far in his life. He could even survive this—whatever this thing was with her.

A dare. The guys had dared him to get her to withdraw the complaint. He could get her to do that. He emptied the wine bottle into her glass.

"Are you trying to get me drunk?" she asked.

"On one bottle of wine?" he asked, and lifting his own glass, added, "One that I'm sharing with you?"

"Maybe you think I'm a lightweight."

Now he studied her face. She had that twinkle in her eyes again. "I bet you could drink me under the table."

"We could have a contest," she suggested.

"Now who's trying to get who drunk?" he asked. He didn't want to be drunk. He had enough trouble maintaining control around her when he was sober. He pushed his glass away from him.

And she made a clucking-chicken noise at him.

He laughed. The woman was one surprise after another, the biggest being that she kept letting him get close to her. Could she feel the same attraction for him that he felt for her?

"I am a little scared," he admitted, and he wasn't just teasing now. "Of you."

She grinned. "You believe your own smear campaign? You really think I'm a man-eater?"

"Yes."

"I am still hungry," she said. But she'd already pushed her food aside. Now she shoved back her chair. Instead of standing up, though, she dropped to her knees and disappeared beneath the table.

Then he felt her hands on his thighs, her palms sliding up them to reach for his zipper. He pushed back his chair now. But he couldn't quite stand, not with his legs beginning to shake slightly.

His cock shook, too, pulsating with the desire coursing through him. "What are you doing?" he asked, his voice gruff.

"Testing control..."

He didn't need to ask whose this time. He knew. His. He was in trouble. Big trouble. But there was no way he could hang onto control with her touching him. Yet he was powerless to stop her. She unclasped his belt and parted the fly of his jeans before pushing down his silk boxers to free his cock. It nearly jumped into her hands. And a giggle slipped through her lips.

"A little eager," she mused.

He'd been wanting this, imagining this, dying for this...the moment when she would close her full lips around his shaft...

She took her time. First she slid her hand up and down the length of him, pumping him into madness.

Then she leaned forward and flicked her tongue over the head.

Ronan nearly lost his head, a groan tearing from his throat as he leaned back. He could feel the cords in his neck straining as the muscles in his stomach knotted. Tension wound tightly inside him. Then her tongue slid down the length of him, right to his balls.

He groaned again and murmured, "What are you doing to me?"

Torture, he suspected, and he couldn't deny that he had it coming. He wanted her so badly, wanted her to close her lips around him and take him deep in her mouth so badly that he would give her whatever she wanted from him.

This wasn't the way it was supposed to be, though. He was supposed to be seducing her. Instead, he had been seduced into total compliance.

This was her chance. Muriel knew it. His big, muscular body was nearly trembling with the passion overwhelming him. He was close to losing control.

If she pulled back now…

If she stopped…

She might be able to make him beg for more. And she might be able to trade her sexual favors for the truth. But would she ever be able to believe what he told her?

At the moment, she didn't care about the truth, though. She only cared about the heat and the passion coursing through her. She wanted him. She wanted to taste his cock and his orgasm. She wanted to drive him as out of his mind as he'd driven her in the elevator a week ago.

So she closed her lips around him and sucked. He arched up from the chair and groaned. Then his fingers clutched in her hair, tangling but not pulling. He wasn't pulling her away. He was holding her close.

He needed the release. She could feel the tension in his body. He fairly vibrated with it. And his cock moved in her mouth; she could feel his pulse pounding madly in his engorged flesh. Hers matched the crazy rhythm of his. She was so excited, so stimulated just from giving him pleasure. Her pulse pounded in her clit and her nipples were taut, pushing through the thin lace of bra and the tank top she wore.

She moaned and sucked his cock deeper, to the back of her throat. Then she slid her lips up and down and around, teasing him to madness.

His fingers clutched her hair more tightly. But she felt no pain, only more excitement. Teasing him was teasing her. She had never wanted anyone the way she wanted him. He was so damn gorgeous—so big.

She stroked her hand up and down the rest of the length of his erection.

And finally he came, yelling her name as his big body tensed and shuddered. She drank him the way she had the wine, savoring every drop. His taste was rich and complex—just like the man.

He panted for breath, his head back, his body limp until she eased away. Then he moved quickly, reaching for her. He lifted her up in his arms and swung her around as he checked out the place.

"Is this a studio?" he asked. He must have been looking for the bed.

She pointed to a door. "One bedroom…" It was a small room. The bed nearly filled the entire space, which was good because he got to it quickly and lowered her to the mattress that was covered with fuzzy white pillows and silky white sheets. She'd wanted to feel as if she was sleeping on a cloud when she went to bed.

He stepped back. And she wondered for a fleeting, anxious moment if he was just going to leave her there. After all, he'd had his release, and he was known for being a ruthless man. But never a selfish lover…

Finally he moved, shoving down his jeans and boxers. Then he kicked off his shoes and lifted his shirt over his head. His washboard abs and muscular chest rippled with the action.

And a moan slipped through her lips. "You could be a model," she mused. He was that good-looking.

He laughed as if she'd told him an absurdly funny joke.

But she was serious.

"No, you really could," she insisted.

"I watched your shoot," he reminded her, as if she would ever forget his gaze on her while she'd been photographed in all those different lingerie outfits. "I couldn't sit still that long. I couldn't hold the poses, couldn't handle the heat of all those lights, and most of all, I couldn't follow the photographer's orders."

"No, you couldn't," she agreed. Modeling was much more grueling work than most people realized. She was oddly pleased that he knew and respected how hard it was. Not that she wanted his respect or anything.

Especially after the way he'd treated her in court.

But she did want him. She wanted him inside her, filling her, like he had in the elevator. He was already starting to recover, his dick beginning to swell and rise again as he stared down at her lying on the pillows.

She lifted her hips and wriggled out of her yoga pants, kicking them off to join his clothes on the floor. Then she lifted her tank top over her head and showed off her latest outfit from Bette's Beguiling Bows.

It was green. Bette had designed it to match Muriel's eyes. And she'd given her the first prototype of it as congratulations after that magazine named her The World's Most Beautiful Woman. This bra had the cups laced together with the bow at the top of them. So she had to take her time, untying that bow before pulling the ribbon loose.

"You didn't model that," he said, whistling with appreciation.

"Bette just made it for me to celebrate that magazine title," she said.

"It's better than flowers," he said with a gruff sigh as he stared at her.

She took her time undoing the lacing, stroking her fingers over her cleavage as she pulled the ribbon free. Even before she pulled off the bra, Ronan was completely hard again.

The panties were designed the same way, laced up to a bow on each hip. Before she could even undo the first bow of the panties, Ronan joined her on the bed. He lowered his body onto hers, but he kept most of his weight off her as he braced himself on one elbow. Then he leaned down and covered her mouth with his. He kissed her gently at first, which was such a surprise that she gasped, her breath shuddering wistfully out between her lips.

Then he deepened the kiss, moving his tongue inside her mouth. He teased hers with the tip of it.

She nipped at it with her teeth, gently biting, and he groaned. Then his hands moved over her, his palms sliding over her shoulders and arms before moving to her breasts. Finally he touched them, and she arched off the mattress, pushing her breasts into his palms. He squeezed gently, massaging the swollen flesh, before focusing on her nipples. He rolled them between his thumbs and forefingers, teasing them to even higher points.

Heat and wetness surged between her legs as her mound swelled and throbbed. She writhed beneath him, needing more, needing him. She was now as desperate as he had been moments before and he had barely touched her yet.

"Ronan…" She murmured his name, not caring how much like a plea it sounded. But she didn't want to be the only desperate one, so she touched him again, stroking her fingers over his chest, down his washboard abs to his shaft. She wrapped her fingers around it.

But he pulled back and moved down her body, his hanging half off the mattress while he pressed kisses to her shoulders and her collarbone and finally her breasts. He closed his lips around one taut nipple and continued to rub the other between his thumb and fingers.

She arched her body up and moaned.

"You are so damn responsive," he said, his voice gruff with his own passion. "You're probably already wet for me."

Instead of fighting with the bows, he just pushed the panties down her legs. And he moved his hand over her mound. His fingers slipped easily inside her, and he groaned. "Very wet…"

Then he shifted farther down her body and made her wetter as he flicked his tongue over her clit. He teased her to madness. She clutched the bed and then his hair and screamed his name as the tension broke with a shattering orgasm.

Her body shuddered.

She clawed at his shoulders and his back, trying to drag him up her body. "I need you," she said. "I need you inside me." She didn't care that she sounded exactly as she'd been portrayed—like a sex addict— a man-eater. He was the only man she wanted to eat at the moment.

He groaned again. But then he pulled away.

And she nearly screamed in frustration…until she heard foil tear. Then he was back on top of her, pushing inside. He was so big. She lifted her legs. And he pushed them higher, over his shoulders. Fortunately, Muriel was flexible. She pushed her legs against her breasts, teasing her already sensitive nipples. Ronan pumped hard—thrusting in and out of her. But Muriel matched his rhythm, arching up and pushing against him.

She was so close…

So close to release, but before she could find it, he pulled out. Then he was rolling her over, moving her around as easily as if she was a doll. Despite being a model, Muriel was no lightweight. Her ex hadn't even been able to carry her over the threshold on their honeymoon. Ronan would have no such problem. Not that he would ever carry her over a threshold.

But he lifted her easily and positioned her with her back to him, her bottom up, and he found her again, sliding inside her. His hand moved over her mound, teasing her clit. He reached farther up her body and teased the nipples of her swaying breasts. And he drove his cock deep inside her.

Muriel rocked her hips back against him, meeting his thrusts as the tension built unbearably. As he touched her and thrust, she shattered as an orgasm overwhelmed her. She shuddered as her muscles clenched before relaxing; she was satiated with pleasure.

Ronan drove deep once more before tensing

and uttering a deep groan. His hand on her breast squeezed, exciting her all over again. Despite the powerful orgasm he'd just given her, she could have gone again. And again and again…

Was she addicted to sex—with Ronan Hall?

CHAPTER SEVEN

RONAN'S HANDS WERE SHAKING. Hell, his whole body was shaking. But he forced his fingers to clench into a fist, and he pounded on the door. There was a bell. He could have used it, but he suspected his hand was shaking too much for his finger to find the small button.

He'd had no problem finding every one of Muriel's buttons. And he'd pushed them. Just like she'd pushed his. They'd driven each other wild. Maybe that was why he was here.

He was crazy. He had to have been crazy to leave The World's Most Beautiful Woman lying naked in her bed. But he'd had the feeling—that urge that he'd had when he was a kid and he'd been overwhelmed with his parents' fighting—the feeling that compelled him to flee.

So he'd fled.

He hadn't gone far, though, just a few floors up to another apartment in the same building. He lifted his hand to knock again just as the door finally opened. He was taken aback for a moment by the face that stared at him. While it was familiar, it wasn't the one he'd expected to see, although he should have known Simon would be with Bette Monroe if she was home. He suspected his friend spent every free moment with his former assistant. Simon's shirt was off and his blond hair was mussed, so it wasn't difficult to imagine what they'd been doing.

The same thing he'd been doing with Muriel...

Simon looked more shocked to see him, his blue eyes narrow and his brow furrowed with confusion. "What the hell are you doing here? Did you get lost?"

Despite feeling a little lost—the way he had when he'd run away all those years ago—Ronan shook his head.

Just as Simon had back then, he took Ronan in. He opened the door to Bette's apartment and led the way down a short hall to a good-sized living room. The apartment was bigger than Muriel's and nicer, with highly polished hardwood floors and dark trim. Maybe designers actually earned more than models.

Or maybe Muriel hadn't been able to afford anything bigger after paying out the divorce settlement Ronan had gotten for her ex...

He flinched as guilt stabbed him. Of course that didn't matter anymore. With all her recent accolades, she had to be back on top now.

On top...

Why the hell hadn't he tried that position with her? But then she would have been able to set the pace and drive him even more out of his mind than she already had. When she'd gone down on him, he'd nearly lost consciousness, the pleasure over-whelming him.

Simon turned back toward him and asked, "What are you doing here? I thought you were going to try to seduce the truth out of Muriel tonight."

"What?" Bette exclaimed as she walked up behind her boyfriend. She was pulling the belt tight on a silk robe that was probably all she wore. "That's horrible!"

Ronan wasn't about to remind her that was what Simon had done with her. He had already caused enough trouble between them.

But apparently Bette hadn't forgotten because she slapped Simon's shoulder and said, "It was bad enough when you tried that with me."

"It was bad?" he asked, as he turned toward her and arched one of his blond brows.

She uttered a wistful sigh, and her mouth curved into a naughty smile. "Very bad…"

Simon stepped closer to his girlfriend and wound his arm around her small waist, drawing her against his side. His hand smoothed over her hip, and his gaze dipped toward where the neck of her robe began to gape over her full breasts.

Ronan snapped his fingers. "Hey, I'm still here!" He didn't mind being part of a threesome—if the other two were women. That was the only way he didn't mind sharing. But somehow he didn't think that would be the case with Muriel. He wouldn't like sharing her with anyone.

But if her reputation was to be believed, she

wasn't seeing only him. There had been all those flowers in her apartment, too, and only people she knew would have known where to send them. According to her ex, one man had never been enough to satisfy her. Of course, that one man hadn't been Ronan.

He could satisfy her. At least, he thought he had.

"Why are *you* here?" Bette asked him. She obviously wasn't very happy to see him, not that he could blame her. He hadn't been very nice to her at her going-away office party.

He wondered if she would ever forgive him. And if she couldn't, Muriel certainly never would. But what was there to forgive?

He had only been doing his job. Ronan was not the one who'd done anything wrong. Muriel was. Wasn't she?

"I came here to ask you about Muriel," he replied.

"Bette already told you she had nothing to do with those documents that were given to the bar association," Simon said. And now his voice was as cold and unwelcoming as his girlfriend's.

"Muriel said those documents were given to her," Ronan said.

And she was the one who'd given them to the bar association. But why? If she had really done what those witnesses had said, why would she have been so upset? And why would she seem so certain that those witnesses had lied?

His blood chilled with the thought that they might have committed perjury. But no. He couldn't be wrong.

"And I don't know who gave them to her," Bette said. "Muriel doesn't even know."

"How well do you know her?" Ronan asked.

Bette glared at him now, and there was a defensive snap in her voice when she replied, "Very well."

He didn't want to piss her off, especially not with Simon present. But he had to ask, "How do you even know her at all?"

"What do you mean?" Simon shot that question at him, and his voice was sharp, too, in defense of his girlfriend. "What are you getting at, Ro?"

Ronan sighed with frustration. "I just don't understand their friendship."

Bette obviously understood what he was getting at because she answered Simon. "He doesn't understand how we can be friends because Muriel's beautiful and famous, and I'm not." Hurt flashed in her dark eyes.

And Ronan flinched. That wasn't what he'd really meant, but it was a valid reason for them not to be friends. They seemed to have very little in common.

Simon's arm tightened around his girlfriend's small waist. "You're beautiful and famous, too, sweetheart."

She laughed, but with no bitterness or resentment. "Not like Muriel." But she didn't appear to be jealous of her friend. "She's The World's Most Beautiful Woman."

Ronan agreed with her, but Simon apparently didn't. Before he could argue with her, Ronan interjected, "That's not what I meant at all. Bette, you're sweet and nice and honest…" At least, he hoped, for his friend's sake and his, that she was. "And Muriel Sanz is not."

Bette laughed again. "Yes, she is. And that's why we're friends. I have never met anyone more straightforward or honest than Muriel is."

He shook his head. It wasn't possible. "But…that's not what all those witnesses said."

"They lied," Bette said as if it was just that simple.

His doubts escaped in a snort of derision. "Really? All of them?"

"Why is it so easy for you to believe that Muriel is the one who lied?" Bette asked. "Because she's a woman? Because she's beautiful?"

Ronan narrowed his eyes now. How much did Bette know about his life? About his past? He turned toward his friend.

Simon shrugged. "She's intuitive."

"And a good judge of character," Bette added. "I trust Muriel. I believe she's telling the truth."

Ronan didn't want to believe it. Because if she was telling the truth, then she had every reason to hate him. Hell, he would hate himself.

He shook his head, refusing to accept it. All of those people wouldn't have lied. No. Muriel was the liar and the manipulator, perhaps better even than his mother had been. He had to be careful. He had to protect himself before he got in too deep.

But he had a sick feeling that it might already be too late for that. He'd been smart to leave her alone in bed tonight and run. He probably should have run farther than he had, though, because he would have a hard time stepping back into that elevator and not pressing the button for her floor, not going back for more of her.

For the first time in his life, Ronan was beginning to understand his father. He was beginning to understand how a woman could become an addiction.

What would it take to cure him?

Losing his license?

Would that finally kill his attraction to her?

The doorbell rang, and even though she'd been waiting for it, the sound startled her. And Muriel realized she'd dozed off on the couch. She opened her eyes and squinted against the sun streaming through the tall windows.

After what they'd done in the bedroom, she wouldn't have been able to sleep there, not on the tangled sheets that had smelled of Ronan and sex. She wouldn't have been able to sleep there because she would have just lain awake, wanting more. But she must have been the only one who'd wanted more, because Ronan had taken off in a hurry.

Had he been late for a date with another woman?

Not that their dinner together had been a date. He hadn't asked Muriel out; he'd just shown up with take-out. And, embarrassingly enough, she had been home alone on a Friday night. But it had been a Friday night, so of course, he'd had plans. No wonder he'd left in such a hurry.

But she'd been certain he would come back, that

he had been as affected by the attraction between them as she was. But he hadn't returned.

Unless that was him at the door, persistently ringing the bell. Maybe he'd brought her breakfast.

Her stomach rumbling at the thought of food, Muriel rolled off the couch and hurried down the short hall to the door. When she pulled it open and found her friend standing in the hall, disappointment flashed through her.

Feeling guilty, she pushed it aside and gave Bette a bright smile. The pretty brunette held a beverage carrier and a bag that was already getting soggy from whatever greasy bounty she'd brought with her. Muriel stepped back, but her friend remained standing in the hall.

"Is *he* here?" she asked.

Muriel tensed. She hadn't told Bette that she'd run into Ronan—a couple of times—lately. No doubt Bette would think she was a fool for even talking to him, let alone letting him get as close as he'd been to her.

Inside her…

She shivered despite the fact that she'd pulled on her yoga pants and a sweatshirt after he left. "Is who here?" she asked, stalling for time.

Could Bette think she'd been hooking up with someone else? Maybe some magazine had printed some more lies about her. But Bette knew better than to believe what she read about Muriel.

"Ronan Hall," Bette said.

The heat of embarrassment rushed to Muriel's face.

"He's playing you," her friend warned. "He's trying to seduce you into dropping your complaint with the bar association."

A pang struck Muriel's heart. Not that she was hurt or anything…

She'd suspected Ronan was up to something, that he'd had a reason for seeking her out in the elevator and at her photo shoot.

She plucked a cup of coffee from the beverage carrier Bette held in one hand. "At least let me have some caffeine before we start this conversation."

She was exhausted. Not just because of the marathon sex she'd had with Ronan but because she hadn't been able to sleep after he'd left.

She'd wanted him again. Hell, she wanted him now.

Bette held up the grease-stained bag. "I brought doughnuts, too."

"I love you," Muriel said as she ushered Bette into the apartment and closed the door behind her.

"You love too easily," Bette said.

Feeling like her friend had struck her, Muriel gasped. "I am not in love with Ronan."

"I should hope not," Bette said.

"I hate his guts," Muriel reminded her.

"Then why are you even talking to him, let alone sleeping with him?" Bette asked.

Muriel silently cursed him for being a tool and herself for being a fool. She should have known that he would brag to his friends, and Bette was seeing one of those friends. Simon Kramer wasn't much better than Ronan. All of the partners of the Street Legal law practice were notorious for being ruthless lawyers and lovers.

"I could say the same about you and Simon," Muriel reminded her.

"You could have in the beginning," Bette admitted. "But I am in love with him now. And he loves me."

She didn't doubt Bette's feelings for her former boss, and he actually seemed invested in the relationship, too. He certainly spent enough time at her place.

"That's not going to happen with me and Ronan," Muriel said. He'd skipped out right after they'd had sex.

"I know," Bette agreed. "So what the hell are you doing with him?"

"We're not *sleeping* together," Muriel murmured as she thought of everything they'd done to each other, everything she wanted to do with him still. "I'm playing him, too."

Bette's brown eyes darkened with obvious skepticism. "How's that?"

"I want to get him to admit the truth," Muriel replied. "I want to make him confess that he coerced all those people to lie about me on the witness stand."

Bette glanced away from her then. Did she not believe that those people had lied?

"Do you think they were telling the truth about me?" Muriel asked.

"No," Bette quickly replied. "Absolutely not. But

I'm not sure that Ronan got them to lie about you."
She dumped out the doughnuts onto the table.

Muriel reached for a powdered one. She knew
it would be custard filled; those were their favorites. Before she took a bite, she asked, "Then why
would they?"

Bette shrugged. "Why does anyone do anything?"

"For money," Muriel replied. "Or fame."

"Exactly," Bette said.

The people who'd testified against her had gotten both. The interviews they'd given after the trial
had brought them their fifteen minutes of fame, and
the magazines and television networks had probably
paid for those interviews.

Could Ronan really have not suborned perjury?

"But what about those memos?" Muriel asked.

Bette sighed. "I think they were forged."

"You believe Ronan?"

"He's too smart to put anything incriminating in
writing," Bette pointed out.

And she was right. Ronan was smart. If he'd done
something illegal, he wouldn't have risked someone
discovering what he'd done. He probably wouldn't
have documented it. Were the memos she'd received
forged, as he'd claimed?

She cursed. She wouldn't have filed her complaint
with the bar association if she hadn't been certain
they were authentic. "But why would someone have
given them to me?"

Bette sighed. "Someone is making trouble for

Street Legal," she said. "They've given case file notes to opposing counsel for another trial…"

"But were those notes real?" Muriel asked.

Bette nodded. "But that doesn't mean the ones you were given are," she said. "I really don't think Ronan would have been so careless." Her throat moved as she swallowed, as if she was choking on her words, before she added, "And I don't think he would have suborned perjury."

"Not even to win?" Muriel asked. Ronan Hall was all about winning. He had freely admitted that in every interview he'd ever given.

"He doesn't take cases he doesn't think he can win," Bette replied. "So maybe he's telling the truth, too."

But Muriel couldn't be certain that was the case. And until she was certain, she wouldn't withdraw her complaint from the bar association, no matter how many times Ronan seduced her. Yet if getting her to withdraw her complaint was what he wanted, why hadn't he asked her to do it?

He hadn't asked her anything during or after sex. He'd dressed quickly and hightailed it out of her bedroom and apartment as if he'd been late for something else.

Or someone else…

Now she felt a curious pang of emotion, one that left a bitter taste in her mouth despite the sweetness of the custard and powdered sugar. It couldn't be jealousy; it must have just been disgust. Anger surged through her.

"Even if he didn't know those people were lying, he treated me like trash," Muriel said. "He dragged my name through the mud. I will never forgive him for that."

"Good," Bette said. "I don't want you to fall for the wrong man again and get hurt."

"I won't," Muriel assured her friend. But she had a sick feeling in the pit of her stomach, and it wasn't the doughnut. She'd barely nibbled on that. It was fear.

No. She wouldn't fall for Ronan. It didn't matter how good the sex was between them. He wasn't a good man. But he was the best lover she'd ever had...

Maybe she would just have to have a lot of sex with him, so much that she would get sick of it, that she would get sick of him.

CHAPTER EIGHT

SUNSHINE POURED THROUGH the wall of windows in Ronan's office. Street Legal's offices encompassed the entire top floor of a building in Midtown. The space was like a loft with high ceilings open to the rafters, exposed ductwork, brick exterior walls and rough-sawn hardwood floors.

Ronan stood at his desk. He had the kind that he could raise, so he could forgo a chair. He didn't like sitting. It was hard enough staying in his seat in a courtroom, which he managed to do only as long as he had to, when the opposing counsel had the floor.

He flipped through the file on his desk, reading over the court transcripts he'd printed out, and he snorted in derision at his opposing counsel in this case. The defendant's attorney had posed no challenge for Ronan at all.

She hadn't raised any of the arguments that Ronan would have, had he been Muriel's attorney. But he hadn't been. He'd been working for her ex.

He remembered Stone's comment at the meeting. The reason Ronan's partner had questioned Muriel's intelligence wasn't because she was a model but because of the man she'd married. Stone didn't have a very high opinion of Ronan's former client, and as Ronan reread his real case notes—not the forged ones Muriel had given to the bar association—his opinion of Arte Armand sank, as well.

Why the hell had he represented this schmuck?

Oh, yeah, he'd felt sorry for the guy. Arte had been a broken man when he'd come into Ronan's office. He'd sobbed out his misery over how horribly his new bride had mistreated him. *New* bride…

They hadn't been married very long at all. Less than a year. The prenup she'd had him sign should have held up—would have held up—had she not been proven at fault in the divorce. Had Ronan not proven her at fault.

Had she been at fault? All those witnesses had claimed she was, that she had treated Arte as horribly as he'd said she had. But if that was true, why had he stayed with her?

Because he hadn't been able to leave, just like Ronan's father hadn't been able to leave his mother? That was why Ronan had taken the case, because Arte had reminded him of his father. But his father had loved his mother for years before she'd started cheating on him. They'd had a child together. He'd had reasons to stay.

What had Arte's reasons been? Money? Or love?

He'd claimed he'd loved Muriel. But if that were true, why had he wanted to hurt her so badly? To publicly humiliate her? And why had Ronan helped him do it?

That twinge of discomfort and regret he'd been having turned into a gnawing ache in his chest now. Had he been wrong? No. That wasn't possible. Not with all those witnesses claiming how badly Muriel had treated her ex…

But as he read their testimony in the transcripts, he noticed how similar their stories were, which had previously convinced him of their veracity. Now he wondered…were they too similar, almost as if every one of them had been reading from the same script?

He felt a shiver of unease chasing down his spine. It wasn't because of the transcripts but because someone stood in the doorway of his office. He turned toward where Muriel leaned against the jamb, watching him.

How had she gotten past Miguel, their receptionist-slash-bouncer? Then he remembered that it was Sunday. Miguel didn't come in on Sundays. Nobody did but Ronan and his partners. Stone had come in, too, to prepare for his upcoming murder trial. And Trev was working on something, as well. Only Simon hadn't come in—probably because he was still in bed with Bette.

Ronan wished he was still in bed with Muriel. He shouldn't have left her Friday night. Right now— as he stared at her, looking so gorgeous in artfully ripped jeans and a sweater with shoulder cutouts— he didn't know how he'd left her at all when she'd been lying there naked in the sheets tangled from their sexual romp.

Remembering how she'd looked—her silky skin flushed from their passion—his body tensed, and his cock hardened. He wanted her again. Still...

She was so damn sexy and looked almost posed against that doorjamb, the way she had posed for that photo shoot. Then she moved, her hips rolling as she walked slowly toward him.

His hand shook slightly as he closed the file—her case file. He didn't want her to see what he'd been reading. He didn't want her to know that she was getting to him, giving him doubts.

He had to clear the desire from his throat to ask, "What are you doing here?" But the question came out brusquely, his voice still gruff.

"It's good to see you, too," she remarked sarcastically.

It was better than good to see her. Despite her face being everywhere, he'd missed her, and that unsettled Ronan. It wasn't like him to miss anyone but his friends. And he and Muriel were not friends.

They were enemies. Weren't they? She'd turned him into the bar association, and he had...

What had he done?

And what was she doing? She stopped next to his desk and glanced down at the surface of it.

He flipped over her file. "I'm working."

"I'm sorry." She held up her palms, but he didn't mistake it for a gesture of surrender, especially when she added, "I didn't mean to interrupt you ruining someone else's life."

"I'm not," he said. At least, he hoped he wasn't. "And I didn't ruin yours."

"Yeah, right…" She snorted.

"You're on the cover of every magazine and all over the news," he said.

She shuddered.

"Isn't that what you wanted?" Why would she have become a model unless she'd wanted to become famous?

"I didn't want it like this, because of a scandal," she said. "I wanted to know I earned it."

"You did." She had been the most beautiful woman in the world even before the scandal.

She snorted again. "I have been half expecting you or that sleazy PR firm to send me a bill."

He wouldn't put it past that PR firm: Allison McCann was nearly as mercenary as Ronan's mother and maybe Muriel's ex had been. If anyone sent her a bill, though, it would probably be Arte Armand…

"I'm not giving you a bill," Ronan assured her.

He couldn't and wouldn't speak for Allison McCann, though, and he wondered now if he should have let her speak for Street Legal, at least for this case. Had Arte and his friends, who were probably now Muriel's former friends, been telling the truth?

"I don't want your money," he said. He just wanted her—like she'd been the other night, naked and wild for him. His fingers twitched now with the urge to reach for her, to touch her.

"I know," she said. She tossed something down on his desk, right on top of that case file.

"What's this?" he asked as he glanced at the big orange envelope.

"This is what you seduced me for," she said.

He groaned. He should have known Bette would tell her about his plan. They were friends. Apparently better friends than he and Simon were, since Simon hadn't kept that dare a secret for him.

"Muriel—" Before he could say anything else, and he wasn't certain what he could have said, she put her fingers across his lips.

"Don't worry," she said. "I was seducing you, too."

Instead of being offended or furious, he was amused and moved his lips against her fingers as he grinned. He'd wondered why she'd let him close to her. Obviously, she'd been after something, too.

She shivered and pulled her hand from his mouth.

And he asked, "What did you want from me?"

What had she wanted from him? At the moment, she couldn't remember. Hell, she wasn't sure she even knew her own name anymore. All she knew was how he made her feel wanton.

She wanted him so damn badly.

"Right now," she murmured, "I don't know."

"I think you do," he said, and he stepped out from behind his tall desk—which put him right in front of her—so close that his thighs touched hers.

She wore heels today, very high stilettos. Since she was already tall, the heels brought her nearly to his height. But he was ridiculously tall and broad and muscular and handsome.

"It's really a waste that you're a lawyer," she murmured. With his devastating good looks, he should have been a male model. He would have been far more successful than her ex had been.

Ronan must have mistaken her comment for an insult, though, because he flinched. "Everybody hates lawyers."

Not everybody.

"Only divorce lawyers," she teased. "I don't have any problem with your partners."

He narrowed his dark eyes and studied her face with obvious skepticism. "Not even Simon?"

"Not now," she said. "But if he hurts Bette, I'll kill him." She'd never had a friend like Bette—she knew that now, after all those people had given false testimony against her. They hadn't been true friends.

Ronan chuckled and reached for her arm, gently squeezing her biceps. She flexed for him. "I think you could take him," he said. "Hell, you could probably take me."

"I wanted to kill you for a long time," she admitted.

And he flinched again. Then he slid his fingers up to her shoulder and, stroking her bare skin, he asked, "And now?"

Now she just wanted him. She shivered in reaction to his touch. But it wasn't enough. She wanted his hands everywhere on her. She wanted his mouth everywhere.

His name slipped through her lips on a soft, lustful sigh. "Ronan…"

He pressed his mouth to hers. His kiss was gentle at first, just a whisper-soft brush of his lips across hers.

Her breath sighed out in a gasp of pleasure. She hadn't known he could be so tender. It was almost as if he cared about her. But that wasn't true.

She had to remind herself of that—of the fact that Ronan Hall didn't care about anyone or anything but winning. And he wouldn't stop until he'd won, until he seduced her into doing what he wanted. While he wanted to find out where she'd gotten the memos, he also wanted her to withdraw her complaint to the bar association. Bette had warned her.

If she was smart, she would stay far away from him. But she was the one who'd sought him out today. Bette had refused to give her his home address, but she'd reluctantly admitted that he could be at the office, that the partners often worked weekends.

Was that why Ronan hadn't come back to her apartment? Because he'd been too busy working? Too busy ruining other people's lives to seduce her again?

Taking advantage of her parted lips, he deepened the kiss, sliding his tongue inside her mouth. He stroked his tongue across hers, teasing her, tasting her.

Desire rushed through Muriel, heating her skin and making her pulse race wildly. She didn't care about anything right now—about his motives or hers.

All she wanted was the pleasure she knew he could give her.

He pulled back and panted for breath, his eyes dark and wild with desire. "Damn you…" he murmured.

Instead of being offended, she laughed because she knew he felt it, too—the overwhelming attraction between them.

His lips curved into a slight, reluctant grin. "You are becoming an addiction."

Apparently he didn't understand the definition of addiction—because if he was addicted to her, he wouldn't have been able to walk away from her like he had the other night. He wouldn't have been able to leave her bed at all.

There was no bed in his office. She wasn't even sure he had a chair. He'd been standing at that odd desk of his. But she didn't care where they had sex; she just had to have sex with him.

Now.

She understood what an addiction was, and she was very afraid that she was becoming addicted to him. Her body ached with desire—with need—for his.

She clutched the nape of his neck as she pulled down his head so she could kiss him back. She skipped the tenderness he'd shown her at first, and she went straight for the passion, kissing him deeply and hungrily. She nibbled at his lips and teased his tongue with the tip of hers.

He groaned and lifted her, the muscles in his arms bulging and rippling as he carried her.

She wasn't certain where he was taking her, and she didn't care as long as he took her.

He settled her onto something that was hard and cold beneath her bottom. And when she glanced down she saw she was on the bar that ran along one wall of his office. The surface was black granite with a vein of gold running through it. The faucet on the little sink was gold, as were the liquor decanters sitting next to her ass on the countertop.

"Need a drink?" she asked.

"I need you," he said. And he dragged her sweater up and over her head. Her hair tangled around her face, blinding her for a moment. So she didn't see his reaction to her bustier. It was black leather and, of course, a bow topped the laced-up front of it. But she heard his reaction in the sharp intake of his breath.

Then he groaned her name. His fingers shook slightly as he fumbled with the button of her jeans. He got it loose, though, and tugged down her zipper, as well. She wore leather panties to go with the bustier. They were also laced up the front and tied with a bow.

"Remind me to compliment Bette on her brilliant designs," he murmured as he lowered his head and kissed her again.

She nipped his bottom lip between her teeth. She wanted more than his kisses. She wanted his dick. So she reached for it, sliding her hand over the fly of his jeans. His cock strained the already worn denim.

She jerked his button loose and pulled down his zipper to free him from his boxers.

Then she wrapped her hand around him, stroking her palm up and down the length of his cock. "I need you now!" she said. "I need to feel you inside me."

He groaned. But he didn't protest. In fact, his control must have snapped because he pulled off her jeans and nearly tore off the bow holding up her panties. The leather dropped away from her. But she was still hot, still burning up for his touch. His fingers slid inside her, and he groaned again. "You're so wet."

So ready for him…

She tugged free the bow on the bustier, and her breasts sprang over the tops of the leather cups. The nipples were already tightened and pointing up toward Ronan. He took one in his mouth and swirled his tongue around it.

She moaned and squirmed against his hand. He moved his fingers inside her while grinding his palm against her mound. Then he flicked his thumb back and forth over her clit. She tensed but then he closed his teeth gently over her nipple and she came, the orgasm shuddering through her.

"Ronan…" She nearly sobbed his name. She tightened her grasp around his cock and stroked harder.

He shuddered and lifted her again. Despite his strength, he stumbled back. Or maybe he'd intended to walk backward, because he dropped into a chair with her astride his lap. He pulled out a condom packet, tore it open and sheathed himself.

Desperate to feel him filling her, Muriel rose up on her knees and guided him inside her. He was so big, so thick, that he stretched her. She arched and took him as deep as she could. He moved his hips and thrust a little deeper.

She'd never been this full, this complete. A moan tore from her throat as passion overwhelmed her. He was so damn good. And as he continued to move his hips, he touched her breasts, teasing her nipples into even tauter points. She bit her bottom lip, but she couldn't hold back another moan.

He drove her crazy. And she wanted to drive him just as crazy. She touched him back, teasing his flat male nipples until they pebbled. Then she reached beneath her butt and stroked his thighs and balls.

He groaned, and the muscles in his neck corded and stood out. "Muriel…" He growled her name like a warning. And sweat beaded on his upper lip and brow as he struggled for control.

She wanted him to lose it, wanted him as wild as he made her. She leaned forward and kissed him deeply before sliding her lips over his granite jaw to his neck. She nibbled on those corded tendons, then suckled.

He clutched his fingers in her hair, tangling it even more than it had already been. He pulled her face from his neck and kissed her, and as he drove his tongue between her lips, he drove his cock deeper into her.

She rocked her hips against him, arching and straining to ease the pressure that had built inside her again. The tension was nearly unbearable. Despite the release he'd already given her, she needed another.

She needed more of the intense pleasure she feared only he could give her. She'd never had orgasms as long or as powerful as the ones he'd given her. Then he stroked his thumb over her clit once more and she came again, screaming his name.

Her name echoed his, as his big body tensed, then shuddered with his own release. Like her, it seemed as though he came and came. As she collapsed against his heaving chest, he wrapped his arms around her. And their hearts pounded in the same frantic rhythm.

Muriel had never felt so close—such a connection—to another human being. But that wasn't possible, not with Ronan Hall. He didn't let anyone close.

And after how she'd been betrayed, neither should she. Remembering how badly she'd been hurt, how badly Ronan had hurt her, she scrambled off his lap. Then she ran back to the bar where he'd taken off her clothes.

"I could use a drink, too," he murmured, as if that was what he thought she needed.

Instead of reaching for one of those decanters, she grabbed up her clothes and donned them in such haste that she didn't realize her sweater was inside out, until Ronan tugged on the tag. Then he reached over her and lifted one of those decanters, and as he did, she noticed his hand was shaking.

Maybe he was as unnerved as she was. He must

have dressed quickly, too, because his jeans were up and zipped again. Once he poured the drink, he walked back toward his desk—leaving the route to the door unobstructed.

Instinct prompted Muriel to run for it. If she was smart, she would. But if she was smart, she wouldn't have come here today—she wouldn't have risked seeing Ronan ever again.

CHAPTER NINE

"THIS ISN'T WHAT I seduced you for," Ronan said as he picked up the envelope. After that mind-blowing sex, he wasn't sure he'd seduced her for any reason but pleasure. He had never had as much in his life before he started having sex with her. "It's just an envelope."

With nothing but her name scrawled across the front of it. He didn't recognize the handwriting, not that it was very easy to read since the thick black marker with which it had been written had smeared and bled through the orange paper.

"That's what those documents were in," she said. "Someone shoved it under my door. When I found it, I thought Bette must have slipped them to me."

"It wasn't Bette." He accepted that now. She cared too much about Simon to put their practice at risk.

"No. I don't know who it was," she said with a sigh. "So I guess I haven't given you what you seduced me for."

"I seduced you so you'd go to the bar association

and confess that those documents were forged," he explained.

She laughed. "If I agreed to that, you'd be suborning perjury all over again."

"I didn't," he said. He'd never had to coerce anyone into lying. They usually did it freely, on their own. But in this case, he hadn't been aware of anyone lying but her. "I would never do that."

He would never risk his license or the reputation of the practice. He'd worked so hard to get off those streets and help his partners form Street Legal. It meant too much to him. Hell, it and his friends were all he really had.

Muriel's beautiful green eyes were intense as she studied his face, as if she was trying to discern if he was lying or telling the truth. "You freely admit that winning is everything to you."

"In interviews?" he asked. "Press releases? We didn't hire that PR firm to make us look like losers. Who's going to hire an attorney who's okay with losing?"

"Apparently not my ex," she murmured.

"You hurt him badly," Ronan said. He needed to remind himself of that, of how dangerous she was. She'd broken Arte Armand. He had to make sure she didn't break him, too.

She shook her head, and her thick, black lashes fluttered as if she was fighting back tears. "I. Did. Not. Hurt. *Him!*"

Borrowing Simon's gesture, he arched a brow to express his skepticism.

"I didn't," she insisted. "He hurt me."

She wasn't broken, not like Arte had been. She wasn't sobbing. But her eyes were bright. He couldn't be certain those were tears glistening in them, though. He couldn't be certain that she was really feeling anything at all.

Was she still playing him? She'd already admitted that she had been.

"Why did you seduce me?" he asked. Not that he minded. He had quite enjoyed her seducing him. In fact, if he'd enjoyed it any more, he probably wouldn't have survived.

She was an incredible lover. But more than that, they fit, as if their bodies were meant to be together. And their sexual appetites were the same—voracious.

He wanted her again. Even after just having one of the most intense orgasms of his life, he wanted her again. Hell, he needed her.

She stared at him blankly, maybe because of the abrupt way he'd changed the conversation.

So he reminded her, "You said you were seducing me, too. Why? What do you want from me?"

Hopefully more of what they'd just done—a whole lot more—because he wasn't sure he was ever going to get enough of Muriel Sanz.

Her beautiful green eyes narrowed as she glared at him. "I wanted to seduce you into admitting that you coerced those people into lying about me."

He shook his head. "I'm sorry I can't give you what you want, either."

Her full lips curved into a small, sad smile and she murmured, "Then I guess we both lose this time."

He didn't feel like he'd lost until she turned to walk out the door. He couldn't let her leave, not like this. He reached out and caught her, wrapping his hand around her wrist to spin her back to him, back into his arms. Her breasts slammed against his chest, and the breath left his lungs. And as he stared down at her beautiful face, his heart began to pound fast and hard and erratically.

She felt so right in his arms, as if it was where she belonged. But that wasn't possible. Nobody belonged in Ronan's arms. He wasn't the type who stayed to snuggle after sex. And he didn't want to snuggle now.

That wasn't why his arms tightened around her, why he pulled her even closer. He wanted more sex. That was all he wanted…

But there was a strange sensation in his chest, as if it was swelling and warming, and he didn't like the feeling. He didn't like feeling at all. Anything.

Lust. That was all this was, all it could be. Just attraction and lust…

Despite the warmth of his body pressed so tightly against hers, Muriel shivered. The look on his handsome face, with his clenched jaw, was so tense, so almost frightened, that it frightened her, as well.

"What's wrong?" she asked, her voice soft and quavering with the fear she felt in him.

He shook his head. "It should be wrong," he murmured. "But it feels so right…"

"What?"

"This," he said, and he slid his hand from her back down to her hip. Then he rubbed the erection that was once more straining the fly of his jeans against her belly. "Us."

"It is wrong," she said. But she couldn't deny that it felt right between them. There had never been an awkward moment, never any hesitation, never anything but passion. So much passion…

He shook his head again, as if he couldn't accept it.

But he had to; she had to make him—and herself—see that this was wrong. "What would the bar association say if they learned you were trying to coerce me to withdraw my complaint against you?"

He tensed and a breath escaped his lips, as if she'd punched him. "Would you go to them and say that?"

She could. She'd once been so angry with him that she would have. But the passion between them, and the orgasms he'd given her, had eased some of her anger.

"I wasn't trying to coerce you to lie to them," he said. "I wouldn't do that…"

And she was beginning to believe him.

"But you admitted that you want me to withdraw my complaint," she reminded him.

"Yes, but I want you to withdraw it because you believe those memos were forged," he said, "because you believe me." And his dark eyes implored her to do just that.

She closed her eyes. She wanted to believe him.

But she couldn't. He'd pretty much told his friends that he was just playing her. So she couldn't believe anything he said.

She shook her head now.

"Muriel…" His breath whispered across her earlobe as he lowered his head and nuzzled her neck. "Believe me."

"I—I can't," she stammered, "any more than you can believe me."

He groaned now and shifted against her again. "I don't know what to believe anymore."

She could understand that. "You don't want to believe me," she said. "Because then you'll have to admit you were wrong."

His brow furrowed. But he didn't deny what she'd claimed. Instead, he lowered his head and brushed his mouth across hers in another of those soft kisses. If she hadn't experienced it, she wouldn't have thought him capable of such tenderness. But just as softly as he kissed her, his fingers slid down her cheek with a light caress.

"What are you doing?" she asked, her voice raspy as she struggled to breathe with the passion overwhelming her. "You have no reason to seduce me now. I'm not going to the bar association for you." No matter how much pleasure he gave her.

But he must not have heard her because he continued to please her. His lips slid down her cheek to her neck, and he nuzzled it again, his breath hot against her skin.

She shivered as sensations raised through her.

Then his lips were on her exposed shoulder. And she shivered again, but it was heat racing through her—straight to her core. Her nipples tightened, and a moan slipped through her lips.

His mouth moved to hers again, but the gentleness was gone. He kissed her deeply, hungrily. When he pulled away, she panted for breath.

Excitement filled her, making her skin tingle and her pulse pound like mad. Madness was what this was—this obsession that Ronan was becoming for her. It was a madness.

She'd lost her mind.

And her breath...

And her ability to think or move...

It was as if his touch paralyzed her. Her body was going so limp that she might have collapsed if he hadn't lifted her up. This time he didn't carry her far; he just put her on the edge of his tall desk.

He stripped off her clothes until she sat naked on his desk, atop whatever file he'd been reading when she'd walked into his office. So intent on whatever he was reading, he hadn't even noticed her standing there.

But now he'd forgotten all about it. He was totally focused on her. He kissed and touched every inch of her skin, every part of her body.

His mouth moved to her mound, his tongue flicking across her clit. She arched off the desk and cried out as the pressure wound tightly inside her. She needed release, needed him. And suddenly the paralysis was over.

She reached for him, tugging at his clothes—tearing them off—until he was as naked as she was. With her on the tall desk, she was the perfect height for him.

She locked her legs around his waist, pulling him closer until he was as close as he could be. His body covered hers, and she was barely able to tell where she ended and he began. They moved together in a rhythm that was theirs alone, like their song.

It swelled to a crescendo, and they both shouted as they came. Her body shuddered and went limp again on the desk.

And his body began to shake, as if he was as overwhelmed as she was. He stared down at her, and she saw the fear again in his dark eyes.

He had been as overwhelmed as she was.

And she *was* overwhelmed. He made her feel so many things, pleasure most of all. No wonder she couldn't get enough of him. No one else had ever given her such powerful orgasms, such strong releases.

He had a reputation for being an amazing lover. That was why his exes were so upset when he dumped them—because he left them wanting more.

Muriel understood that now. Because even though he'd just given her so much pleasure, she wanted so much more.

And now fear coursed through her. She scrambled down from the desk, knocking off that file as she did. She bent over to pick it up—but he was already there, grabbing up the papers and shoving them back into the manila folder.

So she reached for her clothes, instead. As she dressed, she watched him. He hadn't dressed. He was naked and gorgeous and she wanted him all over again.

This obsession was dangerous, so dangerous that she was tempted to do what he wanted. She was tempted to go to the bar association and withdraw her complaint—even if she'd had every reason to file it.

And she had.

She couldn't forget what he'd done to her in that courtroom and in the media. What he must have done...

No matter how much he denied it, he had to have encouraged those witnesses to perjure themselves. Or maybe she was just like him. She didn't want to believe he might be telling the truth because then she would have to admit she had been wrong—about him, about people she'd once thought were her friends.

About everything...

Like maybe what she was beginning to feel for Ronan wasn't just sex. Maybe there was something more between them than just attraction. Too scared to stay, she headed for the door the moment she was fully dressed again.

This time he didn't stop her. He was too focused on that file again, as if he'd forgotten all about her.

That was what she needed to do: forget all about Ronan. They had no future. And because of their past, they never should have been together. She shouldn't have let him touch her. Now she was worried that his touch was the only one she would want. She should have stuck with the vibrator. She didn't have to worry about her mechanical lover betraying her like every other lover had.

Ronan had betrayed her even before he'd become her lover. She would never be able to trust him.

CHAPTER TEN

THE FIRST TIME he'd met with this man Ronan had felt pity. The guy had been so broken, so upset that his new bride had played him for a fool. And Ronan had been determined to avenge the man, like he'd wanted to avenge his father for all the pain he'd suffered.

But Arte Armand and Muriel hadn't been married very long. How much could he have actually suffered?

Ronan hadn't known her very long, either, though, and he was suffering. His body was tense and aching for hers. And it had only been a couple of days since she'd come here and given him that envelope with her name smeared across the front of it. Had someone given her the memos in that envelope? Or had something else been in it and she was just claiming that it had held those forged memos?

He didn't know what to believe anymore. That was why he'd asked Arte Armand to come to the office. They sat back by the bar where Ronan had had sex with the man's ex. Arte sat across from him, his legs crossed. Ronan could almost smell Muriel—in the office.

A twinge of guilt struck him.

But Arte didn't look as broken as he had the day of their first appointment. His eyes were dry and bright now. His face was tanned, his body relaxed. He wore jeans that were as artfully ripped up as Muriel's had been and a bright pink silk shirt with the cuffs rolled back to reveal the black and white polka dots on the other side of the fabric.

"I'm glad you called," the man said. "I was going to set up an appointment to talk to you, anyway."

"You were?" Had the guy gotten married again? Only a little over six months had passed since his divorce had been granted. That was enough time to get into a serious relationship. But to get married again…

Why would he risk it if his marriage to Muriel had been as terrible as he'd claimed?

"Yes, but I've been busy with the musical I've been producing."

With Muriel's money. And Ronan felt another twinge of guilt—this time for her.

"Really?" Ronan asked. "I didn't know you were interested in theater."

Arte laughed. "Oh, goodness, yes, that's why I moved to the city. I'm a triple threat. I can sing and dance and act."

How good an actor was he? So good that he'd fooled Ronan?

"But you were modeling."

Arte grinned, revealing perfect blindingly white teeth. "It was easier to break into modeling than acting. But I've found exactly the right vehicle now to launch my career."

Muriel. She had been the vehicle. And Ronan had given him the keys.

"I can't help you with entertainment law," Ronan said. "I'm strictly a divorce lawyer."

"Oh, that's not why I wanted to see you again," Arte replied. "It's about this whole The World's Most Beautiful Woman thing."

Muriel. She was not a thing. Ronan clenched his jaw to hold back his remarks.

"That's because of us," Arte continued. "So shouldn't we get a part of it?"

"I don't want the title," Ronan said. But he was beginning to wonder about Arte Armand.

His hair was expertly styled, the tresses highlighted in gold. The same color that was Simon's natural hue.

Arte laughed again, and it was nearly as high-pitched as a giggle. "Of course not."

"Then what do you want?" Ronan asked.

"Money," Arte replied, as if it should have been obvious.

And it should have been—from their first meeting—that that was what he was all about. Money.

"I think she should give me a percentage of what she's making now," Arte said, "since we made her so famous."

We. Ronan flinched, and his stomach pitched with

queasiness from guilt. He wanted to shout at the man to stop saying that—stop giving him so damn much credit for what they'd done to Muriel.

"You weren't married long enough to be awarded alimony," Ronan reminded him.

"But you got me a great settlement."

"Yes, I did." Far more than what Ronan now realized the man had deserved. "And you agreed to that settlement, so you can't go after any more."

"But Muriel would still only be a face and a body with no one knowing her name if it hadn't been for us," Arte persisted. "That should get us something, some percentage of her earnings."

It wasn't Ronan or the PR firm that Muriel should have worried would send her a bill. It was her damn ex.

"It got me a complaint to the bar association," Ronan said. "That's why I called you."

"Complaint?" Arte asked, and he tensed now.

"Yes, Muriel claims I suborned perjury," he said. "She thinks I coerced all those witnesses to lie."

Arte laughed again, but this time it sounded hollow with nerves. "Don't worry about it. She can't prove anything."

"There's nothing to prove, right?" Ronan asked. "I believed those people were all speaking the truth."

"They were—of course they were."

"The same truth, nearly line for line," Ronan murmured. "As if they'd rehearsed it…" Why hadn't he noticed that before? Why hadn't he questioned them—and Arte Armand—more?

Maybe it was what they'd said about her cheating, about her orgies, that had distracted him from reality and plunged him into the fantasy of a naked Muriel Sanz, insatiable for sex.

Arte shrugged his thin shoulders. "They all saw the same things," he said. "So, of course, they're going to describe them the exact same way."

Now Ronan knew who'd written the script.

"If they were lying, I could lose my license," he said.

Arte reached out and squeezed his arm. "Don't worry. You had no idea."

"That they were lying?" He needed to know. But if Arte admitted to what he'd done, Ronan would probably be tempted to tear him apart. Even now, his hands were clenching into fists.

"No, no, of course not," Arte stammered. "I don't know why she's so upset, anyway. It's not like the trial hurt her or her career…"

That was the argument that Ronan kept giving her, too. But he heard how self-serving it sounded now. "She is upset," Ronan said. And he was beginning to understand why.

Arte uttered a regretful sigh. "Because of her grandparents…"

"What?"

"They raised her after her mom flaked out and ran off," Arte said. "They're real sweet, real conservative people. They must have been devastated."

Over what had come out of the trial, over what

Ronan, using McCann Public Relations, had put out there for them to see and hear. He flinched.

Arte sighed again but straightened in his chair. "But they know her, so it's not like they believed…" He pressed his hand to his mouth, as if trying to push the words back in.

"It's not like they believed the lies?" Ronan prodded him.

Arte shook his head. "No, no, not the lies. The truth," he stammered some more. "They wouldn't believe the truth about her. They would only see the best in her."

"That she's straightforward and honest," Ronan said.

And Arte turned toward him, his brow furrowed. "You believe that about her?"

"That's what one of her true friends has said about her," Ronan replied.

"Too bad she hadn't had that person testify," Arte said.

Too bad…

Her representation had been bad. But, ultimately, she'd agreed to the settlement once Ronan had had the prenup tossed out. So she was stuck with it now.

At least she wasn't stuck with Arte Armand any longer.

The slighter man stood. "I wouldn't worry about her complaint," Arte said. "You're a good lawyer."

Ronan had believed that until now. Now he wasn't certain how good he was.

"I'm sure you can get out of it," Arte said. "Are you sure you can't get anything more—"

"No!" Ronan snapped as he jumped up from his chair. He wanted to slug the guy so badly, but he held his fists at his sides. "I think she's lost enough already."

Her money and her reputation. And maybe the respect of the grandparents she loved.

Ronan understood now why she was so angry. And he didn't blame her. He was lucky all she'd done was turn him into the bar association. If he'd been in her place, he might have done far worse—like he wanted to do now to Arte Armand.

A knock sounded at his office door before it was pushed open and a blond head appeared around it. "Hey, oh, sorry to interrupt," Simon said. "We were waiting for you to start the meeting. I didn't realize you were with a client."

"We're finished," Ronan said. For now…

He wasn't entirely sure that he was done with Arte Armand, though. Not after what the man had done— and had made Ronan do—to Muriel.

The guy eagerly walked toward the door, as if anxious to escape Ronan. Maybe he'd sensed how close he'd come to getting the crap beat out of him. Or maybe he was just anxious to get a closer look at Simon, because it was obvious he was checking out Ronan's partner.

How the hell had Ronan missed that?

How had Muriel? She couldn't have known or she wouldn't have married the man.

As Arte headed toward the elevator, Ronan walked into Simon's office and dropped heavily into one of the chairs around the conference table.

"What's wrong with you?" Trev asked.

Ronan closed his eyes and shook his head. He couldn't even talk about what he had just learned, how big a fool he had been.

"Arte Armand just left his office," Simon answered for him.

"And you realized the guy's a sleaze?" Stone asked with a shudder of disgust.

"Do you know the guy?" Ronan asked, since his partner had made comments before. What worried him about that was that Stone was a criminal lawyer.

Stone shook his head. "I met him in the elevator a couple of times when you were representing him."

"So you didn't represent him?" Ronan asked.

Stone shook his head again. "He's a sleaze but as far as I know, not a criminal."

"He's a con," Simon said from where he sat at the head of the table. "The guy's a con artist."

Ronan sucked in a breath at the managing partner speaking his worst fear aloud. "Are you sure?" he asked.

"Takes one to know one," Simon said. He had been a con artist himself. If he hadn't, they all wouldn't have survived the streets. His cons had kept them alive and fed.

Ronan sighed.

"What does this mean?" Trevor asked.

"I think I could be in real trouble," Ronan said.

"Those witnesses lied. If the bar association finds out, they might not believe that I didn't know, that I didn't suborn perjury."

"So you might lose your license," Stone murmured.

Losing his license was the least of his concerns at the moment. He was afraid he'd lost more than that, like his chance of ever being with Muriel again.

Her body tense, Muriel followed the man as he led her down a long corridor. She was stiff and achy. Maybe she should have used her vibrator before this meeting. But she doubted that it would relieve her tension anymore. She was beginning to worry that only Ronan could do that.

And that was why she was here.

"I'm surprised you would want to hire McCann Public Relations," the man murmured over his shoulder, his voice pitched low.

Obviously, he knew Muriel and what his company and Ronan had done to her. Because of that, she wasn't here to hire them. Hell, she didn't need them. Not since she'd been labeled The World's Most Beautiful Woman.

No. What Muriel needed was answers.

She hadn't gotten any from Ronan. So she hoped she could get them here. From Allison McCann. The man stopped at the end of the hall and pushed open a door to a corner office. Sunshine poured through the two walls of windows and glowed like a spotlight on the woman behind the desk.

Allison McCann, with her deep red hair, silky white skin and bright blue eyes, deserved the label of The World's Most Beautiful Woman far more than Muriel felt she did. But Allison McCann always remained in the background.

Muriel wasn't sure how she managed that until the woman spoke, her voice so cool it bordered on frigid. "Ms. Sanz, please come in and have a seat." She gestured toward the chairs in front of her glass desk. "Edward, close the door on your way out."

As the man turned to do his employer's bidding, Muriel caught the look that crossed his face. And she shivered. His boss's voice wasn't the only cold thing in this office.

The door snapped shut with a sharp click, and Muriel jumped. She hesitated a moment before walking toward that desk and that woman.

"I'm sorry..." the woman murmured.

"I didn't come here for an apology," Muriel said. She wouldn't have expected this woman to offer one any more than she expected Ronan to do so.

"I meant for Edward..." Allison gestured at the closed door. "So, if you didn't come here for an apology, why are you here, Ms. Sanz? Are you in need of our services?" She sounded politely hopeful—not pushy.

All the PR people Muriel had met were pushy. She was almost pleasantly surprised, until she remembered what this woman had done to her.

"Why?" Muriel asked. That was what she wanted to know the most.

The woman's lips curved into a slight smile. "That is a fair question, given that you are already extremely high profile right now. But, of course, that is the best time to hire McCann Public Relations, so that we can help guide your career in the direction in which you'd like to go. Please have a seat and tell me where that might be."

Muriel hadn't realized she was still standing. But she was too tense, too anxious, to sit. She walked toward the windows, instead, and stared down at Midtown. Allison had a view of a park from her corner office.

"Do you want to cross over into acting?" Allison asked.

"No," Muriel replied. "I'm no actor." She was too honest for that. Arte was the one who'd wanted to act and dance and sing.

"Singer?" Allison asked.

Muriel laughed. "God, no." She held up a hand. "And before you ask, I'm not a dancer, either." She had no rhythm—except with Ronan. With him, she always found the perfect rhythm—their movements coordinated to drive each other out of their minds and to ecstasy.

"So you're happy with your modeling career?"

Muriel turned back to study Allison's face. Did she detect some condescension? Some judgment? "Yes, I'm happy being a model."

"Why?" Allison asked.

That was the question Muriel wanted the publicist to answer. But she answered Allison McCann first. "I admire the creativity of the designers. I enjoy showing off their hard work." Especially Bette's. She knew how long and how hard Bette had worked to achieve her recent success.

Allison tilted her head and studied Muriel, as if trying to gauge if she spoke the truth. "I could use that quote to get you a lot more work," Allison said. "Designers would love hearing that."

Muriel laughed. "You're always working the angles, huh?"

"Is that a problem?"

"It is when you smear innocent people."

Allison jumped up from her chair now. "If you made this appointment in order to attack me, then you should leave right now."

"If I'd wanted to attack you," Muriel said, "I wouldn't have made an appointment. I would have done it someplace public and embarrassing, like your favorite restaurant or on the street outside. I would have wanted to embarrass you like you embarrassed me."

Allison's pale skin flushed, but it wasn't with embarrassment. It was anger. "I was just doing my job, Ms. Sanz," she said defensively. "You should not be taking this personally or making it personal."

"It was personal to me," Muriel said, flinching as she remembered having to warn her grandparents. Well, she'd tried. But she'd been too late. The story had already broken before she'd had the chance.

Allison shook her head. "Is that why you filed a

complaint with the bar association against Ronan Hall? Out of spite?"

Muriel snorted. "Spite? I am not a child."

"You're acting like one," Allison accused her. "Lashing out…"

She was tempted to show this bitch exactly what acting out looked like, but she held her temper. Physically. Verbally she let the other woman have it. "I could sue you for defamation of character," she threatened. "Those witnesses were lying. I have proof of it."

"Forged memos," Allison said with a disdainful sniff.

"That's what Ronan claims," Muriel said. And she was beginning to believe him. "So you've talked to him."

"I work closely with all of the partners of Street Legal," Allison said.

How closely? And did she just work with them? Or was it more than work?

"I know," Muriel said. "That's why I'm here. I want to know whose idea it was to publicly smear me. Yours or Ronan's?" She wanted to cross her fingers in the hope that Allison would take the responsibility. That she would say that Ronan fought her over every press release.

But Allison said nothing. She just sat back down and shook her head.

"I deserve the truth," Muriel said. "Not that I expect you to recognize it."

Allison leaned back in her chair, and her beautiful

face twisted into a tight grimace, like she'd sucked on a particularly sour lemon. "You wasted your time coming here," she said. "Unless slinging your insults will make you feel better...since all your recent success obviously hasn't."

"So you're of the same school of thought as Ronan," Muriel said. "That the end justifies the means."

Allison just tilted her head and studied Muriel through those icy blue eyes of hers.

"It doesn't," Muriel told her. "Not when the means were so mean..." Tears stung her eyes now, and she rushed toward the door. When she opened it, she slammed into the body standing outside it.

And she nearly plowed over Allison McCann's assistant who'd obviously been listening at the door. "If I'd known why you were here," he whispered as he led her through the reception area toward the elevators, "I could have told you that you were wasting your time."

"I should have known I wouldn't get any answers here," Muriel agreed as she blinked back her tears of frustration.

It was Ronan's fault that she was so damn frustrated. She wanted him so badly. But she didn't want him if he was really the man she'd originally thought he was—the liar, the ruthless lawyer.

Who was he?

"You should have asked me," Edward said as he led her toward the elevator.

Muriel stopped. "You know?"

"I sit in on all of Allison's meetings," he said, "except for this one."

Apparently he was the one to whom Muriel should have spoken. Maybe that was why Allison hadn't allowed him to sit in.

The elevator dinged and the doors slid open to the empty car. Before she stepped inside, Muriel turned to him and asked, "So whose idea was it to smear me?"

"Ronan Hall," the man replied.

And Muriel felt as though she'd been punched in the stomach.

"Allison really felt horrible about it," Edward continued. "But she has to honor her client's wishes."

"And Street Legal is her client," Muriel said. Not her.

She'd just been a hapless victim.

"It was Hall's idea," Edward continued. "He's the worst one of those bastards from Street Legal."

"Are they a pretty big client for McCann PR?" she asked.

"The biggest," Edward said with a regretful sigh. "And the most ruthless."

So Allison McCann would probably not help Muriel out with the bar association—even if she knew for certain that Ronan had suborned perjury. And Muriel didn't know for certain. She'd begun to believe him.

But now she wondered if she'd been played—exactly the way he'd bragged to his partners that he would play her into withdrawing her complaint.

Edward continued, "That's why she had to do what Hall wanted. I'm sorry for what happened to you."

Before stepping into the elevator, she squeezed his arm in gratitude. His apology was nice, but it wasn't the one she wanted.

The person who owed her the apology was Ronan.

CHAPTER ELEVEN

RONAN NEVER SAW it coming. Muriel's apartment door barely opened before two hands planted on his chest and shoved him back.

"You son of a bitch!" Muriel yelled at him.

"I guess I had that coming…" he murmured. But she didn't even know about his mother—about how big a bitch the woman had been.

"Yes, you did!" Muriel said, her voice shaking with anger. Then her green eyes widened with surprise as she stared at him. "You admit that you do?"

What did she know? That he'd talked to Arte? He wouldn't put it past the little bastard to have approached her and directly asked for money. No. He probably wouldn't be that direct. He'd be sneaky and underhanded. Like Simon had said, Arte was a con artist.

"What exactly are we talking about?" he asked.

She pushed him again. But she wasn't strong enough to hold him back. He stepped inside the apartment and kicked the door closed behind them.

"What?" she asked. "Are you afraid that someone might overhear us? Are you afraid of making a scene?"

He laughed. "I don't care what people think."

"Yeah, right," she scoffed. "You don't want the bar association thinking you did anything wrong."

"I didn't," he said.

But he was beginning to believe that he had. Even if it was unknowingly.

"I talked to Allison McCann," she said.

"That bitch!" Outrage coursed through him. "She gave you a bill?"

Muriel laughed. "No. She thought I was going to hire her, though." And she laughed again until a snort slipped out. Then she tensed.

And he laughed.

"She is a bitch," Muriel said. "But she's a bitch who's loyal to Street Legal. She wouldn't tell me who ordered the smear campaign."

His stomach churned with the guilt swirling through it. "I did."

"I know," she said. "Edward told me."

"Who's Edward?"

"The bitch's bitch."

He laughed as he realized she was referring to Allison's assistant.

"Why did you do that?" she asked. "Why did you have to smear me in the press, too?" Hurt darkened her green eyes. "Wasn't it enough to beat me in court? You won. Why did you have to win that badly?"

Tears streamed from her eyes, but she squeezed

them shut. Then she turned away from him as if she was embarrassed that she was crying.

He wanted to reach for her, to comfort her. Her tears were killing him. But he knew he couldn't take back what was already done. He owed her something, though.

Maybe it was because she turned away that he was able to tell her the truth. Not about talking to Arte.

He wasn't ready yet to admit how wrong he'd been. But he could explain why he'd been wrong.

"I did it for my dad," he said.

She turned back then, her brow furrowed in obvious confusion. "What? That makes no sense…"

"I take every divorce case for my dad," he said. "Because he should have divorced my mom. But he could never bring himself to do it—no matter how badly she treated him, how many times she cheated on him."

"Ronan…" She touched him, just her fingers on his arm.

But his skin tingled with the contact and he shivered in reaction. Or maybe he was just suddenly very cold as he relived some of those moments from his past.

"They fought all the time," he said.

"That must have been horrible," she remarked, her voice soft with sympathy.

He wasn't looking for sympathy. He just wanted her to understand. "It was…so bad that I ran away. That's how I met Simon and Stone and Trevor."

"On the streets…"

She must have heard the story. Allison McCann had put out several press releases touting the rags-to-riches story of the lawyers of Street Legal.

"So all the stories about you and your partners were true?" she asked.

He nodded. "Yeah."

"It must have been rough."

He chuckled, but with a bitterness he'd never been able to leave entirely behind him. "Living on the streets was safer and easier than living at home."

"Are your parents still together?"

He shrugged. "I don't know. My father and I don't talk about it anymore." But they talked once a week—about the weather, sports, the practice… anything but his parents' marriage. That was the arrangement he'd made with his father—once he'd contacted him again. "And I want nothing to do with my mother."

"I am not your mother," Muriel said. "I didn't cheat on Arte."

"I know that now," he said. "I'm sorry."

But he knew an apology was not enough to make up for what he'd done to her. He wasn't sure what it would take for her to forgive him. Moreover, he wasn't sure what it would take for him to forgive himself.

Muriel watched Ronan turn away from her and head for the door. He was just going to walk away?

"Coward!" she called after him.

He stopped and glanced back at her over one of his broad shoulders. "What?"

"You're running away again, just like you did when you were a teenager," she said.

His lips curved into a slight grin and amusement glinted in his dark eyes. "You think I'm running from you?"

"Maybe…"

Or he was running away from what he'd done.

Or from what he'd admitted to her about his past.

"I didn't think you wanted me to stay," he said.

"I shouldn't have lost my temper like that," she said.

"You're a passionate woman." His dark eyes gleamed with passion of his own.

And Muriel's heart began to pound fast and furiously. Even as angry as she was with him, she had missed him. Badly. Her body ached with an emptiness only he had been able to fill.

He stepped closer to her. "You're the most passionate woman I've ever known."

"Is that a nice way of calling me a slut again?" she asked as she tried desperately to hang on to her anger. It was safer to be mad *at* Ronan than to be mad *about* him.

He chuckled. "I never called you a slut."

"Liar."

"I just let other people call you that," he said, and his handsome face twisted into a grimace of regret. "I'm sorry about that."

"You believe me now?" she asked.

He opened his mouth, but the words didn't come. He wasn't any more sure of her than she was of him.

But did it matter right now?

She wanted him too much to care about the past. Neither of them could change that. It had already happened.

She wasn't worried about it happening again. She wasn't married now. She probably wouldn't get married again. Obviously, she couldn't trust her judgment.

And because she couldn't trust her judgment, she wasn't ever going to risk her heart again. So she was safe having sex with Ronan—because sex was all it would ever be.

She also wanted a little revenge, though, for all the terrible things he'd had McCann Public Relations spread around about her.

"Muriel," he began.

But she pressed her fingers to his lips to stop him. "Shh…" she said. "Don't say anything you don't one hundred percent believe."

He closed his mouth.

And regret tugged at her. But after what he'd told her about his mother, she shouldn't have been surprised that he would find it hard to believe her—especially when so many people, people she'd thought were her friends—had testified against her.

He touched her chin, tipping it up. She hadn't even realized she'd bowed her head.

"I'm sorry," he murmured again.

She shrugged. "I don't believe you one hundred percent, either."

After Arte and those people she'd thought were her friends had betrayed her, she couldn't trust anyone, least of all the divorce lawyer who'd represented her ex.

He flinched but said, "I understand."

"But tonight, it doesn't matter what's truth or fiction," she said. "Tonight, nothing matters but pleasure…"

"I'll give you pleasure," he promised as he lowered his head and brushed his mouth across hers. His lips clung, nibbled, and his breath panted out between them.

It had been too long since he'd kissed her. It had only been days but it felt like years. Long years.

And she knew in this he spoke the truth. He would give her pleasure. But that wasn't all she wanted tonight. She stepped back, away from his kiss.

He opened his eyes and stared down at her, his jaw tense, as if he was worried she had changed her mind. So she reached for his hand and tugged him along with her toward her open bedroom door.

And he chuckled. "So you're going to take me up on my offer?"

She wouldn't have been able to refuse. "I have one of my own," she told him as she dropped her hand and walked over to her closet. "Let me show you a really good time."

"Did Bette design something new for you?" he

asked, and he almost sounded like a kid asking if Santa Claus had delivered presents.

"Bette's always designing something new," Muriel said—with surprise that her friend could think of so many things to do with bows. "I guess she's been particularly inspired lately." Thanks to his friend.

"Lucky for me," he murmured.

"Not tonight," she said. "Lingerie isn't what I have in mind." She pulled out the sashes of a couple of bathrobes and grabbed a couple of scarves. "This is what I had in mind…"

His dark eyes narrowed, and his grin slid slightly away from his handsome face. "What do you want to do with those?"

"Tie you up, of course…"

He laughed, but it wasn't with amusement now. "And what? Take pictures of me lying there naked and helpless to sell to some tabloid? Or will you just leave me here?"

If he was naked and helpless, she doubted she would be able to leave him.

She shook her head. "I want to tie you up so that you can't touch me. Only I can touch you. Only I can please you."

He stepped closer to her and pulled the makeshift bindings from her hand. "This is about control," he said. "And you know it."

Heat rushed to her face as she remembered how smart he was. Of course he would know that she wanted to be in control and she wanted to take his.

That was going to be her revenge for what he'd

done to her—to drive him out of his mind. But maybe she didn't need to tie him up in order to do that.

He'd driven her out of her mind every time they'd had sex, and he had never once restrained her.

But she tugged on the ties he held now and murmured, "Ronan, please..." as she stared up at him through fluttering lashes.

He chuckled and murmured back, "No..." He bunched the ties into a ball, which he threw out into the hallway. Then he kicked the door closed, as if he didn't trust her not to try to use them on him.

"You really don't want me to tie you up," she said.

"I really want to touch you," he told her. And then he proceeded to do just that as he reached for her shirt and lifted it over her head. After he tossed it aside, her hair swirled back down around her bare shoulders.

She had skipped the bra entirely tonight. "Sorry—no Bette's Beguiling Bows..."

His hands were already cupping her breasts. "I don't mind. If I'd known you were braless..."

"What?" she asked.

He leaned down and brushed his lips across one nipple. Then he replied, "I would have done this sooner." And he licked the other one.

She shivered as pleasure coursed through her. She wanted him so badly.

"Aren't you glad you didn't tie me up?" he asked as he moved his hands to the waistband of her yoga pants. After pushing down the knit material, he stroked his fingers over her bare ass. She'd skipped the underwear, too, tonight. "I can give you much more pleasure when I can touch you."

But when he touched her she lost control—and she was losing it now.

Her legs trembled, her pulse raced. She was one more lick or stroke away from an orgasm already. That was how quickly and powerfully he affected her.

And she wanted to do the same to him.

So she reached for him. He must have come to her right from work or court because he wore a suit and tie again. She loosened the tie first and pulled it free from the collar of his crisp white shirt. As she pulled the expensive blue silk through her hands, she stared up at him.

"Don't get any ideas," he warned her, but there was a chuckle in his voice and a glint in his dark eyes. He pulled the tie from her hands and tossed it aside. He definitely did not trust her yet.

So she went to work on his buttons, revealing all the sexy, hair-dusted muscles of his impressive chest. Then she pushed the shirt and his dark gray jacket from his broad shoulders and reached for his belt. He pulled that from her hands, too, though, and undid his own button and zipper before kicking off his pants, boxers and shoes.

Then he was as gloriously naked as she was. And she went wild for him, touching and kissing him everywhere. She stroked her hands over his ass and down his hard thighs as she dropped to her knees in front of him. Then she closed her lips around his cock and sucked him deep into her throat.

He groaned. And she could feel him shaking.

She hadn't needed to tie him up. She could make him lose control without any ropes or bindings.

But he didn't lose it entirely. He pulled her away before she could make him come. Then he lifted and tossed her down onto her bed. She bounced slightly up from the mattress and met his chest as his body covered hers.

They were a tangle of arms and legs, but their mouths met and mated, kissing each other deeply. His tongue stroked over hers as his fingers slid inside her. He moved his fingers in and out of her until she arched up and whimpered at the orgasm shuddering through her.

But it was nothing compared to the pleasure she knew he could give her. He pulled back—only to don a condom—and then the head of his cock eased inside her. He lifted her legs to his shoulders, so he sank even deeper into her.

He filled her and then some.

She reached between them and tried to stroke him. But he caught her hand and held her back.

"This is why I needed to tie you up," she mused.

"Then it would have been over already," he said. "And you would have missed all this fun."

She wasn't sure if it was fun or torture. He teased the tension back into her body, teased her to the edge of an orgasm before he pulled out.

She clutched his butt and pushed him back inside her. Then she used her hands to guide his hips.

But he moved again and took her with him as he rolled onto his back. And suddenly she was astride him.

He'd given her the control she'd wanted. And she used it to tease him like he'd teased her, sliding up until his cock nearly came out, then settling back down hard. Up and down…

He groaned and thrashed on the mattress before his hands clutched her hips. He didn't need to guide her.

Muriel knew the rhythm. With him, she could dance. Together they moved as one until she tensed. Her inner muscles convulsed, her body shuddered, and she screamed his name as an orgasm gripped her.

He was with her, his hands biting into her hips as his body tensed. He shuddered and came, too.

Muriel eased off and dropped onto the mattress on her back, boneless and exhausted. She had needed that. She'd needed him. Completed satiated, she closed her eyes.

But he was already getting out of the bed. She figured he was just cleaning up. But it wasn't the bathroom door she heard opening and closing. It was the front door as he left.

Just as she'd accused him earlier, he was running away. From her? Or from what he felt when they were together?

Muriel wanted to run from those feelings, too. But she wasn't sure she had any muscles left—she was so loose and relaxed—except for the mad pounding of her heart. She was afraid that she was falling for Ronan.

It didn't matter what she felt, though, because Ronan wasn't ever going to let himself feel anything but fear for a relationship. She was going to wind up just like all those other women he'd dated, dumped and left wanting more.

But she realized now, that because of his past, he wasn't capable of giving any more.

CHAPTER TWELVE

RONAN'S HAND SHOOK as he lifted the glass of water to his mouth. "I should have had you guys meet me at the bar," he said. He could have used a stiff drink, instead. But he'd called the meeting in Simon's office, and they all sat around the conference table they used every Tuesday morning for their business meetings.

But it wasn't Tuesday morning.

And this wasn't about business as usual. Of course, ever since he'd been reported to the bar association, it hadn't been business as usual, at least, not for him.

"Do you want a drink?" Simon asked as he stood up and moved toward the bar in the back of his office.

It was Saturday night. Simon should have been with Bette. It was Ronan's fault he wasn't. As if Bette didn't already hate him enough, now she would have another reason. But she wasn't the only one who hated Ronan. Muriel did. And he wasn't too crazy about himself right now, either.

"Pour me a drink," Stone requested. "The trial starts next week."

"Are you ready for it?" Trevor asked him.

"Of course," Stone replied. "I'm just a little worried that I might have some surprises. Like Ronan has."

Ronan had had too many surprises lately.

"Any leads on the mole yet?" Trevor asked Simon.

The managing partner shook his head. "Nothing. I can't figure out who it could be."

And that wasn't good. Simon was the best judge of character of all of them. If he'd been tricked, this mole was good. Very good.

It hadn't taken much to trick Ronan. He'd fallen easily for Arte's bunch of lies. "That's why I called this meeting," he said.

"You know who the mole is?" Simon asked in surprise. Then he sighed. "Don't tell me Muriel Sanz. She doesn't have access to our office."

She'd walked right in one weekend, but Ronan didn't bother sharing that. He didn't believe it was Muriel, either. "I don't know who the mole is, but I'm worried about the practice," he said.

"Why are you worried?" Simon asked.

"I think I'm going to get disbarred," he admitted, and his stomach clenched then sank with the admission.

"You didn't know those witnesses were lying," Stone said. "That'll come out during the investigation of the complaint. You'll be fine."

"Street Legal will be fine," Simon added. Because he was such a good judge of character, he knew that Ronan wasn't worried just about himself.

He wasn't worried just about the practice, either. "I really screwed up," he said.

"The guy's a con artist," Simon reminded him.

He shrugged. "But I took it further than I had to. I used McCann to smear the hell out of Muriel."

Because he'd thought she was like his mother, and he must have subconsciously and childishly been using Muriel to get back at the woman who'd destroyed his father.

"I need to have McCann put out more press releases with the truth about Muriel," he said. It was only fair to undo the damage he'd done.

"Then the bar will think you knew those witnesses were lying," Stone said. "You need to keep your mouth shut and let this play out."

"And keep your zipper up, too," Trevor advised. "It doesn't sound like your plan to seduce her into dropping the complaint worked. Sounds like she seduced you, instead."

She had. He couldn't deny that. But it had made him discover the truth. "I screwed up," he repeated. "And I need to fix it."

"You can," Stone said. "But wait until the complaint has been withdrawn."

"She's not going to withdraw it," Ronan said. And he didn't blame her for not believing him enough to do that. After what he'd done, he would never be able to earn her trust. He, more than anyone, understood how hard it was to trust at all—let alone to trust someone who had already hurt you.

Regret filled him. He was so sorry that he'd hurt her. But sorry wasn't enough.

"So we need to make it go away," Simon said.

And Ronan had an idea about how to do that. "I've got a plan."

"Your last one didn't work," Trevor reminded him. "You should have let *me* seduce her into dropping the complaint. Are you willing to let me try now?"

"No!" Ronan snapped with such force that Stone grabbed his arm, as if he was afraid that Ronan might leap across the table and go for Trevor's throat. He was tempted. But he relaxed back in his chair. "Simon has to do this."

"No," Simon snapped now. "She's Bette's friend. And I'm not cheating on Bette."

"Have her join in," Trevor suggested with a lustful sigh. "That would be fun."

Simon cursed him.

"Two women too much for you to handle?" Trevor teased.

"I can barely handle one," Simon freely admitted.

"This has nothing to do with women," Ronan said. "I want Simon to seduce a man."

"What?" All three of his partners uttered the question.

"Muriel's ex," Ronan said. "He checked you out the other day. I think you could get him talking."

"He's gay?" Trevor asked, his mouth hanging open in shock. "And he was married to The World's Most Beautiful Woman?"

Simon sighed and just murmured, "Con."

"Yes, he is," Ronan said. "And if we can get him to admit that he asked those witnesses to testify and coached them on what to say, I think the bar would throw out the complaint against me."

"I am not going to seduce a man," Simon said.

"You don't have to seduce him," Ronan said. "Just con him."

Simon's blue eyes narrowed.

So Ronan goaded him, "Unless you've lost your touch and aren't up to the task anymore."

Simon cursed him now, but he was grinning. Then he asked, "This isn't just about saving your license or the practice, is it?"

"Of course it is," Ronan said. "What else could it be about?"

"Muriel," Simon replied. "You're falling for her."

Ronan shook his head as panic clutched his heart. That was why he'd run from her apartment the night before—because of the emotions that had rushed through him. He'd wanted to stay; he'd wanted to hold her all night. He'd wanted to wake up and have her face be the first he saw. But it was, anyway; she was forever on his mind.

"No," he said and wished that he sounded as if he meant it. "I am not falling for anyone. I just want to right a wrong." And once that was done, he would forget all about Muriel Sanz. That was the problem. He had to clear his conscience. Then he would be able to get her off his mind and out of his…

Heart?

No. She wasn't in there. No woman had ever been in there.

"I just need for this to be over," he said. And for his life to get back to normal, to picking up women in bars for one-night stands while he focused only on work.

For some reason, normal sounded empty and hollow now.

Muriel's pulse quickened when the doorbell pealed. Had Ronan returned?

She hoped like hell that he had. As wonderful as the night before had been, it had ended too soon. He'd run off too quickly. If he'd stayed…

Hell, if he'd stayed, she would have started getting used to his being around. She would have started envisioning a future with him. And that wasn't possible for so many reasons.

No. It was better that he'd run off. And if she was smart, she wouldn't open the door to him. But she wanted him again—still—so she pulled it open without even looking through the peephole.

But she should have, because if she had, she would have never opened the door. Not to Arte Armand. That was one man she was never allowing back into her life.

Hell.

But she was so shocked that he'd have the guts to come and see her, that she could say nothing. And apparently, her silence unsettled him because he began to nervously stammer, "Mur-Muriel, I—I know that after everything that happened, you probably don't want to see me."

If he was waiting for her to argue, she couldn't. "No. I don't want to see you." Because now she couldn't see what she once had—the sweet, funny man she'd thought she loved.

She could only see the lying weasel he had become. Or maybe he had always been the lying weasel. How had she been so blind? She closed her eyes now, as just the sight of his ridiculously handsome face made her feel sick. Where Ronan's features could have been carved from granite, Arte's would have been porcelain or some other smooth, flawless material. His features were so perfect that he was more pretty than handsome. Had she been shallow? Had she fallen for his almost pretty good looks without seeing his real character?

What character? During the divorce, it had become clear that he had none.

"I didn't think you'd still be mad," he said, as his lips puckered into a petulant pout.

Was he that oblivious to how much he'd hurt her?

"What?" she asked. "How stupid do you think I am?" She had been pretty stupid to fall for Arte in the first place let alone marry him. But she'd thought the prenup would cover her assets. She hadn't realized someone like Ronan Hall would be able to get so easily around it.

"You're not stupid," Arte said. "You're very smart. You used what happened—all the media attention—to take your career to the next level. You're The World's Most Beautiful Woman."

She flinched. The title had begun to wear on her, especially since she felt she hadn't earned it—not like so many other women out there who'd made smart choices. Not someone like her, who kept going for inappropriate man after inappropriate man.

But he must not have noticed her reaction because he continued, "That just goes to prove that there is no such thing as bad publicity."

Maybe Allison McCann would be able to use that for her next ad campaign for her own business. But no matter what campaign Allison launched, she wasn't getting Muriel's business.

"I didn't need any publicity," she reminded him. Since she was fourteen, she'd always had steady work as a model. Her grandmother had worked as a seamstress for a designer who'd given Muriel her first job.

"I do," Arte said. "I'm producing that musical I always talked about."

She didn't know what he was waiting for—congratulations? She knew the only way he'd managed to produce anything was from taking so much money from her in court.

He smiled like a little boy trying to convince his mother to give him a cookie or maybe a puppy. "And I could use some publicity for it," he said, "so people will come and see it."

He'd taken some money from her but not enough

to produce anything on Broadway. So it must have been off-off.

"Is that why you're here?" she asked, as her stomach churned with disgust. "You want me to mention your play?"

"Or you could invest in it."

If anyone deserved a slap in the face, it was her ex. But he didn't inspire any passion in Muriel. Maybe he never really had. Because whatever attraction she'd once felt for him paled into insignificance compared to what she felt for Ronan.

All she could do was laugh in his face. "You're crazy if you think I would help you after what you did." And she pushed the door toward him to shove him back into the hallway.

But he caught the edge of the door and held it. "Please, Muriel."

And she saw the desperation in his eyes. Karma must have finally bitten him in the ass. He was probably on the verge of losing everything he'd taken from her.

"Why don't you go see what Ronan Hall can do for you?" she said. But she only made the suggestion because she wanted to hear what he would say about his former divorce lawyer.

"I already did," Arte admitted. "He said that the settlement was final. I can't get any more money from you." His mouth pulled into that petulant pout again. "Even though all the publicity over the trial has made you even more successful."

And he obviously wanted a cut of it, like he was her agent or something. She felt sick. Why had she not realized what a mercenary little man Arte Armand was? How had she been so fooled?

Because she always tried to see the best in people...unlike Ronan who only saw the worst. Why hadn't he seen Arte for what he was, though?

"No, you can't get anything more from me," she agreed. She would never help this slimy jerk with anything.

"He told me that you filed a complaint against him," Arte continued.

So who had called the meeting between the men? Ronan? Or Arte?

It didn't matter. All that mattered was Muriel finally learning the truth.

"I'll testify against him if you'll give me just a little more money," Arte said. "Or if you don't want to pay me, you could mention the musical in some of your interviews or on your social media."

Her fingers curled into a fist. Maybe instead of slapping him, she should just slug him. But she had to know. "What would you do?"

"I'd claim that he knew those witnesses were lying," Arte said. "That he put them up to it. Isn't that what you want? For him to lose his license?"

She shook her head. "No, Arte. What I want is the truth." But she wasn't sure that he would know what that was, even if it bit him on the ass right next to the teeth marks from karma.

He tensed, as if sensing a trap.

"I'd offer to pay you for it," she said. "But I'd still

have no idea if you were telling me the truth or just what you thought I wanted to hear."

So she wasn't going to learn anything from Arte Armand, at least, not anything she could trust.

"I'm good at that," he admitted, "telling people what they want to hear, showing them who they want to see."

She shivered as she realized she hadn't been as stupid as she'd thought she was. She had been played by a master.

And she had a feeling that Ronan had been played, as well—even before Arte confessed, "I knew about Hall's childhood—how his mother cheated on his father."

"How?"

"Social media," Arte told her with a cluck of disapproval that she didn't spend more time on it.

She had never been big on social media. She wasn't the model who took selfies and posted them all over the internet. She left the picture taking to the professionals.

"Some tabloid reporter dug up the scoop about his past," Arte said.

"And you used it?" she asked, totally disgusted that he had preyed on Ronan's past and his pain.

Arte seemed almost proud of what he'd done, though, as he nodded. "I knew he was the only lawyer who could break that prenup you had me sign. But he had to be motivated."

So Arte had motivated him.

"Why?" she asked. "That's what I don't under-

stand. I thought we were friends." They had been—
before they'd become husband and wife. They had
always been more friends than lovers. And she was
beginning to realize why.

"Things just don't happen for me like they do for
you," Arte said. "You've never had to work for anything. It just falls in your lap."

The modeling. The notoriety. Even those memos
she now realized were forged. Those had just
dropped into her lap, as well.

Maybe he was right. But she still wasn't about to
forgive him for what he'd done.

"It doesn't excuse what you did," she said.

He sighed. "No. It doesn't." He started to turn
away from the door. "I was wrong to come here."

"Yes, you were," she agreed. But she was glad
that he had—because now she knew she wasn't the
only one he'd played. He'd played Ronan, too. "But
you were right about something else."

He turned back toward her.

"There is no such thing as bad publicity," she
tossed his words back at him. "So go to the press
with your scoop."

His brow furrowed. "What scoop?"

"The truth," she said, as if it should have been
obvious. But to a man like Arte, the truth was the
last thing that was obvious to him. "Tell them what
you did to me."

"Would that make amends to you?"

"You don't care about me," she said. He never

had. "But you care about your musical. Get it some attention."

"But I'll be the bad guy," he said, clearly horrified at putting himself in the position he'd forced on her. "People will hate me."

He hadn't minded doing that to her. She grabbed one of the magazines from the narrow foyer table behind the door. Showing the cover to him, she said, "It seems like the media likes rooting for the bad guy lately."

Which was a sad commentary on life.

He took the magazine from her and studied it. But she knew he wasn't seeing her face there. He was seeing his own. He nodded. "You're right... I need to do this."

And she realized now why those witnesses had lied for him. Some people would do anything for even a few minutes of fame. Fortunately for her, in this moment Arte was one of those people.

Finally, he glanced up from the magazine to focus on her real face. "I need to do this for you, too. I am sorry, Muriel."

She doubted it, but she nodded as if she accepted his apology. Then she closed the door on his face and on her past. It was time to let it go. All of it.

Even Ronan. Especially Ronan—because he hadn't let go of his own past yet. It still affected him, still influenced him. He was never going to trust a woman or let one as close as she wanted to be to him. She didn't just want him inside her anymore.

She wanted to be inside him, as well—inside his heart. And she wasn't sure he even had one.

No. It was time to let the past go and Ronan Hall along with it.

CHAPTER THIRTEEN

RONAN STARED AT the screen on Simon's laptop as Arte Armand made a full confession on some internet talk show. "How the hell did you manage that?" he asked.

All those years ago on the streets, he'd known Simon was a good con artist. But so many years had passed since then, he'd figured he might have lost his touch. If anything, Simon had only gotten better. He was in awe and executed a little bow of appreciation and respect.

"Yeah," Trevor chimed in from the other side of the conference table. "What'd you have to do to him to convince him to come clean?"

Simon snorted. "I didn't even meet with him."

"What?" Ronan asked. "That was the plan."

"Your plan," Simon reminded him. "And there was no way it would work."

"Just like your seduction plan," Trevor goaded him.

No. That hadn't worked, either. But he didn't understand.

"Why did Arte do this?"

"Who cares?" Trevor asked. "Now you can have the complaint against you thrown out."

"He doesn't need to," Stone said. "My friend in the bar association said the complaint had already been withdrawn. They sent out a certified letter to notify you of that."

Had Muriel withdrawn it even before she learned the truth? Had she trusted him?

Why? He'd done nothing to earn it.

"This is it," Simon said, as he fiddled with his keyboard. After rewinding a bit of the video, he pushed Play again and Arte's voice cracked out of the speakers.

"I recently saw Muriel," he said.

Ronan flinched, realizing the con had probably gone to her for money. It hadn't mattered to him that Ronan had said he wasn't entitled to any more. Hell, he hadn't been entitled to what he'd already gotten out of her.

Arte continued, "And she made it clear that the only way for me to make up for what I did to her was to tell the truth."

"Wonder if she paid him," Stone murmured.

Ronan cursed at the thought of that con getting another penny out of her. "I sure as hell hope not."

"So, you were lying about your marriage?" the reporter asked Arte.

He chuckled and crossed his legs. "I've been lying about a lot of things."

"But you had witnesses at the trial that testified to the orgies."

"Never happened," Arte said.

"Why would those people lie?" the reporter persisted.

Arte sighed. "I promised them things…like parts in the musical I'm producing." And he began a self-promotion monologue that Simon quickly muted.

"And now we know why he wanted to do the interviews," Stone said. "Free publicity."

It sure as hell wasn't out of any kindness of his heart. Ronan doubted he had one.

"Doesn't matter his reasons," Trevor said. "It gets Ronan off the hook with the bar."

He squirmed slightly in his chair. He really hated sitting. "Yeah, I'm no longer in trouble with the bar, but how does it make the firm look that I was so easily duped?"

He felt like a damn fool for getting played so easily.

Simon shook his head. "You don't think anyone has ever gotten away with lying to a lawyer before this?" He snorted. "People lie all the time."

Not Muriel. She'd been telling him the truth from the very beginning. He should have listened to her. Hell, he never should have taken the case against her.

"I hope not," Stone said. "I hope my client's telling the truth."

"Why do you sound so cynical again?" Trevor asked Simon. "I thought you were all in love."

"I am," Simon freely admitted, when once he would have been embarrassed to confess his feelings—to having feelings. "And Bette would never lie to me. I was talking about clients, about this business."

And all the lawyers nodded in agreement. As they knew, the law was a far cry from black and white. There were so many shades of gray.

"I trusted Bette all along," Simon continued. "She was right about Muriel."

"She was," Ronan agreed. Muriel was as straightforward and honest as her true friend had claimed she was. He could only hope that she would be forgiving, as well.

But could she forgive what he'd done? He didn't think he could forgive himself.

The dressing room lights burned hot and bright above the mirror in front of Muriel. But despite the heat, Muriel shivered. She had been so cold lately—without Ronan's touch, without his kisses and his passion.

Did he know what she'd done? That she'd withdrawn the complaint? Or was he so furious that she'd filed it in the first place that he couldn't forgive her?

The truth was out now—all over social media—and even some of the bricks-and-mortar media outlets had reported about her divorce debacle. Arte was getting all the publicity he'd wanted.

She couldn't help but think he'd been wrong about there being no such thing as bad publicity. The public backlash had not been kind to him, threatening to shut down his musical before it even opened.

And there had even been threats of legal action,

of charges being brought against him and his friends for lying under oath.

Muriel should have felt vindication. Her apartment looked like a funeral parlor again with all the *I'm sorry* flower arrangements. Everyone had apologized to her for believing her ex's lies.

Everyone but Ronan...

She hadn't seen him in over a week—since that night he'd run from her bedroom right after they'd had sex. Maybe wanting to tie him up had scared him off.

She would have expected a man like Ronan—notorious for his sexual prowess—would have loved a little sexual play. But apparently that was only if he was in control.

Was that why he'd run out? Because he'd been afraid he was losing control...?

Was he starting to have feelings for her, too?

Or was she only fooling herself like she had with Arte? He certainly had never been really interested in her—just in her money.

She sighed and made a face at her reflection in the mirror. The shoot was over. She had nothing she needed to change into—no hair or makeup to do.

In fact, from how quiet the photo studio had become, she suspected everyone had left but her. That was good. If there were reporters waiting outside, they might have given up by now. When everyone else left, they'd probably thought she sneaked out somehow. And she should have.

But she hadn't wanted to go home to that flower

shop. She could have called Bette to meet her some-where. Or she could have gone out with some of the other models who'd invited her along to dinner and drinks.

Her stomach growled. And she regretted refus-ing their invitation. But she hadn't been very hungry lately. At least, not for food.

She was hungry for Ronan. For even just a glimpse of him.

The press had been hounding him, too, and they'd caught him outside the office of Street Legal. He'd looked so damn handsome even as he'd lowered his head and ducked into a waiting limo without com-menting to reporters.

What could he say?

That he'd been wrong?

Would a man like Ronan—a man that stubborn and proud—ever admit that he had been wrong?

She had been wrong, too, though, and she hadn't contacted him. Who was the coward now? Or maybe she was so used to things just falling in her lap, like Arte had pointed out, that she expected Ronan to do the same?

She sighed and glanced into the mirror again. And this time it wasn't her face she saw in the glass. It was his...

She met his reflection's dark-eyed gaze and asked, "What are you doing here?"

"Waiting for you to be done," he said. "Every-one else left."

"You were here for the shoot?" she asked. "I didn't

see you." And she looked for him at every one of them, hoping he'd show up like he had that once.

"I couldn't watch," he said.

She turned toward him then. "Why not?" This shoot hadn't been for Bette's Beguiling Bows. It was a perfume campaign. She had been wearing an evening gown instead of lingerie.

"I couldn't watch another man touch you," he said. A muscle twitched along his tightly clenched jaw, and he spoke through gritted teeth. "Like that model was touching you..."

She laughed at his outlandish claim. "You were jealous?" She couldn't believe that a man with Ronan's confidence would ever be jealous of another man.

Unless he still believed all those lies about her. Didn't he think Arte had finally told the truth?

"Is that what this is?" he asked, as if he had a horrible taste in his mouth. "I've never felt like this before."

"Why not?" she asked.

"Because I never cared."

It wasn't a declaration of love. But coming from Ronan , it was nearly as monumental. Muriel's heart rate quickened, and it was suddenly hard to breathe. She parted her lips to drag in some air.

And then his mouth was there, moving hungrily over hers. He kissed her as if he was consuming her, his lips and teeth nibbling at hers. He suddenly pulled back and uttered a deep groan.

"Why do you affect me like no one else ever has?" he asked her.

She could have asked him the same question, but she just smiled with the pleasure his comment gave her. Even if she followed the cardinal rule of gossip and only believed half of what she'd heard, he'd had a lot of lovers. So it was good to know that she was special to him.

"You don't have to be jealous because of me," she assured him. "Because you're the only man I want."

He tensed, and she saw that look of fear pass through his dark eyes. Instead of her words reassuring him, she'd scared him. And she remembered he was a man who would never let himself fall in love—because he didn't want to wind up like his father.

But she was not like his mother. And she wanted him to know that. "I only sleep with one man at a time," she said. "And you're the only man I want to sleep with now."

Yet they had never slept together. He always took off right after they had sex.

"Is that why you withdrew your complaint?" he asked.

She shook her head. "Sorry, you did not seduce me into that."

"Why did you do it then?" he asked.

"Because Arte told me the truth."

"And the rest of the world, too," Ronan remarked. He studied her face. "How did you get him to do that?"

She shrugged. "He must have realized it was the only publicity he was going to get."

"It's bad."

"Yes," she said. "Is it for you? Have you had any backlash?"

"The guys have called me an idiot," he said. "But it hasn't affected the practice any. In fact, I think it's brought in more clients."

"So you've been busy?" she asked. And now she was fishing to see where he'd been, why he hadn't been around. He wasn't the only one experiencing jealousy for the first time.

He nodded. "And I wasn't sure you'd want to see me after the truth finally came out. Or if you'd hit me again like you did in that first elevator…"

She laughed and reaching up, pressed her lips to his cheek. "Poor baby…"

"I had it coming," he said. "I'm sorry."

"Arte duped you—just like he did me," she said. And somehow that made her feel better about it. If a man as brilliant as Ronan had been fooled, she didn't feel like such a fool herself.

Ronan flinched. He obviously hadn't liked being conned. "There was more to it than that."

"I know." But she didn't want to talk about the past now. She'd missed him too much. And her body ached for his.

But she turned away from him, to face the mirror again. Over her shoulder, his reflection's eyes narrowed as he studied her.

"Muriel…?"

Since she'd had to give back the gown she'd worn for the photo shoot, she wore only a robe now. She'd been too lethargic—from all the sleepless nights thinking about him—that she hadn't worked up the energy to change into her street clothes. They overflowed the top of her bag, which sat on the floor beneath the long dressing room table.

Watching him in the mirror, she untied the sash of her robe and pulled it through the loops.

His mouth curved into a slight grin, and he told her, "You are not going to tie me up."

"No," she agreed. "I want you to touch me." She parted the robe and let it drop from her shoulders so that she stood naked before the mirror and him. "I want you to touch me here."

She pressed her fingers to her lips and swiped her tongue across the tips. Then she glided those wet fingertips down her throat and over the curve of one breast. She touched the already taut nipple, stroking her wet fingertip across it. And a moan slipped through her lips. "I really want you to touch me here…"

But it seemed as if he was paralyzed as he just stood behind her and watched as she touched herself.

She guided her hand over her stomach, which, thanks to him stealing her appetite away, was flatter than it had ever been. Then she raked her nails over her mound until she could slide her fingers between her inner lips. She gasped.

And Ronan echoed that gasp. A groan tore from his throat, and his paralysis ended as he reached for her. "Doesn't look like you need me," he murmured as he placed his hands on her shoulders and met her gaze in the mirror.

"Looks can be deceiving," she told him, knowing they were both well aware of that now. Then she assured him, "I do need you." And she placed her hands over his on her shoulders and guided them down to her breasts.

They watched each other in the mirror. She watched him play with her breasts, tease her nipples into even tighter points as tension wound inside her. And with every whimper and moan she uttered, his eyes got darker, his gaze more intense, and behind her she could feel the heat and hardness of his body. His erection throbbed against her bottom.

He wanted—needed—her just as badly as she did him. At least, that was what she tried to convince herself of as her desire for him slipped into madness. She tried to turn around, but he held her the way they were—her back to his front—and he continued to watch her in the mirror even as he undid his pants and freed his cock.

She could feel the slick bare skin of his dick rubbing against her ass now. Then latex separated skin from skin as he rolled on a condom.

Fortunately he seemed as staunch a supporter of safe sex as she had always been. So maybe—someday—they could try it without the condom. But that implied a commitment she wasn't sure either of them was ready to make.

Right now, all she expected from him was pleasure. And he gave that to her. Leaning over her shoul-

der, he kissed her neck. She turned her head until lips
met lips. They kissed hungrily. She was so thirsty
for him, on fire with a thirst only he could quench.

Then his hands moved to her waist and he lifted
her onto the makeup counter so she knelt with her
head toward the mirror and her ass toward him. He
moved his fingers into her before leaning over and
lapping at her with his tongue. He licked her so sex-
ily—as he watched her in the mirror—that she came.
A little squeal of surprise slipped through her lips
over how quickly the orgasm took her.

He grinned at her. But then the grin disappeared
as his control snapped. And he moved between her
legs, guiding himself inside her.

She gasped again as he filled her. Every time it
was a surprise that they fit. But they did fit, so well
that it was as if they were made for each other. And
even though days had passed since they'd had sex
last, they moved together in that perfectly choreo-
graphed dance like they'd been doing it for years.

As he thrust inside her, his hands found her
breasts again. He cupped the mounds, but they overflowed his palms. So he focused on the nipples, gently twisting and teasing them as he built the tension
inside her again.

She felt as if she might split in two—not from
his size or thrusts, but from the unbearable need for
release. He moved one hand from her breasts and
stroked his thumb over her clit.

And she came again, a scream tearing from her
throat that she couldn't stop. The release shuddered

through her with such intensity that tears streaked down her cheeks and her body shook in reaction.

Hopefully everyone had left because if they hadn't, someone would probably have called the police to report an attack. She'd sounded like she was being murdered.

Then Ronan tensed and shouted out her name as he came, leaning his head, hair slick with perspiration, against her back. He uttered a ragged sigh. "You are so damn incredible…"

She wasn't, but what happened between them was. It had started with just an attraction, one that they hadn't been able to overcome despite their anger and mistrust. And every time they came together it was more powerful than the last. The attraction wasn't dying off; it was only getting more and more intense.

Ronan must have realized it, too, because when he lifted his head from her back, she caught a glimpse of his eyes in the mirror. And she saw the fear in them.

But she didn't know if that fear was his or hers. Because she felt it, too. She was afraid that she was falling for a man who would never let himself love anyone.

She was glad he'd found her here instead of her apartment because now she was the one who wanted to run. But she wasn't sure where she could go to escape these feelings for him—feelings that were overwhelming her.

CHAPTER FOURTEEN

RONAN GLANCED AT the address Muriel had texted him on his cell. Was this right?

This small house in the Bronx was where she'd wanted him to meet her. But why?

This wasn't her place. Was it some kind of S and M sex den? She seemed to really want to tie him up. He wasn't sure if he should ring the doorbell or not. But a barking dog from within the modest house must have alerted her to his arrival because she opened the door and smiled at him.

"You came."

Standing two steps down on the stoop made him level with her beautiful face. He closed the distance between them and kissed her, and as he did, he murmured against her lips, "Not yet. But I want to come soon…inside you…"

Her face flushed and her pupils dilated, swallowing the green the way he wanted to swallow her—

"Is your friend here?" a male voice asked from within the house.

And Ronan tensed.

"Muriel, bring him in," a female voice chimed into the conversation.

And Ronan wondered if Arte and his friends had really lied about the orgies.

"Where am I?" he asked her. And why had she had him meet her here?

"Home," she said, and her smile widened.

"You bought a house?" he asked. With the money she had to be making as The World's Most Beautiful Woman, she could have easily afforded something much nicer than this.

She laughed. "No. This is my grandparents' house," she said. "Home…"

That explained why she was there. But why had she invited him? "Did you want me to meet you here?" he asked. Maybe he'd misunderstood the text. Maybe she'd just been telling him where she was because he'd asked her if she was home. He took a step down. "I can leave."

"No," she said, and she tugged him back up the stairs. "I invited you here. I wanted you to come for Sunday dinner."

His breath caught, panic pressing on his chest as he stepped over that threshold. And it wasn't just because he wasn't fond of little dogs like the one that had rushed down the hall to bounce around his feet. It was because he didn't like families.

Any families…

He'd hated his own, and he'd never seen another one he'd wanted to be part of, even the ones that had seemed perfect on the outside. Pitching his voice low, he asked, "Why would you invite me here?"

Hurt flashed through her green eyes. "I wanted you to meet them."

"You should have asked if I'd wanted to meet them," he said.

"I didn't care," she replied, and there was a sharp tone to her voice now. "I wanted you to see why I was so upset about the trial. I wanted you to understand."

And suddenly he did. He hadn't been certain if she'd forgiven him, not even though they'd had sex every day since that night in the dressing room. A couple of weeks had passed, which was a long time for him. Longer than he'd seen any other woman exclusively.

This might have been the point in a relationship where the woman introduced the man to her family. But he didn't know, because he'd never been in a relationship. And it didn't sound as if he was really in one now.

Muriel obviously hadn't forgiven him yet. Not that he could blame her.

"So this is an ambush?" he asked, keeping his voice low so her grandparents wouldn't overhear. "They have to hate me just as much as you did."

Or did she still?

"I explained to them what Arte did," she said, "how he lied to you, too."

He nodded but he wasn't convinced that was really an excuse for what he'd done to her. So he didn't expect her grandparents to be forgiving or sweet. But he didn't turn for the door and run like he wanted.

However they treated him, he deserved it. And maybe when Muriel saw how her family couldn't forgive him, she would realize that she and Ronan had no possibility of a future together.

The silence unnerved Muriel. It was the first that had fallen since she and Ronan had left Papa and Nana's house. All through dinner conversation had flowed easily. Ronan had charmed. Nana had flirted. Papa had teased.

It was the most fun Muriel had had in such a long time. And she'd thought Ronan had enjoyed himself. He'd eaten. He'd drunk. He'd laughed. He'd grinned.

But he had never looked at her.

Was he furious?

She had kind of ambushed him. But if she'd told him that address was her grandparents', he never would have showed up. So she'd tricked him.

"I'm sorry," she said. "I should have told you." She glanced at him across the console that separated the driver and passenger seats.

"You should have asked me," he corrected her. But he didn't take his gaze from the road. And his hands gripped the steering wheel tightly.

"You would have said no," she replied.

"Yes, I would have," he said. And now he glanced across at her, and there was sadness and regret in his dark eyes. "I'm not the kind of man women take home to meet their families."

Heat flushed her face. "I told you that's not why I invited you," she said. "I wanted you to see why I was so upset with you."

"Because of how all that media attention affected them."

She nodded. "They had reporters camped out on their stoop, asking them horribly intrusive questions about me, about my life and upbringing."

"Why are they the ones who raised you?" he asked. "You've never said how they came to be your legal guardians."

She'd fallen into their laps just as so much had fallen into hers. She sighed. "My mother was very young when she got pregnant with me. Just a teenager who'd fallen for an older boy. He left for the Marines, and she had me. But he didn't come back."

"I'm sorry," he said and reached across the console for her hand.

But she pulled it back. She didn't need comforting. "He didn't die," she said. "He just didn't come back to the Bronx. And when my mother realized he wasn't coming back, she wanted to leave, too. She wanted to go to college, so my grandparents said they would take care of me."

"But she never came back, either?" he asked.

"No. She moved to the West Coast. She sends cards and letters and calls sometimes. But Papa and Nana, they're my parents. The people I love the most and who love me most."

"Why did you want me to see that?" he asked. "So I would apologize again?" He had—to her grandparents—repeatedly. "I already told you I was wrong. What more do you want from me?"

His heart. She wanted his heart. But she knew it wasn't something he was going to freely offer her. It wasn't going to just land in her lap like everything else in her life had. She would have to work to earn it.

"I wanted you to see that I'm not a horrible person," she told him. "I don't go around slapping people and filing complaints and…"

"Having sex in elevators?" he asked when she trailed off. And she heard the humor in his voice now.

"No," she said. "Except for you, I've never done any of that stuff."

"I know that," he said. "Well, not the elevator stuff but the rest of it."

It hadn't hurt that her grandparents had gone on and on about what a sweet, down-to-earth person she was. But a man like Ronan wouldn't want sweet and down-to-earth. He'd want the passionate woman from the elevator.

Maybe having him meet Papa and Nana had been a huge mistake. Maybe he would never look at her the way he had before…with such lust.

She reached over the console and slid her hand over his thigh. The muscles rippled and tensed beneath her touch, and something long and hard swelled against the fly of his jeans.

"Muriel…" His voice held a warning, one she ignored as she slid her hand higher up his thigh and then over his fly. "Do you want me to crash this car?"

She didn't want to crash but she did want him

to lose control. Hell, she just wanted him. It didn't matter how much sex they had; she was always hungry for more and the pleasure only he was able to give her.

"You're a good driver," she said.

He chuckled. "You've never ridden with me before."

No. Despite the amount of time they'd spent together the past couple of weeks, they hadn't done much but sex. They hadn't gone out to dinner. They always ordered in. They hadn't seen a show or a concert. Their only entertainment had been each other.

Since she'd been hiding out from all the reporters hounding her, she had been fine with keeping things private between them. But the press wasn't bothering her nearly as much as they had.

Now they could go out in public. But instead of heading toward the city, Ronan pulled his vehicle off into a small wooded area. The two-track road he'd found might once have led somewhere, but nobody had traveled it in a while. Weeds had nearly overgrown it. He didn't drive very far, though, just far enough that the car wouldn't be seen from the street. Then he put the car into Park and shut off the ignition.

Muriel knew why he'd stopped—what he wanted. She wanted it, too. So she pushed her other concerns aside and focused only on the overwhelming attraction between them.

He pushed back his seat and lifted her across the console, and now there was nothing between them.

But he settled her onto his lap so that she was staring out the windshield, too. The woods were getting dark, and the glass just reflected back their images—like that mirror in the dressing room.

And like with that mirror in the dressing room, they watched each other, watched every flicker of pleasure and sigh of desire through parted lips. She wore a dress today, one so short that it had already ridden up around her waist. Ronan pushed her panties aside to slide his fingers inside her. Then he moved his other hand farther up beneath her dress and pushed up her strapless bra to free her breasts. While he played with the nipple of one breast, he slid his fingers in and out of her. Soon Muriel was panting for air, and the windows fogged up. She couldn't see herself anymore. She couldn't see Ronan.

She could only feel him as he lowered his fly, sheathed himself and slid it inside her. He lifted her so that she could slide down on top of him. He filled her completely, perfectly.

The tension inside her spiraled up, then broke, and she shuddered as she came. He tensed and writhed beneath her, losing control until he came, too, and shouted her name. Limp with release, Muriel sagged against the steering wheel and the horn blew.

Ronan cursed and pulled her back. "Damn, someone might see us."

Moments ago her control had snapped. Now her temper did. "And why would that be so terrible?" she asked. "Are you afraid of being seen with me?"

"What are you talking about?" he asked.

Muriel straightened her clothes and scrambled back into the passenger seat. "I'm talking about how you never take me anywhere, how we're never out in public." And as the words reverberated inside the steamed up car, Muriel winced, recognizing that she sounded like a nagging wife.

"You haven't been really happy with the publicity I already got for you," he said. "So I hardly thought you'd want to be seen with me."

And she winced again because he had a valid point. The press had just begun to die down. If she was seen in public with her ex's divorce lawyer, she would stir up the scandal all over again.

Then he continued, "It's not as if we're dating, anyway."

And she felt as if he'd punched her. "What are we doing?" she asked. But the question was more for her than him.

He knew what he was doing—what he was always doing—just screwing around...

She didn't screw around; she fell in love. And once again she'd picked the wrong man to fall in love with. At least Ronan hadn't conned her. He'd been honest from the start that he wasn't the forever kind of guy.

For a man who knew what he was doing, he didn't give her an answer—just opened and closed his mouth as if he couldn't find the words.

"I'm sorry," she said.

"You're sorry?"

She nodded. "I shouldn't have asked you to drive me home—now you have no place to escape."

His brow furrowed with confusion. "What are you talking about?"

"How you always take off and run the minute we're done having sex," she explained. "You can't do that now. Unless you toss me out of the car and have me walk to the city."

"I wouldn't do that," he said. But he started up the car and backed quickly onto the street. He began to drive so fast that it was clear he couldn't wait to escape.

"I shouldn't have brought you to meet my grandparents," she said. "I guess I was hoping you'd see that they have something special, that not every marriage is like your parents'."

"Most of them are," he insisted. "How can you forget I'm a divorce lawyer?"

"I didn't forget," she assured him. "But you have to realize you're only seeing the bad marriages. Not the good ones."

He snorted derisively. "I could read you statistics, too. But I wouldn't have thought I'd have to. Your marriage was a scam. How could you ever consider getting married again?" He shivered as if he abhorred the thought.

"I didn't think I would, either," she admitted. "Arte made me doubt my judgment, not just in men but in friends, too. But then Bette became such a good, loyal friend to me." She blinked as tears stung her eyes. She'd learned that the quantity of friends didn't matter; it was the quality.

"I've been lucky in that regard, too," Ronan said. "I have damn good friends."

"So, if we can choose good friends, why can't we choose good mates?" she asked.

He glanced over at her then looked back at the road. "I don't want a mate," he said. "I never intend to get married. If you thought taking me to meet your grandparents would make me propose."

She snorted now. "God, no. I don't want to marry you. We haven't even been out on an actual date." And that was what she'd wanted from him. Not a proposal—just a date. An actual relationship and the hope that it could go somewhere, someday, when they were both ready.

But it was clear that Ronan would never be ready. At least, not with her.

They were silent the rest of the drive into the city. And when he drew near her apartment building, he double parked by a cab. He obviously had no intention of showing her to her door. She jumped out before he could even put the vehicle into Park.

"Don't worry," she told him. "I have no intention of trying to tie you up or down."

"Muriel…"

"In fact, consider yourself cut loose right now, for good," she said as she slammed the passenger door shut.

He opened his door and called out to her over the roof of the car. "Muriel!"

She sucked in a breath to brace herself before turning back toward him and the car.

His brow furrowed. "I don't understand. I thought you were enjoying…" He glanced around the busy street as if worried someone might overhear them.

But everyone appeared too busy with their own lives to bother eavesdropping on theirs. And for once there were no reporters around.

She was old news again. And, unfortunately, so was whatever the hell they'd been doing. "I'm not enjoying it anymore."

It hurt—every time he ran away from her, it hurt. So this time she was the one who turned and ran…

But she knew it wouldn't matter how far and fast she went. The pain was going to catch up with her. She had fallen in love with another man who would never be able to love her back.

CHAPTER FIFTEEN

"ARE YOU SURE she wants me here?" Ronan asked, as he stood in front of the last empty chair near the stage runway. It was probably the only empty chair in the whole, crowded, loud, chaotic place. He was lucky Simon had saved it for him. But he wasn't certain he should have.

"Who?" Simon asked. "Muriel?"

Her name struck him like a blow, making his breath shudder out in a ragged sigh.

"Don't worry," Simon said. "Muriel has no idea you're here."

He didn't doubt that or he probably wouldn't have made it past security even with the pass Simon had given him and the other partners. Trevor and Stone sat on the other side of their managing partner.

"I was talking about Bette," Ronan said. "She's not exactly a fan of mine, and this is her show." The official launch of her line of lingerie. She'd worked very hard for this, and he didn't want to mess it up.

"Maybe if you become a fan of hers, she'll become one of yours," Simon suggested.

Ronan settled onto the chair next to him. "I'm already a fan," he said. "Huge, huge fan of her work."

And Simon chuckled. "So you've seen some of her designs already…" Then he nodded. "Of course, when you were seducing Muriel."

He wasn't sure he'd ever actually seduced her. But she had definitely seduced him—so much so that he couldn't stop wanting her.

It had been almost two weeks since she'd dumped him outside her apartment building. Dumped? They'd never really been together for her to be able to dump him. Like she'd said, they'd never gone out on a real date. He should have taken her. Or at least asked…instead of just assuming that she wouldn't want to be seen with him.

Because then she'd gotten the wrong idea about him, had thought he was ashamed of her or something.

But that wasn't the only wrong idea. She'd started to think that he might be looking for more than just sex. And that was crazy.

Of course he'd had fun with her no matter what they'd been doing. And he'd really enjoyed that dinner with her grandparents. They were as sweet and funny and honest as she was.

Fingers snapped in front of his face. "What's wrong with you?" Trevor asked from where he leaned around Simon.

"He zoned out thinking about Muriel," Simon said as if he perfectly understood.

Stone snorted. "Just because you do that thinking about Bette doesn't mean Ronan is falling in love, too."

Trevor laughed. "Ronan in love...that would be the day."

"Why?" Ronan asked, and even he was surprised to hear how defensive he sounded. "Why would that be the day?"

Stone stood and stared down at him, his gray eyes full of concern. "Are you okay?"

No. He hadn't been since Muriel had gotten out of the car that day and told him she was cutting him loose.

"You're the one who always says love is a sham," Trevor reminded him. "So of course you're never falling in love."

"I used to say that, too," Simon said. "Now I know the truth."

So did Ronan. The truth was that Muriel was a good person. She was not a cheater or a liar. She was not his mother. And he had been an idiot to ever think she was.

"Love is real, guys," Simon said.

While Stone and Trevor laughed, Ronan did not—because, for the first time, he realized that it was.

Simon loved Bette and she loved him. Sure, maybe they wouldn't last. Maybe they'd burn out like so many other couples did—except for Muriel's grandparents. They still flirted with each other, still snuck hot glances and touched each other—and they were old. They'd been together so many years, but they still saw each other. It was possible to love someone and it was possible for that love to last.

He didn't know if it would for him. But maybe he owed it to himself, and to Muriel, to at least try. He knew that it would take more than flowers and a dinner invitation to get her to give him another chance, though. It was going to take a grand gesture—one that would be humbling and humiliating if she didn't want him anymore.

If she'd moved on to someone else…

He opened his mouth to ask Simon if Muriel was seeing anyone, but before he could get the question out, the lights dimmed and the background music stopped playing. With a swish, the curtains opened to a woman standing behind a podium. Bette wore one of her own designs—a silk robe with bows—and for the first time, Ronan understood why his partner was so crazy about his former assistant.

She was gorgeous. But she wasn't The World's Most Beautiful Woman.

Bette was talking, but he couldn't hear any of it. He couldn't hear anything but his pulse pounding in his ears and his blood rushing through his veins—because Muriel had stepped onto the stage.

She looked gorgeous in a soft pink teddy with bows as the straps. Even her slippers, as she glided down the runway, had bows on them. He wanted her to see him. But anytime she looked away from the stage, so many bulbs flashed that she was probably blinded.

Did every fashion show get this much attention or were they here for Muriel?

He couldn't blame them. That was why he was here. Sure, he'd claimed he was just supporting Bette. But he'd wanted to see Muriel again.

But seeing was never enough…

He wanted to kiss her and touch her and taste her. And most of all, he wanted to hold her, all night long—he wouldn't run away.

He had to convince her to give him another chance. And as the bulbs continued to flash all around her, he realized exactly how he was going to do it. Yeah, he'd be humiliated if it failed. But another chance with Muriel far outweighed any risk of humiliation.

Spots danced in front of Muriel's eyes. She was lucky she hadn't fallen during the show. All those flashing bulbs had nearly blinded her. She wasn't able to see well. But she'd been able to feel…his presence.

Ronan had attended the show.

Before giving tickets to Simon's business partners, Bette had asked if it was okay with Muriel. She'd agreed, but only because she hadn't thought Ronan would actually attend.

Had he been alone? Or had he brought a date? Someone he wanted to be seen with?

Of course, he'd explained why he'd never taken her out. But the press had let up on her; they could have taken their relationship public. But then, it had only ever been sex, and taking that public—more public than the elevator, the dressing room and the car—would have gotten them arrested.

Muriel stepped out of the dressing room where she'd changed from Bette's Beguiling lingerie into a short black dress and boots. She'd promised Bette she would attend her party after the show. But if Ronan was there…

Bulbs flashed in her face again, and she flinched. Ronan was the least of her concerns at the moment. Along with the cameras, there were microphones—all shoved toward her face. How had they gotten backstage?

"What do you have to say about the latest news?" someone asked.

Muriel wasn't sure what they meant, but she focused on what they should be focused on. "Bette's brilliant," she said. "Her designs are amazing. And she's the one you should be interviewing." Not her. She had had more than enough press to last her a lifetime.

"So you have nothing to say about the interview your ex gave?" a woman reporter asked.

She swallowed a groan. What had Arte done now? The man was seriously a pathetic fame whore. "I didn't see his interview," she said, "and I don't care to."

"So he's right—nothing he says or does will compel you to give him another chance?"

"God, no." She shuddered at the thought. What the hell kind of game was Arte playing now?

Did he think declarations of undying love for her would save his musical?

The last thing Muriel wanted to do was feed his need for fame. She shook her head. "You're wasting your time. And so is he. Please focus on the real story and Bette's beautiful designs."

Taking her advice, the reporters put down the microphones and turned away with the cameras. As she did, the female reporter shook her head. "You're a stronger woman than I am, then," she murmured. "There's no way in hell I would say no to Ronan Hall."

Muriel reached out and grasped her arm, jerking the woman to a halt. She waited until the others had filed out of the hallway before asking, "What? What did you say about Ronan?"

"He's the one who did all the talking," the woman said. "About you."

"He—he's the ex you're talking about?"

The woman nodded then laughed. "You thought I was talking about your ex-husband?"

"Yes."

"Hell, no, I was talking about his gorgeous lawyer. Nobody even knew the two of you were dating until he gave the interview at the fashion show."

Muriel hadn't even known they were dating. "He—he told you that?"

"I can show you the interview," the woman offered.

The woman pulled a tablet from her bag and touched the screen. A video began to play. The woman spoke on camera—to Ronan. "You've declined all interviews about representing Arte Armand in his divorce trial from Muriel Sanz. Why have you agreed to talk now?"

"Because I need to publicly apologize to Muriel," he said. "I had no idea her ex had influenced those witnesses to perjure themselves."

"Yet someone reported you to the bar association for suborning perjury," the reporter said on the tablet.

Muriel glanced at the young woman. She wasn't a normal tabloid reporter. She was good.

"That person was misinformed," Ronan said, "and later withdrew her complaint."

"Was that person Muriel Sanz?" the reporter asked.

Ronan offered the reporter a grin and a redirection. "I want to talk more about Muriel," he said. "I want to talk about how beautiful and honest and hardworking she is."

"You sound like a man in love," the reporter remarked. In real life, however, she was focused on Muriel's face instead of the screen.

Muriel felt her watching, but her attention was on the tablet, on Ronan's unfairly handsome face. She looked for fear or panic. But she saw nothing except another grin cross his face.

"I guess I do…" he murmured.

"Are you in love with Muriel Sanz?"

"I was falling for her," he said.

"You were dating Muriel Sanz?"

They hadn't actually been dating, but he nodded as if they had been.

"I blew it, though," he said.

The reporter giggled on camera, and standing next to Muriel, her face flushed with embarrassment. "I find that hard to believe, Mr. Hall…"

"No," he said, his voice gruff with regret.

Or was that just wishful thinking on Muriel's part? Did she want him to regret having run away again?

Actually, she was the one who'd run last. But he hadn't stopped her. Then. What the hell was he up to now?

"I really screwed up," he said. "I don't think there's anything I can do that will convince her to give me another chance."

On the tablet, the reporter reached out and grasped his arm. "I'm sure you'll come up with something—" her fingers stroked his arm "—or someone."

Muriel looked at the reporter now—in real life standing next to her. And she had no doubt that she now knew what jealousy felt like…

Because she wanted to claw out the woman's eyes.

"Hey, he didn't take me up on it," the reporter assured Muriel. "Like I could seriously compete with The World's Most Beautiful Woman."

"There is no competition," she assured the reporter. Because despite what he'd claimed in that interview, there was nothing between her and Ronan anymore. There had never been anything real between them.

Just sex…

She missed that—so much—missed how he'd kissed her and touched her and stroked her.

She missed him, too, though. She missed his smart-ass remarks and his stubbornness and even his fear…

She'd caught a glimpse of that fear at the end of the interview—when he'd said he didn't think there was anything he could do to convince her to give him a second chance.

But if he'd really wanted one, why hadn't he just asked her?

Why had he stayed away these past couple of weeks?

Hadn't he missed her like she'd missed him?

"I am not competing for Ronan Hall," she told the reporter.

"So, you're saying I can have him?" the woman asked—hopefully.

She didn't think anyone could really have Ronan—not for long and never for keeps. She wasn't going to risk her heart. Not again…

CHAPTER SIXTEEN

FOR THE FIRST time in his life, Ronan understood what it meant to fail epically. His hand shook as he clicked off the flat-screen TV that was mounted over his white marble fireplace. He turned toward the windows that looked out over Central Park. He'd seen enough of the news broadcast.

The reporters had ambushed Muriel outside the door of her dressing room at the show. Since she'd been so surprised, she had spoken honestly.

She wasn't going to give him another chance.

God, no...

That had been her reply. He felt sick and hollow inside—even more than he had when he'd dropped her off that night. He missed her so damn much.

Apparently he was just going to have to get used to it, though. She wasn't giving him a second chance.

His doorbell rang, echoing off the high, coffered ceilings of his apartment. He hesitated before heading toward the door. It was probably one of his partners or maybe all of them. Except for Simon.

He would be celebrating with Bette. Her fashion

show had been a huge success. But, of course, her designs couldn't help but look amazing when The World's Most Beautiful Woman was modeling them.

The bell rang again—longer and louder this time—as if someone was repeatedly stabbing the button. Irritated now, he stalked toward the door and jerked it open. "What the hell—"

But it wasn't Trevor or Stone standing in the hall outside his penthouse apartment.

"Muriel," he murmured, shocked to see her. How had she even found him? He had never brought her back to his place. He should have...

But then, he would have found it even harder to sleep in his bed if she'd ever been in it with him. Not that he'd been sleeping, anyway.

He couldn't do anything but think about her— how she'd felt, how she'd tasted.

"Muriel," he murmured again as he reached for her. But before he could wrap his arms around her, she slapped her palms against his chest and shoved him back, just as she had shoved him out of her apartment that one night. But now she was shoving her way inside. After stepping through his door, she slammed it shut behind herself. "What the hell are you up to now?" she demanded.

"Up to?" he asked. "What do you mean?"

"That interview you gave," she said. "Was that to appease your conscience?"

"You once told me that I don't have one to appease," he reminded her.

"Then why did you do it?" she asked, and her gorgeous green eyes narrowed with suspicion. "Why the hell would you give an interview and open everything up again?"

He flinched as he realized now what a bad idea it had been. "Everybody else sends you flowers," he said. "Your place already looks like a funeral parlor."

She glared at him but she didn't argue about the flowers. Instead, a little glint lit up her eyes. "If you'd wanted to send something, there's chocolate or wine."

He slapped his forehead. "Chocolate or wine... I didn't think of those things."

"You went straight for the news interview instead," she said. "And I'm still trying to figure out why."

At the moment, so was he.

She had once seemed offended that he hadn't taken their relationship public. He couldn't have taken it any more public than he just had. Except it was obviously too little, too late. They had no relationship, so the only thing that had gone public was his humiliation when she'd made it clear that she was not going to give him another chance.

He expelled a ragged sigh. "It wasn't a smart move," he admitted, "but I did it because, just like I told those reporters, I have fallen for you."

She closed her eyes, as if she couldn't even look at him, and murmured, "I wish you would have told me first."

He tensed. Was that because she didn't return his feelings? "So did I make a fool of myself?" he wondered. Not that he cared about his pride. He didn't care about anything but her.

She shook her head, tumbling her long wavy hair around her shoulders. He loved when she did that when she was naked and astride him. "No. I just wish you'd told me…"

Oh, no. She had moved on—she was dating someone else already. And probably really dating him, like dinner and movies and shows and art galleries…

"So I'm too late?" he asked. "You're already seeing somebody el—"

"No!" she exclaimed as she opened her eyes. "I am not seeing anyone."

"But you don't want to see me again," he said.

Her brow furrowed with confusion. "I never said that."

"Yes, you did," he said, and he pointed toward the dark television screen. "I believe your words were *God, no* when asked if you would ever give me another chance."

"I thought the ex they were talking about was Arte," she said.

The tightness in his chest eased, and he sighed out his relief. "Okay, that makes sense."

"I didn't even know you were my ex," she said. "We were never really together."

"We were lovers," he said. In more ways than he knew because he had fallen in love with her. Of course, he hadn't realized it at the time because he'd never been in love before.

Her green eyes gleamed as if she was remembering all those times they'd been together…

And hope flared inside him. "I know you won't give Arte another chance. But what about me? Will you give me another chance, or did I completely blow it?"

She narrowed her eyes and studied his face. "Is that what you want?" she asked. "To date me or for me to blow you?"

He chuckled. "I'd be lying if I didn't say both."

She laughed, too.

But she hadn't answered his question or commented on his feelings. Did she have any for him?

"What do you want, Muriel?" he asked her. And this time when he stepped toward her, she didn't push him back. She let him close his hands over her shoulders.

She put her palms against his chest again, but she didn't shove him. Instead she ran her palms up until her arms linked around his neck. Then she pulled his head down and brushed her mouth across his.

The kiss took his breath away. It was gentle and loving and had hope swelling in Ronan's heart. Could she return his feelings?

He asked again, "What do you want, Muriel?"

"You," she said. "I want you…"

It wasn't a declaration of love. But it should have been enough. It had always been enough for Ronan before. But then his heart had never been involved before.

He didn't want to wind up like his father—in love

with a woman who didn't and probably couldn't love him back. But then he reminded himself that Muriel was not his mother.

She was straightforward and honest. And she had a heart—a big one—he'd seen it when she'd defended and supported her friend and when she'd interacted with the grandparents who raised her.

That was why he'd fallen for her. That and the incredible sex. Maybe he could make her fall for him—with incredible sex. He swung her up in his arms and headed toward his bedroom.

She wrapped her arm around his shoulders and snuggled into his neck, pressing kisses against his skin. He shuddered as passion overwhelmed him.

But when he stepped into his bedroom, he brought her to the bed, laid her down and stepped back. Her arms reached out for him, but he turned away and opened his closet door instead of joining her.

"What are you doing?" she asked, her voice thick with passion.

He pulled out four ties and held them up for her to see. "Letting you tie me up," he told her.

Her eyes widened in surprise. "Really?"

He nodded. "That way you'll know I won't run away afterward…"

"I told you I wouldn't try to tie you down anymore," she reminded him.

"I want to be tied down," he said, "with you."

He stripped off his clothes before knotting the end of each tie around one of the posts of his four-poster bed. Then he lay down on the king-size bed. "Tie me up," he invited her.

Muriel leaned over him, her beautiful face even more gorgeous with the big smile that curved up her full lips. "I love you."

The words hit him hard and made him hard, his cock swelling and extending toward her. He wanted to bury himself inside her—wanted to be so close that it wasn't possible to tell where one of them ended and the other began. But before he could reach for her, Muriel cinched a tie around his wrist. Then his other one and his ankles.

He had promised her this—had promised he'd give up control to her. But it was killing him. Then she was killing him with soft kisses and caresses…

With her lips and her fingertips, she touched every inch of his skin—in places he hadn't even realized he was sensitive. Like his knee and his hip…

He wanted to move, but he didn't fight the restraints. He didn't fight the feelings.

And when she closed her lips around his cock and sucked it deep into her mouth, he nearly came. But she just teased him, swirling her tongue around his girth. She even nibbled gently on the head.

He groaned. "Muriel, I want you… I want to be inside you…"

She pulled back and stared down at him. And for a moment, he wondered if this was it—her revenge. She was going to leave him tied up and out of his mind with passion and just walk away. But she'd said she loved him. Did she?

* * *

Muriel saw that fear flicker through Ronan's dark eyes again. And she knew he'd made himself more vulnerable to her than he had ever been.

His gorgeous body was naked and tethered to his bed. His cock pulsated with the need for release from the tension she'd built inside him.

But it was his heart that was most vulnerable—because, for the first time, Muriel could see it. Ronan's heart was in his gaze as he stared up at her. He didn't have to say the words she had. She knew. He loved her.

"I love you," she told him again.

And his body relaxed—slightly—and the fear passed out of his eyes, which warmed with that love she'd already seen. "I love you," he said.

He didn't have to tell her. She knew that was the first time he'd ever said those words to a woman. And she was so damn glad she was that woman.

His woman…

She pulled off her dress and dropped it to the floor on top of his clothes. She wore the lingerie she'd modeled last in the show. The silk and lace was purple and black and sexy as hell with bows holding it together in the back. She turned around, so he could see the bows as she tugged them loose.

Then the lingerie dropped to the floor—leaving her as naked as he was.

He struggled now against those restraints. "I want to touch you," he said, his voice gruff. "I have to touch you…"

And she needed his touch. She untied his silk power-tie bindings.

But when he was free, he didn't automatically reach for her. Instead, he studied her face. "You're not afraid I'm going to run off?"

She shook her head. "Not anymore…"

He leaned closer and kissed her lips. "I'm not going anywhere…"

"Well, this is your place," she reminded him.

He laughed and leaned his forehead against hers. "I love you."

Love rushed through her—along with desire. The power of both stunned her. "I hated you," she said, "after what you did to me in court and the media."

"I'm sorry," he said, his eyes darkening with regret. He lowered his head, as if unable to look at her. "I hate myself for what I did."

She slid her fingers along his hard jaw, tipping it back up so their gazes met. "That's all in the past now," she assured him. "Now I love you far more than I ever hated you…"

He expelled a ragged breath of relief. "That's good. I worried that you would never be able to forgive me."

She wrapped her arms around his neck and pressed her naked body against his. She felt his cock move between them, pulsating with desire. And her clit began to throb. She'd never wanted anyone more—not even Ronan himself.

Love changed everything, made every touch and kiss more intense. He kissed her deeply, and her toes nearly curled with the passion coursing through her.

Then he stroked his hands down her bare back to her hips and lifted her. She wrapped her legs around his waist and rubbed her clit against his penis. A moan tore free from her throat. She nearly came at just that contact. And she couldn't stop moving, couldn't stop shifting her hips against him.

"Muriel," he said on a groan. "You're going to make me…"

"Come!" she yelled as she shuddered and began to come herself. But it wasn't enough. She wanted more. She wanted him buried deep inside her.

And he must have wanted the same, for he quickly, despite his shaking hand, rolled on a condom. Then he rolled her across the bed, parted her legs and slid deep inside her.

Muriel clutched him to her, raking her nails down his back. The muscles rippled beneath her fingertips. Then she grasped his butt. It was so tight, so firm… so damn sexy.

"You really could be a model…" she murmured against his lips as his mouth settled on hers.

He kissed her deeply, his mouth sliding over and over hers. She parted her lips on a gasp of pleasure, and he slid his tongue into her mouth. His cock slid in and out of her, as well. She arched her hips, taking him deeper and deeper.

But he rolled again, moving onto his back so that she wound up on top. She moaned as his cock sank even deeper. She was so close, the tension inside her nearly unbearable. Ronan gripped her hips, lifting her and moving her, as he arched his hips up from the mattress. They found the rhythm that was theirs alone—like a station on the radio that only the two of them could hear.

And the tension broke as an orgasm overwhelmed her. Her body shuddered as her inner muscles convulsed. She screamed as the orgasm went on and on and on...

Ronan's hands tightened on her hips as his body tensed beneath hers. Then he shouted her name as he came. Muriel lifted herself off him and dropped onto the bed next to him. But as usual, he moved quickly—leaving her lying alone on the tangled silk sheets.

Maybe she shouldn't have untied him. But he was back within seconds. He wrapped his arm around her, pulling her against him.

She settled her head onto his chest. His heart was still beating fast and frantically beneath her ear. "Are you okay?" she asked.

His arm tightened for a moment. "I'm afraid," he admitted.

She'd thought he'd already made himself as vulnerable as he could be to her when he'd professed his love and then let her tie him up. But this was even bigger than that.

"Why are you afraid?" she asked.

"I've never felt like this before," he said. "It's overwhelming."

She pressed her lips against his chest. "I know. But I will never hurt you."

His heart beat slowed in pace and intensity. And his hand was steady as it skimmed down her back in a sweet caress. "I trust you," he said. "I just hope I don't screw this up. I don't want you to leave…"

"I'm not going anywhere," she assured him.

He must have believed her because eventually he fell asleep. And Muriel drifted off, as well.

But when she awoke a while later, panic flashed through her. Ronan was gone.

But he hadn't gone far. She felt his lips…on her ankle. Then silk replaced his mouth as he wrapped a tie around it. The other end was already tethered to the bedpost.

"What are you doing?" she asked.

"Tying you up," he said.

"Afraid I might run now?" she asked.

"Not at all," he said. "I'm not afraid of anything anymore."

"Then what are you doing?"

"Showing you how much I love you…"

He showed her over and over again as he kissed and caressed every inch of her. His lips touched her everywhere, the inside of her elbow, the curve of her hip, the back of her knee…

Then he dipped his tongue into her belly button before moving farther down her body. As he rubbed one of her nipples between his thumb and finger, he kissed her mound. Then he made love to it, stroking his tongue over her and nibbling at her with his lips.

She tugged against the restraints, wanting to touch him—wanting to drag him up her body, so that he could bury himself inside her.

But then she arched off the bed as an orgasm shuddered through her. He wasn't done, though. He kept making love to her with his mouth until she came again and again.

The sheets weren't just tangled but damp beneath her. When he finally released her, she launched herself at him. They made love in a frenzy, his cock sliding deep into her wetness.

She shuddered as she came again. "Ronan…" She nearly sobbed his name.

Then he tensed, his body going stiff before he drove deep with one last thrust. He shouted her name and dropped onto the mattress next to her. His skin was slick, like hers. "They got that title wrong," he murmured.

"Title?"

"The World's Most Beautiful Woman."

Unoffended, she brushed her sweat-soaked hair back from her face and wholeheartedly agreed, "I always thought they got it wrong, too."

"Your title should be…" He paused dramatically before continuing. "The World's Best Lover…"

She smiled and settled her head back against his shoulder. "That title is yours," she told him. "All yours…"

"It's ours," he corrected her. "We are amazing together."

But they were more than just lovers now. They were in love. And while her lover might be a little too cynical to totally believe it would last, she had no doubts. They had already survived the worst.

They had nothing but pleasure ahead of them.

* * * * *

LET'S TALK
Romance

For exclusive extracts, competitions
and special offers, find us online:

 facebook.com/millsandboon

@millsandboonuk

@millsandboon

Or get in touch on 0844 844 1351*

For all the latest titles coming soon, visit
millsandboon.co.uk/nextmonth

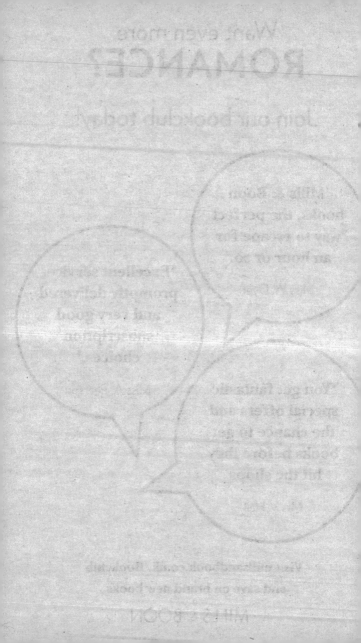